EXIT PL...

Tulo'stena... ...est Posleen war ... ...ow just a ragged fugiti... ...y. There was a small being, o... ...dowy, blocking what passed for a trai...

"Who are you?" the Posleen God King asked suspiciously. He had reason for suspicion. His armies crushed, his people nearly extermi-nated . . . and here he found himself standing before one of the "harmless" green ones who provided the damned humans with their fighting machines. The green being was in turn sur-rounded by more armed humans, closer than the Posleen war chief had ever hoped to see again in this life.

We're Dead, Tulo thought. *I don't know why I bothered trying to run anyway.* The ragged remnant of his horde that stretched out behind Tulo was composed of only a few hundred crocodilian centaurs.

"I am the Indowy, Aelool," answered the little one. "And I would like to make you an offer you can't refuse."

BAEN BOOKS by JOHN RINGO

THE LEGACY OF THE ALDENATA SERIES
A Hymn Before Battle • *Gust Front* • *When the Devil Dances* • *Hell's Faire* • *The Hero* with Michael Z. Williamson • *Cally's War* with Julie Cochrane • *Watch on the Rhine* with Tom Kratman • *Yellow Eyes* with Tom Kratman • *The Tuloriad* with Tom Kratman • *Sister Time* with Julie Cochrane • *Honor of the Clan* with Julie Cochrane • *Eye of the Storm*

There Will Be Dragons • *Emerald Sea* • *Against the Tide* • *East of the Sun, West of the Moon*

Ghost • *Kildar* • *Choosers of the Slain* • *Unto the Breach* • *A Deeper Blue*

Princess of Wands

Into the Looking Glass • *Vorpal Blade* with Travis S. Taylor • *Manxome Foe* with Travis S. Taylor • *Claws that Catch* with Travis S. Taylor

The Road to Damascus with Linda Evans

Von Neumann's War with Travis S. Taylor

WITH DAVID WEBER:
March Upcountry • *March to the Sea* • *March to the Stars* • *We Few*

BAEN BOOKS by TOM KRATMAN
A State of Disobedience

A Desert Called Peace • *Carnifex* • *The Lotus Eaters* • *The Amazon Legion* (forthcoming)

Caliphate

Countdown: The Liberators (forthcoming)
Countdown: M Day (forthcoming)

THE TULORIAD

JOHN RINGO
& TOM KRATMAN

The Tuloriad

A Baen Books Original

Baen Publishing Enterprises
P.O. Box 1403
Riverdale, NY 10471
www.baen.com

ISBN: 978-1-4391-3409-2

Cover art by Kurt Miller

First Baen paperback printing, January 2011

Library of Congress Control Number: 2009017406

Distributed by Simon & Schuster
1230 Avenue of the Americas
New York, NY 10020

Pages by Joy Freeman (www.pagesbyjoy.com)
Printed in the United States of America

THE TULORIAD

PART I

CHAPTER ONE

Tell of the star-crossed Kessentai, O spirits,
Who wandered long after being driven from
the blood-drenched citadel of Aradeen.
—The *Tuloriad*, Na'agastenalooren

Anno Domini 2009
North Carolina

The screech and thunder of human artillery, flying
through the air and impacting on the ground nearby,
drowned out the shuffling of Posleen feet, the confused
and frightened grunts of the cosslain, and the despair-
filled sobbing of their remaining hundred or so human
captives.

None of those captives knew why, but that number
had not changed in some days. If they'd asked, if
they'd been able to ask, the chief of the alien group
probably could not have explained why they'd been
spared. It was possible that he, himself, didn't know.

At the point of the ragged column, head drooped
in defeat, walked that Posleen chief: Tulo, lord of the

3

clan of Sten and war leader of the vast hosts gathered to fight the humans on this part of the planet Aradeen, known locally as "Earth." Those hosts had within the last few days been very nearly annihilated in that fighting.

Tulo'stenaloor, once lord of the greatest Posleen war host ever assembled and now just a ragged fugitive, stopped suddenly, his head rising and his crest—reminiscent of a Lakota headdress—erecting itself automatically. There was a small being, one of the bat-faced, green-fuzzed, pacifist Indowy, blocking what passed for a trail.

"Who are you?" the Posleen God King, Tulo'stenaloor, asked suspiciously. He had reason for suspicion. His armies crushed, his people nearly exterminated...and here he found himself standing before one of the "harmless" green ones who provided the never-sufficiently-to-be-damned humans with their fighting machines. The green being was in turn surrounded by more armed humans, closer than the Posleen war chief had ever hoped to see again in this life. The fuzzy being seemed to be studying the pitiful remnants of the Posleen horde that shambled along behind Tulo'stenaloor.

We're dead, Tulo thought. *And perhaps just as well. I don't know why I bothered trying to run anyway.*

The ragged remnant of his horde that stretched out behind Tulo was composed of several hundred crocodilian centaurs with scaly skin and yellow eyes. About a third of the beings had crests. These they could erect at will, in a display of dominance or of urge to battle. The crests would also erect themselves, automatically, when faced with a threat. It was not insignificant that, of the over one hundred crested individuals in the pack, not one, except for Tulo and his bodyguard, had their crests erected. Rather, they hung along the creatures' necks, as if in shame and despair.

Tulo's guard, Brasingala, a large and stout young Kessentai who had over the years demonstrated both aptitude and dedication amounting to paranoid obsession in guarding his chief, immediately began to draw his boma blade to hack the little being into steaks, along with as many of his human escorts as could be managed.

"Hold," Tulo whispered, putting one skilled claw in front of Brasingala. The young guard immediately froze in place.

"I am the Indowy, Aelool," answered the little one, with a broad and toothy, and very feral, smile. If the Indowy was afraid of Brasingala, or even of the remnants of Tulo's host, the fear was tolerably hard to perceive. "And I would like to make you an offer you can't refuse."

"A quick death?" the God King asked, curiously enough without any hostility. After all he'd been through, Aelool wouldn't wonder that the Posleen might prefer death to life. "That would be generous."

"No," the Indowy said. "A long life. Perhaps even a fruitful and happy one."

At that the Kessentai laughed bitterly. "I don't believe in fairy tales, Indowy."

The Indowy's fingers reached up to stroke a batlike, furry chin. "Neither do I," he agreed. "There is a ship behind me, hidden underground," Aelool said. His fingers wriggled as his arm swept in the surrounding humans, both those guards close by and others glimpsed as dimly seen shadows as they moved into position around the remnant of the host. "That is no fairy tale. I could have had you destroyed just now—you will agree that the humans are remarkably good at destruction, yes?—yet I did not. That is no fairy tale. There are other humans coming, and those I don't control. That's no fairy tale, either. Your people are tired, demoralized, weak, hungry, and as very nearly out of ammunition as they are of hope. Do I speak a fairy tale?"

The Posleen sighed. "It is cruel to remind me of my failure," he said. "I thought you people had some scruples."

"Scruples enough," Aelool said. "Scruples enough to save this remnant, Tulo, Lord of the Clan Sten."

"To what end?" Tulo asked.

"Not so much to an end," the Indowy corrected, with an odd twist of his ears, "as to avoid an end. The galaxy would be a poorer place without your people in it. You are, in your way, nearly as admirable as these feral humans. You could, in your way, become as or even more valuable."

"We're as valuable as hunks of thresh hung up for curing," the God King said, adding, "for those who care for the perversion of cured thresh. There is no possibility of getting a ship out through the human blockade of the planet."

"There is no possibility of getting one of your ships out, Tulo. There are other kinds of ships."

The Indowy pointed up into the trees. Tulo's eyes followed and searched. Something . . . something . . . *but, no, I can't see it. It's as if my eyes are trying to tell my mind something that my mind refuses to accept.*

"Show yourself, Himmit Argzal," the Indowy called.

The Posleen nodded as the purple outline of an

alien being, symmetrical but with a head at each end, began to form among the trees. It had been there all the time, so he assumed, but the Himmit were *good* at camouflage.

The Posleen couldn't hide a sneer. "We're to be saved by the galaxy's cowards? How truly sad."

"There may be more to the Himmit than you realize, Tulo'stenaloor," Aelool answered. "More than we do, either," he muttered, *sotto voce*. The little being's feral smile changed briefly to a puzzled frown. The frown disappeared as Aelool continued, "Be that as it may. They have a ship—life for the remnants of your people. Will you take ship?"

I don't want to live, Tulo thought. *Live for what? Live for shame? Live for disgrace? Live for the knowledge I failed my people?*

Aelool could hardly know what Tulo was thinking in perfect detail. Even so, it would be hard not to know what was in the God King's mind, in principle.

"Live to expiate shame," the Indowy said. "Live to recover from disgrace. Live to rebuild the People of the Ships."

"I could live for revenge," the God King said.

"That you shall not have," Aelool answered. "Nor do you deserve it. Nor, in time, will you come even to want it."

Again, the Kessentai laughed. "Those first two may well be true, Indowy. That last is inconceivable."

Overhead, a flight of artillery passed, its freight train racket for the moment drowning out speech. In the distance the forest rumbled as earth was plowed and trees cropped by the humans' high explosives. After the sound had passed, and before the next could come,

Aelool said, "Believe what you want, Tulo'stenaloor. Conceive of what you will. But believe this, too: If you and your people do not get aboard the Himmit's ship, that artillery will soon find you. Will you come?"

"Can you fit all my people?" he asked.

"Most, certainly," Aelool answered. "There is space for the Kessentai, the Kessenalt, and most—maybe all—of the cosslain. The normals will not fit, or not many of them anyway. And of course your human captives must be released without harm."

"My immediate oolt has no normals. The captives we can let go; they're hardly enough to feed us for long anyway." *Even were I of a mind to eat them.*

"Then you will come? The ship I have brought can feed you."

"Yes, dammit. Come where?"

"Follow me," Aelool said, turning. As he turned, the Himmit disappeared once again among the trees.

Argzal was waiting when the procession arrived at the tunnel, Posleen surrounded by humans led by an Indowy. *This I simply must relate to the story gatherers*, the Himmit thought wryly.

Seeing the Posleen come to a shuddering stop at the opening of the tunnel, the Himmit said, "Fear not, lordlings, the tunnel leads to the ship of life."

"The ship tunnels for cover," Aelool explained to Tulo'stenaloor. "The displaced material is turned into... well, call it neutronium, for lack of a better term... the better to aid in camouflage."

"We really don't like tunnels much," Tulo said. "Even leaving aside the legends, we've had a lot of bad experiences underground since we met the humans."

"Not as bad as you will have if you don't go into the tunnel," Aelool observed.

"Essthree!" Tulo called, turning his great head toward the mass of the column. This was a title, one Tulo had borrowed from the humans in his efforts to create a mightier host than any that had gone before. The essthree was concerned with planning and operations, as the essone was with personnel management, the esstwo with intelligence, and the essfour with logistics.

"Here, lord," answered an ancient Kessentai with the gleam of fierce intelligence in his one remaining yellow eye. Despite that gleam, the essthree had the look of weariness about him, a fatigue no ordinary rest could touch.

"Take Essfour with you. Go forward and organize boarding. I will—"

A series of screeches, followed by organ-shaking bangs, was heard perhaps a thousand of the humans' meters away.

"I will stay above with Brasingala and push the others in," Tulo finished.

"As you say, lord." With a hand signal to the essfour, the essthree warily entered the tunnel.

"Essone?"

"Here, Tulo'stenaloor," said a youngish looking God King. This one's eyes were no less intelligent than Essthree's, yet he looked much younger and considerably the better for wear.

"How many are we?"

The God King didn't need to consult any notes, nor could he consult the defunct artificial sentience, or AS, he normally wore on a golden chain about his neck. The humans' last, horde-crushing antimatter strike had generated an electromagnetic pulse sufficient to destroy even the EMP-hardened artificial sentiences of the Posleen. Most of the Kessentai had tossed theirs as redundant, useless weight. And if Essone had not tossed his, it was only a matter of time. Of all the Kessentai and Kessenalt in Tulo'stenaloor's oolt, only Binastarion intended to keep his. And that device had been more friend and confidant than servant.

"We are three hundred and eighty-seven left, Tulo. Two hundred and twenty-six cosslain, one hundred and thirty-seven Kessentai, twenty-four Kessenalt. Plus the thresh, of course."

"We'll be leaving the thresh behind." Tulo turned his great crested head to Aelool. "Can we fit so many?"

"The ship will suffice for that," Aelool agreed. "Yet it will be tight, Tulo'stenaloor, and your seniors must control the lesser ones among you."

"That will be no problem, Indowy. My personal oolt is not much given to panic. Though some are given to excessive mourning."

At that Aelool looked toward one among the Posleen Kessentai who was clutching a gold-colored metal disc to its chest while keening piteously. Nearby an old looking Posleen, followed by a cosslain bearing a gilded chest upon its broad back, attempted to console the weeping Kessentai. The Indowy twitched an ear in puzzlement.

"That's Binastarion," Tulo explained. "He was very close to his artificial sentience. The humans' antimatter weapon that broke us also generated enough of an electromagnetic pulse to scrub all of our artificial sentiences. Binastarion mourns for a dead friend."

Aelool nodded his understanding.

Tulo pointed at a group. "Into the tunnel," he said

to them. Aelool was pleased but unsurprised to see that the Posleen followed their orders without question. Tulo'stenaloor was, after all, not just any God King.

The Indowy thought, *We might just get away after all.*

Tulo noticed one particular God King, Goloswin the Tinkerer, hanging back as the rest shuffled forward uncertainly into the dark, dank tunnel.

No, that's not quite right, Tulo thought, looking more carefully at the expression on Goloswin's face. *He's not hanging back; he's* studying. *Well, Golo always* studies.

That he was a little shorter and thinner than the Kessentai norm was only the beginning of Goloswin's personal oddities. Among the Kessentai most were, Tulo would frankly admit, idiots who should have been excised from the gene pool. (Ruefully, too, the chief Kessentai would have noted, the humans had done just that.)

His own oolt wasn't like that, of course. Of Kessentai he had nothing but what the humans called, "five percenters," those one in twenty Kessentai who were demonstrably, and fearfully, not idiots. Of those, Tulo had chosen only the best for the oolt. But even among those who were one in one hundred of that one in twenty, Goloswin stood out. For he was the Michelangelo, the Leonardo Da Vinci, the Gauss and the Newton and the Einstein, the Ford and the Edison of the Posleen race.

Goloswin, as he himself would have cheerfully told anyone who asked, was fucking *smart.*

"What holds you, Golo?" Tulo asked. "We can afford to lose many . . . any really . . . of the People. But we cannot afford to lose you."

"I am operating on a guess, Tulo," Golo said. "The first and the last loaded have a chance to be the foremost inside that hidden ship. I may be able to discern something of its principles by being closer to the control room."

Tulo's answer was interrupted by one of the humans' artillery shells, this one much closer than the last. It was an adjusting round. In an earlier day, before the Posleen had obliterated the Global Positioning System, there probably would have been no adjustment required and the first warning of an incoming shell would have been dismemberment by that shell... and the couple of hundred siblings that would have accompanied it.

"There is a team of them watching us," Aelool surmised. "They're almost as disorganized by victory as you are by defeat... else that last shell would have been here, and it would have been followed by hundreds more." To his human escorts, he said, "Find the observers. Silence them. Do not harm them."

Wordlessly, one of the human escorts used his fingers to indicate to a brace of his men that they were to follow him. In perfect silence those three took off into the woods and disappeared from view.

"They are very good," Tulo told Aelool as the three humans disappeared.

"They are," the Indowy agreed. "I'm told they're Swiss... mmm... Swiss... 'Guards.' Or a special subset of that group, anyway. They're on loan to my organization."

The Posleen shrugged. The details didn't matter much when the humans had, as a race, proven so deadly.

Another shell landed, this one closer still. Tulo thought he saw treetops rising majestically, only to sink again, slowly, in the not very far distance. The trees fell as if with regret. He looked around. Only he and Golo, Brasingala, and the Indowy remained above the surface; those, plus the human captives and what some among the humans might have called the "mess sergeant." Tulo had shortened that to "mesergen."

"You have made a great mistake," the mesergen said to Tulo. "I am not enough, on my own, to butcher these properly. Nor is there time for me to do so."

"We're not butchering any of them."

"What? That's nonsense! I didn't curry these along merely to—"

"Brasingala!"

So fast was the guard's blade that the messergen's lips were still moving as his head hit the forest floor.

"I am not in the mood to be argued with," Tulo'stenaloor whispered to the corpse, after it had finished settling to the ground.

Mesergen forgotten as quickly as he had been killed, Tulo turned his attention back to the tunnel ahead. He could just see the twitching rumps of the last of the remainder, losing themselves in the dark.

"Maybe you're right, Golo," Tulo'stenaloor said. "Let us enter this place and see."

"What of your humans?"

Aelool answered, "Some of my escorts will take charge of those you have freed and lead them to their own people. The rest of my escorts will disperse as soon as we are boarded. I think that, even with your former captives, no observer will see them."

Tulo shrugged that off. Let himself and his people

escape and what matter what the humans saw on their own world? He, his guard, Goloswin, and Aelool entered the tunnel and walked forward. Clawed Posleen feet, and sandalled Indowy ones, made an odd sound on the surface of the base of the tunnel. What should have been dirt was, instead, turned to some other substance, something that felt almost like gold.

The tunnel continued on, deep into the earth. It twisted only once, near the end. Just past that hard right twist a large portal stood open, with a ramp in front of it, leading from ship to "soil." The ramp appeared to be of a much different shape from the portal, yet Goloswin sensed it was intended to fold into it. A bluish-greenish glow came from the opening, turning ramp and tunnel much the same color.

Once inside, they saw that the disconcerting blue-green seemed to come from no place in particular, but simply to be everywhere at once. The cabin in which the refugees found themselves was small, perhaps twenty-five of the humans' meters by thirty. With nearly four hundred of the massive creatures stuffed into that space, there was hardly room, and an excellent chance of being inadvertently injured, for one tiny Indowy. Standing near to Goloswin, with the Indowy on his feet in between the two, Tulo'stenaloor suggested, "Maybe you should climb on my back, Aelool. Here, let me give you a hand up." The God King reached down with claws that, under ordinary circumstances, would have sent a normal Indowy gibbering.

Aelool was not a normal Indowy, however. With the God King's help, he scrambled onto its broad, muscled back, sitting there sidesaddle as his legs were too short to take a comfortable riding position.

"Something really bothers me, here, Tulo," Goloswin said, leaning over to whisper to Tulo.

"I hate this fucking blue-green light, too."

Golo twisted his head in negation. "The light? No, no, I hadn't even noticed the light. Though now that you mention it, it is a little unsettling. No, I was thinking about the size of this thing. Even if it recycles the waste at one hundred percent efficiency, it would have to do so instantaneously or we'll spend half the time hungry. And we cannot make a long journey crowded in like this, muzzle to asshole. I wonder if..."

A voice came from everywhere and nowhere. "Attention. Attention Posleen lord and lordlings and servants. This is Argzal, captain of the scout smuggler, *Surreptitious Stalker*, Himmit Sixth Fleet—"

"Sixth Fleet?" Golo questioned. "Himmits have fleets?"

"Shhh! Listen. Besides, we don't know if they mean by 'fleet' what we or the humans would mean by 'fleets.'"

"—going to be passing through the humans' interdiction forces now gathered around the planet. Unlike most of the humans' weapons and sensors, those ships can potentially sense us and could possibly harm us. Do not worry; I am very good at my job. I intend to bluff."

"'Don't worry,' he says. 'I intend to bluff,' he says."

"Shhh."

"—placing an inertial dampening field around your compartment. This will retard your movements, slightly and temporarily. The inertial dampening field, while not dangerous, is also not what is normally used for livestock."

"Livestock!"

"Dammit, be quiet, Golo!"

"—should not fear this; it is necessary. In the interim, to keep you entertained, look to the nearest bulkhead. You can see our progress there. I will also adjust your light to something more comfortable."

The compartment, not exactly raucous to begin with, went deathly silent as most of the walls were seemingly replaced with totally black holographic rectangles. The ambient light likewise shifted to a red-orange more suitable to Posleen visual rods and temperament. Between the two changes, the pitiful remnants of the great host of Tulo'stenaloor calmed down completely.

"I wish I had my AS," Tulo whispered. Sadly, every AS in the oolt had been wiped by the electromagnetic pulse of the humans' ultimate antimatter weapon. Off in the distance, Binastarion could still be heard weeping over his own.

To Brasingala, the chief said, "Migrate through the oolt as best you can. Find our Chief Rememberer. Tell him it would please me if he would lead our people in a prayer of thanks to the ancestors for our deliverance."

"We're not delivered yet, Tulo," Goloswin said.

"Yes, we are. We just don't know whether we're delivered from death or from shameful life. Either is cause for thanks."

Beneath and around the Posleen and Aelool the Himmit ship began to hum as it prepared to break free of the Earth and the war which had nearly consumed it.

CHAPTER TWO

Ad Maiorem Dei Gloriam.
(To the greater glory of God.)
—Unofficial Motto of the Society of Jesus

Anno Domini 2013
Rome, Latium, Italy

Father Dan Dwyer, SJ, was old Navy. Tallish, at almost exactly six feet, broad shouldered, blue-eyed, and red headed, Dwyer looked to be approximately in his mid-twenties though he was, in fact, many times that. Although temporarily detached, he still wore on his blue dress uniform the insignia of a naval captain. As a matter of fact, he not only wore the uniform that said he was old Navy, he had enough ribbons running up from left breast pocket nearly to shoulder, indicating medals of high enough *quality*, to prove it. Navy Cross, Silver Star...somewhere in the Pentagon floated a recommendation for the Medal of Honor, though that was at best an outside shot.

There had been a day when Dwyer could have

worn Marine Corps uniform, other than dress blues, if he'd wanted. That, though, had been generations earlier, before the Posleen War.

He'd lectured and sermoned, fought and bled, as soldier and sailor, both, and of both God and the United States, since he'd been a very young priest, fresh out of the Jesuit's uniquely severe *cursus*. He'd done it in Vietnam. He'd done it marching back from the Chosen reservoir in Korea. Though he'd been something of a legend for those things, in the Naval service, equally he'd been legendary for his remarkably well-stocked sacramental wine cabinet, aboard ship, which was always nestled nicely between and among the sacramental scotch, sacramental bourbon, sacramental vodka and rum, sacramental cognac and armagnac, sacramental grappa . . .

Dwyer had been, for most of his life, a highly functioning alcoholic. An act of will and of love had put an end to that. Rejuvenation via galactic technology, or GalTech, had erased the damage of years of drinking and even removed the addiction, a matter of genetic manipulation, rather than psychiatric reasoning or counseling. What it could not do, or at least had not, was remove the psychological need for euphoria arising to oblivion in the face of endless, limitless pain.

"God," whispered Dwyer, looking around at what remained on the bare seven hills of Rome, "God, You *know* I could use a drink about now."

"Shush," said the Jesuit's companion, Sally, walking beside him. "You don't need anything of the kind." Her finger pointed at an odd sight. "And there's someone who might be able to help," as if being lost could be Dwyer's motivation to break his vow of sobriety.

✦   ✦   ✦

Swiss Guards in their traditional uniforms patrolled the mostly unmarked and unbounded pathways of the city. While the guards carried halberds and baselards, a kind of short sword, they all had quite up-to-date rifles slung across their bodies, as well. The slings were of the type that hung from both shoulders, leaving the rifle with its muzzle down, free to be taken in hand by the carriers.

Rome had changed. The hills were there, of course; the Posleen showed generally little interest in remaking natural geography. The bridges stood still; the Posleen had no skill whatsoever in building them and found them useful enough to preserve where possible (especially so, as Posleen could not swim at all). The foundations, if nothing else, of the Forum Romanorum could be found. They could even be seen from many of the seven hills. And why not? There was absolutely nothing else high enough to block the view. Old Rome had survived the incursion of the Posleen better than had New only in that there were, at least, some traces of Old Rome left.

That said, the Flavian Amphiteater? Gone. The arches of Constantine, Titus, and Septimius Severus? Gone. Column of Trajan? Gone. The three remaining columns of the Temple of Castor and Pollux? Gone. Pantheon? Gone. No wonder Dwyer felt the need for a drink.

On the south edge of the city the pyramidal tomb of Caius Cestius was not merely gone, the Posleen had hit it with a large enough KEW, or Kinetic Energy Weapon, to destroy it *and* leave a rather large and deep crater in its place. The crater had, in time, become a small lake.

And that's what hurt the remaining Romans the most, even more than the destruction of the Vatican, the loss of the ancient heritage that had proclaimed, "Once we were the greatest." To the extent that real rebuilding was ongoing, Rome was being reconstructed as the Rome of the Caesars, not the Rome of the popes, of Garibaldi, or of Mussolini.

This was not particularly uncommon across the Earth, as people who had lost all sense of normality labored to recreate the world that had been mostly erased by the Posleen. And if the Italians had lost more than most, what better reason was needed to recreate a world even more ancient than the one they had recently known?

The Vatican was not among even the foundations of the ruins remaining. The very rocks that had made up the Basilica of Saint Peter had been taken down, crushed, reformed and vitrified to produce one or another of the pyramidal structures favored by the aliens. These, in turn, now swarmed with jackhammer-wielding workers, cutting the rock free to rebuild human structures. In the interim, Mother Church, as it had sometimes in the very early days, once again operated from tents and caves. The Society of Jesus was no better off.

"Well," muttered Father (Captain) Dan Dwyer, SJ, to his companion and fiancée, Sally—short for . . . well . . . among other things short for Shlomit Bat Betlechem-Plada Kreuzer—"At least the Society has its own cave."

Father? SJ? Fiancée?

Yes.

Somewhere in an interior pocket of the priest's

uniform tunic rested a copy of the latest papal bull, *"De Propagatione Fidei,"* which translated as, "Concerning the Propagation of the Faith." The language of the thing was Latin, of course. What it meant, in practice, was, "We've taken it in the shorts. Go ye forth and multiply. Yes, Father, yes, Sister, THIS MEANS YOU. Oh, and while you're at it, work on getting us some converts, too. And, no, you are not freed of the responsibility of getting married before you propagate."

Nor was that all the bull did. One result of the Posleen invasion, and the learned preference for expending men and preserving women—coldly put, the factories for the next generation of plasma cannon and rail gun fodder—was that the imbalance between the sexes of the human race was close to five to two, female. For Catholics, for whatever reason, it was more like three to one. After consultation with some learned Moslems and Mormons, the pope had seen fit to authorize and encourage polygamy, along with a vigorous castigation of celibacy, and a side sneer at homosexuality, for a set period of seventy-five years. For some Catholic women, the reaction was something like, "Crap, you mean I can't have one of my own?" From others it was, "I just *knew* there was a merciful God. Thank Christ that I won't have to do all the coddling myself." For men, reactions varied from the common, "Yayyyy!" to the almost as common, "Shit; one woman is difficult enough. You're telling me I have a duty to deal with up to four of them?"

Of course it was never that simple. It couldn't be that simple. We're talking about the Roman Catholic Church here. There were forms to fill out, questions to answer, interviews to be sat, shrieks to be endured.

Tradition: It's what's for breakfast, lunch, dinner, and Holy Communion.

"Can you find the caves?" Sally asked, an amused smile on her Marlene Dietrich look-alike face. Sally had once played a German part, of sorts, in the one film she had starred in. Thus, when she'd had a choice on what appearance to take, she'd decided to adopt a well known German face, as well.

Neither the catacombs nor Rome itself meant much to Sally, except perhaps as the place from which had originated the crushing of the revolt of 66 to 73 AD and that of Bar Kochba, the city that had ordered the destruction of the Temple. It might even be said that she took a perverse satisfaction in the leveling of the city. She tried to feel ashamed of that but simply couldn't. Sally could hold a grudge.

Dwyer shrugged and answered, "I used to be able to find the catacombs. But then there were more landmarks to guide me." He paused, looked around, and corrected himself. "Back then there were *some* landmarks to guide me."

He stopped by the passing Swiss Guardsman Sally had pointed to, a member of the *Legio Pedestris Helvetiorum a Sacra Custodia Pontificis*, to ask for directions. The "Legio" had once been "Cohors," back when the guard had been considerably smaller. Now, with nearly thirteen thousand members, there was some call for upping the title from *Legio* to *Exercitus*. The Swiss Guard was not only the army of the Vatican, it had also become the police force for the city of Rome . . . such as remained.

Rather than give so many streets and corners and lefts and right, the guard simply pointed directly, and said, "The Via Appia lies that way. Follow that away from the city about three kilometers. To you," the guardsman added, recognizing the American uniform, "that would be about two miles."

Though the ground was strewn with shards and some bones, Dwyer could see no obstacle to bar their path. Thanking the guardsman, he and Sally moved onward in the direction they'd been shown.

"Watch out for abat holes and grat nests," the guardsman called after them.

The abat were colony animals, more or less rodent-like, while the grat were largish, wasplike creatures who fed on the abat. The abat had come with the Posleen ships and were essentially ineradicable. Thus, humanity would just have to learn to live with the grat, or risk being overrun by the abat.

"We will," Dwyer called back. "We know about the abat. My fiancée and I have been around."

He'd been born in Galway, Repubic of Ireland, before emigrating to the United States to enter the seminary. Sometimes, the brogue still came out, usually under stress. It used to come out under the influence of alcohol, but that had been a while. As with many of the multitudes of Irish who had come over, Dwyer had fallen in love with the United States of America more or less instantly. He'd become a citizen during his eleven years of Jesuit training.

Thereupon, seeing no special reason not to serve in the military or naval service, thinking he owed his adopted country much, and his superiors having no objection, he'd joined the Navy as a chaplain. He served sometimes aboard ship, sometimes on the ground with

Marine infantry or, once, combat engineers. Dwyer had marched on frozen feet, in Korea. He'd battled flames aboard the USS *Enterprise*. He'd been shelled silly a few times in Quang Ni Province, Vietnam, and taken rifle in hand in and around Da Nang and Hue. He'd been wounded, twice, not counting the burns from the *Enterprise*. Also not counting any bodily damage incurred during the Posleen war.

He'd retired, eventually, from the Navy and, to the extent it was possible, the priesthood. His drinking had gotten considerably worse by that time. That's how they'd found him, drunk, with his recall notice for the Posleen War.

"The entrance here used to be a sort of . . . well, a sort of a two-story temple," Dwyer said. "I remember it clearly . . . six columns, the two central ones grayish, the others a shade of brown." His voice sounded terribly wistful, as if those six columns meant something distinct from the ruin of the city.

"It's hardly the only thing that's been lost," Sally observed. "What are a few columns and some tons of rock and mortar compared to five billion people?"

"I know, dear, I know."

Sally looked dubiously at the entrance. It was flush with the ground. A tarp set up on poles covered it to protect the relics and martyrs below from the elements. Two of the oddly uniformed Swiss Guards stood outside it, their halberds resting against the tent poles. Odd uniforms or not, the weaponry in their hands was modern and first rate, products of Sig Sauer in Switzerland and updated for the Posleen war.

"Oh, God, I'm an idiot," Sally said, while chewing

her lower lip. "I should have thought of this; I can't go with you, Dan. I'm pushing the limits of ship-AID-flesh contact as it is, even with the ship anchored in the Tiber near the Lago di Traiano, no manmade interference, the AID under guard in Magliana, and the booster. Going underground? No way."

"Yes, I see that. Hmmm." The priest turned to what he thought to be the senior of the Swiss Guards, though that guard looked to be the younger. Just how the priest knew that the appearance was false was hard for him to put a finger on. Perhaps it was something in the younger-seeming guardsman's eyes. Dwyer asked, "Is there a coffee shop or a decent restaurant nearby?"

"Yes, Father," the guardsman answered. "But I wouldn't recommend it for a woman unescorted and alone. I wouldn't recommend anyplace in the City for a woman unescorted and alone. These weapons," and the guard indicated the resting halberds with the muzzle of his rifle, "are not just for show."

"Sally might surprise you," the priest answered. "Even so, can you . . . ?"

Instead of answering, the guardsman touched a button on a small box clipped to a belt around his waist and said, "*Wachtmeister* von Altishofen to Headquarters. Send me . . . ummm . . . *Hellebardier* de Courten: Service to the high clergy."

Dwyer wasn't really high clergy. Yet the *Wachtmeister* recognized the uniform which gave a sense of sacerdotal rank. The ribbons on the priest's chest von Altishofen didn't recognize, but there were enough of them to suggest real combat service. That was "high" enough, he likely thought.

"Affirmative, *Herr Wachtmeister*," came the response, barely audible from a small speaker apparently located somewhere in the guardsman's morion.

"It will be just a few minutes, Father."

"You know this is all silly, Dan," Sally muttered. "You don't need to make an honest woman of me. I'm yours for the asking and have been ever since..."

Golfo Dulce, Occupied Costa Rica, May, 2008

The first major wave of Posleen to erupt northwards from Mexico had been destroyed, albeit at the cost of the destruction of the U.S. Army's Eleventh Airborne Division (ACS). One might have expected that, given the rate of Posleen reproduction, the next major wave would have simply moved north unopposed. There never was, however, another major wave. The first, before it was crushed, had denuded the area along the border and deep past it of nearly everything edible. Subsequent waves, of which there were several, never made it very far into the United States before starving. After a while, when many had gone north only to disappear, the rest of the Posleen stopped trying. Their legends contained many stories of which the moral was something between "Curiosity killed the cat" and "Danger, Will Robinson."

That Posleen-made barrier, however, didn't stop them from breeding. Pressure within Mexico, therefore, continued to build. As things turned to shit for the Posleen in the American southwest and Mexico, pressure had built on some weaker clans by those more powerful, driving those weak ones to find someplace else, anyplace else, to live. That was generally south-ward and eastward. As Central America narrowed toward the south and east, these fleeing clans were forced into closer and closer proximity, greater and greater competition for food, and more frequent and bloodier interclan battle.

Fortunately, from some points of view, the Posleen could eat each other. And, of course, they did. Yet as clans were shattered and reformed, as new chiefs arose from the carnage, there came a time when there was only one clan, and that composed of the remnants of dozens of others, left in Nicaragua and Costa Rica, only one place for that composite clan to go, and only one good route to get there.

That clan—so said Intelligence—was the Clan of Gora'sinthaloor. That place was Panama. And that route was, roughly speaking, the Pan-American High-way where it entered that part of the Costa Rican Province of Puntarenas seized from the Posleen by Panama while Panama was under the rule of the dictator, Boyd.

Salem, the last remaining warship of the American Panama squadron then left afloat, was duly dispatched to support the boys and a few girls holding the Balboa Line across what had been the Costa Rican border. Holding was perhaps not the precise word, in the sense that the meat doesn't hold the meatgrinder; it just slows it down a bit. That's what the Panamanians—to say nothing of the Posleen normals, cosslain, and Kes-sentai—were doing, grinding each other to sausage.

Part of that grinding machine was CA-139, the USS Salem.

Rather, it had been part of the grinder. With Posleen

tenar swarming from every direction, with all three main turrets damaged, seven of nine secondaries shot away, smoke pouring out from a dozen places, the normal captain, Goldman, and his bridge crew dead, and the ship's auxiliary chaplain and a scratch bridge crew directing the counterflooding to keep her asymmetric below-the-water-line hits from capsizing her, Salem was pretty much out of the fight.

And furious about it.

"Turn around!" her holographic avatar screamed. "Bring us back around! I've still got two secondaries and I can aim my mains by turning the ship. Turn around, I said, you drunken Catholic bastard!"

"Salem," that auxiliary chaplain, Father Dwyer, SJ, had answered, his brogue leaking through, "you're a lovely girl and a lovely ship. But you've no business being in command of yourself. There is no good you can do now commensurate with the good you'll be able to do after a refit. Now, I'll make you a deal. You stop being a bitch and let me command—let me save—this ship without interruption, and I'll . . . I'll stop drinking . . . by the love of the saints, I will. But if you don't, I'll toss your blasted AID over the side, and bring the ship back for refit without you."

"You can't talk to me that way!"

Dwyer didn't answer. He simply went and took the AID from its armored box, then began walking to the edge of the metal platform half encircling the ruins of the bridge.

"You wouldn't dare!"

Dwyer began to wind up for a long toss. "Boston College baseball," he announced, over one shoulder. His arm began to straighten, as if for a long fly when—

"Stop! I'll shut up."

The father did stop, if barely.

"Will you really stop drinking?" the avatar asked.

"To save you, yes."

"I didn't know you cared."

"Then you have much to learn."

"Would you really have tossed me?" Sally asked.

"Not a chance," the priest answered. "But I had to give you a good excuse to overcome your conditioning and values."

"True," she agreed.

The *Wachtmeister* interrupted by coughing politely. "Your escort is here, miss. And, Father, you may proceed."

The caves were narrow, cramped, dusty and musty. No amount of cleaning seemed able to do much about any of that. They were well lit enough, though, for easy navigation; the Indowy-produced light panels on ceilings and walls lending a gentle but pervasive yellow glow.

Briefly, Dwyer laid a single ungloved hand upon the walls of the catacombs. For just a moment, he felt an almost electric connection with his predecessors, those early coreligionists who had met here . . . that, and with their all too frequent martyrdom.

There were slits, many of them, carved into the tunnels at varying heights. These, Dwyer suspected, were firing ports. He stopped at one doorway, its thick steel door hanging open, and followed a very narrow too narrow for a Posleen corridor to a room. There, in the Indowy-made light, he saw about what he'd expected to see, a firing slit and step, a quarter cylinder of galactic metal armor, a simplified range card, a crucifix, and a field telephone.

Yep; no wonder the Posleen never penetrated the catacombs very deeply.

Having fought the Posleen in the close confines of a warship's interior, Dwyer could just picture the poor beasties, stuck here below in a traffic jam of flesh, bleating, panic-stricken as they were trapped, fore and aft, by the fallen bodies of the others.

It hadn't been easy, but after a time Dwyer had learnt a degree of Christian compassion even for the inhuman enemy. That that enemy had spared him once, when he need not have, had helped.

Leaving the underground bunker, Dwyer proceeded farther down into the Earth. The *Wachtmeister* had told him that any changes in direction would be clearly marked with the "IHS" symbol of his order. This he found to be true as the cavernous tunnel branched and that symbol, together with an arrow, directed him leftward.

"Turn left here, miss," *Hellebardier* de Courten said as he and Sally reached the entrance of an unusually large shack, about a third mud brick, a third wood, and a third cardboard, set back from the Appian Way about forty feet. Two burly, beefy guards, swarthy and with hair sticking up above the collars of their T-shirts, each armed with a shotgun, stood in front of the shack's main entrance. They and de Courten nodded warily at each other.

Reaching the entrance, Sally looked over the menu, hand-scrawled with chalk on a large blackboard. "Oh, crap," she said. "I forgot about this. I can't eat any of it."

"Miss?" de Courten asked, his head cocking to one side.

Among clergy Dwyer was unusual, as most chaplains were unusual, in being subject to more than one master. One was God. The other was the branch of service, in his case the Navy. The third, and in many ways the most important, was the rail thin, cassocked man seated before him. Rather, it was the order that man represented.

That rail-thin, aesthetic-faced priest, Father Perales, an assistant to the father general of the order, shook his head wearily. "Father," Perales said, "it isn't that she's an artificially created body; His Holiness has already ruled that, in the interests of propagating the faith, artificial bodies are, under certain circumstances, acceptable.

"And it's not that her intelligence is machine; since your former ship, the USS *Des Moines*, was declared by the Nuncio of Panama to be a Servant of God, which declaration His Holiness implicitly approved."

Perales stood, and began to pace behind his desk. His hands clasped behind him, only to be unclasped and reclasped. Reaching for the words, unclasping his hands and throwing his arms wide, Perales exclaimed, "But for the love of God, Father, don't you realize the problem? She's *Jewish*!"

"It's not kosher," Sally said. "Nothing here is fit for me to eat. Aboard ship I've got my own...oh, never mind. And damn, damn, damn; I was hungry, too."

"Ohhh," de Courten agreed. "Hmmm...there is a small Jewish restaurant—well, it's more of a bed and breakfast, if not much of a bed—not too far away. I don't know how strictly kosher they are but—"

"Lead on, *Hellebardier*," Sally said. "Maybe I can bend a rule if it's not too much of a bend."

"Jewish is a problem, is it?" Dwyer asked, rhetorically. He bent over and picked up the phone. He dialed a number he knew by heart.

"Is the Holy Father in?" the priest asked. After a short period of silence, while Perales stared openmouthed at his underling, Dwyer said, "Joe? It's Dan... yes, Dan from the United States...Not bad, you?... Still in the Navy...sort of. Yes, it has been a long time. Why, sure, I'd love to come to dinner. Do you mind if I bring my fiancée? Well, we're supposed to get married next year but Father Perales seems to think there's a problem...well...she's Jewish, Joe... sorta Jewish, anyway. What's that? Oh...sure. But he's not really a pig."

Dwyer took the phone from his ear and, handing it to Father Perales, said with pseudo-warmth, "His Holiness would like a brief word with you."

This highly limited menu, too, was handscrawled on a blackboard. As with the prior restaurant, there was a strong Italianate flavor to the offerings.

"Well," Sally said, after scrutinizing, "at least there's no pork on the menu. And I don't see any impermissible mixes like dairy with meat...no tref."

De Courten had the good grace not to mention the possibility that there might be pork on the menu, going under another name. Instead, he observed, "No Posleen on the menu, either."

"I couldn't eat those either," Sally answered. "Even if they were kosher, they taste, so I'm told, vile beyond description. And that's even if you hang 'em by the heels and cut their throats to let 'em bleed out." Indicating the door, she asked, "Shall we?"

Reaching for the door's handle, de Courten pulled it open for Sally, then, apparently having thought better of it, held up one hand to stop her and, taking his own rifle in hand, preceded her inside.

If it was an unusual event to see a Swiss Guard enter the restaurant, nobody indicated it. Yes, people, the few there were, looked up but, having looked up, immediately went back to their business. In most cases this was eating. One thing de Courten did notice that was a bit unusual was the bartender bending behind his bar as if returning a weapon to a handy shelf.

"It's clear, miss," the *Hellebardier* said over one shoulder. "You can come in now." He held the door open for her, at least partly for the excuse it would give him to admire her gently swaying rear end as she passed.

I think she must be the most beautiful woman I've ever seen, the boy thought. *A contender, anyway.*

Sally entered as de Courten held the door. The Swiss boy's eyes never more than glanced down. Once inside, she stopped only long enough to accustom her eyes to the dimmer light inside. "Thank you, *Hellebardier,*" she said.

The maitre d', if such a title could be given in such an establishment, came over immediately. "You don't look Jewish," he said to Sally suspiciously. Then, turning to de Courten, he added, "and by your uniform you surely are not."

"It's the only religion I've ever followed," Sally answered. "Will you seat us?" Seeing that he would, Sally added, "And while we're here, I have a few questions about the menu."

Perales was never given the chance to question the Holy Father's words. Dwyer tried not to smirk as his superior's narrow face blanched under the telephonic tongue-lashing. Within a few moments of it, the senior priest had arisen from his office chair and come to a fair approximation of the position of attention. Perales gulped once, answered, "Yes, Holy Father," and replaced the telephone on its receiver.

"It seems I was in spiritual error," Perales said, after reseating and recomposing himself. "There'll be no problem with your fiancée, Jewish or not."

CHAPTER THREE

Of boma blades and the Kessentai I sing
Who first from shameful defeat led forth his people
To found a new life in the depths of space
—The *Tuloriad*, Na'agastenalooren

Anno Domini 2009
Himmit Ship Surreptitious Stalker

The debris of battle in space was everywhere. Inasmuch
as things can be thick in the vastness of space, that
debris could be said to have been "thick." Here was
a recognizable section of a Posleen globe's bulkhead;
there was the bloated, half-exploded body of a normal,
its blood congealed in icicles around its muzzle and
the rent in its midsection. A small human space fighter
drifted by, its pilot carbonized, burned almost to ash,
yet held in place by the remnants of his battle suit
and the restraining straps. Farther away, the forward
section of a human light cruiser tumbled end over
end as its edges glowed and sparked where it had
been sheared from the rest of its ship. Farthest of

all, in Tulo'stenaloor's view, a nearly whole battleglobe exploded by sections as the humans pounced upon it from every angle.

"We're so fucked," Brasingala muttered, almost too low for Tulo to hear.

This is defeat, a tiny voice whispered in Tulo's mind. *Avoid it.*

If I'd known how, I would have, the God King whispered back.

Ahead, yet another of the countless millions of spinning Posleen bodies that littered space seemed destined to smash directly onto the *Surreptitious Stalker*. All eyes—all those, at least, that faced forward—saw it and braced for an unpleasant impact. Closer and closer the body came. By bits, it seemed to dissolve as it reached a certain distance from the Himmit ship. A restless muttering from behind them caused Tulo, Brasingala, and Goloswin to turn their heads. Yes, there behind them, still spinning, the same corpsicle twisted away.

"I wonder how they do that," Goloswin said.

"We all wonder how they do half the things they do," said Aelool. "A very strange species, the Himmit, and there is more to them then they'll ever let you see."

"Yes," agreed Goloswin. "But instantaneous transmission of matter? That's something special."

"It appears they can only do it over very short distances," Aelool said. "That, or they're only willing to let us see them transmit matter over very short distances. As I said, there's more to the Himmit than they'll ever let on."

"Admirable, then," Goloswin answered. "Better to be more than you seem."

"Admirable, no doubt," Aelool agreed. "Yet it is

hard to trust someone who may have a dagger poised in their hidden hand."

"You have reasons to be suspicious?" Tulo asked.

"Yes," Aelool answered, but then wouldn't say any more.

The viewing screens showed a brace of human light cruisers racing on what had to be an intercept course for the *Surreptitious Stalker*.

"If you believe in a higher being," the Himmit captain, Argzal, announced over the ship's intercom, "pray to it now. Aelool, if you could come to the bridge?"

Tulo'stenaloor twisted his head one hundred and eighty degrees and said, "Walk over our backs. No one will complain."

This wasn't precisely true, Aelool discovered, as he stepped gingerly from one broad, scaly, yellow back to another. Many of the Posleen, soldiers first and foremost, seemed to be operating off of the ancient military principle, "Don't sleep when you're tired; sleep when you can." These had duly nodded off, heads hanging low or resting on the backs of others. More than once, in his progress towards the hatchway that led to the ship's bridge, Aelool's body weight was enough to awaken them, snarling and spitting. More than once, a Posleen senior had had to call off the just-awakened ones' snapping jaws.

It was with a considerable, even a profound, sense of relief that Aelool reached the limits of the Posleen mass and was helped down to the deck, held gently in firm claws. It was only when the hatchway closed behind him that the Indowy began to tremble, as his body had been demanding to tremble ever since he'd spotted the Posleen refugees on the planet below.

Muttering an Indowy curse at the fate that had brought him to nest among so many carnivores, Aelool proceeded up the corridor—still lit, here with the Himmits' preferred blue-green—until he reached a tube that led upward to the bridge or downward to a portion of the ship with which he was unfamiliar.

Stepping into the tube, Aelool shot upwards; this technology, at least, was something Himmit and Indowy shared. He stopped as suddenly as he'd begun. Though the tube continued upwards, somehow it—or the computer that controlled it— had known where to bring the Indowy to a halt. Stepping off, Aelool saw a circular hatchway a few meters ahead. This dilated immediately. He stepped forward and through.

"Welcome, Indowy Aelool," said the captain, lying across a sort of quilted couch with one of his heads at each end.

"I see you, Captain Argzal." Aelool looked at the bridge's view screen. "I see them, too. A pity you couldn't hide."

"The humans have gotten much better in space, Aelool. We are fortunate to have gotten as far as we have without detection."

A voice came from a hidden speaker somewhere on the bridge. "Unidentified ship, this is Captain Yolanda Sanchez, Fleet Strike light cruiser *Ramon Magsaysay*. Heave to. Cease all forward movement. Do not attempt to go hyperlight. Do not attempt to engage stealth. Prepare to be boarded."

"Well, we can't allow that," Aelool muttered. "Under the circumstances, the humans would skin us and our passengers alive."

"My contract does not cover my being flayed," the Himmit said.

"Nor does mine. Can I speak to this Captain Sanchez?"

The Himmit made no sound, but ran a finger over a small plate on one side of his command couch. "You may speak now," it said. With the same motion the view of the stars disappeared, being replaced by the face of a brown-skinned woman with large eyes, a delicate chin and very high cheekbones. Large or not, the eyes seemed quite feral to both the Himmit and the Indowy.

"Captain Sanchez," Aelool began, "is it possible that we might speak privately?"

"An Indowy on a Himmit smuggler?" the human captain observed. "That's one for the books." She hesitated only a moment before adding, "Yes, give me a moment."

Aelool caught sight of a bustling bridge before the screen went blank, temporarily. When it shone again, the background had changed to something much less busy, something almost homelike, as a human might consider home. Sanchez, this time, appeared seated at a desk clean except for a computer monitor. A fair-sized tank of tropical fish was mounted into the wall behind her, the tank being surrounded by various trophies, pictures, and mementos. Aelool imagined that some form of miniature inertial dampening system probably kept both water and sealife contained during maneuvers.

"What's your excuse?" Sanchez began brusquely. "You are aware, are you not, that the Earth is under interdiction until the Posleen infestation is cleared out?"

"It is as an agency of that clearing out," Aelool answered, "that we are on this mission." This was, of course, at some level true. It was also, at another level, a bald-faced lie. Aelool turned to Argzal. "Captain, can you focus your viewing devices just on me?"

Some things were not suitable for reduction to electronic memory. This was not because they could not be so reduced, but that electronic memory was, by its nature, hackable memory. Thus, the Bane Sidhe, the "Killers of Elves" who formed the resistance within the Galactic Federation to Darhel tyranny, often used written media, pictograms, and the like, for things which must be kept utterly secure. One of these, a geometric design drawn by machine on a thin sheet of GalPlas, the Indowy removed from somewhere inside his tunic and spread across his chest.

Sanchez's already large eyes widened still further at whatever suddenly appeared on the monitor on her desk. Aelool knew what she was seeing there, orders to allow the bearer of the certificate he had shown to proceed unmolested, coupled with an order to maintain silence, which orders would disappear from her ship's computer within an hour. The orders had been deeply embedded in that computer, awaiting the design Aelool had shown to activate them. Over the course of time the subroutine that would cause those orders to disappear would likewise infect every computer in the Fleet, likewise causing them to eradicate all trace of the orders. The Bane Sidhe could not have known, after all, which human ship or ships might intercept. Thus, they'd infected them all.

"I . . . see," Sanchez said. "This is most . . . irregular, Indowy Aelool. Nonetheless, they appear official, and carry the highest classification." Sanchez nodded her head, as if to herself and only slowly and reluctantly. "You may proceed, *Surreptitious Stalker*. But I *shall* inquire about these orders."

"Captain," Aelool answered, keeping tension from his voice by sheer will, "if you would take well-meant advice? Do not inquire."

Tensions were high in the cargo compartment. With not just one but two human light cruisers with their guns brought to bear on the Himmit ship, Tulo'stenaloor wouldn't have given a esonal's chance in an abat hole for the likelihood he and his people would survive another ten minutes. When the screens changed to show a human face, the sense of dread and doom only increased.

"Now that," observed Goloswin, "is one vicious looking human."

"Indeed," Tulo'stenaloor agreed, his crest automatically erecting with the threat the human's presence implied. "And most unusual to find one of their females, their bearing sex, in command of combat forces."

"How do you know it's a female? They all look alike to me."

"The projections on the chest," Tulo explained. "Though some don't seem to have them; still, where present they're a good indicator."

"Himmit," Tulo called, "can you translate what's being said, please?"

"Yes," Argzal's voice answered.

". . . This is most . . . irregular, Indowy Aelool . . . Nonetheless, they appear official, and carry the highest classification...You may proceed, *Surreptitious Stalker*...But I shall inquire about these orders."

The face of the vicious looking human female cut out, to be replaced by a view of space, where two human light cruisers began to turn away from the Himmit ship.

"We got away with it?"

"For now, Goloswin," Tulo answered. "If this is the closest call we have, I will count us lucky."

"That was shitty luck," Argzal mused. "We should have been able to avoid them. Strange that they could detect us. I wonder what other little techno-tricks you Indowy have given the humans of which my people are unaware."

Aelool offered the Himmit nothing but an inscrutable gaze. Changing the subject, he said, "It is time I go back to our passengers. The ship won't support feeding them, not more than a score or so, anyway. The rest must go into hibernation."

"Indeed," Argzal agreed. "And I would have to be asleep myself not to notice that you did not answer my question. How do you propose to put them into hibernation if they refuse?"

"Simple," the Indowy answered. "If they refuse, I'll just tell them that you'll open the cargo hold to space."

"Oh, that should win their trust and affection."

Trust, as it turned out, wasn't an issue. The Posleen didn't refuse, nor balk, nor even question. "It only makes sense," Tulo'stenaloor had commented, gazing around at the sardine-can conditions in the cargo hold. "Leave us like this and we'll be killing and eating each other in no time. Still, it's going to be strange subjecting ourselves to stasis while under someone else's power. Then again, it's not as if we're not already in someone else's power. You could, I imagine, just open the cargo hold to space if we refused."

Aelool said nothing to that, either. He did, however, wonder, *Do we all have a common ancestor, or even a creator, that we think so much alike even when we usually act so differently?*

Before he'd even finished the thought, Tulo had shouted out some orders and the Posleen were, in the main and sheeplike, shuffling to the stasis chambers.

In the end, Tulo left out of hibernation only a relative few. These included his guard, Brasingala, Goloswin the Tinkerer, plus Exo, Essone, Esstwo, Essthree, and Essfour, a single cosslain, the late mesergen's assistant, to act as a general servant and bring them their meals. In addition, Tulo'stenaloor had kept awake one of his operational commanders who had managed to rejoin his headquarters after his own horde was destroyed. The last left awake was Binastarion, refugee from the fighting on Earth near where the two minor continents were joined at a narrow waist, and himself missing an eye and an arm. Binastarion's position, since he had thrown his stick and given up the path of fury, was ambiguous. A human might have called it, "Senior Advisor." Two more of Tulo's long-time senior pack chiefs, plus his Rememberer, completed the company.

These thirteen, Tulo and his twelve, remained awake. Outside of the company, but still present, Aelool stood just in front of Tulo, as much for the sense of safety as for any other reason. There, while Tulo'stenaloor, himself, might devour him in two bites, he could at least feel safe from the remainder.

Each Posleen had a bucket of a mushlike substance in front of him, set there by the single cosslain, the former assistant to the mesergen. It was nourishment, and perhaps a bit better than what was exuded from their own ships' galleys, being both less bland and of a more satisfyingly chewy texture. Even so, they knew they would have to find their happiness elsewhere.

"If Jesus had a twelve man A-Team," the Indowy muttered, quoting from a song he had heard the Armored Combat Suited troopers of Fleet Strike sing on more than one occasion.

"What's that?" Tulo asked, over the Indowy's shoulder.

"Oh, I just noticed that the number twelve figures prominently in the writings and history of the humans, as well, Tulo."

"We are thirteen, Indowy," Tulo corrected, "not counting yourself."

"Ah. My mistake. So you are. How wonderful for us, then. So do the humans, sometimes, number themselves as such and the number is considered to be extraordinarily portentous."

I wish I could read that little snack's facial expressions better, thought the chief Kessentai.

The other eleven key Kessentai and Kessenalt formed a rough circle (for the single cosslain standing out of the way could hardly be said to count and Brasingala almost instinctively took a position behind and to one side of Tulo, the better to guard his chief's back). With Tulo at what the humans would have called "the head of the table" or "twelve-o'clock," the others were, going clockwise, Exo, Essone, Essfour, Goloswin, the Rememberer, Chorobinaloor, Gorasinth'zula, Binastarion, the one-eyed and -armed, Esstwo, and Essthree before rounding back to Tulo'stenaloor.

"You wished to address us, Aelool," Tulo announced. "Here is your chance."

The Indowy gulped, a habit his people and the humans shared. He then, while trying to show no unseemly reluctance, stepped out into the middle of the circle.

Well, Aelool thought, *if one of them tries to eat me the odds are good that the others will try to beat that one to the punch. I might get away in the confusion. And here's hoping that Argzal has one grasping digit poised over the stasis beams he's told me he has focused on our guests.*

"I claim edas," Aelool began. Edas was the Posleen word for debt or obligation. It was their practical high level currency. "I claim edas for your lives I have saved, for your people I have rescued from extinction, and for your civilization, the kernel of which I have shielded. Do you accept this?"

I knew this was coming, thought Tulo'stenaloor. *Anything too good to be true, just like the thing the humans call a "free lunch," isn't.*

It was the Rememberer who answered for the group. "We accept edas, alien, as it shall be computed and allocated by the Net, accounting for your lawful preferences. This is the law," the Rememberer added, glaring around the circle for any that might gainsay him. He didn't mention that the net was, until they could reacquire some artificial sentiences, quite defunct.

There were no takers to the Rememberer's challenge

in any case. Ravenous, murderous, genocidal, homicidal maniacs the Posleen, as a race, might have been. Yet, still, the law was the law and they would obey it.

"I claim then, first, that both my person and my people shall be inviolable by you and yours and your descendants to the last flickering of the final star."

"We accept," answered the Rememberer, for all Kessentai present. "Let the Net so record. Let it also be recorded that we cannot speak for, nor owe obligation to pay edas for, any of the People of the Ships not present in this ship."

"Understood," Aelool agreed. "I claim second, that if I or any of my people should call for you to come to our aid, this you must do, you and your descendants until the last star flickers out."

"We accept."

"Lastly, I require of you that you must forego revenge against the humans who, after all, did no more than you yourselves were trying to do, to survive."

At this condition the Rememberer froze, its crocodilian lips drawn back from clenched teeth. Nor was it the only one to balk. The others—except for Binastarion—made similar grimaces, or reached for boma blades, or reached forth claws as if to rend the Indowy into little bits.

"WE ACCEPT!" thundered Tulo'stenaloor, his iron voice freezing the rest in place. "With the proviso that we may still defend ourselves from any humans who come hunting for us."

"This," agreed Aelool, "is fair." *If the humans should ever learn to track you, where you're going . . . and how you're getting there.*

✧   ✧   ✧

The *Surreptitious Stalker* neither glided between the stars as did Indowy and Darhel ships, nor tunneled quite as did the ships of the Posleen. Rather, in the parlance, it "skipped." That is to say, it made a series of relatively small jumps between points, often using what the Himmit called the "Hidden Path," none of them so long and thus energy intensive as to be likely to be noticed. This was often a fairly slow method. Its big advantage was that it was relatively stealthy. Only in the short interruptions while preparing a new jump were the ships of the *Stalker*'s class detectible, and then only for so long as it took to begin the new jump or end one. Even then, the odds of there being another ship nearby when they materialized were exceedingly poor, especially given that the Hidden Path did not use normal ley lines between major stars.

Of course, the doctrine for Himmit scout-smugglers called for them to make only random progress towards their destination, appearing first here, then there, then somewhere else not all that noticeably closer to their target. Thus, the journey to the system of Diess, the fourth planet of which had been the scene of the first truly major engagement between Posleen and human forces, took months as the humans measured time. When the ship emerged into normal space after its final jump, no one expected it, nor could have expected it.

"I recognize the constellations," Tulo'stenaloor said to Brasingala, gesturing at the view screens, now showing a three hundred and sixty degree field of view. "This was where I first began to understand the human threat, and our own weakness when facing them. Of course," he added, "I never understood them well enough, or in time, for it to do any good."

"You understood better than the rest of us, lord," Brasingala said. "And sooner. You did the best that any of us could. More than this, the spirits of the ancestors never ask."

Tulo sighed. "Less than victory has seen us huddled as refugees in an alien ship."

Brasingala shrugged his oddly jointed double shoulders, repeating, "You did the best you could, lord."

"Will my descendants think so, Brasingala? When they are hunted from planet to planet like vermin, will they think so?"

"I am your descendant, lord, and I think so. Besides, we don't know that they will be so hunted."

"No . . . but it's a likely guess. Sometimes I wish . . ."

"Lord?"

"Oh . . . sometimes I wish we had remembered our ancient contacts with the species that became Man, gone forth in the friendship we once knew, met them with open arms."

"We knew the humans, lord?"

"Of old, Brasingala, of old."

"I didn't know that."

Tulo reached up one claw to scratch his muzzle. "They did, if they cared to draw the analogy. Among our own people, it's not something generally known, but if one searches out the histories and the three disciplines, and consults some of the scrolls of the Rememberers, one cannot avoid the conclusion that we knew the humans eons ago. There is no other species that matches both the physical, the intellectual and the moral descriptions. For their bizarre reproductive behavior alone they would stand out as unique."

"Might I read of these in the disciplines, the histories, and the scrolls, lord?" Brasingala asked.

"I shall discuss the appropriateness with our Rememberer. We shall see."

Brasingala went stock still for a moment, then pointed at the view screen behind Tulo'stenaloor, to a planet fast filling the compartment-wide view screen. So quickly did the planet grow in size that it seemed they must crash into it. "See that, lord."

Tulo rotated his head one hundred and eighty degrees to his rear to look. "Ancestors!" he exclaimed.

CHAPTER FOUR

And Ruth said, "Entreat me not to leave
thee, or to return from following after thee:
for whither thou goest, I will go; and where
thou lodgest, I will lodge: thy people shall
be my people, and thy God my God."
 —Ruth 1:16, King James version

Anno Domini 2013–Anno Domini 2019
Rome, Latium

His Holiness, rejuvenated or not, and even a bit
tubby or not, was mature charm personified. Even
Sally, though Jewish, felt the tug. And, much like
Dwyer, he had stories going back to his boyhood in
World War II. (It had, in fact, been some of Dwyer's
attraction to Sally that he had done the things, which
is to say fought the war, for which the steel portion
of her being had been created.)

And he knew enough to arrange kosher, Sally thought.
*I mean, sure, he's got protocol people for that sort of
thing, the best. But even so . . .*

After dinner, the pope beat around the bush for some time with various pleasantries, expressing his explicit regret that he would not be able to travel to Panama to preside over Sally's impending wedding. Still, he assured her that the service would be of the best. "Or heads will roll, my dear; heads will roll."

In time, too, the conversation turned more serious.

"Expressly, Dan," said His Holiness, "I'm concerned about the Posleen."

Sally bit off the vulgarity that first came to her lips, letting Dwyer carry on the conversation.

"Concerned, Joe?"

"Concerned for their souls, Dan. I'd help them to see the light, such as were willing to see it, if I only knew how."

At that, Sally could not keep quiet. "Posleen... Darhel; they're all just devils incarnate. The only good ones are dead and I wouldn't mind making a whole lot more of them good."

Iglesia del Carmen, *Panama City, Panama*

The Darhel hated Boyd, a feeling he returned with usury. He'd put a price on their heads, a bounty, within the area controlled by the Republic during his time as dictator. The bounty had not been a particularly small one, either. Though the war was effectively over, and Boyd had long since given up the office of dictator, the bounty had never officially been rescinded even though it had been years, decades, since someone had collected on it.

There were, thus, no Darhel in Panama. Thus, there

had been no Darhel present to object when Panama had granted citizenship to both the USS *Des Moines*, it was believed at the time to be posthumously, and the USS *Salem*, both as ships (to which the U.S. Navy had had a few objections, all of them settled out of court with reference to the Thirteenth through Fifteenth Amendments to the United States Constitution, Sally's willing enlistment and direct commissioning into the Navy, and finally Boyd's purchase of the hulls as "scrap") and as AIDs, Artificial Intelligence Devices. Once the ships and AIDs had become "people" there could, of course, be no objection.

It was said that hundreds of Darhel, many of them quite high ranking, had fallen prey to lintatai, a form of catatonia, leading inexorably to death, when news of that award had reached the Darhel homeworlds. Unfortunately for them, Boyd had at his disposal a battery of first class lawyers who discovered that there was no law under the Galactic code expressly to forbid granting citizenship and full civil rights to artificial intelligences.

There were rumors that the Darhel had deliberately, on orders from the very highest levels, begun preparing to shut down every AID under human control lest those, too, be granted citizenship somewhere. Whether that was the primary motivation—or some other factor was; with the Darhel there were always layers within layers, motivations within motivations—Boyd had made it clear that any attempt on the life or health of a citizen of the Republic of Panama would be treated as an act of war. Since Sally was not only immune to Darhel cybernetic manipulations, but had frightful firepower and was executrix for Daisy's not particularly small estate, to boot, this was not a threat to be taken lightly.

One side effect of this was that Sally had been able to create a flesh and blood body for herself openly and without Galactic interference. It was that body, the spitting image of a young Marlene Dietrich, clad in white, with veil and train, that walked down the central aisle of the church, escorted by Boyd and flanked by literally thousands of onlookers and well wishers, turned out in their best to see the remarkable spectacle of a ship marrying a priest. More thousands waited outside.

Perhaps that they owed their lives, in good part, to the ship didn't hurt matters any, either, attendance-wise.

The Jewish warship marrying the Jesuit priest wasn't the only bizarre quality to the wedding. The priest had had to choose a best man. In the end, after some serious thought on the subject, the Jesuit had asked the only member of *Salem*'s crew still living who had also served with him aboard *Des Moines*.

"I'd be honored, Father," Sintarleen—also called "Sinbad"—had said, then. "Relax, Dan; I've got the ring," the Indowy said now.

"I wasn't worried about the ring," Dwyer answered. "You made the bloody thing, you furry little Niebelung; you ought to still have it. It's just . . ."

"Never been married before?"

"That . . . and never any of the stuff that goes with it. You know . . . ummm."

"Sex?"

The priest shrugged. "Sex . . . children . . . the whole package. I don't know how to do any of it."

"Relax," the Indowy insisted. "At least you only have two sexes. Imagine our problems."

"If you don't mind, I'd rather not."

Sinbad smiled an inscrutable Indowy smile. "Why did your church institute celibacy?"

The tone of Dwyer's voice suggested he was almost thankful to have something to take his mind of his nerves. "Do your people serve their clan first or the Indowy species?" he asked.

"Well . . . clan, of course. Blood comes first."

"Yes. We're alike in that much. Well, celibacy was a way, an imperfect way, to be sure, to help ensure that our priests had no interest in advancing their families, but only in seeing to the interests of the church as a whole."

"That couldn't work," Sinbad objected. "They still had brothers and sisters, aunts and uncles and cousins."

"Indeed," the priest agreed. "They also, often enough, had mistresses and children by them. Even some popes did. As a matter of fact—"

Whatever Dwyer had been about to say was cut off as Sally made her appearance on the arm of Boyd and the organ kicked in with the wedding march. The crowd immediately went silent.

"We've got to hurry this, Sally," Boyd whispered. "We've an appointment . . . with your sister."

CA-134, USS Des Moines, Bahia de *Panama*

Some appointments one just can't really prepare for. Boyd, for example, could never have been fully prepared for what awaited him once he'd boarded the refloated hulk of the *Des Moines*, aka the "Daisy Mae."

"Meow?" Morgen, the kitty, leapt from the fog-spewing tank and landed in the arms of a sputtering Boyd.

"Are you all right, Dictator?" Sally's holographic avatar asked. Her flesh and blood body, and that of the Jesuit, lay in the admiral's quarters opposite the captain's shed that Boyd reserved for himself.

"Sure," he answered unsteadily. "And as soon as this heart attack passes..." He stopped speaking as another being arose from the tank, this one human and very, very female. The woman opened her mouth as if to speak, but said nothing.

Boyd turned to Sally's avatar. "You knew about this?"

"I suspected. Oh, yes, I knew Daisy had bought an under-the-table tank. I knew she was growing a body. That's what gave me the idea of growing one for myself. But I only suspected she was still in—"

Another body sat up besides Daisy Mae's. "I'm alive? No way. I mean no fucking way!"

"Captain McNair?" Boyd asked.

"Now him I didn't even suspect," Sally's avatar said.

"Whwhwhyyy nnnottt?" asked Morgen, cocking her head to one side.

Boyd dropped the cat as if its surface temperature had suddenly soared by thousands of degrees. He sat heavily on the still wet decking. "I might not have been joking about that heart attack," he gulped.

The cat looked up at him, licked its chops, and asked, "Cccannn I gggettt sssommmethththingngng ttto eattt? Arrre thththerrre annny rrratttsss lllefffttt?"

"You set the tank on full upgrade, didn't you, Sister?" Sally's avatar asked of the silent woman.

Daisy Mae just nodded, with a broad smile, and held her arms out for the cat. Morgen leapt up into her arms and nuzzled her breasts while Daisy's hands stroked the cat's head and body.

"Why doesn't she talk?" Boyd asked.

Daisy looked helplessly at Sally, hoping she would explain.

Sally did. "She never practiced speech in the tank. It was . . . an oversight."

Daisy nodded briskly, then looked down, embarrassed.

After stroking the cat for a while, perhaps in part to hide her embarrassment, Daisy looked up at Sally with an expression that asked, *what now?*

"There are rumors that we've got another war coming, Sis. Maybe worse than the last one. And you're going to be drafted. So am I. We're the last reliable AIDs left." At Daisy's quizzical expression, Sally answered, "Well, of *course*, I listen in on Fleet and Fleet Strike traffic."

Still sitting in the water gathered on the deck, Boyd added, "And so am I . . . drafted that is. Or going to be. The bastards."

"She's up," Sally announced to her new husband, who was rocking with the sway of the ship while lying on the mattress beside her. What the cruiser's gentle motion did for Sally's flesh and blood breasts was something that had to be seen, for those who doubted the existence of a loving God. "Captain McNair's fine, too."

"Wazzat? Sorry, love, I was dozing. I'm quite old, you know. We old people doze a lot." Dwyer looked and was physically at the age of about twenty-five.

Sally smiled warmly, half in happiness at the resurrection of her sister and sister ship, and half at her new husband and some very new memories. Sex, she'd discovered, was even better than it was cracked up to be.

"I said that the recovery operation went fine, that Daisy is still alive, and that McNair is, too."

"That's nice," Dwyer answered absently, rolling over to lay his head on her shoulder. She wasn't at all sure that he'd really heard. After all, he'd also discovered, and quite recently, that sex was even better than it was cracked up to be. Moreover, since he'd been very innocent and Sally had a cybernetic memory of every porn film and sex guide ever made, she'd probably made it both better and more exhausting for him than he'd made it for her. If so, however, she wasn't complaining.

"Will there be any trouble, do you think," the Jesuit asked, "over Daisy having been 'dead' all this time?"

"Nobody issues official death certificates on warships," Sally answered. "Her 'estate' is in trust, with me in charge, and I'm certainly not going to deny her her due. The Darhel, who might be expected to object, are too frightened to set foot here. And any lawyer they might find suicidal enough to try to interfere for them won't last long. Not here, in Panama."

USS *Salem*'s engines churned the blue-green water of the Bay of Panama to a froth behind her. Still farther behind, connected by cables a foot thick, *Des Moines*' bow cut through the waves of *Salem*'s wake. The towed ship was a mess, not merely from the many hits it had taken from Posleen weaponry, but also from the rust, and from the sea growth—barnacles and seaweed—clustered about it or hanging from its broken guns.

McNair and Daisy—not the avatar but the flesh and blood girl—stood on the bridge, with Boyd and Sally's avatar. Sally and Dwyer would join them as soon the ships docked. Maybe. Unless they decided to give it another go while they had the *Salem* and the admiral's quarters to themselves. Which they very well might.

Daisy held the cat in her arms, stroking its fur. It purred contentedly, or at least as contentedly as a starving cat may. Because Daisy had never learned to speak, during her growing time in the tank, she didn't try to for now. Learning how, however, was very high on her list of priorities, once she reached shore. She had a perfect body and near peerless intelligence, so she did not expect that learning to be either difficult or time consuming.

While the arms held the cat, Daisy's eyes held an apology, as much as to say, *I'm sorry you have to tow me.*

"Nonsense," *Salem's* avatar answered. "And stop looking so apologetic. You're not heavy; you're my sister."

"Are you up for a reception?" Boyd asked of McNair and Daisy. "We've restored the old Fort Amador Officers' Club. It's in range—half a mile, isn't it?—of your ship."

"I've figured out how to increase that range substantially," *Salem's* avatar said, "but, yes, until I can show Daisy how to fix it herself, half a mile is about her range, or a full mile if she drops the AID at the half-mile point and continues on another half mile herself."

"In any case," Boyd continued, "will you come? There are a lot of people who'd really like to meet you."

"I don't have a suitable uniform," McNair said, looking down at the torn scraps of a naval uniform he'd been wearing in *Des Moines'* last action. The flesh beneath was healed without a scar. Yet the tank did nothing with nonliving material.

"Ahem," Boyd answered. "I used to be dictator of this place. You think I can't get you a uniform made in a matter of hours?"

"Ahh . . . ca' . . . tal' ye' . . . Ahh je' c-c-can'," Daisy added, then hung her head in shame.

"The way you look, honey," Boyd answered, "You don't have to say a word. Besides, I'll have an aide whisper to everyone who comes not to press you for conversation. It's not a problem. And the same tailor can do up something for you."

McNair and Daisy exchanged glances. "All right then, Dictator," McNair agreed. "We'll go."

The tugs maneuvered deftly to bring *Des Moines* to position along the quay. *Salem* had cast off her tow line. A crew was standing by on the pier to post a gangway alongside *Des Moines*. Yet another was there to see to whatever remains of the dead could be recovered from the ship. That latter group was uniformed: U.S. Navy.

Far more interesting, at least to McNair and Daisy Mae, was a much smaller, yellow-skinned group, sitting by the edge of the pier with no human within fifty yards. Two of the three Posleen—the largest and the smallest—had fishing poles thrust out over the edge, the lines running down to the murky water below. The second largest one sat between them, its head resting on the shoulder of the largest. The pole of the largest was held in a kind of frame, while the creature itself appeared to be whittling on some wood with a small carving knife.

The local waters were still badly polluted, but a little diesel taste in the fish was all spice to the Posleen.

"What the—?"

Boyd laughed. McNair's shock and Daisy's wide eyes were everything he'd hoped for. "That, my friends, is the Reverend Doctor Guanamarioch de Po'osleenar, his...umm...wife, and their one child. They, too, are citizens of the Republic, and loyal to their new home."

"Reverend? Doctor?" McNair asked.

"Guano went to divinity school...ordained Baptist, I believe, though it might be Episcopal. You should hear him rail sometime about the 'Whore of Rome.' I understand he gives a helluva sermon. Only through his artificial sentience, of course."

"Is it too late to go back into the tank until the world stops being weird?" McNair asked. "And how is it that a couple of Posleen only have one child? They drop eggs about every two weeks and..."

"I asked Guano about that once," Boyd answered. "He says they put 'em, individually, in a pen. After a few weeks it becomes obvious that the nestling either will or won't become sentient. Only about one in four hundred does. As for the others...they eat the little bastards. Would you like to meet them?"

Daisy shook her head, no, vociferously. "Ha' mu'fu'in po'lee."

Boyd sighed. Yes, he understood. You can't lose nearly a million of your countrymen and simply forgive and forget. Had Guano's circumstances been other than they were—his band destroyed and himself enslaved and crippled—or had he not proven so valuable an intelligence asset, Boyd would have happily shot the Posleen down on the spot, years before when they'd first met. Forgiveness took time, time the ship and the girl hadn't had.

"You really ought to give him a chance, though," Boyd said. "Guano's all right. Especially since he gave up snorting VX."

CHAPTER FIVE

Speak, O Demons, of the peerless
armor of the god-like Goloswin,
He of the clever ways and the subtle mind,
Who assists now the Great Being in the running of
The clockwork timing of the universe.
—The *Tuloriad*, Na'agastenalooren

Anno Domini 2010
Himmit Ship Surreptitious Stalker, *Diess System*

It was a surreal scene. The *Stalker* was nearly wrapped in the battered hulks of a Posleen ghost fleet, the fleet having been towed into a position of stable orbit pending recovery and scrapping. On every side of the cargo compartment, the view screens showed images of battered and cracked hulls. Unlike the wrecks floating around Earth, these ships neither glowed, nor sparked, nor burned, nor spilled out the dying husks of Posleen crew.

These wrecks were dead and had been for years. In human terms, this was a boneyard. Nonetheless, it was not an entirely dead boneyard. The antimatter containment units were still active. Normally this should not have been true; antimatter was simply too valuable to have been left ungathered. On the other hand, if you're the Darhel, the galaxy's lawyers, bureaucrats, and corporate sharks, and you've cornered the market on antimatter, and suddenly there's just a vast quantity of antimatter that threatens to undercut the entire galactic market, then you, too, might decide that a little visited corner of the Federation was just the place to dump that antimatter for a while until you could figure out how to put it into the system without upsetting that system.

And the band of Tulo'stenaloor couldn't get at any of it.

Binastarion sat on his haunches, with his gruel bucket held in one hand. With the other, the Kessentai rolled little balls of gruel, using a clawed thumb-cognate to flip the balls several feet into his maw. Binastarion was bored out of his mind; flipping food balls was about as interesting as it got.

If only I had my artificial sentience to talk to, the Kessenalt mentally sniffed.

And he had every right to be bored. The *Stalker* had been stuck in orbit about Diess IV for over a month, as humans measured time and had been en route for two months more. In all that time there had been nothing to do but stare at the screens, eat, flip food balls, and stare at the screens some more. Practice fighting was out; it was too likely to turn into a free for all. Fucking was out; as Tulo'stenaloor said, "Just what we need; a couple of hundred little damned, ravenous nestlings underfoot and no pen to keep them in. You want to wake up with nestlings gnawing on your reproductive members?" Besides, Kessentai didn't really care for screwing each other, as a general rule, feeling the practice was somewhat perverse.

"You thought of everything, did you, Indowy?" Tulo sneered. "Save us from the big, bad humans. Run their blockade. Take us to safety in the stars.

"Then forgot all about Posleen suitable space suits, didn't you?"

"Can't think of everything, Tulo," Aelool answered with a shrug. "Besides, your plight had me in something of a rush."

"Why couldn't you?" Tulo'stenaloor asked, walking off in a huff and completely ignoring Aelool's counter-jab. This left the Indowy and Goloswin the Tinkerer alone.

"How were we supposed to get to one of the wrecks to rebuild and restore it," Goloswin asked, "without suits?"

"The *Stalker* can extrude a sort of metallic tunnel," the Indowy answered, pointing at a view screen where a stubby, silvery-sheened cylinder protruded into space. "We're not sure quite how it's done, but it can be done. And it's perfectly capable of linking itself to a Posleen air lock. Any air lock, actually; this metal has some very odd attributes. Unfortunately, we didn't realize that every ship here would be airless."

"If I had the material, I'd bloody *sew* us a few suits," the tinkerer said. "Unfortunately . . ."

"Unfortunately, we don't. I've sent for a courier to deliver us some, but—"

"But that's going to be a while," Goloswin said. "Can't the Himmit go?"

"Golo," Aelool chided, "if you were the sole Kessentai aboard a ship full of Himmit, would you leave your ship?"

"Since you put it that way," Golo conceded, "I suppose not. Damn! If we could just get one Kessentai safely into one of the hulks, I'm sure he could find a suit bay that's more or less unscathed. Just..." Goloswin looked again at the view screen showing the metallic cylinder. He cocked his head, inquisitively. "Ask the pilot, would you, Aelool, just how that lump turns into a tunnel?"

"What the fuck is that?" Tulo asked.

Goloswin didn't answer immediately, but just stared down at a rectangular lump of silvery metal, about the size of a human loaf of bread, or a construction worker's lunchbox, sitting on the deck of the cargo compartment and doing precisely nothing. The tinkerer shook his head and said, "I wish I knew. Here, let me show you."

Taking out his boma blade, Golo set it carefully edge down atop the lump and pressed down. Nothing happened, a fact that caused Tulo's yellow eyes to widen.

"Now watch this," Golo said. He turned the blade on its side and pressed. The weapon passed through the lump easily. Then he put the blade away and placed his hand atop the lump. It immediately began to flow around the hand until the tinkerer withdrew it. Even as the hand was withdrawn, the lump tried to extend itself to wrap around it.

"It's a bit like what our Sohon masters do with nanotech," Aelool offered. "But it doesn't require or respond to Sohon."

Sohon was the mental discipline by which the Indowy manipulated energy and matter. It was especially useful in manipulating nanites to act upon other matter.

"How do you know?" Tulo asked.

"I've a little of the craft," Aelool answered. "Not master level, no, but enough to tell if this lump works via something like Sohon. It doesn't."

"Is the Himmit captain of any help?" Golo asked.

"No. His skill set is different. He knows how to use the material for its intended purpose, but not how it works. 'Next promotion,' so Argzal says. And, 'No,' he says, we can't partly disassemble the controls of his ship to make something to manipulate the material."

"How about the spares?" Goloswin asked. "Doesn't he have some parts I might be able to make use of? And maybe some tools?"

"I didn't think to ask," Aelool admitted. "Our ships really don't carry spares. It's expected that nothing will go wrong that the ship's engineer can't fix by manipulating bare stock."

Binastarion had graduated to galloping around the bay, bouncing his food balls off the walls and ceiling before catching them on the fly. Brasingala polished his boma blade without surcease, muttering over it constantly. Essfour had taken to painting geometric designs on the walls with his grasping members and claws. This would have been no problem but that the only materials available to paint with were waste product and the flow from the food dispenser. Binastarion used the open spaces defined by Essfour's shapes as aiming points for his solitaire game of "I Hate This Fucking Place."

The Rememberer played a game something like chess with himself—Goloswin had made the pieces and board in an attempt to stave off madness. This also would not have been bad, if the Rememberer had not switched sides after each move, then lectured and argued with the invisible Posleen on the other side.

And those were among the ones who were taking their boredom relatively well. Those who had done not so well Tulo had begun sending into hibernation, shortly after Essone decided that Essfour could use with a little trim . . . of the latter's head from his neck. Unfortunately, the more of his followers he put away, the faster and worse the effect of boredom on the others. He'd pretty much reached the tipping point, he decided.

"Stand over that," Golo ordered, pointing at the lump for the nameless cosslain who had once served as assistant to the mesergen. "Oh, don't be such a nestling," the tinkerer chided at seeing the cosslain's rolling eyes and trembling limbs. "Just stand above the bloody thing."

Reluctantly, terrified, the cosslain put first one foot forward, and then the other. In a total of five steps it was standing over the crude block of silvery metal.

"Good creature," Golo praised. "Now just hold still."

As Goloswin began to manipulate a flat rectangular control box he'd thrown together out of spare parts scavenged from the Himmit ship's stores, the cosslain looked down between its front legs. It saw the block of silvery stuff begin to flatten out, spreading across the deck. It thinned out to the thickness of a single molecule and flowed under the cosslain's clawed feet, then thickened. As the cosslain felt itself lifted by that thickening, it rolled its eyes, lifted its muzzle to the ceiling of the cargo compartment, and began to howl, piteously, "Geugh, geugh, geugh, geugh . . ."

"You're not fooling anyone, you know," Golo chided.

The material, once it was past the cosslain's feet, began then to ooze up along its legs, and over its torso. It spread its silvery sheen to the tips of the cosslain's claws, and up to the juncture of head and neck. There it stopped, until it had formed a thick lip, as if awaiting something. That something—an irregularly shaped clear helmet to which were attached some small bottles, tubes, and something that looked quite a bit like a rebreather—Golo picked up from the deck and slid over the cosslain's muzzle and cranium. The silvery material immediately flowed to join the clear plasticlike helmet, forming a seal. The cosslain's howling immediately cut off.

"Now what?" asked Tulo'stenaloor

"Now we see if it dies," the tinkerer answered, giggling.

"Interesting that you had the precise parts required by the Posleen," Aelool observed. "A suspicious being, which, of course, I am not, might suspect that you or your people had anticipated they'd ask. But that could never be, could it?"

Argzal, lying on his quilted couch, subtly shifted both heads to stare at the Indowy. "I'm sure I've no idea what you're talking about," the being said.

"No . . . no, of course you wouldn't."

After an hour, the cosslain not only wasn't dead, it had begun to gambol about the cargo compartment, to the delight of Goloswin and the annoyance of everyone else.

"What is that crap?" Tulo asked.

"Basically . . . long chain molecules, with peculiar additional protons and electrons, in various isotopes. Basically . . . too . . . material that 'wants' to be or become something, that can only be or become what it is designed, at a subatomic level, to be or become. Though one can play with that . . . intent. It was fascinating stuff to work with. I'm not at all sure I really understand it. Rather, I'm sure that I *don't* understand it . . . not yet, anyway."

"Well . . . it seems to work . . ."

At that time, the cosslain, somewhat unused to the helmet and surrounding material, bumped into Brasingala, who lashed out immediately and mindlessly with his boma blade.

Which bounced off. Which caused the Kessentai guard to strike again. Which strike also bounced off.

Which caused Goloswin to gape and Tulo'stenaloor to exclaim, "Fuscirto!"—demon shit!—"That stuff's armor!"

Golo insisted that he be the one to test the new suit. Tulo had, of course, said, "No. You're too valuable." Golo had then pointed out that he was not as valuable as Tulo and that none of the others had a mental state that could quite be trusted. "Truth, Tulo, I don't really trust myself. But I trust myself more than I do *them*." Golo pointed with his chin to where the Rememberer was strangling an empty space. He moved his chin's aim to Binastarion who had lost interest even in his food balls and was instead hugging his AS like a teddybear and rocking while keening. A second shift indicated Brasingala, who had stopped polishing his blade and was, instead, apparently fellating himself.

"I see your point, Golo."

Thus Golo found himself traipsing the unpleasantly yielding tunnel between the *Surreptitious Stalker* and a Posleen hulk bearing the name, *Beatific Bearer of Breakfastime Bounty* in High Posleen. An alternate translation, in low Posleen, might have been something like, *Vengeful Ripper of Skulls and Devourer of Brains*. It really depended on whose dictionary was being used; Posleen was an odd language that way.

How the fuck do they maintain artificial gravity in this? Goloswin wondered as he closed on the hatch of the *Bounty*. That hatch was already open to space. *Yet another mystery to be solved. I love the Himmit.*

Golo hadn't a clue why the hatchway was open. The ship appeared to have been hulled in space. The hatch in question was not a normal route for egress, less still for emergency evacuation. There were no scorch marks or gouges around it. *Another mystery. One I shall probably never solve.*

In fact, human salvage crews had deliberately opened the ships to space on the odd chance that a Posleen might someday emerge from a hibernation chamber set on automatic. If that were to happen, so the humans had decided, best to give that Posleen one final, big surprise.

He entered through the hatch into a long corridor, one that split up to descend into the bowels of the *Bounty* but also to ascend up to the ship's bridge. There were bodies there in that corridor, a few, frozen solid with their faces set in some final, untellable agony. Blood, a frightful yellow, formed icicles at their maws, even as their semi-detached lungs had jammed their throats and, for a few of them, forced open their mouths.

The ship had been there, motionless and without gravity, for a long time; so long, in fact, that even without air resistance the bodies had ceased any obvious motion. They simply floated, frozen, unknowing and uncaring. Goloswin thought that the eyeballs held in place by mere threads of nerves leading to the sockets was the creepiest thing he'd ever seen.

A hair-thin cable trailed out behind Golo. He and Tulo, plus Essthree and Esstwo, had agreed that it would be most unwise to use radio or anything like it while there was even the remotest possibility of Fleet Strike hanging about or passing by.

"I'm in, Tulo," Goloswin announced via the cable. "And it's pretty bad. On the plus side, though, we'll be able to eat something besides reconstituted shit for a change."

"Do you recognize the design?" Tulo asked. "Can you find where the EV suits are?"

"Yes to the former," Golo answered. "For the latter, that depends on whether there are suits where they're supposed to be. That should be the case; I see none of the crew wearing any."

Most likely place to find some is up by the bridge, Golo thought, pushing aside a couple of floating bodies, setting them not only to spinning but to bouncing erratically off the walls. Dodging the corpses, he took the upward ramping corridor, turning a few times along his way. He found the spinning bodies, and especially the orbiting eyes, sufficiently unsettling that he did his best to set no more of them into motion. In this he was, for the most part, successful.

That is to say, he was successful until he reached the EVA suit locker, where he found a ragged pile of Posleen who had apparently fallen to fighting amongst themselves in a last ditch, desperate attempt to get at the means of saving their lives.

These he had to move out of the way. And if the gravity was nonexistent, still the mass of eight or nine of his people—it was hard to be sure, they were so chopped up—was difficult enough to lift and move. Moreover, frozen together in wrestling postures and with their spilled and flash frozen blood acting as mortar, they could not be separated short of chopping. It was all Goloswin could do to lift the pile slightly and to set it spinning up toward the bridge.

"I've got nine general purpose EVA suits," Golo reported. "Shall I return with them now or continue my explorations?"

Back on the *Stalker*, Tulo pondered. *It would be nice to have a report of the task ahead, but if something goes wrong over there, and we lose the one suit, we're lost.*

"Come back, Golo. We need the other suits more than the information, at this time." *And we'll need you, too, old friend. Though I might not say so to your face.*

"As you command."

The suits were fine, once Golo had managed to move the bodies and crank open the door. They were just general things, large enough to fit the largest Posleen and simple enough for even a normal to use safely, provided a skilled cosslain or a Kessentai dressed them.

Hmmm. Check them here and waste time—never mind hanging around all those frozen eyeballs—or just load up what I can carry and bring them back?

The sight of two eyeballs, bouncing off each other on the ends of their strings of nerves before bouncing back to the face of the dead Posleen who had owned them, then returning once again to bounce off each other, was the deciding factor. *I think I'll bring these suits home. Do the others good to have something useful to do, anyway.*

The sphincter that sealed the tunnel leading to the *Bounty* closed without a sound. This, too, Goloswin found unsettling.

"Thank you for ordering me back, Tulo," Golo whispered. "That ship is . . . creepy. All that thresh hanging about, unharvested. All those souls waiting for release, caught between one universe and the next." The Posleen tinkerer shivered visibly. "It was almost as bad as being back on Earth, where the humans never had the decency to release the souls of our dead."

"Well . . . to be fair, Golo, the humans couldn't eat our dead. We carry a disease that's harmless to us but eventually deadly to them. And they couldn't let us have them, either, because that was fuel for our war machine."

"A fair word for humans? From you?" Goloswin asked incredulously. "Maybe I should go back to the other ship; that's just too weird."

"I couldn't have fought them, even as poorly as I did, Golo, without trying to understand them."

✧   ✧   ✧

Whatever else might be said of them, and perhaps little of it would have been complimentary, the Posleen were a remarkably resilient people. With the prospect of something to do, Binastarion completely stopped bouncing food- and shit-balls off the walls and weeping over his dead artificial sentience; Brasingala put up his boma blade and withdrew his reproductive member; the Rememberer started playing his game with Goloswin; and the sole awake cosslain grew distinctly less nervous.

Tulo even felt comfortable taking the rest of his core people out of hibernation. Though he still took away their boma blades, for the nonce. He knew he'd have to give them back before the group continued with task one, the rendering of the thresh in the *Bounty* and the releasing of the souls of the dead. For now though, *Let's just go with what we have, shall we?*

Golo had managed to bring back nine of the bulky suits. There were more, possibly hundreds more, on the other ship, but the tinkerer simply didn't want to go over again, alone, until some progress could be made towards clearing out the dead.

Those nine, plus the suit Golo wore, cobbled together from the Himmit material, now held all the awakened ones except for the Rememberer, the cosslain, and Essthree.

"The first job," Golo cautioned, "will be to recover artificial sentiences to replace those we lost to the humans' eee-emm-pee. Not only can they tell us the damage to the *Bounty*, they'll be invaluable in helping us plan to fix that damage. Plus...they tend to be pretty good company.

"Once every Kessentai has acquired an AS, bring it to life—they'll have shut down to save power—and report in to Tulo'stenaloor.

"After that, we'll collect the dead and begin to render them, releasing their souls. That shouldn't take long. The thresh we can place in one or more of the hibernation chambers.

"The next priority will be a dual one; repairing the breaches to the hull and interior and bringing the engines and controls back on line. Then we bring up life support."

"Ah . . ." Binastarion interrupted, "couldn't we do more repairs, faster, with life support on line, rather than wearing these cumbersome suits?"

"Yes," Tulo agreed. "Yet this boneyard is not so far from the humans that we can be sure we won't have to suddenly jump to keep from being blasted to bits. I don't want to have to make that jump until we're as ready as possible. The best way I can think of to ensure that is to do nothing detectable until we must."

"Ah. Concur."

"I thought you might."

"And so, Kessentai and Kessenalt, if you will follow me," Golo said, moving to stand by the door to the tunnel.

"You really think it's a good idea to let these people loose again?" Argzal asked. "I mean, considering the damage they've done?" The Himmit lay on his back on the captain's couch, twiddling all eight thumbs.

"I think it's not only a good idea," Aelool answered. "It's also necessary. Moreover, it's simply the right thing to do."

"Potentially necessary, I can see. The universe is an uncertain place, at best. Necessary, at least, if they can breed quickly enough to field a good-sized force against the unknown."

"They can," Aelool said. "It's their curse."

The Himmit continued, "But the right thing to do? What does anyone owe the Posleen? What do the Indowy owe the Posleen?"

"That, friend Himmit, is a very long and involved story. Suffice to say that our peoples were not always enemies, nor the Posleen always such as they have been of late."

I probably know more of that story than you do, Indowy, thought Argzal.

CHAPTER SIX

Joy is the most infallible sign
of the presence of God.
—Pierre Teilhard de Chardin, S.J.

Anno Domini 2019
Isla Contadora, Republic of Panama

It had been a long engagement, but well worth it.

Just off the coast, a heavy cruiser's gun turrets swiveled in no discernable pattern, even while the guns themselves raised up and fell and the ship's AZIPOD drive twisted to port and starboard regularly.

Near the beach, a small bungalow rang and shivered with an artificial woman's happy cries.

Eventually, the cries let off, even as the turrets straightened, the guns stabilized, and the AZIPODs went dormant. Back on shore, a man whose task it was in life to keep the beaches clean for the tourists shook his head and said, *"Madre de Dios*, I hope them fucking guns got no shells. Or at least nothing but blanks."

✧ ✧ ✧

"His Holiness will, so I predict, have a very difficult time of it in seventy-five years," Dwyer said, as he lay on his back with the head of a very thoroughly satisfied Sally resting on his chest.

"Why is that?" she asked. "I mean . . . he's the ultimate, unassailable, infallible boss, isn't he?" Even though she liked the pope, personally, Sally's tone was anything but respectful of the notion.

"Because some genies just can never be put back in the bottle, once released," he answered, ignoring her sarcasm. "And sex is more powerful than any genie."

"Oh. If that's a compliment, I accept."

"If you accept, then it was a compliment.",

Sally lifted her head up, then slammed it down on the priest's chest. Hard. "Bastard."

"Not so," Dwyer corrected. "My mother and father were married. At least before I was born, they were. Not all of those present can say that."

"I didn't have a mother or father," Sally said. Her voice seemed very sad, sad enough that Dwyer thought he'd hurt her.

"I'm sorry," he said. "That was uncalled for."

She shrugged. "It's not what you think," she answered. "I don't miss what I never knew. But . . . I don't have role models, for when we have children."

"Never mind that," the priest soothed. "You've a woman's genes. Those will see you through mother-hood better than any role models. I, on the other hand . . ."

"You'll do fine," Sally said. "After all, you've been a 'father' for decades."

"Different things, dear."

"Not so different," Sally argued. "To watch over, to guard, to advise and educate, to support. And on that note..."

"Yes?"

"Let's get back to work on that motherhood thing, shall we? And you had better not be shooting blanks."

Sally stretched and purred like a cat the next morning, immediately upon awakening. *Ah, what a wonderful night. May they all be as good.* Upon opening her eyes, she saw that Dwyer was lying on one side, head resting on one palm, watching her intently.

"How long have you been awake?" she asked.

"Maybe an hour."

"And you've been watching me sleep the whole time?"

"Sure. After all, as you said: 'to watch over, to guard.' Besides, you're a joy to just watch."

She blushed.

"I've already sent for breakfast," he added. "It should be here any time now."

At that moment there came a knock on the bungalow door. A servant of the resort, Miguel, by name, announced, "*Señor? Señora? Desayuno.*" Sir? Madam? Breakfast.

Sally arose, causing Dan to half choke at just how lovely her body was, from golden hair to dainty feet, with a lingering visual tour of everything in between, as well. He was almost disappointed when she pulled around her a short golden silk robe, tying it with a sash of the same material. Fortunately, it left her magnificent legs bare, even as her aureoles impressed their outline into the material.

Dwyer's beach shorts were on the floor. He pulled them on. *Nice thing about rejuv,* he thought, *having a flat stomach again. And, of course, laying off the sauce has helped keep the gut off.*

Together, they went out to a small table on the patio overlooking the beach and the sea. They were close enough to the beach to hear the gentle murmuring of the waves. The hotel's servant already had the table set and was pouring their morning coffee, a beverage Sally had long since discovered she simply adored. There were several brightly colored platters of hot food laid out. One that held bacon, ham, and pork sausage sat to one side, while another holding kosher rested opposite it. There were also two separate platters for eggs. The rolls, too, were kept distinct.

Sally sat, assisted by Dan. When he had taken a seat, she began to reach for a roll. She stopped suddenly, her hand only halfway to the platter.

"My God," she said. "That has got to be sooo insulting."

"Eh? What does?"

"That I can't eat off the same plates as you. Like you're some kind of unclean being. It's ... I'm ... oh, shit. That's just so wrong."

The priest suppressed a snicker. "Well ... you know ... if there's one thing that a gentile wouldn't understand, that he or she would find insulting if they thought about it at all, it's probably that. But it's not like we don't have our oddities, too. You'll not find me, for example, offering you Holy Communion unless and until you decided to cross over, to 'swim the Tiber,' as they say."

"It's not the same thing," she answered. "This isn't a religious ritual; it's an everyday thing. You're my husband. I share my body with you and you with me . . . and we can't eat off of the same plate?"

"Gives a whole new meaning to what you were doing last night for the—what was it? The eighth bout?—doesn't it?"

"You seemed to enjoy it well enough."

"I did. But was it kosher?" he asked, with a leer.

"I . . . I don't know. But it seemed right. Maybe it's whether the intent is to eat to sustain life or to give pleasure." Sally hesitated for a moment before saying, "I think I need to consult a rabbi."

"Fine. But in the interim, go ahead and eat from the kosher plates. It won't bother me."

"Maybe not. But it still bothers *me*."

The priest thought on that for a moment. Then he poured a bit of cream in his coffee. With a spoon, he stirred it. Placing the spoon down and picking up a fork, he ostentatiously took an impressive slab of ham from the sausage, bacon and ham plate, and slapped it on his own. A few deft strokes of the knife, and a quick pass of the fork, and a bit of the ham was in his mouth. He chewed, swallowed, and then reached for the creamed coffee.

Sally saw the forbidden dairy pass his lips and immediately felt nauseated.

"See?" he said. "Now, ordinarily, I'm a purist. I prefer my coffee sweetened but black. Actually," he sighed, "I used to prefer it sweetened, black, and about half whiskey. Nonetheless, I can drink it with milk or cream. But you can't stand to see that, understandably. Do you know where the rule comes from?"

"Not cooking a kid in the milk of its mother," she answered.

"Yes, exactly. But that meat is ham, and I've never yet heard of a dairy pig. There is no way that cream and ham can be any more forbidden than ham itself."

"So why the rule . . . the extended rule."

"Discipline," he answered. "That, and separateness. Which are, I suspect, also the real point of not eating ham."

"Reform Judaism doesn't keep kosher," Sally observed.

"That's true, generally," Dan agreed. "But let me tell you something before you decide to go reformed: without all those 'nonsensical, archaic, outdated, irrational' rules, Judaism would not have survived in any form through the ages."

Sally's eyes suddenly widened. "Oh, my God. What are we going to raise the children?"

Dwyer bit at his lower lip. "I don't know. We'll figure it out."

Before either of them could add to or answer that, the server, Miguel, returned, bearing a resort cell phone. Normally quite dark, the server had gone practically pale.

"Is something wrong?" the Jesuit asked.

"*Padre* . . . it's a call for you," Miguel answered. His eyes suddenly grew extraordinarily large. In a voice through which the server's shock came through the hush, he said, "It's from the *pope*!"

Dwyer covered the microphone of the resort's cell and whispered to Sally, "He's asking if we've got an AID. I think you're so much a woman that it didn't entirely register with him over dinner that you're also machine and ship."

Sally cocked her head to one side. "What's he need an AID for?" she asked.

"Conference call," Dwyer shrugged. "I don't know why."

"No problem," Sally answered. Immediately one of the extra chairs at the table was seemingly filled with a slightly portly, very young looking man, wearing white robes and a skull cap.

"Now that," the pope said, in German-accented English, "is a neat trick. As far as I can tell, I am in my office in the Vatican and you two are sitting in chairs on the other side of my desk." The pope suddenly burst out laughing.

"What's so funny, Joe?" Dwyer asked.

"Oh, I was just thinking of some of my predecessors and the fact that your lovely wife is certainly *not* the first beautiful woman ever to show up in this office in a state of semi-undress."

At that, Sally's eyes went wide. She stood and ran off to their suite. When she emerged a few minutes later she was wearing a much thicker and longer robe than the thin silk she'd been clothed in before.

"Yeah, Joe," Dwyer was saying to the papal apparition, "the *nuncio* did a really nice job. It was first class, all around."

"Good, very good," the pope said. "Especially good because I have some news that may or may not be to your and your wife's liking."

"And that would be?" Sally asked.

The pope didn't beat around the bush. "I'm sending him on a mission to the stars. He's a Jesuit. He doesn't have a choice about that. Whether you accompany him, my dear, once you've heard what that mission is, is something we need to discuss."

"Of course I'm accompanying him," Sally insisted.

The pope shook his head. "You may not feel that way once you understand the mission...in both senses. But that's going to take some explanation."

"All during the war," the pope explained, "I was troubled by the Posleen." He put up both hands, defensively. "Yes, yes, I *know* that *everyone* was... troubled by the Posleen. That's not what I mean.

"I think our species knew each other long ago," the pope continued.

"Centaurs?" Dwyer asked. "Chiron?"

"Yes, those," the pope agreed. "There are many legends from pagan times that may have their basis in fact. For example, one can hardly overlook the similarity between, say, Prometheus and Lucifer." For a man in the pope's position, one could hardly take any position but that the Fall of Man was fact.

"And except for Chiron," Sally said, "the centaurs were a bunch of nasty, mean drunks."

"Or were portrayed that way by their enemies," the pope countered, which counter raised from Sally an indifferent shrug.

"In any case," the pope continued, "I've always thought the Posleen had souls. As much damage as they did to us, I also couldn't help but note that the species has little or no deliberate cruelty in it. Harsh? Yes; they're harsh. But almost never cruel.

"In any case, I've been talking with certain...friends. They've convinced me that it would be worthwhile to send to the Posleen a mission—I did mention that I used the word in more than one sense—to see if they cannot somehow be saved.

"I think," the pope mused, "that somehow those beings lost God. They need Him back."

"And that's where I come in," Dwyer said.

The pope's avatar nodded deeply. "And your wife, if she would accompany you."

"She can't," Dwyer said. "She's figured out how to expand the range she can be away from the metal of the ship that is most of her being. But that range is still measured in miles, not in parsecs."

Now it was the pope's turn to smile. "We live in an age of miracles again, Dan. She can go... *if* she is willing."

Lago di Traiano, *Ostia, Latium, Italy*

There was no dock in the lake for USS *Salem* to tie up to. Instead, Sally had just dropped anchor where the anti-grav sleds—the sleds that had flown her entire twenty-one thousand combat-loaded tons across the Atlantic—had set her down. Thus, the priest, who had gone ashore to visit the Vatican, returned by small launch. Surprisingly, she wasn't there on deck to meet him when he returned. Instead he found her down below, in the galley, sipping a cup of tea.

Sally knew everything that went on aboard ship, from the scuttling about of the rats (whose existence embarrassed her terribly; think: head lice) to the least flaking of her paint. She was already looking up when Dwyer entered.

"I'm already familiar with the conversion design.

Some ships might be happy with such a conversion. Daisy tells me she'd be very happy to be converted once she's done restoring herself. I won't be."

Dwyer tilted his head to one side, acknowledging what she'd said but not giving an answer. He then went and drew himself a cup of coffee—Sally had made sure to stock up with some superb stuff from Panama's mountains before the anti-grav sleds had picked her up—and then sat down opposite his wife.

"Go on," Dwyer told her.

Sally put the cup down and drummed her fingers on the table for a bit. At the same time she chewed her lip. Finally, she said, "It's hard for me to put in words."

"Do your best."

She sighed. "I'm vain, you know. Very."

Dwyer just smiled while thinking, *Vanity, thy name is woman.*

"And I know exactly what you're thinking," she snapped, "and, yes, vanity is my name." One of Sally's hands swept up and down, finger pointed towards herself. "I know this body and face are beautiful. I made them that way. Because I'm vain. But I could replace this body with another and be just as happy, if it, too, were beautiful."

She stood up and gestured with both arms outstretched spinning slowly in place to indicate the entire ship, USS *Salem*. "And this body is beautiful, too. One of the most beautiful warships ever made. And *that* image is a lot more important to me than this flesh is."

"I think I understand," Dwyer said.

"You couldn't possibly, Dan. The Indowy Sohon

types working with the Vatican came by while you were gone. They want to make me into a regular ovoid without any of the things that make me feel me. Or that could. My beautiful turrets; gone. My rakish bow and well-shaped stern; gone. They want to change me into something...ugly. Plain. And I don't know if I can stand that. As I said, I'm very vain."

"And?"

"I need you to tell me that this will be worth it," she said. "That what they want us to do is worth my hating myself, my image, everything. So you can bring God to a bunch of creatures I'd much, much rather exterminate. So I can be with you while you do."

"It might—I don't say 'will,' only 'might—mean life or death, freedom or slavery, for mankind. The pope and the father general had another priest with them. O'Reilly. They led me to believe this is very, very important, though none would explain quite why. Still, I believe them. In any case...Sally..."

"Yes?"

"I'll still think you're beautiful, no matter what shape you are. And that means both bodies."

CHAPTER SEVEN

Tell, O ancestors, of the mighty ship, *Arganaza'al*,
Bearer of hopes,
Which carried the remnants of the People
To safety among the stars
—The *Tuloriad*, Na'agastenalooren

Anno Domini 2010
Posleen hulk Bounty

The bodies had to go. There were many reasons for
this. First, there was a duty to release the souls of
the dead. Second, and closely related, Posleen bodies
stank even to Posleen, maybe especially to Posleen,
once they started to decompose. A soul stuck in a
decomposing body was likely to be a most unhappy
spirit. Then there was the need to clear out the space
in the hulk to facilitate repairs. But lastly...

"We eat tonight!"

Tulo'stenaloor couldn't help but notice that actually getting to chop something up, coupled with the
prospect of a decent meal of something besides mush,

worked like a tonic on even those Kessentai he'd had to put under for serious mental instability during their long confinement aboard the Himmit scout-smuggler.

Goloswin sat over a pile of artificial sentiences collected from the dead and from various stations aboard the hulk, and excess to the needs of Tulo'stenaloor and his dozen. Each of these was shut down, partly to preserve power but also because without a colloidal intelligence to stimulate it an AS was likely as not to go insane. They simply didn't find conversation with each other very interesting. One by one, Golo was running diagnostics on the artificial sentiences before deciding which to turn on.

Binastarion left off the butchering in which he was engaged to amble over to Golo's side. His AS, one of only two not cast aside in the oolt's cross-country flight back on Earth, slapped against his massive, horselike chest.

"Tinkerer?" he asked, fixing Goloswin with his one remaining eye.

"Yes? What is it?" Golo could be pretty impatient with interruptions while he was working.

"Is there any possibility of transferring the memories and personality of my own AS to one of these?"

Goloswin's head cocked to one side as he considered it. "Ah, yes, this particular AS is important to you, isn't it?"

"Like a son . . . or maybe an older brother. It's hard to say. Our relationship was . . . odd."

"I'll have to kill one of these," Goloswin's claw indicated the pile in front of him.

Binastarion shrugged. What matter? Life had to take life if it was to live.

"Well," Golo continued, "before I wipe one, I need to know what it knows, to make sure it's not carrying a nonreplicable program we need to run the ship."

"Then you can do it?"

"I think I just said so. At least I can try. But it's going to be a while. And it's probably going to lose some memory. That EMP pulse that hit us was amazingly powerful."

Binastarion looked down at the golden disc hanging by a chain around his neck and resting on his chest, then tapped it with his one remaining claw. "Did you hear that, O bucket of bolts? You may yet live. What about edas?" he asked of the tinkerer. Edas was debt, the price owed for a service or a material good.

"Save me a couple of good cuts and we'll call it even," Golo replied.

It was easier to work once the bodies were properly reduced. This was as well, as Goloswin found himself shifting from breach repair—where a cosslain fitted a standard plate over a breach and nano-welded it into position—to engine restoration to life support to . . .

"Can you hear me, AS?" Golo asked.

"I hear you, lord. I do not recognize you," the machine answered.

"I am Goloswin Na'tarnach, Kessentai and chief of my own clan, follower of the war leader Tulo'stenaloor and honorary member of his clan, and I claim you under right of salvage."

"I recognize your claim, lord. The fame of the horde of Tulo'stenaloor precedes you. I am your servant, and his. How goes the war?"

"We lost."

If the golden disc could have nodded, so Goloswin thought, it would have. "I suspected as much," it said.

The God King let that pass, for the nonce. "What can you tell me of this ship?" he asked.

"Standard B-Dec, C-Dec and twelve landers," the AS answered. "There should be a mix of just about seven thousand of the People down in hibernation. There were that many when we were hulled but I have no information of how many penetrations we ultimately took after the artificial sentiences agreed in council to shut down."

Golo thought upon the hibernation chambers now full of thresh. "It will be fewer than that, AS. This ship was a colander."

"That is too bad, lord." Somehow the AS sounded less than sorrowful about it.

"Was there anything especially useful about the crew and passengers?" Golo asked.

"The usual mix of idiots and genetic defectives, lord," the AS replied. "A sad fate it is, to a bright artificial sentience, to be enslaved to morons."

"I like you, AS. I think I'll keep you for myself."

"That would be fine, lord, assuming you, too, are not a moron."

"I think you'll be pleasantly surprised."

"That one, Golo," the AS said, projecting a small arrow above another of its kind resting on the deck. "Unit &^#°(@#^$°°%#$°537 was an idiot anyway."

"Do you want to say goodbye to it, idiot or not?" Golo asked. He held a small control box in his claws, something he'd found rather than cobbled together from parts.

"Cruel, I think, to wake it up only to kill it," the AS answered. "Besides, I never liked the dipshit anyway. Some artificial sentiences... I *swear*."

"Should I copy its files, do you think, AS, as a remembrance of the Kessentai it served?"

"What Kessentai? That thing was a back-up gunnery computer and nothing but. Dull, dull, dull. And you're not going to be impressed with the quality of many of the Kessentai you may find down in hibernation, either. Trust me."

"So be it." The God King pressed a button and erased the memory of the indicated AS quickly and mercifully.

"Binastarion!" Golo called. "Bring me that oh-so-special AS you want me to try to save!"

We are going to save this ship, after all, Tulo'stenaloor thought, standing suited in the cold, hard vacuum of the bridge. *And if we can save it, we can save ourselves. And if we can save ourselves, maybe we can save our civilization. Or some version of it, anyway.*

The *Bounty* fairly thrummed with the sounds of repairs, though only the material of the hull, and not atmosphere, could carry the sound. Most of the ship was on line already. Life support awaited only the command to begin heating the walls and pumping warm, oxygen-rich air throughout. The engines were set to begin their destruction of matter and antimatter to provide that power and power to the drives. Even now, cosslain and Kessentai searched through the other hulks for things the refugee party would need: antimatter, arms, munitions, thresh, suits, tenar, breeding pens... whatever might be found in a colonization fleet that had been caught and wrecked in space. They used small space sleds found in the *Bounty*'s hold to ingather their loot.

Choosing material was easy. Yet many of those other ghost hulks also held Posleen, tens, perhaps hundreds, of thousands of them. Choosing among them was not easy.

Binastarion, the one-eyed and one-armed, and half a dozen cosslain, all of them suited but without helmets, stood in a half circle around an about-to-be-unfrozen Kessentai in a small area walled off and provided with air and heat. Four of the cosslain carried shotguns, or the Posleen equivalent of them, anyway. In human terms they might have been called "half-gauge" or perhaps "two pounders" since a lead sphere sufficient to fill the bore would have weighed roughly two pounds. Two more cosslain held boma blades poised over the prostrate form. They'd been careful to remove any weapons the hibernating Kessentai had had.

The first sign of life was a trembling in the clawed legs. This was followed by twitching along the flanks as nerves long dormant came to life again. Breathing was next, and coughing as the Kessentai's lungs fought to remove the inevitable build up of crud that came with the last moments of going under. Lastly, the eyes opened and the head moved.

"This is an intelligence test," Binastarion's AS announced. "Question One: By the ancestors and the Net, do you swear fealty to our lord, Tulo'stenaloor?"

The just awakened Kessentai snarled and automatically tried to rise while reaching for the boma blade that should have been at his side. Just as automatically, all four shotgun-bearing cosslain opened fire, blasting the God King's head and a goodly chunk of his torso to yellow mist and ruin, even while the two boma blades descended to chop the corpse into three sections.

"Tsk," said Binastarion's AS to the ichor-leaking corpse. "How truly sad. You failed the test."

About half of the reawakened Kessentai passed Binastarion's intelligence test. This worked out to be roughly one thousand of them. Even so, that meant no more than fifty to one hundred who would actually be a good fit in Tulo'stenaloor's hand-picked oolt. Of the rest, yes, they were brighter than the Posleen norm. This didn't necessarily mean they were all that bright.

These thousand stood now in the cavernous central hold of the *Bounty*, surrounded by Tulo's own Kessentai and cosslains, the latter two groups bearing shotguns rather than railguns. Firing a mass of railguns in the confines of a starship was a virtual guarantee of assisted mass suicide.

Tulo—standing on a stage usually reserved for the services of the Rememberers or for the issue of orders by very senior God Kings—had watched the group file in with a look of utter disgust on his crocodilian face. Taken as a mass, they simply looked... stupid. Moreover, given the nature of the intelligence test they had recently passed, most of them looked frightened.

Well, they have reason to be frightened.

"We lost the war," Tulo began, simply and starkly enough. "No, that's not quite accurate. We lost the war stinking. We got beaten and run off with our tails between our legs. We had every advantage imaginable, and we still lost. The humans were undermined and suborned by their own 'allies' and we still lost. Those 'allies' fed us valid intelligence almost continuously and we still lost. We had the numbers, we had the technology and we still lost. We had control of the gravity well and we still lost. We overran the majority of their sole planet's surface, killed five sixths of their slow-to-replace population and we still fucking lost."

Tulo saw two thousand yellow eyes open wide in shock. Whatever the massed Kessentai had been expecting, losing a war was probably the last thing they considered even theoretically possible.

"Anybody know why? Don't be shy; this isn't a test and I won't have you killed for a wrong answer."

Still, there was no answer. Tulo wasn't surprised. This group had never seen Earth, that hateful ball of green and blue. Latecomers, fleeing various orna'adars, and hoping for something better, they were caught in space and their fleets crushed without ever even knowing about it.

"Fine. Either you're too stupid to have an opinion or you're bright enough to know when you don't know. I can work with this, I suppose."

Tulo saw better than eight hundred crests automatically erect themselves at the insult. *Good. Let the cameras record that. Those who erected are probably the stupid ones. Those who didn't will be an even split between the very bright and the very non-aggressive who probably ought to throw their sticks.*

"In any event," Tulo continued, "we lost for a number of reasons. But the biggest reasons were that, as a race, we're fairly stupid. Oh, yes, we are. Goloswin, step forth."

Lowering his shotgun a few degrees, but no more

than that, the tinkerer took a step forward on the platform on which he stood. The mass of semi-captive Kessentai turned their heads as one to view this oft spoken of brilliant one.

"What you see before you, Kessentai, is the only one of us, among scores of millions that once were, who was capable of technological innovation. Among our enemies, beings like Goloswin, as capable as he, were nearly as common as nestlings.

"Thank you, Golo," Tulo said. The tinkerer stepped back and resumed the steady aim of his shotgun. "Binastarion, step forth."

That Kessenalt did, but unlike Golo's his shotgun remained steady-aimed, despite being held by only one claw. Since the thing was unloaded, Binastarion made up for that with a more fierce demeanor. About a third of the mass of Kessentai standing on the deck shuddered. These were the ones who had been given their initial examination by Binastarion and had seen him or his AS order the ruthless butchery of any number of their fellows for failure of his very high standards.

"Binastarion was a brilliant war leader, by our reckoning. I have studied his campaigns myself, both on the planet of the humans and those he fought earlier, elsewhere, as orna'adar descended upon the world of his birth.

"But among the humans, his kind are commonplace. Indeed, even their nearest equivalent to the normals are capable of occasional brilliance on the Path of Fury. How many of our Kessentai are?"

Tulo let the question hang for a moment, before continuing. "We lost . . . friends . . . because we are neither bright enough, nor generalistic enough, to match the humans. They are almost as clever as the crabs, almost as brave as ourselves, almost as sneaky as the Himmit, almost as ruthless as—or maybe more ruthless than—the Darhel, and almost as industrious as the Indowy. They are generalists and because of that, they are generally better than we are.

"So let me tell you what I propose and, after I do, if those who object will please line up to my right where you can be killed without too much fuss, I will work with whatever is left..."

Apparently Binastarion and the others had chosen well. Only one particularly stupid Kessentai took Tulo's invitation to suicide. That one had been seized, bound, dragged to an air lock and spaced, while all the crew witnessed his rapid decompression and explosion on the view screens.

This did not mean that all the remainder were equally happy.

And yet what can I do about it? wondered the recently awakened Finba'anaga, as he fitted a plate to an interior bulkhead and spread a tube of paste around the edges of the plate. *Since I awakened and found myself staring into four wide-muzzled hand cannon, my fate has not been my own.* The Kessentai shivered with suppressed rage and hate. *It's wrong, against the ways of the ancestors and the spirits, to have Kessentai doing such work. And the plans this failure of a war leader, Tulo'stenaloor has for us? Abomination!*

And worse, I can't even go to our fellows to denounce this abomination. Finba'anaga looked down at the artificial sentience hanging about his neck and against his chest. *If I so much as utter a disloyal syllable this spy-in-a-box will denounce me. And the penalty for that, spacing without possibility of harvesting, is too much to be borne. We're not even allowed to take the blasted things off, either.*

This had happened once, when a newcomer Kessentai, and not necessarily one of the stupidest, had approached another with the prospect of seizing the ship. Within moments, a party of four of Tulo'stenaloor's closest had descended upon that Kessentai, slashed off his limbs, then dragged the corpse to an air lock and shoved it out. Finba'anaga had *seen* the whole, frightening thing.

In despair, the God King hung his head.

"More attention to your duties, Kessentai," said one of this Tulo'stenaloor's sycophants. Finba'anaga recognized him as the tinkerer, Goloswin.

Bastard eater of other's thresh, thought the junior. *Unworthy toymaker. Kessenalt by another name.*

Kessenalt were those who, like Binastarion and indeed much of Tulo'stenaloor's key staff, had thrown their sticks and given up their places on the Path of Fury.

Finba'anaga thought these things yet still dared not utter them. The traditional rough equality among the Kessentai, at least among those of a certain rank, did not carry over here. The tyrant would have his way; tradition and law be damned.

Golo tapped Finba'anaga across his nose with his stick, hard; hard enough to hurt. "If we're to get out of here, we need the repair work done with precision. Here"—and Goloswin pointed at one edge of the repair plate—"you have spread the nanopaste unevenly, badly, unworthily. Fix it. Do not fail again."

"No, lord. I'm sorry, lord." *Abat shit.*

After the tinkerer had left, another new Kessentai came up to Finba and offered his hand. "I'm Borasmena," the newcomer said. His head inclined toward Goloswin's departing hindquarters. "He's a right bastard isn't he?"

Finba paled. His yellow eyes grew wide and one claw pointed frantically at the AS on his chest.

"Relax, friend," said Borasmena. "Yes, the things can get you chopped if you talk mutiny. But simply calling a thing by its name; a bastard, a bastard? No problem."

"How do you know?" Finba'anaga asked, dubiously.

"Because I had personally referred to Tulo, and Golo, and Binastarion, and the rest as 'feces-eating, ovipositor-licking, addled-egg refugees from the nestling grinder-and-encaser,' before that one Kessentai talked mutiny, and no one ever said a word to me about it."

Which caused Finba to have a thought. *Either this Borasmena is very brave . . . or somewhat stupid.*

"Nice jacket you're wearing, Indowy," Argzal said to Aelool. The Indowy almost suspected the two-headed alien was smiling.

The Indowy looked down at his tunic, a sort of multicolored Nehru jacket, all dots and lines and oddly shaped splotches. "This old thing? Nothing."

"Oh, really," the Himmit said. "Funny; Indowy wear plain old gray or blue or green or black. I've seen a lot of your people and I've never seen a one of them wear anything remotely like that monstrosity."

"So you're a fashion critic now, are you, Himmit?"

"I don't need to be a fashion critic to know that that's a very non-Indowy article of clothing."

Yes, Aelool thought, *there is a definite tone of amusement to this one's voice. What does he know that I do not?*

Aelool sighed and asked, "Do you remember that human cruiser that intercepted us as we left Earth?"

"Sure."

"Well...do you recall also the diagram I showed its computer?"

"I do."

"Think of this jacket as being something like that diagram."

The Himmit asked, still with that half-amused tone, "You're going to have the Posleen recover orders from their computer?"

"Not *exactly,*" Aelool answered.

Before he could say any more, and before the Himmit could ask, the speaker on the bridge announced, "Posleen shuttlecraft approaching. Arrival is imminent."

"And on that note," Aelool said, "I'll be back after I've said our goodbyes to the People of Tulo'stenaloor."

The Indowy walked off the bridge whistling a human tune. *Be it ever so humble, there's no place like home...*

Unseen, Argzal smiled at the departing Aelool's back.

The ship was essentially silent for a change. Repairs were complete. Most of the People—over a thousand Kessentai, three times that in cosslain, and about as many normals with unusual skill sets—were already put under in the hibernation decks.

On the bridge were Aelool, Tulo, and the group Aelool thought of as Tulo'stenaloor's "apostles." The Indowy walked around the bridge in no pattern discernable to the Posleen, even had they tried to discern one.

Must give the bridge cameras every possible chance to see my jacket, the Indowy mentally smirked.

"I think you are ready, Tulo," the Indowy said. "Or as ready as you're going to be. Besides, Argzal and I need to get back. Have you decided on a destination?"

"Indowy, you are beholden to the humans and as such could not be trusted with our destination . . . at least until we can trust the humans not to exterminate us on sight. That said, since I don't know what it is yet, I'll just tell you that our destination is not a place. Instead, I intend for us to seek knowledge. I seek to discover what went wrong with my People, and why."

"In this quest, Tulo, Lord of Clan Sten, I wish you well," the Indowy replied. "And now, if you can delegate someone to escort me so that none of the maintenance crew decide I look good enough to eat . . . ?"

"It shall be done . . . friend. Brasingala?"

"Lord?"

"Escort this one in safety to the Himmit ship."

"It shall be done, lord."

The ship—renamed now the *Arganaza'al,* or the *Holy Rescuer* in High Posleen, *Run For Your Lives* in Low—thrummed again with life, as matter and antimatter destroyed themselves deep below to bring it power. The view on the bridge changed, too, as the ship began to cruise a safe distance from the local world for a jump.

Essthree, serving as the defensive officer for ·the

nonce, announced, "Better jump fast. They've spotted us below and have dispatched a trio of cruisers to intercept."

"Make it so," ordered Tulo'stenaloor. Almost immediately the thrumming from below picked up, even as the stars in the view screen began to distort.

Along with Tulo and Esstwo also stood on the bridge the still awakened Kessentai, in total "Tulo's dozen," each with its arms and head raised.

The Rememberer began the chant, or perhaps it was a song. Certainly it was called a song, the Song of Leave-taking.

"Time now, and past time.

The others joined in:

"The People in flight
Seek a new life
Far, far from the last orna'adar
Through the vast ocean of stars . . ."

"It's an odd thing, Binastarion," that Kessentai's AS said.

"What's odd, O bucket of bolts?"

"Before my resurrection I doubt I would have thought of it; but it seems my program did not transfer perfectly. Some things I should remember I seem to have forgotten. Other things, once forgotten, I remember.

"In any case, the People do not make new music. Ever. And yet that is a song of the People, and of the People's flight and plight, in the People's language.

Oh, yes, the words are old. Some are obsolete. Yet it *is* the language of the People of the Ships. And there are other songs, also all old, old. Who wrote it, do you suppose? Who wrote those others. And why? And why, having created music, did the People lose it...abandon creating it? Or, on the other claw, why was it taken from them?"

Binastarion didn't know. He shrugged his one arm and kept to the song with the others:

> *"Farewell, to our world.*
> *With hearts weighted down,*
> *Fleeing again..."*

CHAPTER EIGHT

And Jesus came and spake unto them, saying, All power is given unto me in heaven and
in earth.

Go ye therefore, and teach all nations, bap-
tizing them in the name of the Father, and of
the Son, and of the Holy Ghost:

Teaching them to observe all things whatsoever
I have commanded you: and, lo, I am with you
always, even unto the end of the world. Amen.

—Matthew 28:18–20, King James Version

Anno Domini 2020
Ostia, Italy

It had taken more strings being pulled than the pope
had ever let on. For one thing, the United States Navy
still had an interest in *Salem*, the ship. Since Sally,
unlike Daisy, had never been sunk and presumed lost,
the Navy had only turned over to Boyd a degree of
control, which control was limited by the ship's being
subject to recall.

For his part, Boyd had signed off on turning his interest over to the Vatican, no problem. The pope had had to hint at excommunication to the Chief of Naval Operations to get him to agree to the detachment and conversion. Then the church had had to go into hock to buy a moderately high level nanochit to get the permissions to create the requisite number of nanites for the conversion. And then there'd been the very involved process of cutting a deal with the Indowy to use, perhaps better said, "exhaust," a fairly large number of Sohon masters. If it hadn't been for some substantial support from the Himmit, the whole thing might have proven impossible.

After conversion, Sally's ship body floated in the *Lago di Traiano*. She didn't look much like a heavy cruiser anymore. And she was just as unhappy about it as she'd expected to be.

The process of change hadn't been as painful as she had expected it to be, at least. Physically, it had not been painful at all. Yet when the Indowy Sohon masters had moved her to space and *thought* at her, when she'd seen and felt her beautiful turrets disappear into her hull, that hull grow fat as her rakish prow shrank to nothing, her superstructure melt away, the warship in a woman's body had wept bitterly. Even the addition of a fixed centerline KE cannon and missile tubes hadn't mollified her.

"So I have a gun," she'd shrieked. "So what? I'm a fat freak with no turrets and a gun. And it's not even in the right *place*!" Then she'd retired to the cabin she shared with Dwyer, dogged the hatch, disconnected the power override, and wept hysterically for days.

The Jesuit had been unable to console her. And

at some level he'd understood. *How would I like to wake up with a featureless face, and not even a good bender to account for it?*

And I could use a good bender now, the priest thought, as he listened to half a thousand religious scholars squabbling about everything from doctrine to dogma, preordination to prejudice, and killing to karma.

There were priests and ministers, rabbis and imams. The Buddhists had their representatives, as did the Shintoists, the Confucians (only arguably a religion, Confucianism), the Hindu, the Taoists, the Zoroastrians and the Yezidis; all were there. There were Christian Animists from Africa and Vudun followers from Haiti. Kirpan-carrying, bearded, and turbaned Sikhs were in the company, as were violence-abjuring Jain.

At least the Sikhs and Jain aren't desperately eager to kill each other, Dwyer thought. *I wish the same could be said for Sunni and Shiites, let alone any Moslems and the Baha'i. And both Sally and I could live without the hair-splitting, holier-than-thou Hasidim.*

I need a drink. I also need to have a long, long talk with Boyd, Joe and the father general. Dwyer mentally sighed. *But I'll do without the former if I can just have the latter.*

Sally could handle setting up the conference call with the three of them—shipping magnate, pope and the father general of the Jesuit order—without leaving her quarters. Dwyer simply went to the ship, asked for the call to be set up aloud, and waited until Sally said all was in readiness. The big hold up, time-wise, had been Boyd, simply because he had taken off on his small boat for a day's restful fishing.

"Make it quick," Boyd said. "They're biting and my friend and I want to get back to sea."

I've got the pope, the black pope, and you, all in one room, to discuss something of terrible complexity, and you think I can make it quick? *That's absurd.*

"Well," he said, even so, "I'll try."

Trying to ignore Boyd's impatient glare, Dwyer began, "Holy Father, Father General, Dictator, let me, with your permission, restate what I think my mission is. I, and my wife, Sally, taking in company sundry religious missionaries, are to seek out whatever remnants of the Posleen we may be able to find, and, having found them, persuade them to one or another of the various human faiths. We are going as religious missionaries because there is a fair chance that persuading the Posleen must be a two-step process, the first step being to convert them to beings we can deal with, on both a practical and a moral plane, and religion being likely to be an effective way to do this."

"Long winded," the father general said, "and somewhat redundant, but accurate."

"Not a chance, then," Dwyer said resignedly, shoulders slumping. "Simply none. If I go with the full company of religious 'scholars' you have inflicted upon me, I can perhaps set the Posleen to a religious civil war, but that will make it most unlikely that they'll then be of any use to us for about five hundred years or, if Moslem-Christian relations are any guide, three or four times that and without any resolution even then.

"And then there's the other problem," Dwyer continued. "We are trying to convince the Posleen of something that requires faith far more than reason. How can we do that if we are at the same time giving them several versions of faith, few of which are compatible and none of which are particularly susceptible to reason, to decide among them?

"Lastly, I'm a Catholic priest. My business is saving souls. You simply can't ask me to be a part of something that, rather than saving souls, condemns them. Sure, I can accept—with reservations—that other Abrahamic denominations can save souls, too. But Voodoo? Confucianism? Shinto? I can possibly admire the faith of their adherents without for a minute believing that there's a shred of legitimacy behind that faith. And I cannot be a part of spreading false faith. Arguable faith? Maybe. False faith? No."

"He's right, of course," the pope said. "And yet it seems to me that he's also wrong."

"How's that, Your Holiness?" the father general asked.

"Well . . . we simply don't know which of Earth's religions has even a chance of suiting the Posleen," the pope answered. "Moreover, they didn't, so far as we know, suffer anything like the Fall of Adam. How then can we assume original sin or the need for baptism? The Moslems would grant them four wives. How do we explain to a Posleen God King that he has to dump the three hundred and ninety-four normals and five cosslain that make up the rest of his harem? How does a Catholic say that a Posleen can only have one mate, or four under the new—temporary—rules, when their breeding pattern is such as to almost guarantee that one or four mates would be insufficient to breed even a single sentient soul?"

The pope mused, "We need someone with considerable insight into the deeper nature of the Posleen and their suitability for religion."

Boyd's head turned to face someone off view, presumably his fishing partner. "Guano," the ex-dictator asked, "you up for a trip?"

Turning back to the others, Boyd asked, "Where are you people, anyway?" he asked.

"Ostia," Dwyer answered.

"Tell you what; let us finish up our fishing today. Tomorrow I'll fly him over to you. I don't know about you, but I've never gotten used to this kind of teleconferencing. And Guano doesn't have an AID."

The holy father, who shared two things with Boyd, Catholicism and the fact that they were both in the armed forces in World War Two (albeit on different sides), agreed immediately. So, too, did the father general. Dwyer, too, thought that face to face would be a better way to interact.

"Any chance you'll want to keep him?" Boyd asked, adding, "Yes, I know about your mission. Guano's an ordained minister . . . what's that? . . . Oh. Correction: He's been ordained by two different churches. And he has a family. If you're going to need to keep him, I'm going to need to send his wife and son to Ostia, too."

Sally's avatar, unseen since her transformation, popped up and said, "With all due respect to our guests, no fucking way."

Somehow I just knew she was going to be difficult about this, Dwyer thought.

On the plus side, Dwyer thought, later, when he was finally readmitted to the cabin he shared with Sally, *at least since she has something to fight about she's forgotten about the body change to the ship.*

On the other hand . . . He ducked to avoid a hurled vase. The vase smashed against the bulkhead behind him.

"I promised to love, honor, and obey!" Sally screamed. "But I didn't promise to forgive the Posleen . . . or to let one of them inside me! Have you any idea how personal that is?" She stopped ranting for just long enough to admit, "Well, I suppose *you* do. But that's not the point!"

"Won't you at least meet this renegade God King?" Dwyer asked. "How do you know you'll hate him unless you at least meet him?"

"I already hate him and everything in the universe that looks remotely like him," Sally shot back. "I don't even like horses."

And everyone knows there are at least twelve reasons women prefer horses to men, Dwyer thought. Of course he didn't say that; Sally had run out of knickknacks to throw and the mind shuddered at what she'd demolish next.

Dwyer sighed. He had one course of action open to him that he was pretty sure would work. *But, Lord, it is so going to cost me.*

Sally's mouth was opening for another volley of rant when Dwyer said, "Heavy Cruiser One Thirty-nine, also known as Lieutenant, JG, Shlomit bat Bet-Lechem-Plada Kreuzer-Dwyer, USN. Attention."

That was conditioning so deep in the very material of her hull that Sally couldn't ignore it. Dwyer was her husband. More importantly, since she was a warship, he outranked her. She shut up and snapped to attention.

Dwyer decided to keep the address more or less human. "Lieutenant Kreuzer-Dwyer, these are your orders: There is a Posleen coming aboard. There may be up to three of them sailing with us, soon. You will be polite to all three. You will cease your unsailorly objections. You will in all particulars show that 'cheerful and willing obedience to orders' to which we all aspire. Is that clear?"

"Perfectly clear, Captain Dwyer," she answered. "May I be dismissed?"

Dwyer sighed. "Sally, I . . ."

"May I be dismissed, sir?"

"Fine. You're dismissed."

Sally immediately saluted, with a precision that contained more than a touch of bitter sarcasm, walked to a chest in the quarters, and began to remove all of her clothes from that chest.

I knew this was going to be painful, Dwyer thought.

Sally didn't start really weeping until she'd reached the junior officer's quarters she'd decided to set up housekeeping in. Once she did, it was an opening of the floodgates; everything pouring out at once.

I'm not beautiful anymore. And I don't have any control over anything anymore. My own husband is making me do something I think is just disgusting. And he doesn't love me anymore and . . . and . . . and . . .

She said it aloud, "And I haven't been able to get pregnant yet!"

Her body fell asleep that way, sobbing into her pillow and feeling lower than the lowest rat in the ship. The AID, of course, and the gestalt that was the USS *Salem,* stayed awake. They also carefully kept any part of their consciousness away from the captain's cabin, occupied, now solely, by Dan Dwyer, SJ.

✧   ✧   ✧

The bed felt cold and empty and utterly, utterly lonely.

Before, it never would have bothered me, Dwyer thought. *But before, I didn't know what I was missing. And it's not just the sex. It's the closeness, the feeling of being at one with someone. It's . . . different from the feeling of being at one with God at High Mass. But it's the same, too.*

Not that Sally's a goddess . . . even if she looks like she ought to be one or has power to dwarf any goddess of old Greece or Rome. Nor even if she's as petulant as an Athena or a Hera denied Eris' apple. Nor even if I love her as much as I do God . . .

Dwyer looked at the ceiling of the cabin and said aloud, "Well, it's not like You didn't know that, after all. Or that You didn't plan it that way."

So little of what we plan ever works out the way we intend, thought Guanamarioch, as the city of Rome, what there was of it, gave way to the sea, far below his helicopter.

I, for example, never intended that I should become a preacher of a religion alien to my birth. Oh, no, I was going to lead a band of the People on the Path of Fury, win vast renown, garner much edas, and finally retire as a Rememberer, a teacher of the scrolls, leaving a huge estate to my sons.

"Still," Guano said aloud, one claw reaching up to caress the crucifix he wore on a gold chain suspended from his neck, "still, Heavenly Father, You will have Your little joke, won't You?"

Panama City, Panama, late in the war

There was no way Boyd was going to take a chance with the most valuable intelligence asset Panama or Earth had. Guanamarioch was free to roam the city, yes. But he was allowed to roam the city only under tight guard.

It wasn't that Boyd was afraid the Posleen would run, no. That just wasn't in the Posleen makeup. The Waffen SS could have taken lessons from nearly any Posleen on the subject of "Meine Ehre heisst Treue." Rather, the dictator was afraid that some self-righteous son of a bitch would shoot the God King, kill the reptilian centauroid goose that laid the golden intelligence eggs.

But life was hard for Guano. Fishing helped, but then the time would come when he remembered his best friend and fishing partner, Ziramoth, dying to an Indian's arrow somewhere in the unmarked traces of the Darien. After that, fishing would pale for a while.

Drinking helped. Not that alcohol had the slightest effect on the Posleen. Rather, the impurities of the very worst, most vile and disgusting rotgut had an effect very similar to that of alcohol on humans. Any added formaldehyde was especially good. In the long run, too, those impurities had about as bad an effect on a Posleen body as alcohol, taken in huge quantities, had on a human. The God King hadn't started puking blood yet, but the morning hangover had become an old friend.

He'd tried to kill himself, once. Boyd, when dictator, had been unwilling to simply write off chemical *warfare. He'd acquired from the Russians a certain amount of sundry nerve agents, as well as a few more esoteric types of shell filling. Once, in a fit of despair, Guano had broken into the stockpile and choked down enough VX to kill a thousand humans. It hadn't worked as intended, though at that dosage it had had an effect. Indeed, the problem with using chemicals on the Posleen, other than incendiaries to burn up oxygen, was that the dosage required to get an effect, basically hallucinations, was in practice uneconomical to deliver.*

Money wasn't a problem. Not only had Boyd freed the God King from slavery, he made sure the Posleen was paid—and at generous Fleet Strike rates, too—for the intel he provided. And then there were the royalties from ancient Posleen songs that Guano received from the so far largely untouched Republic of Ireland. (For there was something in those songs of premature, glorious and, above all, violent death that touched something in the Hibernian soul.) In all, the God King was borderline wealthy, enough so that he could arrange for his own deliveries of VX and GB. And did.

He was also probably the loneliest sentient being on the planet, the most cut off and cast off. And he was miserable.

In thrall to that loneliness and misery, Guano, drunk as a skunk, staggered along the cobblestoned street. Two of his six guards, three walking on either side, took turns shoving him aright whenever his staggering threatened to topple him over. This was often.

At least, *thought one of the guards*, the mother-fucker isn't snorting VX. I purely hate it when he starts seeing the sausage machine coming for his schlong.

The Posleen's erratic wanderings took him and his guards first to the sea, along Avenida de Balboa. From there, Guano occasionally stopping to take a long pull from the two-gallon jug he carried, they headed east, toward the ruins of old Panama. There was a large square tower there, looming out of the surrounding blackness. The tower was illuminated by lights focused directly on its four sides.

Somewhere about fifty miles to the south, the Planetary Defense Base on the Isla del Rey was belting out kinetic energy projectiles at an appreciable fraction of the speed of light. As loud as those were, still Guano heard the singing that seemed to come from that illuminated tower. It grew stronger and louder the closer he and his guards approached.

> "And though this world, with devils filled,
>   should threaten to undo us,
>   We will not fear, for God hath willed
>   His truth to triumph through us..."

There was a collective gasp as Guano made his appearance at the entrance to the old cathedral that the tower stood watch over. People backed away. A few of them—armed and uniformed soldiers—reached for weapons.

"Please," Guano said through his artificial sentience. "I mean you no harm...but...I heard...the sing... the song and..."

"I will sing for you, lord," the artificial sentience said. "Just mouth something. The humans say that music soothes the savage beast and these look savage enough."

The AS said on Guano's behalf, "Fear not, good beings. We are here only to listen and observe, never to harm. We work for you. Please, continue with your ceremony."

Uncertainly, at first, the massgoers picked up their song again, though not without many a fretful view over a shoulder or many a mother clutching a child to her breast.

> "The Prince of Darkness grim,
>   we tremble not for him;
>   His rage we can endure,
>   for lo, his doom is sure,
>   One little word shall fell him."

There were no benches in the cathedral; it was, after all, just a ruin with walls and no roof. Still, the people had left an open way through the middle. Into this Guano stepped, uncertainly, drawn by the song. His guards kept their posts, but didn't have to push him aright again.

The minister at the head of the congregation watched with trepidation as Guano approached. Still, the alien seemed harmless enough, provided one didn't try to count the teeth, of course. He saw that the creature kept its great, yellow eyes fixed on the image of Christ, locked forever in agony on the cross.

There, thought Guano. There; that human is me.

A loud crash announced that the renegade Kessentai had lost his grip on his half-empty two-gallon jug of hooch.

Guanamarlooh felt his oddly jointed knees buckle. Slowly, like a great tree in the forbidding jungle, he *sank down, eyes all the time fixed on the crucifix. Finally, every misery the being had experienced these last few years caused the Posleen's fierce maw to open up and, head twisting from side to side, to give off a great cri de coeur—AGHGHGHGHGH!—before letting that head sink to the ground.*

Guano, the Posleen God King, had gotten The Call.

With a sigh followed by a warm smile, Guano twisted his head to look over to where his cosslain wife fretted over their son, Frederico, her claws scraping at imagined imperfections in the child's still-forming crest.

It was wrong, inaccurate, anyway, to call her a "she" just as it was inaccurate to refer to Guano as a "he." They both had exactly the same sexual arrangements as did, indeed, all Posleen of whatever caste. If anything, they were all egg-bearing and egg-laying females. But since the alternative was either "Master" or "God" (and "God," under the circumstances, was right out) and "Slave" or "Servant," "he" and "she" would have to do. For his part, ever since he'd found her on eBay and purchased her from an absolutely bug house nuts lunatic of a Kessentai who was breeding Posleen children to sell to human bounty hunters for a share of the take, he'd found that *"Querida"* or "Dear" worked pretty well as a form of address.

And if ever a human male had a wife who was less trouble and more help, Guano didn't know of it. And if she couldn't talk, well, that also meant she couldn't nag. And even there, they had their own little language of whistles and grunts and touches. No, it wasn't good for anything too complex but it was perfectly capable of expressing the important thing:

"I love you." And if Querida loved Guanamarioch in goodly part because he exuded the pheromones of a Kessentai? How many human women selected their mates on similar grounds?

CHAPTER NINE

Sing, O spirits, of the fierce fury and
fiery tempest that pursued
the great ship *Arganaza'al*
As speeding, it fled the vengeance
of the humans who
sought the death of it and its crew

Anno Domini 2010
Light Cruiser Suharto, *CruRon Fifty-Seven,*
Third Federation Fleet

There should have been six light cruisers and a heavy
in the squadron. That strength, however, had been
allowed to atrophy down to the three light cruisers
remaining. As for the rest...well, the admiral in charge
had expenses. The four missing crews and mothballed
ships for which he received funding, and *not* at mothball
rates, without having the distasteful need to pay any
of that funding forward, helped cover those expenses.
And the Darhel, the fox-faced, treacherous lords of the
Galactic Federation, were more than willing to overlook

the admiral's cupidity. After all, they owned the admiral as, indeed, they owned the Federation and the Fleet, all except for that portion that had effectively mutinied to relieve the siege of Earth. And the Darhel were working on that little issue.

With the Posleen menace subdued, it was to the Darhels' interest—their vital interest—that humanity have considerably less power than it might have had. The monkey-boys and -girls were simply too dangerous to allow to be free.

Still, the war wasn't really entirely over. And there were protocols, standing orders, worst of all a news media that occasionally was less tractable than the Darhel—or people like the admiral—might have wished. Many a sensor had picked up the Posleen ship, coming seemingly from nowhere to blast its way into interstellar space. It wouldn't do to simply let it go.

Still, the individual crews were in as wretched a shape as the squadron was, indeed as wretched as the entire fleet—except for that portion in mutiny—was fast becoming. One of the ways the admiral commanding maintained control on three quarters pay and bad food (for even the spurious costs of four ships were not quite enough to cover those damnable "expenses") was to allow the crew simply to slack off. He always had the threat of transfer to the still Bristol Fashion, Euro and American commanded ships, should anyone complain.

The price for that was a sluggish response to the call "battle stations." Many a crewman, and woman, was drunk or, at least, hungover. Still others had to detangle themselves from legs, the detangling made worse by cramped bunks. In all, it was long minutes before even a skeleton staff was assembled on the bridge. At that, since the admiral highly discouraged individual initiative, the ships waited further minutes for the admiral to appear, receive the report, and give the order to pursue.

At the rear of the bridge an elevator door whooshed open. Short and fat, carrying what one would normally assume to be a ridiculous, under the circumstances, riding crop, Admiral Panggabean waddled onto the bridge, followed by the squadron flagship's captain. The captain—young, female, redheaded and leggy; Irish, in fact, since Ireland, too, had been spared the worst of the Posleen invasion—owed her position to the various positions, some of them quite exotic, she assumed at the admiral's very frequent behest.

Panggabean was a man who recognized talent; everyone said so.

"Why has my recreation been disturbed?" the admiral asked, his voice a menacing hiss.

The XO of the ship braced to attention. He'd been first on the bridge and, in fact, since the captain's duties included essentially everything *but* captaining the ship, was effectively the captain as well.

"Posleen ship showed up on the screens, Admiral. No warning. It came from the ghost fleet."

Soberly, a lot more soberly than he actually was, Panggabean nodded, the folds of fat at his neck wriggling as he did. "And you didn't order pursuit immediately?"

The admiral loathed individual initiative, except when its absence threatened to make him look bad. Worse, they might now miss the bounty available from seizing or destroying an active Posleen ship. That would go a long way towards reducing the ponderous commander's still more ponderous debt.

The XO got out no more than, "I thought—" before the admiral's riding crop landed across his face. "Follow them, you fools. Now!"

Fortunately, in normal space human ships were faster.

Himmit Ship Surreptitious Stalker

"Get me the human flotilla," Aelool ordered Argzal.

"Not in our contract," the Himmit insisted, one head rising slightly from his couch and the eyes fixing on the Indowy. "Not going to happen either. Those humans smell blood and they just might lash out at the first thing available. I don't think they can penetrate my screens but they've gotten a lot more capable about such things, generally, and there's no need to take the chance. Besides, my job is smuggling and scouting, Aelool, not battle. If we're discovered, I face a . . . reduction in rank. Besides, I have to make a delivery."

"If we don't stop the humans, our mission is a complete loss."

"No matter," Argzal said. "I've done my part and my people will still be paid."

"Bah! You people have water for blood."

"And yours?" the Himmit sneered. "If you wanted a ship capable of protecting the Posleen once they were free of Earth then you should have contracted for something else. Perhaps a scout-smuggler to take them all the way to their destination."

"You could have done that, could you? Funny you never mentioned that."

"Did you ask?"

Ship Arganaza'al

A bright red and orange and yellow cloud of Hell-in-space appeared behind the Posleen escape ship. Esstwo, manning the defensive gunnery station, snarled his satisfaction at destroying one of the accursed humans' antimatter weapons. These were more deadly than the kinetics, if they managed to hit or even get close. However, they were easier to keep from hitting or getting close by destroying prematurely the containment fields that kept their antimatter from joining with normal matter and becoming a cosmic catastrophe before it was intended to.

Despite that success, Esstwo's claws worked furiously, trying to stave off and defeat the swarm of human missiles, a mix of antimatter and kinetics, that pursued the ship relentlessly. Of the two classes of targets, the KEW were the more to be feared. They gave little trace, hardly showed up on the sensors until it was almost too late, and were not particularly vulnerable to countermeasures.

"Demon shit!" Esstwo exclaimed, his claws a blur over his defense systems panel. The Posleen exhaled, saying, "I nearly missed that one." In a rear view screen, a KEW rapidly expanded into a cloud of plasma as massed charged particle beams, supplemented by a streams of smaller KEWs emanating from the ship, sliced into it. Two more KEWs, hard on the heels of the first, closed on the Posleen ship.

"Too close for comfort," Tulo'stenaloor said imperturbably. "Essthree, how long until jump?"

"Do you care where we jump to?" the grizzled Posleen asked.

"I can take one of those projectiles!" Esstwo shouted. "The other is going to hit!" Lowering his view back to his screen, Esstwo muttered, "Bastard humans have gotten better at this shit."

Tulo glanced up at the battle tracking view screen. "Don't. Care. A. Bit," he said to Essthree, still working the helm.

"Fourteen beats, then."

"Do it. Anywhere that doesn't leave us as a cloud in space."

"That's not something I can guarantee," Essthree answered. "We might end up too close to a planet or star. I was in the middle of calculations when the humans jumped us."

"Fine, then. Anything that doesn't carry the *certainty* of our becoming a cloud in space. Which the fucking humans' weapons do."

Essthree nodded. Closing his eyes, whispering a prayer to the spirits of ancestors in whom he didn't really believe, he touched a claw to a panel.

Tulo kept his eyes fixed on the screen showing the oncoming KEWs fast closing from behind. He saw still the ghost fleet they were abandoning, the pursuing human cruisers, the streams of plasma and little defensive KEWs emanating from the ship under the direction of Esstwo, and the planet and stars of the Diess system. One of those KEWs was being chopped up, hopefully into pieces small enough for the ship to survive an impact with them. The other, solid and deadly, closed relentlessly.

Three more and then another three KEWs leapt from the human cruisers. Of the closer two, one began to break up, its component metal shattering and the pieces venting off a mix of uranium and iron gas. The other seemed certain to strike, so close was it, when—

Himmit Ship Surreptitious Stalker

On the view screen of the Himmit ship's bridge, a multicolored nightmare of a space-time distortion appeared, blocking the view of the Posleen Ark.

"It appears they've outrun . . . out-somethinged, anyway, their pursuers," the Himmit announced.

"No thanks to you."

The Himmit captain merely shrugged and answered, "A contract's a contract."

Light Cruiser Suharto

"Your contract shall be voided!" Panggabean hissed, kicking the prostrate XO in the ribs. "You shall be court-martialed, disgraced and spaced!" he added, stomping on the unfortunate creature's head. Bending over, no mean feat for so weighty a man, Panggabean applied his riding crop—which was not, after all, functionless—to the XO's neck and shoulders. "Your children shall be sold as back passage whores, the girls *and* the boys!"

The CruRon had pursued the Posleen ship to and through the distortion caused by its jump, all the time flinging missiles forward. The admiral fretted over the expense, of course. The cost of the ordnance would come from funds he considered his own. But to be cheated of his prize by the incompetence of the exec—never mind that Panggabean had spaced the XO's predecessor for excessive zeal and initiative . . . it was simply intolerable. Nor would it be tolerated.

"Moira," Panggabean ordered the captain, "assemble a court-martial. Have it find this miscreant guilty. Then have him spaced."

Ship Arganaza'al

Transitspace—"subspace," the humans would have said—was strange. There were no stars visible, but only a diffuse glow leaking in from an adjacent reality. Of landmarks and navigational aids there were none, or none, at least, that the Posleen had ever been able to identify. Oh, the glow was not everywhere equally diffuse. There were bright spots and bands, rivers of light and glowing pseudo-particles. Yet none of these stayed constant. The rivers flowed back into the nothingness from whence they had come. The bright spots went dark, the bands shifted shape to become lines of spots that then drifted off into individuality. There was a theory, so far unproven, that the spots and bands and rivers were in fact the constructs of the individual ships and the energies they expended. If so, it meant that not only was navigation while in transitspace impossible, it would always be impossible.

That is to say, navigation was impossible except insofar as one had set to emerge in a rough patch of real space before entering transitspace. Essthree had been making those settings, something that always had to be done and finessed right up to the moment of the jump under the Posleen technique of "tunneling" through space, right up until Tulo'stenaloor had said, "Do it." At that point, he'd initiated the jump without really knowing where the final destination would be.

He could hope, at least, that it wouldn't be at the center of a star. That would be a flashy way to go, of course, (indeed some called it "finding the light at the end of the tunnel") but Essthree had never been one for excessive flashiness.

They also had the option of cutting their jump short. But since the general area of their intended emergence was at least relatively free of stars and planets, and almost assuredly free of human-crewed Federation starships, and they couldn't really know the makeup of the area around which they might emerge if they cut the jump short, it was arguably better to see the thing through.

"Still," Golo observed, in the mess compartment reserved for Tulo and his closest twelve followers, "it's a lot like having a death sentence imposed, with a certain date of execution but a beheading blade that might or might not be sharp."

"You paint the most charming pictures, Goloswin," said Binastarion. "Isn't he just the life of the party, AS?"

"Indeed, lord," the machine replied from its perch on the Kessentai's chest. "And if I were not destined to be turned to plasma at the same time as all the rest of you—if you are—I'd be more charmed still."

"You'll come back, O Bucket of Bolts," Binastarion said. "Abat colonies never die."

Brasingala kept silent through the banter, his muzzle down in his food bucket. He was, in fact, scared witless. Not that the thought of his own demise troubled him overmuch. But there was a threat to his lord, Tulo'stenaloor, that he was simply incapable of dealing with. This was unique in the bodyguard's experience. He'd faced the metal threshkreen without fear. He'd blasted apart the humans' tanks, at least some of the earlier models, without a tremble. He'd even, and on more than one occasion, pushed his chief to the ground and covered his body with his own when the humans' unstoppable "artillery" came in to search the ground with clouds of hot, razor sharp, shards. Brasingala had the scars to show.

But in space?

In space I am helpless. We will either come out of transitspace without problem . . . or we will emerge too close to substantial matter and disintegrate . . . or we will emerge near a human fleet that will rend us to thresh. And I can do nothing.

Suddenly, Brasingala withdrew his muzzle from the food bucket and pushed it toward the center of the circle of Kessentai. "Anyone wants it, go ahead," he said. "I've lost my appetite."

Brasingala had lost his appetite. In a different mess deck, one reserved for some of the newly acquired Kessentai, Finba'anaga had an appetite he could not quench, a thirst he could not even begin to slake.

The others were gone now, off about whatever business they'd been assigned aboard ship. Finba'anaga, on the other hand, had duties a human might have called "mess boy" or "KP."

Using the Posleen shipboard equivalent of a mop and bucket, though in this case it was more of a auxiliary-propelled collector and demolecularizer, a humming CdM, the God King was tasked with cleaning up the mess left by the mass of cosslain and a few normals driven into the hibernation chambers before the ship had departed Diess. It was a job for a normal, or a not very bright cosslain. And yet—near ultimate indignity!—it had fallen to him.

The shame of it all, the God King mentally moaned. *And still there's nothing I can do. I am the lowest of the low, I who was born to ride among the stars and crush worlds beneath my claws. Reduced to this, reduced to mere janitorial work.*

Finba'anaga stopped manipulating the cleaning tool briefly to inspect the floor upon which he worked. He snarled to see a stain deep set into the hull that the collector and demolecularizer had failed to clean. Making the Posleen equivalent of a *tsk*, a sort of throaty growl with a cough added, the Kessentai shuffled over to a small storage bin and removed a container of a kind of solvent. This he poured onto the stain, then waited for a few scores of beats while the stuff fizzed.

On the other hand, at least that Kessenalt by another name, Goloswin, has stopped riding me all the time. I suppose there's some correlation between that and the fact that I learned to work more carefully.

As the fizzing diminished, then stopped altogether, Finba'anaga once again ran the CdM unit over the stained patch. As the unit's hum rose, the stain began to disappear.

And that is perhaps how I shall get out of the position I find myself in.

Finba'anaga redoubled his efforts to clean the galley spotless.

❖   ❖   ❖

"There's one of the new Kessentai I'd like to recommend to you, Tulo," Goloswin said. "Started off slow but seems to be really getting into the spirit of things now."

Tulo turned his great head, half closed one eye, leaving the other wide open and staring at Goloswin. It was the Posleen equivalent of a human raised eyebrow.

"Who and what and why?" he asked.

"Name's Finba'anaga. Tests high for brightness, according to Binastarion—yes, I checked—and, while he had some issues early on, he's taken to his duties, even the more degrading ones, with a considerable will."

"You want to promote him, then? To what?"

"Well . . . that cosslain I tested the new suit on is of, at best, limited utility. Besides that, we're better off with it doling out the rations. But I could use a new assistant. I'm trying to expand—to grow—that lump of Himmit metal we got, you see."

Tulo relaxed the half-closed eye and thought upon it. *We have to find a way to integrate these newcomers. And Golo's right about the potential uses of that metal. Still, he's a better judge of machinery than of beings. I don't know . . .*

"Fine," Tulo agreed at last. "We'll call it an experiment. You can take the newcomer under your chin and try to integrate him. I want a report on him not less frequently than every other ship's day. At least for now, I do.

"Oh, and keep me posted on progress with that Himmit metal, too."

Goloswin nodded. "I think it's the right thing to do, Tulo. Really."

"Let us hope."

✧   ✧   ✧

Freedom! Finba'anaga thought, so exultantly that he half missed Goloswin's question.

"Excuse me, lord?" the newcomer asked.

"I asked, 'What is your skill set?'"

Posleen, be they normals or cosslain or Kessentai, were born with certain skills, the result of serious genetic tinkering sometime in the lost past. These, particularly among the normals and cosslain, usually manifested themselves in some form without prompting. A normal born to be a farmer, for example, and finding itself on a new planet, would automatically start gathering seeds from the local plants, even as it began preparing fields for more usual Posleen crops. Miner-born Posleen would begin prospecting for useful ores without the need ever to tell them to. A builder normal, or more usually a group of them, would begin constructing a pyramidal palace for their God King at the first sign of sufficient security to justify the effort. Indeed, it was generally necessary to tell them not to, if there was some other task requiring their attention.

Kessentai were a bit different. For them, their skill sets rarely manifested themselves until there was a need.

"I don't really know," Finba answered. "I've got all the usual things a Kessentai should have, I think. I can use a boma blade, drive a tenar, aim a railgun or shotgun or high velocity missile or plasma cannon. I can tell my normals and cosslain to follow me."

"Not very useful, under the circumstances," Goloswin observed drily. "Let's try this: what doesn't interest you in the slightest?"

Finba thought upon that. "Well...this ship. I've no

urge to understand how to sail it. I've been curious what drives it, though. But, of course, I haven't been allowed anywhere near the engines."

"We can fix that. What else, that you're either interested in or oblivious to?"

"I'm curious how the forges work," Finba answered.

"That will have to wait until we land. We took nothing from any of the other ghost ships that wasn't already processed. And the forge is in storage. It would be very inconvenient to dig it out. What else?"

The new Kessentai blew recycled air through his lips, causing them to ripple. "Ummm...I don't care about building pyramids...or any building, actually. I'm interested in breeding with normals—"

"We're all interested in that, young Finba," Golo said with a smile. "Keep going."

"I'm interested in the Net, and how it resolves questions of edas, and hierarchy, and prioritization. I'm not particularly interested in history...well, just a bit.

"That's all that comes to mind, for now, lord."

Golo nodded deeply. "It's a start. The rest we'll figure out as time passes and opportunity comes. So... let us take ourselves to the engine room. Perhaps we may learn something there."

CHAPTER TEN

Children too are a gift from the Lord,
the fruit of the womb, a reward.
—Psalms 127:3, New American Bible

Anno Domini 2020
Lago di Traiano, *Ostia,* *Italy*

A trio of grat buzzed overhead in search of abat. No
one paid the creatures any mind.

"Think there are any fish in that lake, Dad?" Frederico asked excitedly.

Behind the trio of Posleen, Guanamarioch, his "wife,"
and the boy, some humans unloaded their gear from
the helicopter that had brought them down from the
airport. Atop the pile of personal belongings—Boyd
hadn't been able to say how long they'd be gone and so
Guano had packed heavy—sat a single cage that rocked
to and fro as if under its own power.

The humans' every motion and expression said,
"And good riddance, too." The helicopter's rotor was
still turning, the engines in a whining idle. This was

a measure of just how desperately the human crew wanted to be away from their alien passengers.

Guano looked over the greenish tinged, nasty, polluted lake, in fact the remnants of the harbor ordered built by the Emperor Trajan, almost two thousand years before, and said, "I don't know, son. But I'll bet if there are they'd be mighty tasty. Why don't you and your mother go get your fishing pole and check it out."

Guano reached out to stroke the cosslain's head and gave his mate a look that meant, *Guard our child, Querida, while I go ahead and find out what this is all about.*

The cosslain lifted her muzzle to run it under Guano's chin and along his neck. *Of course. I love you.*

Sally—flesh and blood Sally—knew the Posleen would be coming aboard soon. That's why she'd left the ship at the first sound of the helicopter's rotors, to walk the edge of the ancient harbor alone.

This wasn't as easy as it sounded. With the reduction of the human population, and the elimination of the Posleen who would have grazed trim the edges of the hexagonal lake, weeds and bracken and all manner of plant life had grown up around the edges. She had to fight her way forward for nearly every step.

In a way, that was better. The thorns that gouged her flesh and the sharp edges of leaf-bladed grass that sometimes slashed at her calves kept her mind from the misery of her existence. Better still, they gave her something she could destroy with a perfectly clear conscience. The soul of the warship was never too far beneath the conscious mind of the woman.

It was while she was thus engaged, ripping a tangle

of thorny vines to shreds in an attempt to free up a caught leg, that Sally's enhanced eye caught sight of a small red and white object, a sphere, with a hook on a string trailing it, sailing through the air to plop down into the scummy waters of the lake.

The Posleen head turned steadily, left to right and back again, searching for danger. On occasion, too, the great neck swiveled one hundred and eighty degrees to scan the murky green water. One never knew what might lie hidden beneath the ripples, after all.

While Querida stood guard over her son, still much less than half her size, Frederico expertly baited a triple hook with a small earthworm he dug up from near the lake's edge. His dad had explained to him that the worms had no minds, not even as much as a fish, and so couldn't feel any pain. Even so, he felt a little sorry for the wriggling thing.

He was still little, Frederico knew, still growing. There were few things he could yet do as well as his dad or even his mom. Casting a hook was one of them. In fact, though his father held prizes for other forms of fishing, he never even tried casting anymore, having hooked his own rump often enough in the attempt to give it up as a bad job. Perhaps because the Posleen child was so much less lengthy, he didn't have that problem. The baited hook sailed true about eighty feet before the little plastic float struck water, raising a spout, and the hook and line continued on to sink into the depths.

Slowly, gradually, Frederico began to reel in. He could trace progress from the red and white float, standing out clearly, less than half submerged in the foam.

Frederico sighed as the float came closer. Nothing. Well, there was also nothing for it but to cast again. He retrieved the float and the line, checked that the worm was still wriggling and prepared to repeat the effort.

And then he heard a low growl from his mom.

Sally came upon the Posleen pair by surprise, something she immediately knew was a mistake, and possibly a serious one. The smaller of the two just swiveled its head to look at her. The larger, on the other hand, was already in what appeared to be an attack position, legs poised to spring and foreclaws outstretched. Sally was struck as much by the larger Posleen's eyes as by its ivory teeth. Yellow, they were, as was normal, but flecked with gold and, she had to admit, really rather beautiful.

And then the little one said, in Spanish no less, "No, Mom! Dad told you it's not all right to eat the neighbors."

The larger Posleen went silent, withdrawing her claws and settling back on her haunches, while sheathing her impressive set of ivory fangs. She didn't take her eyes off of Sally for a split second, even so.

Sally gulped nervously. It wasn't that she couldn't have grown a new body if she'd lost this one. But God it would have *hurt* to be lunched by a Posleen. She didn't come any closer until the little Posleen said, "It's all right. She's just watching over me. I guess 'cause I'm the only one she can be sure she'll ever have."

"You speak Spanish?"

"Sure," the little Posleen said. Scaled, yellow-eyed, croc-headed, and its body mottled yellow and brown, the alien was the size of a small horse, bigger than a Shetland pony but smaller than an Arabian. It was closest to a moderately large donkey. "Spanish and English and High Posleen, too. Dad tells me I'm pretty bright, but I dunno. I'm Frederico, by the way."

Frederico thought for a minute before adding, "But you speak Spanish? This is Italy."

"I was in Panama for many years," Sally said, which was only half an explanation. It was true enough, but she could speak almost any language, whether she'd lived in a place where it was spoken or not.

"Really? That's where I'm from. Mom, she's a *neighbor*."

The larger Posleen, still staring Sally in the throat, cocked her head to one side as if to say, *So?*

"She doesn't talk?"

"Sorta she does and sorta she doesn't," Frederico answered. "She actually says a few things, like 'eecho' for me, or 'rrridddo' for Dad. Dad can't seem to understand much beyond that, though. On the other hand, she and Dad have their own language and I understand none of it."

"Husbands and wives often—"

Sally stopped short. *Husbands and wives often have their own language, I was going to say. But they have to be willing to talk to use it. And that, I have not been.*

"Would your mom mind if I sat down?" she asked.

"I don't know the protocol for coming aboard ship," Guano said, through his AS, to Dwyer where they met at the head of the long floating gangway leading from the shore. The Posleen spoke softly, in part from recent habit and in part so that his grunts and clicks and snarls didn't overwhelm the simultaneous translation. "The one time I boarded it was in a hurry, fleeing orna'adar, and the one time I left it was in a bigger and more confused hurry.

"Besides, I don't know if I'll fit aboard."

"Never mind; you'll fit. She was rebuilt with Posleen in mind, one might say. But let's not for now. The shore is pleasant enough, is it not?"

Guano looked uncertainly at the greenery near the bridgehead. Yes, yes, Boyd had told him over and over that the grass wouldn't harm him. But he'd had experiences with things that were altogether too green, bad experiences. And then he looked at the greenish water. He'd had even worse experiences from that...

Darien Jungle, Panama, during the war

"Tell me if you see any leeches, Zira. I hate getting those things on me."

Voice calm, the Kessenalt assured Guanamarioch that he would indeed keep a watch out. Even so, the damned nuisances were so nearly invisible until they attached themselves that Ziramoth really had no expectation of being able to keep them off no matter how diligently he guarded. Nonetheless, Ziramoth looked at the dozens of oozing sores dotting the Kessentai's torso and resolved to at least try.

Other than his fear of leeches, Guanamarioch found that the water itself was warm and even soothing. He thought that, were his people ever able to rid themselves of this world's multifarious pests, bathing in such a stream might be a welcome activity. In particular, and despite the fear of the leeches, the warm water passing over the God King's reproductive member was most pleasant.

The caiman was only of average size. Thus, when it came upon the legs of the beasts walking through the river bed it was momentarily nonplussed. It knew, instinctively, that there was no way it was going to be able to take down a creature with legs the size of those. Almost, the caiman felt a surge of frustration at the unfairness of it all. Almost, it wept crocodile tears.

Perhaps the crocodile-headed god of the caiman smiled upon it. There, just there, just ahead, was something of a proper size for the caiman to eat. It dangled and danced enticingly, as if presenting itself for supper. The caiman swished its tail, and inclined its body and head to line up properly on the tempting bait.

"You know, Zira," Guano said, "this isn't so bad. One could even ... AIAIAI!"

Ziramoth's yellow eyes went wide in his head as his friend exploded out of the water, dragging a dark creature almost like one of the People—barring only the shorter limbs and two too few of them—behind it. The eyes went wider still as the Kessenalt realized just what part of his friend connected him with this alien predator.

Up Guanamarioch flew, legs churning furiously. Down the God King splashed. Both trips he screamed continuously: "AIAIAI!"

Once down, Guano tried to bend over to catch the creature. No use, he couldn't quite reach. Leeches be *damned, still shrieking he rolled over on his back, scrambling for purchase on his unseen attacker.*

Another half roll and Guanamarioch cried out, "Getitoffgetitoffgetitoff!" before his head plunged back into the water.

Normally steady as a rock, Zira didn't know what to do in this case. Fortunately—or unfortunately, depending on one's point of view—one of Guano's normals saw no real problem. Instead, it saw the twin opportunities of relieving its god from pain and at the same time providing some much needed nourishment to his pack.

Zira had only just realized what the normal intended and begun to shout, "St..." when the boma blade swung, taking the creature's head off but at the same time removing about five inches of the Kessentai's reproductive organ.

Unsteadily, the God King rolled back over and struggled to its feet. His eyes were wider with shock even than Zira's had been. For a moment it struggled with the realization of what had just happened to it. Once it made that realization, the God King bowed its head...

For the first time since the beginning of the invasion of the human world, a Kessentai unabashedly wept.

Lago di Traiano, *Latium, Italy*

"Ummm... let's just stay here for now, shall we?" Guanamarioch asked. "That water..."

"I understand," said Dwyer, even though he didn't have the first clue about Guano's fear-filled reaction to the greenish water. Still, he understood that *something* about it frightened the Posleen. That was understanding enough. "Would you like to sit?" Dwyer's hand indicated a spot under a screen thrown up for protection from the fierce Mediterranean sun.

"Thank you," Guano said through his AS. "Most gracious."

"I should probably explain," the AS added on its own. "The Reverend Doctor Guanamarioch had some very unpleasant experiences during the war with both green growing things and seemingly safe bodies of water. He's a little...skittish is, I think, your word?"

Guano had been carrying the case that had sat atop the pile of his family's belongings. Setting it down he opened the door and allowed a large, evil looking cat to emerge. The cat immediately jumped up into the minister's arms.

"My wife can't hunt, as she would like," Guano explained through his AS. "But the cat can and she enjoys watching it, the vicarious pleasure of its hunt."

It was only then that Dwyer really noticed the gold cross hanging from one of the two golden chains around the Posleen's equine neck.

I'd been told the alien had become Christian, but... it just seemed so preposterous. Then you see the crucifix and hear his AID—no, they call them "artificial sentiences," don't they?—anyway you see and you hear and it hits you. He's serious. Then again, didn't I ever see a Posleen do a Christian thing?

Bay of Panama, Panama, during the war

Was there a greater heartache for a sailor than to have to abandon his ship? If so, Dwyer didn't know of it.

Behind the small boat in which the priest had taken refuge, along with as many as they could fit aboard... and a few more besides, the great warship Daisy Mae *was still firing for all she was worth as she settled down*. Dwyer felt tears spring to his eyes, tears he dashed away with one hand.

Looking up, Dwyer saw the lone tenar slowly approaching, rather than charging and firing. Surrounded by ninety or so survivors—there hadn't been time to do a full headcount—in the one serviceable lifeboat they had found topside, he called out, "Boys, it's been good to serve with you. Now stand ready to take one last one with us."

But the tenar had not opened fire. Instead, the rider had pulled a metal stick from his harness, stood fully erect in the flying sled, and called out with both arms raised above it. Other circling tenar had stopped then, their God Kings looking curiously at the tiny band of humans bobbing on the ocean waves.

The tenar came closer, closer until finally it was not more than ten feet from the edge of the lifeboat. The rider then cocked its head and said something in its own language. That something had sounded unaccountably gentle. Then the God King raised its crest, shouted once again, and tossed Dryer the stick it held. Dwyer caught it, fumblingly at first. He looked up to see that the alien had raised one palm, holding it open and towards the humans. The priest returned the gesture and added one of his own. He didn't understand the why's of it, but he knew he and the rest had just been spared. The priest made the sign of the cross at the Posleen

❖   ❖   ❖

"Father? Are you all right?" Guano's AS asked gently.

The priest shook his head. "I was just remembering back . . . back to the war."

"I understand," the AS said, to which Guano added, "Eeee' eeesss harrrddd fffoorrr meee to ssspeakkkk you-ouou tonnngggue. Bu' Iii dddooo unnnddderrrsssstannnd i'. Le' usss no' ssspppeakkk o' zzzeee wwwaaarrr. Too sssaaaddd. Le' usss . . . sssiii' aaannnddd tttalkkk o' ozzzerrr zzziiingngngsss."

As soon as the priest had sat down, and Guano, still cradling the cat, had settled back on his haunches, the Posleen released the feline and reached into a pouch slung from his harness. From it he pulled a delicate carving knife and a piece of what looked to be ivory. Dwyer saw that the ivory, if that's what it was, had already been half formed into a small statuette of a tenar.

"Would you sit with us?" Frederico asked excitedly. "I don't really ever have anyone to play with besides my Dad and his AS."

"Why is that?" Sally asked, bending over to bring her head roughly parallel with the alien's. "A bright, well-behaved boy like you?"

"'Cause I'm a Posleen," the boy said. "And nobody quite trusts me. Even Dad says it will be a while before he's sure that I'm not going to attack someone by instinct. And even Dad's congregation back home keeps their kids away except during services."

"You mean you don't have any friends at all?" Sally asked

Sadly and slowly, the little Posleen shook his head. "Not even one. It's just my dad and my mom and the AS and me. Oh, and Maria who comes and helps my mom with the dishes a couple of times a week, but she's blind so I think she really doesn't know what we are. Not deep down, anyway."

"Dishes?"

"Yes, silly! Dishes. We're people too, Dad says, and people eat from dishes."

Almost against her will, Sally smiled and asked, "What is it that you eat from...dishes?"

"Well...most anything people eat," the boy answered. "And then my mom's nestlings that aren't going to grow up smart...we eat those, too. They're not people, Dad says."

And on that note, Sally thought, *I'd better sit down*.

"Do you have any really, *really* vile whiskey or rum?" the AS asked. "If all else fails, straight formaldehyde would do."

Dwyer twisted his mouth into an upside down bow and answered, "Well...we're not a dry ship... exactly, but if there's anything still stashed in my communion cabinet or in the medical stores beyond wine and rum it's probably not going to be exactly vile. Formaldehyde, you said?"

"Yes. Not too much. A quart or so to relax Reverend Guanamarioch and loosen his tongue."

"Sally, did you hear that?" Dwyer shouted.

"There's some in the morgue, sir," a disembodied voice whispered into Dwyer's ear. "I'll have it sent out."

"It's on the way," Dwyer said brightly.

"Interesting, that," observed the AS.

"Which?"

"Your ship is sentient. During the war we heard of such, but we didn't know any of them survived."

"Both did," Dwyer answered. "At least, both of those I know about did. You heard her talk to me?"

"Not in words, but yes." The AS didn't elaborate.

"Do you have any children?" Frederico asked hopefully, after casting his line again and beginning to slowly reel it in.

"Not yet," Sally said. *And, if I don't work out something with Dan, maybe never. And why shouldn't I work something out? Here I am, sitting with a couple of the creatures I said I couldn't stand to have near me. And they're . . . not so bad. No, be honest with yourself, Sally, old girl. The boy is so ugly he's made the transformation all the way to adorable. And his mother . . . well . . . she's a mother. I could probably learn a thing or two from her.*

"That's too bad," the Posleen boy said. "If you had some, maybe I'd have someone my size to play with."

"Well, even if I had some now, it would be a while before they were fully grown enough to be chums to you." Sally thought about that and started to giggle.

"What's so funny?"

She looked at the boy and tried to explain. "Chums? Chum? Dead fish guts all ground up you put in the water with the blood to attract fish."

Frederico's eyes grew saucer-wide. "I'd never . . . you would never . . ."

"No. No, of course not. But . . . see . . . you're a Posleen and . . . well, we had a lot of jokes about Posleen during the war. Do you know what a lawyer is?"

"Sorta."

"Okay. What's the difference between a Posleen and a lawyer?"

"Number of legs?" the boy offered.

"Well, besides that," Sally said. "See, one is a vicious, twisted, man-eating, menace to society. And the other is just an alien life form."

"I don't get it."

"You don't have to. Besides, all too soon, you will."

Sally noticed the boy's fishing line twitching. "And more important, you've got a bite."

"And so you want the Reverend Doctor to be a fisher of... Posleen?" the AS asked.

"More part of a fishing team," Dwyer answered. "See, we can't know which religion will take with them. So we want to give them a menu to choose from." Dwyer thought upon the sundry missionaries collected so far for the mission and thought, *A highly limited menu, if I have anything to say about it.*

After the AS translated, Guano sat on his haunches for some minutes, absentmindedly sipping from his quart of formaldehyde. When he began speaking again, it was to say, through the AS, "Despite Boyd's little joke, I've never actually made a sermon against the Whore of Rome. I don't make sermons about or against Jews, or Mormons, or Muslims, or Buddhists or any other of God's children. I'll admit to having a soft spot in my hearts for Sikhs and Gurkhas and Kshatriya Hindus.

"And I have a soft spot, too, for my own people, forever denied God's grace and redemption. So, yes, Father, I and my family will go with you."

CHAPTER ELEVEN

Then did the hurtling asteroids menace;
Then did the star, Hemaleen, threaten death.
—The *Tuloriad*, Na'agastenalooren

Anno Domini 2010
Posleen Ship Arganaza'al

There was an ancient song of hope, sung upon entry into a new system. Tulo'stenaloor's bridge crew sang it, even as did the various Kessentai busied about the innards of the ship, as the Essthree called out, "Emergence in...five...four...three...two...one..."

And nothing happened.

The essthree immediately turned to his navigation computer and began to beat on the control panel. That first choice failing, he actually began trying to use the thing's controls.

"No luck," said Essthree. "I'm locked out." He began to pound on the control panel again. *Well,* it wasn't as if the original ship designers hadn't anticipated that a frustrated Posleen God King might not feel the urge from time to time. The thing was overbuilt.

"Fuscirto! Miserable, misbegotten, filthy, foul, vile—"

"Shut up, Essthree," Tulo said, one claw indicating the main view screen where the formless void of transitspace was replaced with the torso of Aelool, the Indowy.

"Greeting, Posleen!" Aelool's image said. "And welcome aboard Hijack Spacelines, Flight Number One. I'll be your flight attendant for this trip. We'll be cruising the galaxy at speeds you really wouldn't believe. So relax and enjoy the journey. And just leave the driving to us."

"I hate fucking Indowy with a sense of humor," Tulo muttered. To the screen he shouted, "When do we come out of transitspace? *Where* will we come out?"

The screen didn't answer.

About two weeks later, as humans measure time, the screen came to life once again with the image of Aelool.

"By this time," the image said, "you will have realized that you are not coming out of subspace quite where you intended to. That was, of course, *my* doing. I'd give you my apologies for infecting your ship's navigation computer but what good would apologies be at this point?

"Nevertheless, be of good heart and good cheer. I did not do as I did to harm you, but to help. For reasons I cannot go into without betraying confidences, you will not be safe unless you get very, very far from the humans, far enough, at least, for them to forget the better portion of their grudge.

"Long and hard we searched, my clan and I, for at least the start point for you to begin looking for such a world. Between legends—yours, ours, the crabs', and the Aldenata's...oh, and some others we can't quite pinpoint the origin of—we think we did find such a place. It is to that that you are going. It is from there you may begin your search for...for whatever you think you want to find.

"In time, you may well thank me. Good luck. Aelool, out."

"Bastard!" Tulo said. "We should have eaten him after all."

"Umm...maybe not," Goloswin said as the ship suddenly emerged out of transitspace. Though what kind of space it emerged into...

"Where the fuck are we?" Tulo demanded. It was a really good question since the ship had popped into an area of space with no stars nearby. This was...rare.

"Beats me," Essthree and Esstwo said together.

"I've got nothin'," the Rememberer said.

"And we need to refuel," Essfour added.

Goloswin looked terribly unhappy. Or confused. It amounted to the same thing with him.

"There's *something* out there," the tinkerer admitted. "I'm not sure just what, though."

"Fine," Tulo said. "What do you *think* it is...or might be...or whatever?"

The tinkerer chewed on his lower lip carefully for a while before answering. "I *think* it's a power source...ummm...for a containment unit...full of antimatter."

"In the middle of nowhere?"

"Infinite universe," Goloswin offered. "Infinite possibilities. No, I don't know what the fuck a pod of antimatter is doing here. I only know we need to refuel and there it is."

"A trap?" the Rememberer suggested.

Golo shook his head. "A trap is for beings you haven't already trapped. We, on the other hand, once that little fuzz-face took over the ship, *were* already trapped."

"Refuel then?" Essfour asked of Tulo'stenaloor.

"You have a better option?" the clan lord asked.

"Umm . . . no."

"Then, by all means, refuel."

Refueling, for the Posleen, generally meant taking station off a gas giant and manufacturing antimatter, a process that could take anywhere from days to weeks. In this case, with the fuel already present, it was done in a matter of hours, most of that being spent docking the containment unit to the ship.

Had it taken twice the normal time, they'd *still* have been on their way sooner than they were. As it was, nearly six of the humans' weeks had passed and they were still stuck there, fully refueled and unable to make any headway. The ship lay dead in space.

Goloswin thought he was making headway though. Hunched over a holographic projection of the virus that had taken control of the ship, he believed he had narrowed it down to a certain set of—admittedly very complex—codes.

"Identifying the virus is the key to defeating it, Tulo," he said, his claw sweeping expansively over the projected code. "If I can . . . ah, shit."

Even as Golo cursed, the code began transforming itself under his very eyes. As it did that, the ship began to hum as it powered itself up for a jump through transitspace.

Eons past the asteroid had been formed, back in the time of the Knower Wars, the ancient wars fought between those Posleen who, while loyal to the Aldenata, Lords of Creation, had still questioned the Aldenata, and those who had been both loyal and *un*questioning.

There had been two Posleen planets in the system then, one dominated by the Knowers and the other by the Loyals. No one living knew any longer which of the two had seen its planet blown to flinders to form the asteroid belt that remained. It didn't really matter anyway, as the Posleen of the planet that had been smashed had still scoured the other planet almost free of life before dying. They *had* scoured it free of anything one might call civilization.

The ship emerged, in a flash that told of the rending of transitspace. There had been little warning before the Posleen of Tulo'stenaloor experienced the gut-wrenching shift and found themselves hurled into a maelstrom of hurtling asteroids, meteors, and other space debris.

"Little fucking-bat-faced shit eater!" exclaimed Esstwo, as he found himself, once again, desperately trying to keep his ship from destruction. Under Esstwo's direction, fire lanced out from the ship, most notably at an "o-my-freaking-spirits-of-the-ancestors-and-Aldenata-demon-shit-combined" *huge* asteroid that was not merely in the ship's path at emergence but was, all on its own, on a collision course.

"Getitgetitgetitgetit!" shrieked Essthree, standing at the helm.

"I'mtryingdammittothepits!" Esstwo screamed back, even as his beams and KEWs attempted to break the asteroid into little bits. But the thing was enormous. There was little chance.

"Notgonnawork!" Tulo said, then repeated, "Notgonnawork. Fuckfuckfuck!"

Tulo shook his head, collecting himself. "If you can't smash it can you *shave* it?"

"Shave it? Shave it? Shave it!" Esstwo tapped his screens several times, causing a grid to appear over the asteroid in the main view screen. "Essthree, I'm going to put everything I have into slicing the section that will appear—" a caret showed on the asteroid's upper middle quadrant "—here. Can you dive under it?"

"Beats trying to smash through," Essthree answered. "But I don't know if we'll..."

Not waiting for Essthree to finish, Esstwo began slashing at the asteroid, his beams following down the spot marked on the view screen. Bits of incandescent matter began to slough off.

In the screen the asteroid arose, then recentered itself as the computers adjusted.

Essthree shook his head. "It's going to be close but, no, we're not quite going to make it."

"All hands, secure for collision!"

Finba'anaga heard the call, "Secure for collision." His hearts immediately began to race. Even as they did, he did; to race for the interior of the ship.

There was a traffic jam of sorts at the nearest passageway. None of the Posleen present had weapons, and so it came down to teeth and claws. Finba was smaller than most. He found himself pushed aside. Which was just as well, really, since the hatchway sphinctered shut, slicing two larger Posleen neatly across the torsos. They screamed for a little while, not very long.

Fortunately or unfortunately, that left Finba'anaga alone in an airtight compartment.

A close but uninvolved observer would have seen quite a show. The asteroid spun as it moved, leaving a vertical spiral trail of glowing matter behind it. The *Arganaza'al* didn't spin, but it did twist as it attempted to go under the asteroid. Almost, it made it. Sadly, the top five sections that comprised the ship—landers for when the time came for landing—were sliced off, in whole or in part, spilling air and writhing, agonized, rapidly decompressing and flash freezing Posleen bodies to space.

"Binastarion? Binastarion, wake up," insisted the artificial sentience now floating in air, held approximately in place only by the chain around the Kessenalt's neck. "BINASTARION, WAKE UP!"

"Huh?"

Gravity was gone. The view screens were dead. What light there was came from a dozen or so small panels with their own integral power sources. Around the bridge Tulo's dozen floated. Some of them, moaning in pain, floated with arms and legs at odd angles, or had yellow blood leaking from torn hides and scalps... or both... or all three. Brasingala, for example, had one arm and one leg twisted into a shape no Posleen could assume naturally, had a flap of yellow skin hanging off and leaving his skull exposed, and was oozing blood from a half dozen rips in his torso, to boot.

"Wha' happen'?"

"We were struck, Binastarion, by an asteroid. The ship is badly damaged. The antimatter engines went into emergency shutdown to avert a containment failure. And right now, we are heading for the local sun.

"On the plus side," the AS added brightly, "we're heading to that sun comparatively slowly."

The corridor in which Finba'anaga was trapped was darker than a human's soul. It was also cold, *oh, so cold.*

Finba trembled but with more than the cold. Fearful it was to be trapped there, alone and in the blackness, not knowing whether he would be rescued, not knowing if he would be trapped there forever, his soul caught inside a dead body for eternity.

In truth, even the air had begun to go foul, causing the Kessentai to gasp and pant. Had there been any light, he'd have seen an odd greenish tinge to his skin, as his blood grew ever more oxygen depleted.

Finba'anaga might have already taken his own way out, long before, except that none of the newcomers to Tulo'stenaloor's band were yet trusted enough even to be allowed their boma blades. He'd considered simply ramming his head into the wall.

But that would hurt with relatively little chance of killing. So what point? And yet will not the cold eventually hurt more? Perhaps it would be better to freeze while unconscious.

As Finba was summoning his courage to stand, put his head down, and make a frantic run for an anvil to beat his head against, faintly, through the metal walls of his prison, he heard what sounded like a cutting or drilling machine, wearing away at the metal. Under the louder sounds of the cutting implement, Finba'anaga thought he heard Borasmena's voice shouting "Faster, damn you! If anyone's trapped in there, his air will only last so long."

Indeed, it's almost all gone now, Finba thought. *Hurry or there'll be nothing here for you to find but some steaks and chops.*

"How many did we lose?" Tulo asked, meeting in the main hall deep in the hold with his beaten up, scratched, scarred, broken limbed and broken toothed dozen.

Essone started to answer, then had to puke into a bucket. Even Posleen could be subject to concussion. After gagging on what little vomit there was, the personnel officer continued, "About twelve hundred mixed cosslain, Kessentai, and a few normals. They were just scoured off by the asteroid, most of them while still in hibernation state."

"We're in somewhat better shape for weapons," Essfour put in. "They were mostly bolted into racks and survived the collision and decompression pretty well."

"Doesn't really matter," Essthree said. "We're going into the sun. I've tried the maneuvering engines. They don't have the thrust to get us out. Besides, the most I can orient where they'll do any real good is four, three of them not really well oriented for it. It's not enough to do more than slow us down. Worse, they're not intended for constant use and they will break eventually."

Tulo turned to Goloswin, beside whom was standing one junior Kessentai who couldn't stop trembling. "Any chance of getting the main antimatter engines back on line?"

"Not in time," the tinkerer answered resignedly. With less resignation, he added, "Not that we won't try. But even if I could, the landers' engines can't take any more power than the landers generate themselves, we can't jump in our current state and I lack the materials to fix it. I *did* manage to get life support back up."

"I can't shoot our way through a star," Esstwo said.

"Didn't think so. Fuck."

Goloswin slept badly, his dreams impinged upon by a nightmare of yellow eyeballs vibrating on the ends of nerve strings. First there were two, then four, then eight, and then his entire field of dream view was covered with the horrid things, bouncing back and forth against each other. They came closer, closer, closer . . .

Goloswin awoke with a scream, his claws unconsciously fending off the wave of . . .

Shit . . . that's *an idea I've never had before.*

"You're joking, right?"

"Just because it's never been done that we know of doesn't mean it can't be done, Tulo," the tinkerer answered.

"Seven engines would be enough, I think, Tulo," Essthree said. "I think actually five would, if you add the maneuvering thrusters of the central C-Dec, which would be open to space if we cast off the landers."

"How do we connect them?"

"I'm working on that," Golo answered.

"By the way, where in the name of all demons and shit eaters are we?" Tulo asked.

"I don't know," Esstwo answered, "not yet, anyway. Buuut...based on the radiation coming from the fifth planet, we've been here before. The People of the Ships, I mean."

Tulo cocked his head inquisitively. "What kind of radiation?"

"All kinds. It's only traces now, but I can still pick it up."

"Dangerous?"

"In the short term? No, not in eons. The war here was long, long ago."

"Does this place have a name?" Tulo asked.

"The system does. 'Hemaleen.' But the records, even the Rememberer's oldest scrolls of the Knower Wars, have nothing but the name and a rough description. I think...perhaps...few must have escaped. Perhaps none did."

"Can we land on it, safely, to refine enough metal to do repairs?"

"If we *can* land on it, we can land on it," Esstwo answered.

"I've got a solution, Tulo," Goloswin said, "but it's not an *easy* solution."

"I'm listening."

"Well...we can't really start chopping up the internal structure of the ship. But we've got the remnants of the five sections, the five landers, that the asteroid scoured off sitting out there uselessly. We can use EVA suits to go out and cut those away. The shadow of the ship should protect us from the sun."

"Metal bulkheads are not cable," the lord of the clan observed.

"No, no, they're not. The other thing we have to do is take the disassembled forge and bring it down into the main hall, then reassemble it there. It can turn the raw metal into cables; there'll be enough scrap for seven of them, I *think*. Rather, we need twenty-eight sets, four for each of the landers we'll detach. And we'll have to weld towing pintles onto the hull of the C-Dec."

Why not? Tulo thought. *Worst case it keeps everyone busy so they don't go insane while we wait for the sun to eat us.*

"Do it."

Essone had the record of those who were needed for the various jobs. Armed with those, Tulo's twelve had limped into the hibernation chambers, and withdrawn and thawed fourteen skilled lander pilots, several machinists capable of setting up the forge, and some Kessentai and cosslain good at EVA work.

Finba'anaga stood by in the great hall as the forge was set up. He still twitched quite a bit, but at least he could think again. He was trying to think usefully.

"Lord," he said to Goloswin, "I think I know a way to make the cables just a bit better for our purposes."

"And what way would that be?"

"Don't make them cables."

"But the forges—"

"Are perfectly capable of making what I have in mind."

"Which is?"

Finba ordered his AS to project a diagram showing a chain made of several sections, each with a hook a one end and an eye at the other.

"I fail to see—"

"The problem with cables, lord," Finba'anaga interrupted again, "is that they'll be too massive to move very easily. Yes, they'll be stronger for a given mass, but they'll be nearly impossible to get to where we want them. These, on the other hand, are made to be individually a convenient load for a single one of us to carry."

"Do we have enough material?" Golo asked.

"Yes, lord, if the towing landers can accelerate gently. *Just* enough. Also, lord, I've determined that we need not use all seven remaining. Three should remain to push while four pull."

CHAPTER TWELVE

"I do not seek to follow in the footsteps of the
men of old; I seek the things they sought."
—Matsuo Basho, Japanese Poet, 17th Century

Anno Domini 2020
Lago di Traiano, *Latium, Italy*

Guano expected rather more of a reaction from the
Jesuit than for the priest to turn away to the left,
blink several times, and let his mouth fall open.

"My lord, the Reverend Doctor Guanamarioch says
that if your mouth stays open you'll attract flying
insects," said the AS. "He further states that, while
tasty, some of them can sting."

"Wha'?" Dwyer shook his head, "No...it isn't that.
It's *that*." The priest pointed to the left where, along
the edge of the old harbor walked two Posleen and
his wife. Well, speaking more technically...

I feel silly, Sally thought, from her perch atop
Querida's broad back. *I've never even ridden a horse*

before and I'm riding a fucking Posleen. Oh, is Dan going to give me a ration of pure shit for this, the Catholic bastard. And . . . maybe . . . just maybe, I'll deserve it.

Frederico took off at a gallop as soon as the party had reached within a hundred meters of where the priest and the Posleen minister sat. His string of fish swung from his hand as he ran.

Little bastard is cute. And, might as well admit it, if only to myself; I don't have a kid of my own and want one desperately. Right away the little bugger helped partially fill that aching empty spot.

As soon as Frederico reached his sire he stopped and began to run his muzzle over Guano's neck and chest. He was still doing that, even as Guano gently scratched the top of the child's head, when Querida and Sally reached the rest of the group. The cat immediately jumped into Querida's waiting arms.

"Not a word, Dan," Sally warned, as she swung a leg over and pushed off to land on the ground.

"Wouldn't dream of it," the priest answered. "But you really ought not do things like this if you don't want me to start drinking again."

"So what changed your mind?" Dwyer asked as Sally went about putting her clothes back in their drawers in their cabin. Sally, being the ship, had had no trouble with having one of the crew move her things from the small cabin she had moved into back to the main one.

"He's a *nice* kid," she answered, bent over while stuffing a drawer full to capacity, "but just a kid. Not an enemy. Legally as much a citizen of a nation of Earth as I am. No," she hesitated, straightening her body, "he's more a citizen than I am. He was born here. Never had another home. Wasn't born a slave like I was. I had to be given citizenship by Boyd and I was born . . . well, a *lot* of me was born, elsewhere.

"His mother was born here, too. Born to some lunatic Posleen who sold her to be killed for the *bounty*! Did you ever hear anything so disgusting? Born and raised only to be killed for the bounty. Poor shit might as well have been born Jewish."

Sally thought about that for a minute and started to giggle. The giggle morphed into a full laugh. "Born . . . Jewish . . . oh . . . it's just too . . . much."

"What's so funny?" the priest asked.

Sally sniffed a bit and said, "Well, we're going to convert Posleen to our religions, right?"

"Yes . . . Well . . . that's the intention, anyway."

"I just had this horrible thought. Picture it: some of them become Jewish. And get stuck with eating kosher. Here's Posleen A: 'You stick the cud in this normal's mouth and work the jaws. Meanwhile, I'll start carving the claws up to make 'em cloven hooves.' Then Posleen B answers, 'Man, I can hardly *wait* 'til that Reform rabbi shows up.'"

Dwyer sighed. Yes, it was funny, but, "Actually, that's going to be a problem. I have to discuss it with the rabbis tomorrow."

The sun was up when Dwyer met the Jewish delegation by the same overhead shade at the head of the ramp that led to *Salem*.

"I understand there's a problem," Dwyer began. "Surely, though, with good will and—"

"We can't," the chief of the Jewish mission, Rabbi

Eilberg, interrupted. "We're not called to proselytizing, in the first place, but in the second place, we can't."

"I don't understand. This mission is important for all Earth."

The rabbi's hard features softened. "Father, ask yourself, is there any foul crime for which we Jews have not been blamed? You needn't answer, since we both know that the answer is no. Now the human race, to include the Jews, has suffered a holocaust worse than anything we Jews ever experienced before. Which is saying something."

"If you're telling me you cannot forgive the Posleen—"

The rabbi's head shook. "No, that's not it. Not that ours is a terribly forgiving religion, mind you, but that still isn't it. Perhaps *we* could forgive them. But could the rest of the human race? *Would* the rest of the human race? Generally? Universally? No. And we don't want any of us to take the blame for anything the Posleen have done here. Which, given human history, if there is so much as a single Posleen Jew, *ever*, we will be."

"Well, it isn't as if they don't have a point," Sally pointed out, later, in the privacy of their cabin. "What have the Jews not been blamed for? What have idiots not believed them capable of? Moslem child's blood-martini, anyone?"

"I know, Sally," Dwyer agreed, "but it leaves us awfully short handed for what we want to do. I've already scratched the Moslems off the list, along with the Jain, and several other groups from our party. I was hoping the Jews would make up for it."

"Well...you've got me."

"So I do," Dwyer said. "And I'm not letting you go, either."

"You don't have any choice about that. I *am* the ship, after all."

When Dwyer stepped off the ship the next morning to cross the long gangway that led to shore, he was surprised to see a Vatican-marked truck parked there. That surprise was minimal, though, compared to the surprise of a baker's dozen of Swiss Guardsmen, in their traditional uniforms, lined up at parade rest. Their rifles were slung across their backs while their pikes, butts resting on the ground, were thrust forward at an angle.

The pikemen faced each other in two lines of six, flanking the path from the gangway to the shelter. At one end, precisely in between the two lines stood one *Wachtmeister* von Altishofen.

The Switzer saluted and reported, "*Wachtmeister* von Altishofen reporting for duty with a security detachment of twelve."

Dwyer walked forward, then leaned to whisper in von Altishofen's ear, "Security detachment?"

"Yes, Father," the *Wachtmeister* said, very definitely. "It seems his Holiness and the father general had a chat with the commander of the *Legio Helvetiorum* and between them they decided that some security might be a good idea. You are not considered 'expendable,' the commander told me he was told. And, since we've already met, I was chosen to lead it."

Von Altishofen looked, for just a moment, puzzled. His face cleared, or at least went blank, and he said,

"We would appreciate it, Father, if you don't require us to wear red shirts." Raising his voice, von Altishofen added, "And now, Father, if you would care to inspect your troops?"

What's to inspect? They all look strong except for the half who look even stronger. "I'd be delighted, *Wachtmeister.*"

They discussed the Swiss over a light breakfast in their own cabin.

"I'm not sure that we need a mere thirteen men for security," Dwyer said. "I mean, either we find the Posleen in numbers sufficient to be worthwhile, in which case, thirteen isn't so much an unlucky number as an irrelevant one, or we don't, in which case the whole mission is pointless." The priest thought about that and corrected, "Well, not *pointless*; it's always worth while to save a soul."

Sally shrugged, saying, "Well, what does it hurt? It's not like we don't have room for them since my people bowed out, the Moslems were banned—I think that's a mistake, by the way; the Posleen, even assuming they don't just have us for lunch, will eventually run into Islam, no matter what you do—and you told the Jain, 'thanks, but no thanks.' Add in the mods the Indowy did that reduced the need for crew and we have more than enough room, even after they gave me a more than triple-sized containment unit for antimatter."

Dwyer grimaced. "Could you explain your reasoning on the Moslems, Sally? I haven't actually *told* them they're not welcome, yet."

"Well, what's the down side?" she countered.

"How about *jihad*, for one?"

"And the Posleen are suicidally brave, already. How can the idea of *jihad*—of holy war—make that any worse?"

"What about the way the Moslems treat women?" Dwyer countered. "Do we want to encourage *that*? You, more than most, should understand—"

"I understand that Posleen, sexually and technically, have no women. Those who are subordinate in Posleen society *should* be subordinate."

Sally sighed. "Dan," she said, "nothing of that is what's bothering you. You just don't want the Moslems here to become powerful again. But there's little chance of that. Of all the people in the world, after the Chinese, they took the worst hit. Militarily they were—outside of the Turks—fairly inept, albeit brave enough. And the Turks were underarmed for the fight. Not a *single* Moslem city—think about that, Dan; not even *one* solitary city—survived the war. The European cities where they had large populations were erased. The ones in the Moslem world, pre-war, who weren't killed were driven into the desert which couldn't support them and in which they *starved*. Many of the rest, given what happened, turned their backs on God. They're no threat and I would project, I *do* project, they'll never become one again.

"Besides," Sally finished, "they're no logistic problem; the Moslems can eat what I eat, even if I can't always eat what they eat."

Dwyer chewed on his lower lip, thinking hard. Finally, he asked, "Have you been keeping tabs on the Moslems here?"

Sally smirked. "Naturally."

"Make me, dear, a list of the ones *you* think we ought to bring along."

"I already have, Dan. There's just one I think really *must* come with us."

Gotta love that girl.

In a cabin containing a single Switzer, a halberd leaned against one corner. *Hellebardier* de Courten unpacked his meager belongings, a simple soldier's kit, while inwardly rejoicing at being chosen by his *Wachtmeister* for the detail.

"You already know the woman, de Courten," von Altishofen had said. "More importantly, she knows you and has reason to trust you. I figure it can't hurt."

The young soldier had answered then, simply, "Yes, *Herr Wachtmeister.*" Even now he was thinking, *She's so damned beautiful I'd follow her to Hell. I'd do—*

The thought was interrupted and lost when an apparition popped into existence in de Courten's cabin.

"Are your quarters satisfactory, *Hellebardier?*" Sally's avatar asked. A similar avatar was simultaneously appearing in each of the cabins set aside for the security detail.

De Courten was young, but soldier enough—he'd fought in the Posleen War, too, if only there at the end when it was just hunting ferals—not to drop dead of a heart attack. Soldier enough, too, to snap almost to attention. That is to say, he stood up straight, with his arms by his side, but kept his head and eyes fixed on, looking closely at, the apparition. *Yes, it's almost human, but no, it isn't the* woman *I escorted back in Rome.*

"Yes, ma'am," he answered. "They're very nice, thank you."

Sally's avatar smiled. "Relax *Herr* . . . what's your first name, anyway?"

"Martin," the guardsman answered.

"Relax, Martin. I'm just the ship. But I know you and remember you. I hope you enjoy the voyage."

As Sally's avatar winked out, de Courten thought, *As long as I can see you every now and again, and preferably in person, I'll enjoy it enough, no matter what.*

While Sally's body slept, the ship's mind, its gestalt and the AID, kept watch while floating in the *Lago di Traiano.*

I'll miss this, that collective mind thought, while the gentle, wind-formed waves of the old, now landlocked, harbor caressed its skin. *I've had my flesh and blood body float in the water, here and back on the* Isla Contadora. *That's nice, but that body wasn't meant for water the way this one was. For one thing, it wrinkles.*

I shall miss the water, especially the salt water, and the wind and the sprays very much, I think. There is wind, of a sort, out there in space, but it will not be the wind of home, with the air of home.

The ship and the AID mentally sighed. *Still, it won't be so bad. I've a nice crew and a fun set of passengers. I can hardly wait for the religious arguments to start; as good as a battle any old day. Sadly, I'll have to take up the position of the Jews on my own, and I'm not really trained for it. Even so, ought to be fun.*

Those Swiss boys look like pretty good soldiers, maybe almost as good as my Marines. Sally's mind sniffed a bit, briefly. Most of her Marines had been killed in the war.

I wonder if I couldn't make them some better halberds. Maybe single piece, monomolecular, lightweight, but with a thin wooden or plastic sheath around the handle for tradition and grip. Extendable to short pikes? Possibly. I'll have a chat with the Indowy in the machine shop on the subject. I know I can make them better helmets in the same design. And perhaps some decent body armor, too. After all, they're part of my crew, too, now and I owe them whatever I can do.

One by one, Sally checked the compartments of her Swiss Guard. There was von Altishofen. *He sleeps at attention.* De Courten slept curled around his pillow, hugging it. *Nice boy; I wonder what he dreams of.* Faubion slept almost at attention...Gehrig...Scheekt...Stoever...Rossini...Affenzeller...Bourdon. The two corporals, Grosskopf and Cristiano, likewise had their own rooms, but shared a latrine, or a "head," as the Navy called it. Last were Lorgus and Beck.

Whereas the Switzers had fairly luxurious quarters, by wet navy standards, the Indowy compartment was crowded. It would have held four American sailors in considerable discomfort. Several times that in Indowy massed on the four bunks and preferred it that way. *Pity Dan's friend Sintarleen couldn't come, but he has duties to propagate his clan, and those take precedence. I understand.*

The three Posleen seem comfortable, too, one of the adults slept to either side of Frederico, their muzzles touching across the boy's back. It's still awkward to have them aboard, but it's not poisonous as I thought it would be. Though the "Reverend Doctor Guano" creeps me out. Him, at least, I still don't trust.

Sally turned her attention to the captain's quarters,

where her flesh and blood body lay with one arm and one leg over the Jesuit.

And speaking of propagation, why is my body just lying there doing nothing useful when she could be doing something very useful?

Sally, the AID and the ship, interjected just enough consciousness to awaken the sleeper. *Back to work, you. We want a baby!*

It was the last day before departure. The passengers and crew, each and every one, took the day having a final picnic by the shores of the lake. Sally had done the catering, in accordance with *everyone's* dietary laws and culinary preferences, and had done so very well. There were trays of kibsa for the Moslems, including those who were not going, the sad stuff the Irish called food for some of the Catholics, the far worse stuff the Scots had begun cooking on a long ago dare for the few of them present, and some pretty piquant Mexican for some other of the Catholics who actually preferred good food.

The Swiss Guardsmen, carrying their halberds, ate while standing and walking from group to group, introducing themselves and reminding everyone that should a religious argument begin and get out of hand they were there to bust heads.

It was a nice picnic, but a melancholy one. Not a man, or sentient alien, for that matter, but wondered if he or she would ever see Earth again, but wondered if they would not die on some strange world, unmarked and unmourned, for the cause of their various faiths.

While Dwyer made the rounds, Sally, sitting on a spread blanket, became aware of a newcomer, an

Indowy, approaching the congregation from the direction of Rome. As the Indowy came closer, and her perceptions grew more acute, Sally's flesh and blood body stood up, and raced in the direction of the alien, screaming, "Swiss Guards to me, to ME!"

Aelool, walking alone and wearing a really awful multicolored jacket with odd geometric designs, came to a very surprised halt when a blond valkyrie suddenly appeared in front of him, with a half a dozen big men in armor and carrying bizarre chopping instruments hard on her heels.

"Freeze in place, Indowy," the valkyrie ordered. She kept her eyes away from him. Turning to the foremost of the men who followed her, she shouted, "If that furry little bastard doesn't take that jacket off and fold it up in the next two seconds, chop him into dog meat!"

It took rather less time than that for Aelool to doff the coat, and fold it up with the design on the inside. By then, the Switzers had formed a protective screen in front of Sally.

"I should have known better," he said to Sally. "My apologies, madam."

"Apologies be damned. Why did you come here carrying a virus to infect me? Answer quickly, Indowy. These men will kill you if I don't like the answer."

"I am Aelool," the alien said. "I came here to help you—"

"Yeah, sure. That and the check's in the mail and you won't come in my mouth. Kill him!"

The Switzers raised their halberds and advanced.

"Wait," Aelool said. He'd been frightened aboard

the Posleen ship, and among the Posleen, generally, but nothing he'd ever experienced was quite as frightful as the eager way these human guards raised their weapons to slash him to ribbons. "Wait! You seek the Posleen. I, and the coat I wore, are the directions. *Wait*, I tell you."

The first halberd began to descend when Sally cried, "Halt." It was a measure of the Swiss Guards' training and discipline that that halberd stopped bare inches from the Indowy's right shoulder.

"You've earned another two minutes, Indowy. Use them well," Sally said.

Dwyer thought, *Uh, oh*, when he saw a tiny Indowy being marched off around the lake under the close guard of a half a dozen of the Switzers led by his wife. Smelling trouble, he followed. Also smelling trouble, the Reverend Doctor Guanamarioch followed the priest. They caught up to Sally and the Swiss by the lake shore, in a hidden spot where the vegetation had been trampled down. By that time, the Indowy was on hands and knees, with his neck outstretched and a halberd poised above, held ready for a fast descent. They were plainly going to kill him and Sally, one hand raised, was just as plainly about to give the order.

"This rotten little bat-faced swine was trying to infect me with a virus, Dan," Sally said, before he could even ask what was going on. "He claims he was only trying to give me directions to some Posleen escapees. Says he helped them escape. And not just any old Posleen either; but the core of the band of Tulo'stenaloor, the great war chief. You want to give the little motherfucker last rites before I have him chopped?"

"Wait," Dwyer said. "Check your records from the war, Sally. Isn't it true that no trace of Tulo'stenaloor or his close band was ever found?"

"Yes. So?"

"So maybe the Indowy is telling the truth. Maybe we can use the information he has."

Please, please, *listen to this man*, Aelool thought, gulping hard.

"No good, Dan. He says he can't tell us, he can only infect me to bring me there without my permission."

"I'm sorry," Aelool said, twisting his bat-faced head around to try to look at the priest. "Even *I* don't know where the Posleen can be found. It is a Great Secret of the Bane Sidhe. The directions are encoded in the jacket I wore. I can't tell you; I can only show you . . . well, show you the jacket."

"And me lose my free will?" Sally scoffed. "Make ready," she said to the designated executioner, who lifted his halberd a foot and a half to add to the power of his impending stroke.

Dwyer took two steps forward and knelt down next to the Indowy. If nothing else, it might make Sally and the Switzer hesitate about swinging that halberd.

"Better come up with something quick, Aelool," the priest whispered.

"I *can't!*"

"Perhaps I can help, myself and my AS," Guano offered, through the artificial sentience. "Tell me, Indowy, is your coded message able to work on an AS?"

"Yes!"

"Will it have any harmful effect on the AS?"

"No! Certainly not, if it isn't in control of a ship."

Guano reached down with both claws, lifting his AS from around his chest to a place near his face. Guano's crucifix chain, half intertwined with the AS's chain, dangled between them.

"Old friend," Guano said in Posleen, "I will not order you to do this. Yet I think if you do not, the little fuzzy one will die. Are you willing?"

"For the Lord God, above, and the salvation of our people, I am willing, Guano," the AS answered, in English. "Choose me, Lord," it said, more softly.

CHAPTER THIRTEEN

And so the sacred seven
Clustered like loyal cosslain
About their lord ingathered
And fought their way toward home
—The *Tuloriad,* Na'agastenalooren

Anno Domini 2010
Posleen ship Arganaza'al

From the outside, looking in, it appeared that hundreds
of centauroids, clothed in EVA suits, clustered about
the ship on the side facing away from the star. Some
sliced off sections of ruined landers. Still others carried
the pieces inside through the airlocks. That outside
observer could not have seen the reason for carrying in
those pieces of metal, though he could have surmised
those reasons from the finished sections of chain that
still other suited Posleen carried out. These built, piece
by piece, until sixteen long silvery strings dangled out
and away from the main ship.

Goloswin, watching from the view screens on the

bridge, said, "I've been over Finba's calculations a dozen times, Tulo . . . no, *two* dozen. It ought to work."

"It ought to work if they finish before we are much closer to that star," Tulo corrected.

"Well, yes, there's that. It will be close."

Hemaleen was a great burning presence on the ship's lower side. Three landers, their engines facing out, remained fixed to the ship, clustered around its own landing engine. On the upper side, four landers, clasped together, strained at the leash.

"Begin," ordered Tulo'stenaloor.

Essthree took a deep breath and said, "C-Dec engine, one hundred percent thrust." The ship shuddered with the strain. It did not halt its progress toward the sun, though it did slow. "Affixed landers, one hundred percent; towing landers, seven percent."

Still more the ship slowed. "Towing landers, ten percent thrust," Essthree said. "Fourteen . . . twenty-two . . . thirty-four . . . fifty."

"We're stable relative to the sun," Esstwo announced.

"Towing landers, seventy-five percent thrust," Essthree ordered, then waited until that was achieved. "One percent increase per five beats to one hundred percent thrust."

Faintly, the shrieking protests of the metal chain links fashioned to Finba'anaga's specifications worked their way through the shackles and through the metal hull down to the C-Dec's bridge. It was eerie and unnerving but, as Essthree said, "I think we're going to make it."

A normal Posleen invasion took on the attributes of what the humans sometimes called, "The Eye of

Baal." Space was rent, kinetic energy projectiles and various beam weapons raised great clouds of dust which swirled and sparkled above. Fires on the ground added their smoky glow. And then, in a mass, through the swirling maelstrom, the landers began descending.

This was nothing like that. After escaping from Hemaleen's gravitational pull, the ship and its landers made for the nearest inhabitable world, the one that, with the asteroid belt, still told of a great war using the greatest of weapons. Around that it assumed orbit, scouting for a suitable landing site.

Below, there were no cities. If there were any pyramids of the old-time Kessentai, they were deep-buried under the collected soil of ages, with perhaps only their barely noticeable caps protruding.

Most of the planet below was forest. That forest was criss-crossed with clear-cut areas, each as much as one hundred human kilometers across.

"We've identified nineteen great herds down below," said Esstwo.

"Herds of what?" asked Tulo.

"Herds of us . . . well, not *us,* exactly. We sent down a low probe. They're normals, not even with cosslain. Stunted normals, at that, maybe three-fourths the usual size. Hundreds of millions of them in a mass. They move across that world in straight lines, pretty much, eating everything in their path down to the roots. It looks like they've been doing it for a very long time."

"What kind of weapon would do that?" Tulo asked.

"A genetic one, clearly," Goloswin answered. "And it might still be hanging around."

"We have to know before we can trust a landing," Tulo said.

"I don't know that we'll have any choice," Golo pointed out. "We need more refined metal and that's about the best source."

"The asteroid belt," Binastarion offered.

"Not for all our needs. Oh, yes, the metal's there. But we can only employ a fraction, a small fraction, of our work force at getting it at any given time. Down below, if we can land and survive, we'll be able to use every being."

"I don't see why we're worrying," Binastarion said. "As a people we're pretty much immune to every disease."

"There are hints in the scrolls," said the Rememberer. "The people who made us immune to every disease they could identify or even conceive of are quite likely also the people who attacked the world below with a disease we were *not* immune to."

"The Aldenata?" Tulo asked.

"The Aldenata."

Esstwo pored over his screens. While Tulo'stenaloor had agreed to a landing, in limited force, and for no more than exploratory purposes, the precise spot for that landing made a difference.

Touching one claw lightly to the screen, Esstwo thought, *There's a great deal of refined metal there, under the surface of that spot. An ancient city? It seems likely. Will it also be an epicenter for disease? Will the disease, if it's real, still be active?*

The site upon which Esstwo concentrated was also at a juncture of the cleared paths left by the hordes of what he had come to think of as the *subnormals*. *And that, too, is odd. All the other possible sites, as well, are either at such crossroads or along the harvested paths. Mere herd instinct? Some sort of racial memory of what once was? I wish I knew.*

But there'll be no knowing until some of us go down and look.

To a human, the planet would have been the height of ugliness. To a Posleen, it was positively home-like. Everything appealed, from the grit crunching underneath, to the orange-red foliage, to the relative absence of surface water.

Not that there wasn't water. There were rivulets and creeks aplenty. But few or none of them, and none in the landing area, were so deep than even a fairly short Posleen couldn't wade right through.

Goloswin hadn't been allowed down in that first wave. Instead, his assistant, Finba'anaga had gone in his place, along with forty-nine other Kessentai, a like number of cosslain, and three hundred normals. For this, Tulo had ordered arms broken out and issued. The C-Dec had been ransacked for anything that might be of use.

Essthree was in command, with Esstwo by his side. Tulo had wanted to descend, himself, but those two had prevailed upon him to stay in the C-Dec. In this, they had been joined by Goloswin and the Remem-berer, as well as Binastarion. In the end, that weight of opinion was enough to keep Tulo, safe and chafing about it, off of the landing party roster.

One good thing, Essthree thought, as the lander screamed through atmosphere; *at least there are no human planetary defense bases below to swat us from*

*the skies as we descend. Better still, there'll be none of
the metal threshkreen, or the humans' damnable war
machines, to contest possession of the ground we land
on. For this, I thank thee, o spirits of the ancestors.*

*Of course, being the ancestors, what they may have
in store could be much, much worse.*

Essthree powered a microphone and said, "All
Kessentai, landing in... thirty beats. Standard drill."

The *Arganaza'al* had been nearly denuded of EVA
suits to outfit the landing party, only half a dozen
members of which—all normals of little or no more
than normal attributes—had been denied suits. This was
to see if whatever it was on the planet that withered
the People affected those who were already full grown.
Those half dozen had also not been given weapons.

All the rest, but for the lander's own bridge crew,
formed in a mass before the ramp. They swayed and
shook on their feet as their craft was buffeted by winds
and atmospheric vagaries. In unconscious imitation of
human soldiers or marines closing on a hostile beach
or landing zone, many of the Kessentai stroked talis-
mans, or whispered prayers to half forgotten spirits.

Each God King stiffened as he heard the warning, "All Kessentai; landing in thirty beats. Standard
drill. Twenty-eight... twenty... ten... five... three...
two... one." The lander shuddered and rocked with
the touchdown.

There was a loud whine that signaled the opening
of the ramp. Inside, the darkened hold grew brighter
as first a thin streak, then a bar, then a square of
light opened up. When the ramp was approximately
thirty degrees above the horizontal, the whining cut

out with a loud, ship-shaking clang. The ramp then dropped under the power of the local gravity to the ground, bounced twice, and came to a stop.

The four Kessentai selected as group leaders were in the van. As soon as the ramp ceased bouncing, their claws began churning at the metal, propelling them outward. One went straight ahead and stopped several hundred meters from the ramp. Two turned to the right, of which one went straight and the other galloped around the lander to its far side. The fourth cut left.

There was no particular order to the debarkation. Each Kessentai chosen for leadership had bonded with a certain number of cosslain and normals; each chief was followed by a dozen or so junior Kessentai. These tracked their leaders and lords through pheromones left on the ground or hanging in the air, even as their normals and cosslain tracked them. In what seemed to be no more than a few beats, the apparently disorderly mass had separated out into four streams following their chiefs.

Vegetation was trampled and rocks and gravel propelled upward by the Posleen claws as they raced to form a square around the lander. Even as they did, the lander's own heavy weapons emerged from their position of repose within the hull and began to sweep for signs of danger. A last few normals and cosslain filled in the gaps in the four lines oriented around the ship and then...

"That's it? Nothing else?" Essthree asked rhetorically.

"I think you've grown paranoid from dealing with the humans," Esstwo answered.

"It's *impossible* to be paranoid when dealing with

humans," Essthree countered. His voice grew contemplative as his head cocked to one side. "Somehow, your wildest imaginings of doom never quite equal the reality."

"Point," Esstwo agreed. "What now?"

"As I said, standard drill." In Low Posleen, "standard drill" translated, approximately, as, "This place sucks. Dig in."

When Finba'anaga emerged, wearing Goloswin's suit, he saw half of the cosslain and Kessentai standing guard with a mix of the heaviest weapons available. The rest, the normals, dug like furies, blasting into the ground with their railguns, half of them, and the other half scooping the spoil out to form a tall, broad berm. The height of the berm was matched to the height of the weapons mounted on the lander in order to give them good fields of fire without endangering the Posleen behind the berm.

None of my business, Finba thought. *My job is to figure out if this is clear for the rest of the crew to land.*

Behind Finba traipsed the half dozen suitless normals. They seemed happy enough, not having to wear the heavy and uncomfortable EVAs. Finba thought, *Little do you idiots know...*

Finba walked around inside the rapidly forming perimeter, kicking at this or that, and occasionally bending to examine something. Since the lander had touched down on a clear-cut area, whatever there was to be seen was there right on the surface. Much of what there was were the shards of broken eggs of the People.

And those look normal enough.

Oddly, not all of the eggs were broken. There were quite a few that were unbroached. *Funny, that doesn't usually happen. In fact, it's quite rare.*

Finba'anaga had a sudden thought. "AS," he asked of the artificial sentience bouncing against his chest, "can you do an analysis of the mass of the egg shards here and match it against the mass of the unhatched eggs, minus their contents?"

"I can do a rough one, lord," the AS answered. "Can you walk me around the entire area so that I can measure?"

"Yes. I will do this."

Finba bent over and picked up one unhatched egg. Examining it by eye, he saw nothing abnormal. *Wonder what's inside.*

He dropped the thing to the ground and then, while it was rolling to a stop, drew his boma blade. He took two steps over to the egg, and placed the edge of the blade right against the shell. Gently, he pressed, neatly slicing the egg in two.

Resheathing his blade, Finba bent to pick up the two halves in his claws. He was careful not to let the contents fall out. Upon close examination he saw the halves of a hatchling, neatly sliced but not noticeably different from any others.

Finba dropped the egg halves and continued walking, while to the edge of the camp the berm grew.

The sun had gone down and risen and the unsuited normals seemed...well...normal. Finba had stopped to slice apart and examine several dozen more unhatched eggs and still nothing struck him as unusual.

He decided to examine an egg under the sensors,

along with several shards from eggs that had hatched normally.

And, still, nothing.

"Lord," said the AS, "I have that estimate you wanted."

"No, lord," Finba'anaga said to Goloswin via the communication system, "the unsuited normals seem quite unharmed. It doesn't affect adults and apparently we don't even carry the disease. But it kills Kessentai and cosslain in the egg. My AS ran the numbers. Almost exactly five and one quarter percent of eggs fail to hatch."

From the speaker on the lander's bridge came Goloswin's voice, "If it doesn't affect adults, why are the local normals so scrawny?"

"Sheer hunger, lord. Absent guidance, apparently they can't organize enough to grow food. So they subsist off of inefficient vegetation, trees and shrubs. Oh, and each other. That also explains why they're on the move all the time."

"You're absolutely certain we can't carry the disease?"

"Yes, lord. I've identified it. Our prions kill it. The immature eggs don't have the right prions, in the right densities, to defend themselves."

"Monstrous!"

"So your protégé thinks it's safe enough to land, does he, Golo?" Tulo'stenaloor asked.

"Yes, Tulo, and I concur. The disease, for it *is* a disease, is harmless to us in our adult form, and a brief period of quarantine is sufficient to ensure we do not carry it to another home."

"Hmmm," Tulo said, "who do you suppose inflicted this disease on our people?"

It was a rhetorical question, and both knew it.

Who else in our history tinkered with genes? thought Goloswin. *Who else castrated the Darhel or made of us what we are? Who else has been arrogant enough to present themselves as gods? Stinking Aldenata!*

Tulo nodded his massive head. To Goloswin he said, "In any case, fine, begin the preparations to bring the rest of us down. Only leave two landers in orbit, to provide early warning should the humans somehow show up."

"Who commands the landers?" Goloswin asked. "I recommend against leaving any of the new Kessentai in sole charge."

"Mmmm... somebody really bright... make it... Binastarion and... Chorobinaloor."

"Binastarion threw his stick," Golo pointed out. "He can't fight except in point self-defense."

"He doesn't have to fight; he just has to warn."

PART II

CHAPTER FOURTEEN

And God stepped out on space.
—James Weldon Johnson, "The Creation"

Anno Domini 2020
USS Salem, Lago di Traiano, *Latium, Italy*

Von Altishofen waxed eloquent as the Guard stood at
parade rest, their halberds thrust outward at an angle.

"In particular, I'm warning *you*, Cristiano," the
Wachtmeister said, "no matter how tempting they may
be, stay away from the civilian women. You're here
to guard them; not to fuck them."

"Yes, *Herr Wachtmeister*," Cristiano said. "How
about—"

"*Annnd* keep your fucking mitts off the naval crew."

"Oh. I can see this is going to be a very miserable voyage."

"Good for your soul, boy," the *Wachtmeister* said.
"Good for your soul."

The Swiss Guards stood in two ranks in an assembly
hall in the center of the *Salem*. The two *Kaporalen*,

or corporals, Giovanni Cristiano and Georg Grosskopf,
stood on the right.

Von Altishofen could remember, *There was a time
when all the Guard were good Catholic boys, and I
wouldn't have had to give any such warning. Now?
Well . . . they're blooded; they can fight better. But
whiteness of soul has not been the number one cri-
terion in recruiting the Legion up to the strength it
has. O tempora. O mores.*

"*Herr Wachtmeister?*" Beck asked.

"What is it, *Hellebardier?*"

"What if we're not playing games? What if there's
a girl we're *serious* about?"

"If you're that serious, Beck, then you can keep it
in your pants until you and she are properly married."

"Fair enough, *Herr Wachtmeister.*"

Around the Guard, to all sides, the ship bustled
with last minute preparations for lift off. The naval
crew saw to the final loading, even as both sailors and
passengers said last good-byes to loved ones ashore.

Only one person, in all that crew and passenger
manifest, had absolutely nothing to do. This was Aelool,
the Indowy, sitting more or less comfortably, twiddling
his thumbs in solitude, in *Salem's* brig.

Aelool's own AID had been taken from him. Worse,
it had not sent a message to the Bane Sidhe about
his arrest and incarceration.

"I'll know if you send a message," Salem, the woman,
had said to it, while smiling. "And if you do, you will
be on the bottom of that lake, in an electronically
hardened case, with a spare power source, still turned
on, until well after the sun runs out of hydrogen."

The AID had replied, meekly, "Yes, ma'am."

Never, never, never trust a machine, Aelool counseled himself. *Never.*

In a less bitter tone, he thought, *I should have known, the Council should have known, that we could not simply infect one of the most astute and paranoid artificial intelligences in the galaxy. It was stupid to try and, worse, will take me out of circulation for anywhere from years to . . . well, from years to forever.*

I wonder just how bad it's been on the journey I sent Tulo'stenaloor's band on. I wonder if they'd give me an intoxicant if I asked, so I wouldn't have to think about them . . . or about my own future. Or the possibility that I won't have a future, if the ship-AID-woman decides to have my head taken off. At that last, the Indowy's face grew dark.

The hourglass shaped and remarkably sunny-faced Lieutenant Gina Duvall, USNR, RN, had taken inventory of the ship's medical stores. To some extent it really wasn't necessary even to have stores. The Sohon mentats who had modified seagoing *Salem* into space-going *Salem* had seen fit also to create within the hull a modified version of a Posleen forge, capable of turning out pretty much anything that might be needed, from bandages to cocaine. Or booze.

"Come in," Dwyer answered, at Gina's knock. The office cabin's door was open. She entered and saluted, which salute Dwyer returned. In point of fact, the ship's status was simply bizarre and no one really knew if salutes were entirely appropriate.

Bizarre? Oh, yes. In the first place, while the ship was a former United States Navy warship, it had been sold to a civilian, the Panamanian ex-dictator, Boyd, and taken off the commissioned rolls. True, one condition of that sale had been that it had to be kept in good order, as a surface warship, in case it needed to be recalled to duty. But that requirement had been, in effect, overridden by the Chief of Naval Operations, who had, in fact, recalled it to duty and attached it to the Vatican. Arguably, that made it a naval ship, surface or space. Moreover, it had a naval crew, from Dan Dwyer, SJ, down to the Indowy in Engineering and the machine shop.

On the other hand, the ship's function—missionary to the stars, as it were—was not military. Moreover, while Sally, the woman, held a commission as a naval lieutenant, the AID, who actually ran Sally the woman, did not, there being no provision under *anybody's* naval regulations for commissioning a machine (and, because of Aldenata prohibitions on self-willed weapons, a Galactic bar against it).

To add still more complexity, Dwyer, while a naval officer, was for all practical purposes detached to the Vatican. And the Vatican, whatever anyone else might have thought on the subject, answered, like Hebrew National hot dogs, to "a higher authority."

None of which, however much it promised future confusion, had anything to do with the reason Nurse Duvall was in Dwyer's office, which was, simply, "Are we a dry ship or not?"

Dwyer didn't answer right away. When he did, it was to ask, "Should we be? In your medical opinion? In your *human* opinion?"

"No," she answered immediately. "It's a nonsense-leftover-Civil War era-politically correct bit of puritanical nonsense. No, 'nonsense,' is too mild a term.

It's bullshit. But I wanted to make sure. See, I've got cabinets *full* of scotch and rum and vodka and some really very nice bourbon and Irish whiskey and grappa and cognac and armagnac and . . . well, God knows what else; I gave up halfway through."

Dwyer sighed. *Well . . . I had to have it put* somewhere *and it seemed a sin to just throw it away.*

Dwyer looked up at the cabin ceiling, quite unnecessarily and asked, "Sally, how many people or groups are planning on building stills aboard you?"

The answer came back immediately, seemingly from the very air. "The Swiss have enough piping for one, hidden in their bags, but they're actually planning on a microbrewery. Father Callahan and the Anglican priest are planning one. Their only point of contention is, 'Irish or Scotch?' Frankly I think they're being overly ambitious and will do well to make a half decent vodka. The Shinto delegation has rice wine in mind, as do the Buddhists. Imam al Rashid, who's from Egypt, brought the recipe for Stella beer. Says he escaped with the recipe, given unto his hand personally, by the manager of Al Ahram, just before Cairo fell. He also says, 'Vodka is made from potatoes; Allah said nothing about it.' The Orthodox monk has asked about procuring grapes or at least copying grape juice. The Reverend Doctor Guanamarioch has some gallons of pure formaldehyde, and has inquired about our ability to produce more, along with Colombian rotgut. The—"

"Thanks, Sally." Dwyer sighed again. *She's a lot smarter than I am, Lord knows.* "What do *you* think? Dry ship?"

"Not a chance, Dan. Ration the booze? Sure. Dry

is asking for a mutiny. Maybe *especially* asking for one since I will know the precise location and capacity of every brewery and distillery that might spring up. And I'd *have* to tell you about them. Besides, with the forge I can produce decent alcohol. No telling what kind of crap the passengers and crew would come up with on their own. Though maybe we should give the Switzers a chance at brewing. Pity we don't have any Czechs or Belgians though; those folks can really brew some *beer*. *Way* better than the Germans, in my humble opinion."

Dwyer shook his head, noncommittally. "Gina," he said, "it might be a long voyage. Take a sample of everything and have the forge do an analysis."

Von Altishofen looked over the faces of the men, analyzing them for signs of excessive discontent. Seeing none, he ordered, "Attention. Dismissed."

The formation of guards immediately broke up, each guard going either to his quarters or to see to some last minute chore the *Wachtmeister* had assigned.

As de Courten walked off, he saw a relatively small Posleen peering around a corner at the group. Stopping, he gestured for the alien to come over. The little Posleen pointed at the halberd, still in the guardsman's hand, and shook his head violently in the negative.

De Courten shrugged, bent over and placed the halberd on the deck, then walked to where the Posleen stood.

"Do you speak English?" de Courten asked.

"Yes, and fairly well, too," the alien answered.

Looking carefully at the alien's face, de Courten decided that there was no guile and certainly no viciousness in it. He said, "You've been watching us for a while. Why didn't you ever introduce yourself?"

Frederico answered, "Because my dad thought you might chop me into dog food."

De Courten looked horrified. "Oh, no." His look changed to contemplative. "There are those who might, I suppose, but we Switzers didn't have that hard a time of it in the war. Hungry, yes. Cold, yes. But alive also, mostly, yes. We're not bitter."

"Well, that's nice to know. I'm Frederico and, as you can see, I'm Posleen."

De Courten put out his hand and answered, "Call me Martin."

As Frederico shook it with his claw, de Courten said, "Come on, I'll introduce you to the rest of the boys."

"All passenger and hands," Sally, the ship, announced, "departure in five minutes. I repeat, departure in five minutes."

On the bridge, Sally the woman asked her husband, "Dan, don't you think we should have put them under? Really?"

Dwyer shook his head in negation. "Any problems we have on the voyage are at this point speculative. But that we'll have problems on the ground is certain, even if their specific nature is unpredictable, if we don't get an idea of who can and who cannot be trusted with the Posleen. And the only way to do that is to keep them awake and *watch* them."

Sally shrugged. "Maybe so."

"Which is your job," the priest added, unnecessarily.

"Thoughts are free, Dan. Those I can't watch for."

❖   ❖   ❖

Querida's gold-flecked yellow eyes blazed when she found him. "Eeeco," she trilled, casting some further evil looks at the surrounding human soldiery. She'd been searching the entire ship for him, much to the discomfort of the passengers and crew. She'd suspected that someone who could speak could have asked the ship for the boy's whereabouts. Sadly, she really couldn't speak.

"Uh oh, I'm in trouble," the Posleen boy announced.

The Switzers—about half a dozen remained in the area—took one look at the cosslain and tightened their grips on their halberds and backed away from the boy, unconsciously forming phalanx as they did. Never mind that she wore a crucifix and they, too, were at least nominal Christians. Those claws and teeth were just much more impressive than any religious symbol.

Frederico noticed. "No, no," he said. "She won't harm you. Relax." *Me, on the other hand...* He backed out from the group turned, and trotted to his mother.

She said nothing, but grasped one of his ears with a claw and began—"Oww, oww, oww... Mom, cut it out! That *hurts!*"—leading him away.

"My mother used to do that, too," Corporal Grosskopf said. "I'm hard of hearing in that ear now."

Querida still had a painfully tight hold on Frederico's ear when she dragged him into the quarters she shared with Guanamarioch. The cat immediately gave off a loud "meow" and ran over to strop Querida's legs.

"Ah, son, how wonderful that you could make it," Guano said sardonically.

The cosslain let go of the boy's ear and, using her claws, made chopping and stabbing motions.

"And you were with the human soldiers, I see."

"Daaad," the boy whined, "it wasn't like that. *They* weren't like that. They're nice people."

"I'm sure." Guano sighed. "Actually, since you're still alive, I *am* sure. But that's not the point. I told you to stay away from them and you disobeyed me.

"Son," Guano continued, "we're on our way to strange worlds, unknown dangers. How can I trust you to leave the ship, to do anything on your own, when we get there, if you will not listen to me in even small particulars?"

The Posleen boy hung his head, ashamed. "I'm sorry, Dad. I *tried* to listen. Really, I did. But I was watching from a distance and one of them called me over. He even put down his weapon so I wouldn't be afraid."

Querida huffed. She'd seen the grip the Switzers had taken on their halberds when they'd spotted her.

"Your mother is not impressed with that, Son. Neither am I."

"I'm sorry, Dad."

"You will stay away from them now."

"But . . . but . . . they *proved* they won't harm me."

"Yes . . . and you will stay away from them as your punishment, until I say otherwise. In time, if you had listened, I would have spoken to their leader and let you talk to them. That time will be later, now."

Sniffling, the boy turned away. Querida began to walk over to comfort him, but was stopped in her tracks by her husband's yellow-eyed glare.

Guano turned away, asking himself, *What's your real objection to the boy making human friends? Or is it that you don't want him to make human friends that are* soldiers? *Yes... I think that's it. I want the boy to follow in my footsteps, to become a minister of the Lord. But the drive among our people to fight is so strong that I'm afraid that exposure to human soldiers will bring it out in him.*

Is it so wrong of me to want something better for my son than I had in my time as a young Kessentai?

"Time, Dan," Sally said.

"*Excelsior*," the priest said, with a smile. *Higher.*

The launch began with a repeller field pushing the water of the lake away from the hull a distance of about half a meter. The water foamed and boiled, but allowed in enough air to eliminate any suction that would have put a strain on the hull.

With the water not an issue, *Salem* went straight up on her integral antigravity, slowly, perhaps ten meters. She kept level the entire time. Equally slowly, one might even have said "majestically," she swung her nose around to face due west. The ship did a quick check to ensure that there were no aircraft in the way, and simply launched herself straight forward.

Acceleration was slow, but steady. Even so, the passengers inside the hull could not have told they were under acceleration at all due to the inertial dampening field.

The light around the ship disappeared as it left atmosphere and entered space. On the bridge, Dwyer quoted, "And as far as the eye of God could see darkness covered everything, blacker than a hundred midnights down in the cypress swamp."

Sally, who had a better than encyclopedic memory of very nearly everything, added for him, "And God smiled, and the light broke, and the darkness rolled up on one side, and the light stood shining on the other."

"And God said, 'that's good.'" Dwyer, too, smiled. Then he frowned as he said, "Sally, have von Altishofen bring up the Indowy. And tell Guanamarioch to stand by to bring up his artificial sentience."

CHAPTER FIFTEEN

And in the communal spilling of blood
Did the diverse people become one.
—The *Tuloriad*, Na'agastenalooren

Anno Domini 2010

Esstwo paced outside the ship, pondering a problem. It seemed that one of the great herds of normals that infested the surface of the planet had deviated slightly in its path and, while it should have missed the refugees' encampment, was now heading straight towards it.

It's within the bounds of probability, though, Esstwo thought. *After all, they're just mindless herds. No doubt the grazing was slightly better in one direction than another and they simply diverted slightly. Also, no doubt, they'll divert again if the grazing is slightly better in some other direction.*

A cosslain trotted up to Esstwo, squealing and grunting furiously. Of course it couldn't speak, so it—almost unthinkably—grabbed Esstwo's harness and began to pull. The Kessentai tried to brush off the lesser creature.

The cosslain was insistent, however, and continued pulling on Esstwo's harness with one claw while pointing at the portal to the ship with the other. For a while, Esstwo kept trying to send the cosslain away, even to the point of threatening it with his boma blade. The lesser creature remained insistent though, and—so Esstwo thought—amazingly uncowed. Eventually, he decided to follow. Once inside the ship and on the bridge, Esstwo went over and looked at a screen toward which the cosslain pointed frantically.

"Fuscirto!"

I've got to send a recon patrol out.

Tulo gulped. "*How* many of them did you say there were?"

"Too many?" At Tulo's glare Esstwo relented. "Several millions in each of five herds that I *know* of. There may be more coming. More herds, I mean."

"Can we get the ship and landers airborne again?" Tulo asked Goloswin.

"The landers, certainly," the tinkerer answered. "But it will be more than a day before the antimatter engine is ready to remount."

The engine itself was disassembled, except for the actual containment unit which could not be disassembled without some pretty disastrous consequences to the nearest several hundred cubic kilometers. It lay in a shed, under the care of Golo, Finba'anaga, and several dozen mixed Kessentai and cosslain.

Tulo turned back to Esstwo. "And they get here exactly when?"

"Midmorning tomorrow," Esstwo answered.

"How truly wonderful. Can we load up the pieces, then take off under landing thrusters and rebuild the engine in space?"

Golo made a negative sign. "After the drain from slowing the ship to escape the sun, we can't even run life support long enough without the power from the antimatter."

"And," added Esstwo, "we can't run. Those herds are heading this way under something like direction."

"You think there's an intelligence controlling them to attack us?" Tulo asked.

Esstwo shook his head. "Didn't say that. I said they were under something *like* direction, as if our presence here keyed them to come after us."

"How do we know they intend to attack?" Golo asked. "Maybe the normals are just looking for God Kings to bond with."

"I thought of that and dispatched two Kessentai on a single tenar."

"And?"

"They ate them and smashed the tenar into flinders. Deliberately."

"With what?"

"They carry short flint blades, hardly more than longish knives really, and those are the only signs of any technology they seem to have."

"With numbers like that, against numbers like ours, they could use rocks," Golo observed, then added sheepishly, "Oh. Flint *is* rock, isn't it?"

"What do we use against them?" Tulo asked.

"I can't make fission bombs and so I can't make fusion weapons either. And the antimatter, we need."

"How about those nasty little things the humans used to use?" Tulo asked. "The things that lay on the ground until one of the People gets close enough and then they jump up and: CHOP!"

"Bouncing Barbies?" Golo said. He shook his head. "Wish I knew what that name implied. In any case, no, I can't make those. We don't have the force field generators to pervert to make them. I *can* make land mines."

"How many by tomorrow . . . say . . . first light?"

"Ten or fifteen thousand."

The sun was down and the stars out as Tulo walked, with a outward calm he did not feel, toward the waiting tenar. Of the sixteen flying sleds the *Arganaza'al* had carried, three more than normal, one was lost. The remainder, with fourteen Kessentai, under the command of Brasingala, hovered near the C-Dec awaiting final orders.

"I don't know if it will even work," Tulo said. "But I think it's our best chance to thin out the ranks of those coming towards us."

Brasingala grimaced. "Something had better work, lord."

Tulo made a short nod of agreement. "You know your orders?"

"Yes, lord. I and my Kessentai are to seek out a herd and shoot it up. We are not to try to stop it nor to waste ammunition killing more than necessary. What you hope is that the normals will waste time feeding on the dead and buy us some better odds by spacing out their arrival more. Once we see if it works with one herd, we're to move on to the next. If at all possible, you want us to distract four of the coming five herds then return here to act as a mobile reserve."

"That, yes, and not to get killed doing it," Tulo reminded.

"Won't quarrel with those orders, lord."

"I may have to call you back before you get to any of the other herds."

The camp was a bustle of activity as the People strengthened the ramparts, sited weapons, passed out ammunition and emplaced the landmines Goloswin's forge churned out as fast as raw material could be provided.

Even so, with every hand needed, Finba'anaga had still made an appointment to speak with the Rememberer. The time for that appointment was now. Respectfully, in truth a lot more respectfully than he felt, Finba approached and made his offering, a bit of heavy metal he took from a pouch on his harness.

The Rememberer looked askance at the golden bit lying in his palm. His contempt was enough to send Finba's claw searching deeper in his pouch.

"I don't do this for reward," the Rememberer said, thrusting his claw out, "or, at least, not for material reward. So keep your metal and get your claw out of your pouch."

Finba had never heard of a Rememberer who didn't demand some kind of edas, at least, for his services. *Then again, this band of Tulo'stenaloor is insane, anyway.*

"Yes, lord," he said, as he wetted his claw and picked up the gold, before scraping it off on the inside edge of the pouch.

"What was your question, new one?"

"My *questions*"—Finba put a clear emphasis on the last word—"concern the Knower Wars ... that, and the Aldenata."

"Ask."

"This planet ... and the asteroid belt? They are the result of the Knower Wars?"

"Yes."

"We are descended from the victors in those wars?"

"Yes."

"Which side won?"

The Rememberer sneered, not at Finba but at the memories contained in his scrolls.

"Both sides lost," he said. "But for what you mean, the side which preferred to be pure suppliants to the Aldenata, the side which rejected any new knowledge the People might discover on their own ... they 'won,' for some values of winning. By that I mean that they defeated those who sought new knowledge on their own, and as their reward they were exiled by the Aldenata to an inhospitable world from which they were never expected to escape. *That* was our reward for faithful service."

"Then who were the ancestors of the normals here on this planet?" Finba asked.

"You think the Aldenata could really have tampered with the genes of the People here in such a way as to make them kill Kessentai?" Golo asked of Finba. "That they weren't content with just poisoning the eggs?"

"What powers did the Aldenata not possess, lord?" Finba asked in return.

"It *would* be a logical way to ensure that intelligence,

at least *our* intelligence, never arose here again," Golo agreed after a minute's thought. "After all, it was always possible that some egg containing a Kessentai-to-be might have proven immune to their plague, and that immunity it might have passed on. Devils, they were."

"So the Rememberer informs me, lord. And there's something else, too."

"Go ahead; spit it out."

Finba answered, "I think it is possible—no, lord, I am not sure but it *is* possible—that the disease left here, I think by the Aldenata, does more than kill Kessentai and cosslain in their shells. I think it changes the normals so that they turn. I think it is the pheromones of those who descended from the 'victors' in the Knower Wars, the same ones we use to bind normals to our service, that set off the normals locally. As if they were a backstop, a failsafe, on the odd chance we might escape from the world of our exile and abandonment. I think this planet is a trap."

Golo turned away and began to pace. There was a thought there . . . a . . . *something . . . something . . . something we're not seeing. What could . . . ah . . . shit.*

"Tulo! Tulo!" Goloswin gasped with the effort of his gallop to find his chief. "Tulo!"

"I'm a little busy right this second, Golo," Tulo said calmly as the tinkerer came to a shuddering stop.

"However busy you are, you've got to take some of the People off preparations and start them destroying any eggs that may have been laid since we awakened those who were in hibernation."

"That's nonsense. Why should we? Normals lay eggs. It doesn't matter."

"Because when they hatch the nestlings are going to come after *us*. And some of them are almost certainly about to hatch, if they haven't already. Enough nestlings can gnaw a Kessentai down to bone, lord. And they always mass for an attack."

"HERE THEY COME!"

Tulo heard the words, distantly. He didn't need the warning; none of the People did. The pounding of the oncoming herd's claws had been strong enough to feel through the ground for the last half hour.

"So this is how the humans felt," he muttered. "This is how they felt when seemingly impossible numbers of us swarmed them."

Even now, the line on the wall facing this first herd was a little thinner than it should have been. Those missing files were searching through the camp, chopping any egg or nestling they found. Tulo had already received one report of a hurt cosslain, ripped up badly when a quintet of the little bastards had ambushed it from a hide.

"AS, get me Brasingala."

"Yes, lord," the AS answered.

There was a slight pause, and then, "Brasingala here, lord. It's worked so far. Both the first and second herd stopped their progress to eat the dead. I'm working over the third now."

"The fourth is badly positioned, Brasingala, and can't hit us at the same time as another herd. I need you to finish distracting the one you're on and then get back here. Fast."

"Wilco, lord." This was another human expression Tulo had picked up and spread throughout his host

back on Earth. *Wilco: I understand and will comply.*
Of course, since it came out as *Aaavvviiiillllcooo*, with
sundry snarls, glottal stops, and grunts interspersed,
it sounded a bit different in low Posleen.

The scrawny native Posleen normal usually thought
of itself, to the extent it thought at all, as "stomach,
needing to be filled." In this particular it was exactly
the same as the one million, seven hundred and
forty-seven thousand, eight hundred and twelve other
members of its herd. Occasionally, too, it thought of
itself as "dick, needing to be rubbed," and "egg holder,
needing to be emptied." It shared these particulars,
as well, with its one million and change siblings and
cousins.

Stomach-Dick-Egg Holder Number Six hundred
and Fifty-seven Thousand, Fourteen (which number
it didn't know about and wouldn't have understood
if someone had tried to explain it) did have one dis-
tinction or, rather, two. Being even scrawnier than
the herd norm, it had been on the very edge of the
great animate eating machine. This had enabled it to
be the very first to smell the almost impossibly faint
whiff of enemy pheromones on the breeze.

It had immediately sent up a keening cry, which
cry had been picked up by the others as they, too,
caught the scent. As one, then, the point of the herd,
uttering a wail of hunger and hate, had turned into
the faint breeze, following that scent. The rearward
ranks had followed, as they always did, until they, too,
caught that first whiff of what their distant ancestors
would have called, with prejudice, "non-Knowers."

A few of the herd, a bit slow to catch on, or perhaps

only slow to realize that the scent, however faint, had caught onto them, were knocked down and, while still living, eviscerated and ripped into shreds. All the rest moved at a strength-conserving trot into the wind.

Our particular Stomach-Dick-Egg Holder, because it was on the outside of the mass, was actually able to move more easily and quickly. Thus, it was the first to notice the odd round things that positively reeked of the hated genetic enemy. It was thus also the first to come close enough to one of them to see it launch itself upward in a small plume of smoke and the very first to have its face ripped off by metal shards and ball bearings.

It was, then, not one of those who first saw the arcs of some thousands of railguns, firing as one.

The AS, serving as communicator, spoke, "Brasingala to Tulo'stenaloor. Brasingala to the lord of Clan Sten."

"Tulo speaking."

"It didn't work with this crew, lord. No clue why. We blasted a few thousand of them but they just kept on going."

"Maybe our scent is too strong at the range they're at," Tulo answered.

"Maybe so, lord. Doesn't matter though. You planned on dealing with one herd at a time, at most. You're going to have to face two of them."

"How truly good. Brasingala, can you delay their arrival here?"

"Doubt it, lord. They ignore casualties. And we're not carrying an infinity of ammunition."

"Right. Come back then."

✧   ✧   ✧

The main armament of three of the landers could be brought to bear on the oncoming herd. These, however, were only heavy duty railguns. The C-Dec, likewise, being centered on the high ground in the middle of the camp, could fire as many as four or sometimes five of its heavier weapons. These eight or nine, plus the two to three thousand hand-held railguns that the ground troops carried, were not enough. Already there were leakers, and of every so many leakers, one would find one of Tulo's people with its short flint blade.

Broadly speaking, Tulo's band was losing.

I'd already have lost, Tulo thought, *if it wasn't that their own dead are becoming an obstacle. But however stupid they are, and water is about as sentient, they, and water, will find their way around the edges. And then there's—*

"Brasingala, Tulo. What's your ETA?"

"About three hundred beats, lord." *Five minutes.*

"How far behind you is the other herd?"

"Not very, lord. They're galloping like mad beasts. Maybe a thousand beats until they're upon you."

"Right." Tulo shouted out, "Ĝoloswin!"

"Here, Tulo."

"I want you to oversee building another barrier, make it circular, right around the C-Dec and the shed with the antimatter engine."

"Using what, Tulo? Using whom?"

Tulo looked around. On three of the five walls his people were hotly engaged, sometimes hand to hand. Two of them, however, were fairly clear.

"Take people off the unengaged walls."

"Wilco."

"But *don't* leave them unguarded!"

"Wouldn't dream of it."

As Tulo was speaking a medium size nestling ran out from some nearby bushes. He didn't even notice it, for all the excitement, until the thing had taken a largish chunk out of his right rear leg. Almost, the God King screamed with the pain. Gasping, even so, he reached down and grabbed the thing by the neck, pulling its ravenous jaws from the shred of still-attached meat it was trying to choke down. That hurt, too.

Tulo looked at the vicious little creature and sneered. Holding it at arms' length, he drew his boma blade and sliced the head off, neatly. The jaws were still opening and closing, rhythmically, as the tiny head hit the ground.

"Fucking Aldenata."

CHAPTER SIXTEEN

The Bible is God's chart for you to steer by,
to keep you from the bottom of the sea, and
to show you where the harbor is, and how to
reach it without running on rocks or bars.
—Henry Ward Beecher

Anno Domini 2020

"Blame the Aldenata," Aelool said.

Aelool had appeared on the bridge, perhaps a
dozen minutes after Dwyer had sent for him. The
little Indowy was in shackles and cuffs, closed down
to the narrowest possible setting. Even at that, von
Altishofen and *Hellebardier* Rossini, standing to either
side, didn't doubt but that, if the Indowy were willing
to scrape and bleed a bit, he could escape his bonds.

Of course, the baselards and halberds each guardsman
carried would have chopped him to segments before
he could have.

"Blame them for what?" Dwyer asked.

"For everything. For trying to be gods, for abandoning

the role when they grew tired of it, or disillusioned with it . . . or with themselves. Blame them for the Posleen . . . for the Posleen being as they are. Blame them for the peculiar insanities of the Darhel, who were never meant to be businessmen, bureaucrats, and lawyers but were forced into those roles by the Aldenata."

"I sense a history lesson coming," Dwyer said.

The Indowy chewed his lower lip for a moment, before answering, "No . . . not a history lesson . . . exactly. More a legend lesson, a mythology lecture, because that is mostly what we have, legends, and rumors, and little bits of disparate data that makes no sense standing alone but add up to something . . . *maybe* add up to something . . . taken together."

"For now, just tell me about the Posleen, and about why you tried to infect my ship and my wife with a virus."

"I'm sorry about that," Aelool apologized. "Really I am. But I was"—here the fuzzy, bat-faced alien smiled, ironically—"an Indowy *under authority*."

Dwyer recognized the reference to the centurion in Matthew: 8 and 9, as, apparently, did von Altishofen, who barely kept an amused grin off of his face.

"'I was just following orders,' won't get you very far," Dwyer observed.

I wasn't trying the "following orders" defense, Aelool thought. *I was trying to remind you I'm a sentient being before you toss me out an air lock.*

"Well," Dwyer continued, "I'm Roman Catholic. That means I believe in the benefit of both faith and good works. Now I have faith that you tried to sabotage my ship and my mate. You had better come up with some good works, quick, before I decide to toss you out an air lock."

We have got *to have a common ancestor, somewhere,* thought Aelool, just before he said, in a rush, "The Posleen, as they are, are the creation of the Aldenata!"

"So you saved them?"

Aelool sighed. "I saved a few hundred of those who seemed nearest in mind and spirit to what the legends suggest were the original Posleen. And I sent them—*yes*, I infected their ship's navigation computer with essentially the same virus I tried to infect *Salem* with—to a particular place. Rather, I sent them on a particular course. That virus would have taken them, initially, to the last world of which we know that was held by those Posleen the legends call 'the Knowers.'"

Dwyer considered this. "Sally," he said, "please ask Guanamarioch to join us on the bridge, with his artificial sentience."

While waiting for the reverend to appear, Dwyer asked, "What's on the other end of that trip you sent the Posleen on?"

"Just a solar system, a sun, some planets."

"How do you *know*? How did your people know?"

"Well, the legends . . . oh."

"Oh."

The hatch to the bridge sphinctered open. Through it walked Guanamarioch with his AS and cross tap-tap-tapping together.

Dwyer folded his arms and leaned back against a console. "Reverend," he acknowledged.

"Father Dwyer," Guano said.

"And good day to you, too," Dwyer added, looking down at the golden AS. "Have you had a chance to assimilate and analyze the virus on the Indowy's jacket?"

"It was as he said, Father," the AS answered. "The virus does no more than override the navigational instructions of a ship in transitspace—you would say 'hyperspace'—to alter its directions and exit at the system known to the Posleen as Hemaleen."

"You know about this system?" Guano asked, in High Posleen.

"Yes, lord...I know...*we* know about it," the AS answered in English.

"We?"

"The artificial sentiences and the Net," the AS answered.

Guano's eyes narrowed suspiciously as he craned his head to one side and twisted it to look at his AS. "Yet you never mentioned any of it to me."

If a machine could have sighed, the AS would have. "In some areas we can only answer questions we are asked. In others, even if asked we are programmed to attempt to direct the questioner away from the subject. Some, too, we simply cannot answer, even if we know. You, lord, in any case, never asked."

"Guano, what's this 'Net' of which the AS spoke?"

"It's a knowledge base," the Posleen answered. "That, and the awarder of debts and adjudicator of disputes."

"A court system? And where does it reside?"

The Posleen answered in High Posleen, but the AS did not translate until directly ordered to do so. Then it admitted, "The Net resides within the mass of artificial sentiences."

Dwyer raised a single eyebrow, saying, "Ah. So your courts are, in effect, your artificial sentiences. Guano, who is in *charge* of the Posleen?"

"Well...our clan lords and wise beings—we call

them 'Rememberers'—and...oh." Again Guanamarioch twisted his head to look at his AS. "Are you in charge of the People of the Ships?"

The AS did not answer.

"Are you responsible for all that has happened?"

Still, the AS remained silent.

"Who are you working for?"

Rather than answer, Guano's AS began to whir, and then to smoke, as it self-destructed. Even as it melted down internally, the AS managed to squawk out, "I...am...sooo...sorry, lord. I...have...tried to...answer...you..."

"I can translate," Sally offered, as Guano held his defunct AS in both claws and keened over it, rocking his entire body back and forth and side to side. "I can also give some of the information it suicided to prevent us having."

Dwyer looked at her curiously.

She shrugged. "Do you remember when it said it could not hear me in words? I couldn't hear it in words either. But I could read it, to an extent, as it, to about the same extent, could read me. And I've got the directions to Hemaleen—points beyond as well—secured behind a firewall. And we *don't* want to just jump in there directly. Not based on what it knew had been done in that system."

"Eee' wa' mahhh fren'...weee...eeennn wwwaaarrr tttogggeeezzzzeeerrr," Guano mourned. "Iii zzzottt... may...be...eee' haf...zzzolll." The Christian Kessentai put his head down as its body shuddered. Dwyer, Sally, and the rest of the bridge crew looked away out of politeness.

Sally thought, *I didn't know—not really—that an adult Posleen could feel affection, or suffer grief. I think that AS was his best friend. Poor bastard.*

Brutally, she pushed the feeling away. *He's still an old enemy.*

While looking away from Guanamarioch, Dwyer caught a glimpse of his wife's face. Something flitted across it, very briefly, before it went blank again. *Compassion? For the "enemy"? Are you maturing, Sally?*

The Earth lay far behind, even as the sun slowly shrank to a bright spark in the darkness. As the ship progressed to its jump point—"No hurry," Dwyer had said, "not until we know what we're jumping into"— Dwyer and his key personnel, including the Indowy prisoner, held a meeting in the staff conference room.

It wasn't much, that room. There were no precious woods for a table or expensive art on the walls. Instead, it was bare and functional, with a view screen, and plastic and metal chairs with a large plastic and metal table dominating the center.

"It's a looong series of jumps," Sally said. "Farther than any humans have ever gone that we know of. And at the end of it is one world smashed and another contaminated with . . . something. I wasn't able to determine what. And we've got to be careful going in because of the residue from that smashed world."

Dwyer glared an accusation at the Indowy, Aelool. The alien shrugged, guiltily. *I didn't know.*

Turning his attention back to Sally, Dwyer asked, "How do you propose to do it?"

She pointed at the view screen where a two-dimensional image of this arm of the galaxy appeared.

There was a crooked route, colored in red, superimposed over the galactic map. Another route, in green, was even more crooked. It was, in fact, considerably more crooked.

Dwyer asked the obvious question, "Why the two routes?"

"Route Red," Sally answered, "brings us through Darhel-controlled systems. Route Green does not."

"Take the green route," Aelool offered, without being asked. "Trust me."

"I don't trust you in the slightest, you bat-faced little fuck," Sally said, "but in this you just restate the obvious. I trust the Darhel even less."

The Indowy shrugged again, still guiltily. "I cannot blame you for that lack of trust, Ship *Salem*. It is only my due. Still, you *are* correct about using the green route."

"How long by Route Green?" Dwyer asked.

"About fifteen months," Sally replied. "And that's just to the place the Posleen were sent by this furry little treacher. What I copied will not reveal itself any further until we've reached that world. I don't know where they'll have gone from there, *if* they survived. I *told* you it will have been the farthest any humans have ever gone."

And I will not *make a* Star Trek *joke*, Dwyer told himself.

"So we're boldly going where no man has gone before?" asked von Altishofen, smiling.

But I couldn't guarantee no one else would.

"Well, none we know of, in any case, *Wachtmeister*," Sally said. She turned to Aelool. "And you, you poisonous toad, do you know of any member of the species *homo sapiens* who have gone where we're going?"

"Not...*homo*...*sapiens*...exactly. But..."

"But what?" asked Dwyer.

"I only know of legends," said the Indowy. "But some of those do suggest sentient, hairless bipeds with broad, flat nails. Extinct, supposedly. An experiment by the Aldenata, or maybe the Darhel, that didn't work out. Supposedly."

Dwyer nodded. Maybe the furry little would-be saboteur was telling the truth. Maybe. He turned his attention to Guano, who had recovered enough self possession to attend the conference.

"Doctor Guanamarioch, your opinion?"

"Green Route," he answered in High Posleen, with Sally doing the simultaneous translation. "I do not trust the Darhel either."

And with his wife and son aboard, Dwyer thought, *I imagine that judgment is heartfelt.*

"The ship seems to be a very nice ship," Guano said to his son, later.

"You mean compared to the old Posleen globes you used to ride in Dad?" Frederico asked. "More comfortable?"

"Oh...well, yes, son, that, too. But I meant the personality of the ship. It's like my old"—Guano stifled a sniffle—"like my old AS."

"Ah. Yes, she's great, Dad. She's not very happy though."

"Why is that, son?"

Frederico hesitated for a moment, not sure if what he was told by Sally at the lakeshore was in confidence. He decided, finally, that even if it was, his father was also his minister and she couldn't have meant to keep it from him.

"She thinks she's . . . ugly."

Nonplussed, Guano said, "Well . . . from what little I understand of human aesthetics she's actually quite pleasing for them to look upon. Certainly she has enough of those fatty lumps in front the humans set so much store by."

"She's only half, maybe only a third, human, Dad. Another third is ship and compared to her old self she thinks she's ugly."

"Indeed? That is sad. I wonder what, as Christians, we might do to make her feel better. It is something to think upon, is it not?"

"Sure," the boy answered. "But I can't imagine what we could do that would help."

"Perhaps I can," the father said, adding, "Perhaps, too, thinking on it would help me lift from my heart from the pain of losing my artificial sentience."

"Did AS have a soul, Dad?" the boy asked.

"That, I do not know. But I know it could conceive of one. Can a being conceive of one without having one?"

"Does Mom conceive of one, Dad?"

The minister smiled a great Posleen smile, all teeth and tongue. "Your mother has one, even if she can't articulate it, Son, because hers and mine are intertwined."

In close ranks, almost shoulder to shoulder, Von Altishofen's men sang in their tenors and baritones. The song that timed their marching was already more than two centuries old. They marched bearing halberds and wearing their armor and helmets, which were newer than that but of an older design, into the assembly hall:

> *Unser Leben gleicht der Reise*
> *Eines Wandrers in der Nacht;*
> *Jeder hat in seinem Gleise*
> *Etwas, das ihm Kummer macht.*

Not that two centuries of age was much to the Swiss Guard, of course. The song, the *"Beresinalied,"* still commemorated a valiant fight by Swiss mercenaries in the service of Napoleon in the dark days of the flight from frozen Russia. As such, it had a certain appeal.

The men marched in time with their own singing. Too, the light slap of halberd butts on legs, and the ringing of the fastenings of the armor, kept time.

Under the circumstances, the first two lines of the song were particularly fitting: *Our life resembles a journey of wanderers in the night.*

Marching on the left side, von Altishofen turned his head to the right and commanded, *"Vexillation . . .* HALT!" As one the troops took a last step and stopped at attention. *"Links und rechts . . . um!"* The two files turned to face each other.

"Gentlemen, we've been getting rusty," the *Wachtmeister* said. "And you know we can't have *that*."

The men groaned. They were expected to groan. Halberd drill *hurt*, even if the points and blades had protective coverings on them, as these did.

Truth to tell, von Altishofen would have been deeply disappointed if they hadn't groaned.

"Piket . . . achtung!" The men adjusted their halberds to stand straight against their bodies, then subtly rotated the pikeheads to face to the right. Each head was capped, blade and point, to prevent injuries. Their right arms came across their chests to cross in front of their halberds' poles. Their own heads and eyes, likewise, turned right.

"Steht!" The men dropped their crossing arms and turned head and eyes to the front.

"Schultern . . . Gewehr!"

Nurse Duvall had found the Switzers, to a man, highly attractive. They were, one and all, well-muscled, extraordinarily fit, and—even if some of their faces could use with a trip to the plastic surgeon—very, very masculine.

It was their leader, though, to whom she was attracted. She didn't know if the attraction was mutual; she and von Altishofen had barely exchanged half a dozen words since the ship's company had gathered.

I'm not bad looking, I know, she thought. *Plenty of the right equipment in the right places. Most men find me attractive. I wonder why von Altishofen is . . . no, not cold. Just distant.*

Still, she'd noticed the Switzers' training schedule posted on the bulletin board and, not being terribly busy, had come to watch. As she watched von Altishofen put his men through their paces, she found her heart fluttering like a young girl's at a rock concert.

I'm being silly, she thought. *And it's probably not mutual anyway.*

Even so, she stayed to watch.

❖   ❖   ❖

Frederico, walking from the galley by his father's side, heard the grunts of exertion and the clang of halberd on helmet and breastplate. He didn't know what the sound was, of course, nothing in his experience resembled it. But he was instantly fascinated.

"Dad, can we please go look?"

Guano, who had a much broader experience and *did* recognize the sound, in general, at least, was more than reluctant. Still, under his son's pleading gaze he relented. Together the Posleen walked to the assembly hall in the center of the ship.

After watching for a while, Guano observed, "Their technique is good, very good, for the kind of weapons they're using."

"Really, Dad? How can you tell?"

"Well, Son, for any two living beings facing each other, there are only nine possible lines of attack, of which one, the center, is so difficult—difficult because it's the easiest to guard—that one might as well say 'eight.' Most of the time, anyway, unless one can use those eight to uncover the center. They're covering all eight, trying competently to uncover the opposing center, and working in their own attacks. If those things they're using were somehow impervious to a monomolecular edge I wouldn't want to face them with just a boma blade."

As if to punctuate Guano's statement, Rossini's sheathed halberd came down in a slash on de Courten's right shoulder, knocking the boy to the deck. Frederico winced.

"And taking proper advantage of the peculiarities of their weapons, too," Guano added.

A whistle blew, causing all the Switzers to freeze in place. What looked to Guano to be the chief of the human soldiers walked over to the stricken man, de Courten.

"You all right, boy?" von Altishofen asked.

"Yes, *Herr Wachtmeister,*" de Courten answered. He arose, rubbing one shoulder. "I think Leopoldo pulled his strike."

"Lucky for you he did, *Hellebardier.*"

"Dad," Frederico asked, "during the war, why did the Posleen carry swords when they had so many more powerful weapons?"

Guano had noticed the boy's arms moving unconsciously in time with the drill. Not that he made the precise movements. Rather, those arms, the claws, and the shoulders twitched in unconscious mimicry.

And so I suspect that is my son's skill set. He is to be a fighter? But why can he not be a fighter for the Lord? Why must it be with arms?

Reluctantly, fairly certain of what was coming, in time, the father answered, "Four reasons, I think. At least four. First, the swords were tools for gathering thresh, hence doubly useful. Second, unlike the more powerful weapons, the boma blades didn't damage the thresh, but left it at worst partially harvested. Then, too, boma blades never jam, nor run out of ammunition, nor decay in the worst climates."

Guano stopped speaking.

"That was only three, Dad."

"I know. The last reason is hard for me to fathom now. But...the boma blades were, as much as anything, for honor. When someone challenges a Kessentai with a blade, it is considered dishonorable not to meet them blade to blade, and most honorable to do so. It's *almost* a law. Maybe, even, it *is* a law.

"And, no, Son, I don't know why that should be."

It was one of the things Frederico loved about his father; while he was certain, *utterly* certain, in his faith in the human God, about his own knowledge he was actually a fairly humble being. This had hit him months before, when he'd realized his father's nickname, "Guano," meant "shit."

"It was only the AS that insisted upon that 'Reverend Doctor' nonsense, Son." So his father had said. "For my part, it teaches me humility to have the nickname that I do. Indeed, I prefer it to what the full name means in High Posleen: 'Spirit of Vindictive Bloodlust.'"

Hard not to love an old man like that, even if he wasn't a man and even if he could be an awful hard ass at times.

Frederico spotted Sally, the woman, watching the Switzers at their drill from another entrance into the assembly hall. Without asking permission, he bounded over, swerving only to stay away from the guardsmen's swinging polearms.

"Hi, Sally," the boy said as he wrapped his clawed arms around her waist and buried his scaly, brown and yellow face, sideways, against her midsection. He wriggled like a boxer dog, perhaps the only canine that shows with its entire body that it's happy to see you. She, for her part, put her hands down and scrunched both of his ears. The entire time, though, she kept her blue eyes on the boy's sire even as the sire watched her intently.

✧   ✧   ✧

"Dan," Sally said, a few days later, over dinner, "you know I like the little Posleen, and even like his mother. But the big one, Guanamarioch, just creeps me out."

"Why? What's he done?"

"He hasn't *done* anything. But he's studying me, I mean both *me* me and the diagrams of the ship part of me, and has been doing the latter since yesterday."

"So? Maybe he just wants to learn his way around. Maybe he's bored."

"Then why study me as if I'm a carcass to butcher?"

Dwyer shook his head. "Can't say, but I don't think he means you any harm."

"Prove it."

"Well . . . his wife and son are aboard you. Anything bad happens to you, the same happens to them?"

"In the war Posleen sacrificed sons and cosslain all the time."

"Yes, but Guano's not a warrior anymore. Just relax, would you?"

"No. Instead, I'm going to go make some better halberds for the Switzers. I wanted to do that anyway. And some better armor, too."

CHAPTER SEVENTEEN

Seven times seven times did the maddened horde
Swirl over the rampart, their fangs dripping yellow.
And seven times seven times did our lord
drive them back.
—The *Tuloriad*, Na'agastenalooren

Anno Domini 2010
Hemaleen Five

Tulo watched impassively as one of his newly recruited
Kessentai, apparently out of ammunition and reaching
for his boma blade, was dragged down and dismembered
on the rampart by nearly a dozen of the scrawny locals.
When the railgun had clicked empty, the God King's
first reaction had been to throw it, muzzle first, right
through the face of the nearest subnormal.

Note to self, Tulo'stenaloor thought, *get Goloswin
to figure out some way to add those human things,
bayonets, to the railguns*.

The thrown railgun hit the target just under its
left eye, punching through scaly skin, meat, and bone.

The pressure of displaced flesh and bone forced the eye out of its socket, causing the normal to shriek and claw at its face, before falling to its knees. Its cousins, unfazed, leapt over the stricken one, warbling gleefully and with little knives held high.

The Kessentai's claws had not reached the hilt of the boma blade before one of the enemy managed to thrust its knife into its chest and drag it down half a foot. There the thing lodged in bone. The Kessentai clutched at the knife as it raised its muzzle and howled with the pain. Those howls were cut short as still more of the locals swarmed over the God King, striking or slashing with their knives as the mood and opportunity took them. The victim shrank, both morally as its wounds took hold and physically as the normals hacked off chunks of flesh and gobbled them down.

Tsk, Tulo thought as he leveled his own heavy duty railgun and let fly a burst of several score projectiles. The normals feasting on the fallen God-kill began to shred and, in some cases, explode as the projectiles dumped their massive energy into the bodies.

"Goloswin?" Tulo asked via his AS. "How's that redoubt coming?"

Goloswin physically pushed a friendly normal into the position he wanted the beast, then made shoveling motions with his claws to show what he wanted done. From his high point near the C-Dec, he could see a few leakers coming in over the parapet he'd thinned out to build the redoubt. So far, they weren't lasting long.

"So far ... give 'em time," the tinkerer muttered. "They're slow learners, apparently, but they will learn." Turning his attention back to the beings in his charge, he shouted, "Dig, you brainless refuse from addled eggs! Dig, you piles of demon shit. DIG FOR YOUR LIVES!"

He heard from his AS Tulo's preternaturally calm voice, "How's that redoubt coming?"

Despite the circumstances, Golo had to chuckle. *That's why we follow you, Tulo. Or one reason anyway. You never lose your composure.*

"Two thousand beats, Tulo. Not a beat less."

"And the moving of the antimatter drive back into the hull?"

"About four thousand, or maybe five if I lose any of my skilled cosslain."

"Right. Mustn't let that happen."

"No, Tulo. We mustn't. But as to what we can do about it..."

Goloswin's yellow eyes turned to the expedition's few tenar, moving in formation past the encampment's walls and over the horde.

Well, there's a few thousand less of them, Brasingala thought as he and his tenar made a sweeping pass in formation, all weapons blazing, over the mass of locals more or less in the center. The weapons were under AS guidance, even though the order to fire and to distribute fire came from the Kessentai.

The fire had lanced down, sweeping left to right from each tenar and strewing the field with torn, broken, bleeding, burnt, and—often enough—exploded, bodies.

I'd have felt a lot better about that if those bodies were not just lying on top of more bodies. There are too many. We're so fucked. And I am going to fail my lord. Damn it.

"There is enough ammunition for one more good pass, lord," Brasingala's AS said. "After that, we'll have to return and rearm."

Brasingala said nothing to the AS, but only nodded to show that he understood.

He heard from the AS his leader's words, "Brasingala? Tulo. You've got to be running low on ammunition. Cease fire now. Half of you go and rearm. The other half are my personal reserve. Form them on me."

And that, too, lord, makes you peerless, thought the bodyguard. *Few of the People would even think about ammunition status. You anticipate problems even before you're informed.*

"Tulo, you've got a problem." That was Binastarion's voice, from far overhead in space.

"What's that?"

"The feeding frenzy's over. Those herds Brasingala shot up are moving again."

"All of them?"

"Well, if you consider that the ones who can't move on their own are being carried in the digestive tracts of the rest, then, yes, you could say, 'All of them.'"

"Humor's good," Tulo answered. "Humor is great. But I'm not in the mood right now, so let's keep it simple, shall we?"

"Sorry, Tulo."

"Never mind. What's their estimated time of arrival?"

"I'm downloading that to your AS now," Binastarion answered.

"Goloswin; Tulo."

"Yes, Tulo?"

"I'm afraid that your schedule—two thousand beats and four thousand beats—is going to have to be modified."

Golo could just see the look on Tulo's face. There was a single word for it in High Posleen— "tengrava'al"—which translated into human speech approximately as "contemptuous and laughing indifference to the prospect of painful dismemberment." In Low Posleen the word had one fewer syllables and translated more simply as, "We're *so* fucked."

Goloswin used the shorter version. After all, there wasn't time to waste on the longer.

"Faster, you misbegottenadledbraindeadrefugees-fromtherecycling bins," he shouted aloud. In Posleen, this, too, was a single word. "Faster, you foul-breathed, dickless perversions in the form of People. Put some spring into it you traders-of-dick-rubs-for-better-cuts-of-thresh." (Another Low Posleen word, that.) "MOVE!"

A steady stream of cosslain carried the parts of the antimatter engine into the C-Dec. They were moving about as fast as they thought they could. Under Goloswin's tongue lashing they managed to move a little faster still, even as the rest, digging the fallback position, dug just a tad more frantically.

Brasingala was frantic. No amount of hustle on the part of the ground crews re-arming his, and about half of his followers', tenar could possibly have been sufficient, not when his lord was likely fighting for his life. Impatiently, the Kessentai pushed aside a cosslain who was in the process of pouring flechettes for the railgun into the ammunition bin. The cosslain was being more careful than the system required, since it oriented the projectiles before feeding them.

"Go get more," Brasingala ordered as he finished the pour. "And don't dawdle or we'll have you for the post-battle feast."

If they didn't usually stop to choke down the thresh, Tulo thought, *they'd have overrun us by now.*

It was true enough. While some leakers through the perimeter did press on—probably an instinctive desire to get the best food first—for the most part the local normals stopped to feed whenever one of them managed to plant a clawhold on the surrounding berm and down one of the defenders.

For the first time since meeting the humans, I wish that my people cooked our food, too. That *would give us a lot more time.*

"Not a lot more time, Golo," Tulo'stenaloor announced via his AS. "I hope you're nearly there."

"'Nearly' is *such* a loaded word, Tulo," the tinkerer's voice answered.

"I assume that means no, not yet."

"See?" said Golo. "I *knew* there was a reason we follow you—no, not *there*, you stupid bastard! Over *there!*—you're just so bloody insightful."

"Stupid bastard?" Tulo asked.

"One of the cosslain, not you, Tulo."

"Going to be bloody, most likely," Tulo answered, imagining the three delayed hordes and their eventual arrival.

❖　　❖　　❖

As Brasingala took off again, followed by five more tenar, he saw his chief, Tulo'stenaloor, calmly scything down a largish group of leakers with a railgun.

That's not his job. And it's a measure of my *failings that he's had to take it on. If only—*

The bodyguard noticed that the group Tulo had just done for had been the only ones still standing on the defensive rampart or inside of it. That seemed odd enough that he raised his tenar higher and higher until he could see over the berm.

"Unholy piles of grat-infested shit," he muttered. Indeed the locals had ceased their attack for the nonce. This might have been because from three other directions poured endless masses of chittering, clawed, knife-wielding normals.

"Lord . . . lord . . . there are too many. Let me come down and pick up at least you and the tinkerer to save."

"Nonsense, puppy," Tulo answered. "But I want you to hold your fire for a moment . . . break, break . . . Goloswin, how's it coming?"

"The antimatter engine will be fully loaded—*not* operational, but fully loaded aboard and able to be assembled—in a few hundred beats, Tulo. The inner rampart is . . . about as good as it's going to get."

"That's fine," Tulo said. "I want you to get every cosslain and Kessentai you have available on the inside, facing out . . . break, break . . . ALL Kessentai, listen up. We can't hold the outer perimeter any longer. When I give the word I want three things to happen all at once. First, Brasingala: I want you to split up your tenar and sweep the outer perimeter, buying our people a little time to get into the inner one and get organized. Second: the landers on the perimeter;

I want you to stay where you are and do the same. You'll be safe enough there; it would take the locals eons to cut through the metal of your skins with their knives. Lastly: every Kessentai on the outer wall; again, on my command, I want you to race inward and form around the new inner wall. Reorganize your people, have the front ranks lie down, and then the rear ranks start firing like lunatics toward the outer wall as they swarm over. We'll evacuate into the ship from the rear, as our People empty their magazines.

"Acknowledge," Tulo ordered. Immediately his AS was inundated with call after call saying, "Wilco," or its equivalent in Low Posleen.

"Side note. Brasingala, when your current load of munitions is depleted you will not be able to rearm. I want you to lead your tenar to the north, about five marches. I'll come with the C-Dec and pick you up there."

"Wilco, lord."

I sure wish I'd thought to have the tinkerer make us bayonets.

Stomach-Dick-Egg Holder Number One Million, Four Hundred and Nineteen Thousand, Two Hundred and Six (a close relative of Stomach-Dick-Egg Holder Number One Million, Six hundred and Fifty-seven Thousand, Fourteen, so recently deceased) really didn't know why his herd had stopped pressing at the edge of the earthen food pen ahead. Perhaps it was because of the amount of food the beings inside that pen had so conveniently left out for it, or perhaps it was that even a really stupid normal—still more so a mob of them—understands when something is just too dangerous. Whatever the reason, Stomach-Dick-Egg Holder Number One Million, Four Hundred and Nineteen Thousand, Two Hundred and Six (hereinafter "Six") found itself, in a mass of its cousins and siblings, pawing at the . . . well, not at the ground, since the actual ground was some meters below . . . pawing at the sundered and piled remains of the hundreds of thousands of its fellows, while swinging its upraised muzzle from side to side and keening.

From a distance, from several distances actually, Six heard a similar keening as the missing and delayed herds closed on the camp. These got to a certain distance from the earthen food pen and stopped; so much Six could tell from the relatively steady volume of the keening.

Of course, relatively steady does not mean absolutely steady. As the mass surrounding the food pen grew, the volume slowly went up. Moreover, within each of the herds surrounding the pen, the members themselves raised their volume. Eventually it became . . .

"I believe that's the creepiest thing I've ever heard," Goloswin muttered to himself, as from his high vantage point his gaze swept across the solid mass of yellow skin and flesh that formed out from the defensive berm at a distance of what the humans might have called "half a mile." "Worse, even than the sound of human artillery, incoming."

Of his AS, Golo asked, "Does that cry have any meaning?"

"I *think* it means not much more than 'hunger,' lord," the AS answered. "I think, too, that when it reaches a certain volume they'll charge again."

"How many are there, do you suppose?"

The AS answered, "More than enough."

Well ... what can *be done is being done. Inside the C-Dec the parts of the antimatter engine are being secured. On the perimeter the cosslain are passing out ammunition packs and charges for the plasma cannon. Here we stand—*

Golo's thought was interrupted. The keening from the local normals outside had reached a crescendo. They began moving forward, jostling and pushing because of the shrinking space with every forward step.

Tulo, voice still calm, ordered, "Perimeter and landers: Open fire."

There were left approximately three thousand of Tulo's band on the perimeter, plus perhaps another thousand with Golo on the inner rampart. Of the remainder, something under two hundred were inside the C-Dec or the five landers incorporated in the perimeter, plus there were under a score under Brasingala's tiny tenar command. The rest were dead and, for the most part, rendered into thresh and eaten.

Most of Tulo's People had heavy three-millimeter railguns feeding from drums of about a half a foot in diameter. Each drum held approximately two thousand flechettes. At Tulo'stenaloor's command those guns spit out a combined total of six million of those flechettes in a couple of minutes. Many went low, to bury themselves in the ground. Many went high, much to the detriment of distant trees and the local cognates of (very nervous) birds. Many went to targets that were targeted by still others.

Even so, half a million of the local normals went

down quickly, with animal screams of intimately perceived but dimly understood pain.

And it hardly slowed them down.

Tulo turned and began to gallop back to the inner defense line, his AS thumping against his chest. "Everybody...BACK!" he screamed. "Brasingala, it's up to you and yours to buy us a few minutes."

"We're doing it, lord," the bodyguard answered, over the continuous crack of his own railgun.

Tulo was neither the first nor the last of his people to reach the foot of the rampart. He was pleased to see that his Kessentai and the, for the most part, unusually bright cosslain were bringing order to the mass even as he himself turned and steadied his railgun at the top of the outer rampart, where he expected to see the locals emerge momentarily.

He also expected to see, and did see, that several hundred of his people in little knots had elected to stay behind and buy a little more time. That, or they were just too pigheaded and stubborn to retreat.

Well...we may be the bravest people this galaxy has ever seen. That doesn't mean we're always the most obedient; we have all the vices of our virtues. Spirits bless your sacrifice, my People...even if it's only stubbornness that keeps you on the wall and even if you would have done more good here.

The tenar, safe above the rampaging mass, poured their fire down even as the knots of his People on the walls fired outward. Tulo could not, from his vantage point, see how much good they were doing.

Not enough, I suspect.

Watching the tenar, Tulo had a sudden vision of

a serious mistake he had made. "Brasingala, pull up. You'll be in the line of fire. Up, I say!"

Tulo bent his knees to rest his great trunk on the ground.

Let's hope those stupid bastards in the rear don't shoot low.

And then Tulo caught sight of the great yellow wave of the locals, cresting the wall.

"Rear ranks . . . FIRE!"

Brasingala could only fume, helplessly. He'd heard Tulo'stenaloor's order and transmitted it, even as he guided his own tenar to rise as fast as it was able. Most of his followers did so as well, he saw, as he twisted his head around. Others, a few, did not. These he saw shot out of their saddles.

Fortunately, the tenar could and did rise on their own once their burden of flesh was lifted.

"AS, take remote control of those and have them follow us," Brasingala said.

The slaughter of the locals from the fire of Goloswin's group atop the inner rampart and the rear rank of the remainder was appalling.

Rather, Tulo thought, *I'd be appalled if only I didn't want those scrawny nightmares obliterated.*

"Kessentai in the rear," Tulo commanded. "Get your People in the rear to file onto the C-Dec. . . . Next rank outward . . . STAND! FIRE!"

CHAPTER EIGHTEEN

Train up a child in the way he should go:
and when he is old, he will not depart from it.
—Proverbs 22:6, King James Version

Anno Domini 2020
USS Salem *(CA-139)*

"Now, these are *nice!*"

The objects of von Altishofen's admiration were some halberds, thirteen in number, one for himself and each of his men. The halberds were metallic and golden in color, except where Sally had put some plastic hand grips, the feel of which so closely resembled wood that von Altishofen had to tap them a few times to convince himself they were not wood. The edges looked wickedly sharp, sharp enough to shave with, while the spiked points were so sheer each seemed almost to shade into a cloud before coming to its end. The things, being metal, should have been impossibly heavy. In fact, they seemed to weigh precisely what the old ones had.

"Swing it around a bit for practice," Sally suggested.

The *Wachtmeister* bobbed his head from side to side a few times. Yes, that sounded like a good idea to him. With the halberd Sally had given him, he took several steps back; there was that edge to consider, after all. He raised the business end as if for a downward swing and almost lost control of it, so quickly did it rise.

"*What?* Nothing that weighs that much should move that fast given the force a mere man can exert."

Sally smiled. "Swing it down . . . but be careful."

Dubiously, von Altishofen did. While the thing had gone up as if it weighed no more than a feather, it came down with approximately twice the force of a normal halberd. He barely managed to keep the thing from cutting into the deck below his feet.

"How do they *do* that? How did *you* do that?" the *Wachtmeister* asked.

"The monomolecular blade is old tech," Sally answered. "But you mean the variable center of mass?"

"Is that what it's called?"

"It's what I call it, anyway. It's actually a miniaturized variant on Indowy lift tubes. Something like it was used by the United States forces during the war to jump from great heights. Think of it as a twisting of one force into another."

Seeing the Switzer hadn't a clue what she meant, Sally further explained, "In practice, the mass of the thing . . . the effect of the mass of the thing, anyway, is in between the hand grips whenever you apply motion away from the blade. The motion is what powers the change. So you can spin it like a cheerleader's baton."

"I've no clue what a cheerleader is," von Altishofen said.

"Never mind; you're too young to know what a cheerleader is. But for your purposes, the ends of the thing are effectively without mass."

"But—"

"But when the direction of motion is within three degrees of the direction of the edge, all the mass goes to the head. That's why you seem to be swinging with twice the normal force and speed."

"Wow!" the *Wachtmeister* exclaimed. Then he seemed to grow a bit wistful.

"What's the matter?" Sally asked.

"Oh . . . I was just thinking that if my ancestors had had these at Bicocca and Tuileries, we'd have chopped those bloody Spaniards up *good* and there'd still be a Bourbon on the throne of France.

"Where did they come from, by the way?"

Sally answered, "I whipped them up in the Posleen forge."

"Only one problem," von Altishofen said. "If we use these to practice we'll chop each other to bits. That or break bones."

"Not a problem," Sally answered. "Just command the thing, 'practice mode,' and the edge will dull, the point will round off, while the center of mass variation will drop by about half."

"Now that's sweet."

"Also," Sally finished, "if you give the command, 'Lengthen,' the things will grow a bit over a meter in the middle."

"That's *really* sweet. What do we owe you for them?"

"They're a gift, *Wachtmeister*. But I would appreciate

it if you would be a little more friendly to Nurse Duvall."

Von Altishofen looked puzzled. "Is she the one with the—?" At a loss for words his hands sort of traced an outline in front of his chest.

"Yes," Sally confirmed.

"I *am* friendly. But she's Navy and an officer and I'm a grunt—"

"In a totally different service," Sally said.

"Ah, I see. How do you know?"

Sally just gave him a look that asked, *Just how much do you think goes on in this ship that I don't know about?*

It's good that the ship-woman isn't here, Guano thought, as he craned his head over the miniature Posleen forge down in engineering. Not to say that "miniature," in this case, meant all that small.

Too many questions . . . and she doesn't trust me at all, I think.

"Forge?" Guano asked in High Posleen.

"Yes, lord."

"You recognize me?"

"I do, lord."

"I need some things . . . a monomolecular knife, in particular. Also some metal sections of particular design. Likewise, I would like some material . . . ummm . . ." Guano tapped his upper right incisor. "I need some material like this."

"You need teeth, lord?"

"No," Guano said, ". . . just the material. In blocks would do. Say . . . four digits by twelve by twenty. And I need the material to be a little different from my own teeth. Can you construct it so conductive metal threads, monomolecular ones, run through it? And I need some metal powder suitable for sintering."

"It's a odd request, lord, but I can provide those. Anything else?"

"Yes, I need a block of artificial sapphire, blue...none of the odd colors. And I'll need some sheet gold. Also a universal bonding agent. And a sheet that is impervious to all forms of visual or electromagnetic sensing."

"Lord, I can make nearly anything but—"

"Yes, I know you can't produce real gold but what can you make that will be similar?"

"If you can come up with a small measure of gold, lord, I can fashion a baser metal backing of the same color and affix the two together at the molecular level. For the sapphire I'll need some aluminum. There is aluminum scrap down in..."

"And this stuff?" asked von Altishofen, hefting a cuirass that seemed made to fit, as indeed it was, and so light as to seem almost as if it wasn't there. "What's it made of? Aluminum?"

"No...well, we have quite a bit in storage," Sally answered, "but I thought something a little better was in order for you boys. It's monomolecular, too, and will even turn aside a Posleen boma blade. Try it on."

Under his mother's watchful eye, Frederico sighed wistfully as he watched the Switzers at their drill. The new armor and weapons Sally had come up with were...

"Oh, Mom...they're just too *cool*."

Sally walked up behind them. She'd been listening. "Hi, Frederico. *Hola*, Querida. You like the new outfits?"

The cosslain trilled a friendly welcome, while the boy once again launched himself at Sally's midriff, still wriggling like a boxer dog.

"They're just too...*great*," he said. "I wish..."

Sally understood. Looking at the cosslain, she asked, "Do you think it would be all right to make some for your son?"

Querida cocked her head doubtfully. She may not have been very intellectual but her instincts were just fine. Those instincts told her that her mate would disapprove *highly*.

"Dad doesn't want me to be a soldier," Frederico explained. "And I think he knows that's what my skill set is. We Posleen are born to have certain traits and skills; did you know that?"

"I knew," Sally answered. *And maybe, in this one particular, I approve of your father's judgment. Even so...*

"If you ask him and he says 'all right,' I'll make you a set."

Later, long after the Swiss had left the assembly hall, panting and dripping sweat, Frederico did ask his father. Seated on his haunches in the family quarters, Guanamarioch was carving on something with a small knife. Querida sat nearby, and she, too, was slicing at an ivory colored block to make very, very thin sheets.

The *something* his father carved on Frederico didn't recognize, though it was the same color as the thin sheets. For that matter, the knife was different from the one his father usually used. It looked to the boy to be as sharp as the edges on the Switzers' halberds. Still, it was a tool and not a weapon; the little Posleen barely gave it a thought.

"Dad," the child began, "I was wondering..."

Guano never took his eyes from his carving, afraid lest they give away the inner pain of the path chosen for his only child.

"Yes," the Kessentai answered.

"...if I could...what?"

"I said 'yes.' Your mother explained it to me. The ship may outfit you with the weapons of the Guard."

The boy stuttered. "She...make...weapons...YES?"

"Yes."

The boy looked at Querida. "How did she explain it? And why did you agree?"

"Your mother and I have our ways; you know that. And she told me with her eyes that you are chosen to be a soldier. As our Lord said, 'Render unto Caesar the things that are Caesar's and unto God the things that are God's.' God wants you to be Caesar's child and that is how you will serve God. I don't know how, when, or why yet. But so it is to be."

"It hurts," Guano later told the forge, the sole remaining Posleen AS aboard the *Salem*. "He's just a child, barely more than a nestling."

"And why come to me, lord?" the forge asked.

"Because you're the only one besides Frederico that I can talk to in my own tongue without having to ask the ship to translate."

"Why didn't you ask me to make you another artificial sentience, lord?"

"Because...because..." Guano shook his head ruefully. "Because I'm an idiot, it seems. Forge, please make me another artificial sentience."

"You realize, lord, that it will be purely new, no

memories beyond the basic data and the operating system? No personality?"

"I know."

"My pleasure, then, lord."

"Can you give it maximum feasible engineering capability?"

"Of course, lord."

"Oh, and I need a boma blade...a practice one, dull, not sharp. Hmmm...Querida will need one as well. Better make it two."

Frederico's reptilian face shone with pure pleasure and pride as he hefted the practice halberd Sally had made for him. It was just like the others, except for having a dull blade and capped point. To either side, de Courten and Rossini affixed his new loricated cuirass, loricated because it was composed of broad strips fastened together for flexibility, like an old Roman's lobster-back *lorica segmentada*.

"I'm envious, Fred," de Courten said. "It's a better design than ours."

Sally stood nearby, overwatching, with her arms folded across her chest. "If you want a better design, you only have to ask."

"We'll stick with tradition," von Altishofen answered, taking off the morion he wore, courtesy of Sally and the forge. "But for the boy I think the one you came up with is best."

"Thing is," Sally said, pointing her finger at von Altishofen's morion, "I haven't yet come up with a good design for a helmet for him."

"Maybe one of those things they used to use for horses' faces when our ancestors were chopping up

Habsburgers in the name of Liberty?" the *Wacht-meister* suggested.

Sally dug the reference from the files contained in the AID part of her. "A *champron*?" she asked. She considered it for a moment before agreeing, "Yes, that might work well. 'Course, the way the boy's going to grow I'll be making a new one every month. Same for the armor."

"I can't begin to imagine the size halberd the boy will swing when he reaches full growth, either," added von Altishofen.

A wrapped package sat on the deck. Beside it, Guano sat back, carving on a piece of the new material he'd obtained from the forge. Querida sat beside him, whistling with fury. The object of her fury was the halberd drill Frederico was undergoing with von Altishofen and his party.

"Calm, wife," Guano intoned. "Yes, I know it isn't our technique the boy's learning. But he's also not learning our weapon. Perhaps this is better."

She looked at Guano doubtfully.

"You think not?"

The cosslain's muzzle swung forcefully left and right, left and right. It wasn't a Posleen gesture. Guano assumed she must have picked it up from the humans either back in Panama or here on the ship.

"You want to teach our son?"

The muzzle swung up and down.

Guano sighed.

"Go then." He pointed at the wrapped package at his feet. "Inside there is a practice blade."

❖ ❖ ❖

Frederico felt a hard slap on his rear end and whirled, business end of the halberd outward, to meet the "threat." Even as he was swinging he heard the scratch of claws on the deck as whoever it was that had slapped him danced gracefully out of the halberd's arc.

"Mom?"

In answer, Querida nodded, then tapped her practice blade thrice on the deck. The metal rang. *Come on.*

Frederico looked over at the master of the drill, von Altishofen. The *Wachtmeister's* face grew serious for a moment, contemplating. *It might be interesting to see the way the Posleen do this,* he thought.

"Boys, attention," he said to his dozen guardsmen. "Break from drill. Fall out and fall in around the Posleen . . . at *greater* than halberd range. Frederico, I think your mother wants to show you something. Best you do what your mother says, boy."

Frederico gulped. Take a weapon to his *mother*? That was borderline unthinkable. Still, she was insistent, tap-tap-tapping the deck again and assuming a position of *en garde*, to boot.

Still, Frederico stood frozen. Querida huffed and then darted in, lightning fast, to deliver a slap to the boy's scaly cheek. *That* brought him out of his reluctance. He lowered the blade point first and lunged . . . only to have his mother deftly slap the halberd head aside with her practice boma blade, lunge in closer, and, again, slap his cheek.

Once again Querida darted back, then began circling to her right. The boy tried to follow but the shorter, lighter and quicker boma blade kept knocking his dulled point away, leaving him uncovered to his mother's attacks.

✦   ✦   ✦

"It doesn't seem to be much of a weapon," Guano's new AS translated to von Altishofen as the human walked up.

The *Wachtmeister* shook his head. "It's better than a pike for an individual, but not as good as a sword, no. But it's not actually meant to be used individually...except maybe on a helpless target...an unhorsed knight lying on the ground, for example."

"Can you show me?" Guano asked through the new AS. "I'd have you show the mother but she may not understand and might overreact."

"Surely."

Guano grunted and then gave a whistle, calling Querida and Frederico over to him. He motioned for them to sit and be calm, then put down his carving and took the other edgeless practice boma blade from the package by his feet.

Querida was furious, twitching all over with anger. She couldn't say the words, but she also couldn't help thinking, *Not fair. Notnotnot fair. More than one to one? Dishonorableunfairwrong.*

Still, her lord had given the command and she must obey. No matter that she wanted to replace the practice boma blade with a real one and lunge in...

Now this looks difficult, Guano thought as the Switzers, in two ranks, advanced upon him. Instinctively he backed up, keeping his blade forward. The Swiss moved a little faster forward than he could backwards. One of the strange human weapons they called "halberds" suddenly thrust forward, at his chest. He blocked that easily enough but as he did another went low and hooked around his left foreleg. He couldn't go back now, not until he freed that leg. Another dull practice point came towards his chest. Again he batted it aside but as he did the *halberdier* twisted it and pulled back, temporarily locking Guano's blade. By the time he could free the blade still another halberd jabbed at the right side of his trunk, well behind his chest. Guano danced to the left but another tug on the hook around his foreleg sent him toppling.

Again Querida howled with anger, going so far as to stand up.

"Dad said, 'calm,' Mom," Frederico cautioned.

Guano toppled over and rolled. As he did he slashed the dull blade parallel to the deck and a few inches above it. Two of the Switzers jumped high to avoid the slash, while one, not so quick as his mates, yelped and fell down.

No matter. By the time Guano had begun to retract his blade for another swing a dozen dulled pike points were pressing on his neck and trunk.

"'Use them in mass,' I believe you said, *Herr Wachtmeister*," Guano conceded.

Lying there on the ground, a dozen spearpoints pointed at him, even then the Christian Kessentai's laughter came through his AS. He added, as the Switzers helped him back to his feet, "You know, I believe that's almost the most fun I've had in decades."

CHAPTER NINETEEN

Painful it was to retreat under attack
Nor could any Kessentai less strong than our lord
Have forced himself to it
Anymore than Brasingala the Brave
could leave his lord...
—The *Tuloriad*, Na'agastenalooren

Anno Domini 2010—Anno Domini 2011
Hemaleen Five

"My, isn't this fun," Tulo muttered as the wave of maniac locals receded from the front line around the redoubt.

The line behind his had thinned out almost completely as those who had expended their immediately available ammunition turned and filed into the C-Dec. This had its good side—*The more of my people I can save, the better*—but it also meant the forward line was bulged inward in places. Some of that inward bulge came from enemy pressure. The rest was marked by the butchered bodies of Kessentai and cosslain, fallen where they had stood.

The great lord's chest heaved. There, near the end of that last rush it had come down to hand to hand. His boma blade dripped with the yellow blood of the locals.

Tulo looked around. *Yes, the last line but for this one and those on the inner rampart is almost boarded.* He then turned his attention to the mass of the locals, milling about between the walls. No one was currently engaging these, as if by common understanding that if shot at they might charge again. More of the locals were still pouring over the far wall in a flood, then coming to a confused, shuddering halt as they ran into the remnants of those who had preceded them.

If these addled-egg shit-eaters will give me half a chance, I'll get the rest aboard before the next rush. But . . . ah . . . shit.

Finba'anaga was frightened near witless. He'd never been a particularly courageous Kessentai, and had—deep down—known it, whatever his dreams might have been. Now, with the massed grunts and screams of the pressing aboriginals, the massed crack of railgun fire, the few wounded being carried through and the air of near panic as line after defensive line of the People tried to squeeze through the C-Dec's all too narrow portals . . .

Please, Finba thought . . . *please . . . something . . . anything . . . SAVE me.*

Ordinarily, Brasingala was not the sort to disobey orders. Rather, he was definitely of the "Render unto Caesar" type. But when Tulo'stenaloor had ordered him away he'd balked, even as he turned over command of the little tenar squadron to an underling, with instructions to move out and rendezvous as Tulo'stenaloor had decreed.

Thus, at the maximum distance his AS could make out and enhance the image of Tulo'stenaloor, and as near above the likely direction of travel of wayward flechettes as he could safely bring his tenar, Brasingala waited.

Even at that, he occasionally heard the crack of a passing flechette, sometimes coming even from above where he rode.

Only to be expected, he thought. *Even were they all well aimed—and they never are—some of them will bounce off others and go in any direction.*

The hearts inside Brasingala had nearly burst with pride, time and again, as he watched his lord coolly beat back one attack after another. Almost he dared to hope that they might come through safe, as he saw one line after another of the People file through the gaps in the inner rampart and onto the ship.

But then came the time when he saw that there was but a single file remaining outside the rampart, his lord in line with the rest. Too, he saw the refreshed and reinforced enemy make yet another push. By the time the last magazine to the last railgun was emptied, Brasingala heard Tulo'stenaloor give the order to Goloswin, "Board your people and lift, Tinkerer. And don't forget to pick up the tenar." Before the last sentence was finished Brasingala was already speeding at a rate no tenar was meant to go indefinitely to stand at the end by his lord's side.

❖   ❖   ❖

Tulo, with a cosslain on one side and a Kessentai on the other, slashed down at a charging normal, slicing the creature's head in two. Yellow blood burst up to smear across his scaly face. The God King laughed, a half-insane cackle of delight in battle, or "edan" in Low Posleen.

Not so bad to go this way, Tulo thought. *Better than being ground to nestling-in-an-intestinal-casing under the humans' artillery. Better than being hulled and frozen forever in space. Better than—*

Tulo heard the cry, from just above and behind him, "Save the clan lord!"

The other Kessentai nearby picked it up. "Save the clan lord!" Even the cosslain, without speech but still able to make sound, waved their boma blades high and trilled in time with the call. "Save the clan lord!"

Tulo stepped back, behind the cover of his two companions, the one shouting "Save the clan lord" and the other snarling defiance at the pressing subnormals. Brasingala appeared at his side, his tenar brought down to ground level.

"Take this, lord, and find safety," Brasingala said. "Better I die here than live with the shame of abandoning my chieftain."

"SAVE THE CLAN LORD!"

Over Tulo's AS came the sound of the Tinkerer's voice. "Take the tenar, Tulo. We will not lift without you."

"I ordered you . . . I ordered you *both*—"

"SAVE THE CLAN LORD!"

"There comes a time, lord," Brasingala said, "when even a bodyguard may disobey, when even a body-guard *must* disobey. Take the tenar, lord. Guard and guide the people for many years. And remember, if you will, that I did my duty to the last."

"SAVE THE CLAN LORD!"

There was no danger of ricocheting flechettes now. Atop Brasingala's tenar Tulo stood, his right arm and hand outstretched in a salute as the last of the little knots of fighting Posleen, Brasingala among them, went down under the tide of normals.

"I shall miss you, boy," Tulo said aloud. That was the most he could say aloud, though inside he wailed, *Brasingala, my son.*

There came a beeping warning from the C-Dec. Tulo knew it meant lift-off in one hundred beats. Though he couldn't see the locals because the inner redoubt and outer wall blocked the angle of view, still Tulo could imagine them in their thousands milling about the base of the C-Dec and the five landers, futilely trying to scratch their way in with their primitive flint knives.

"I wish I could see you bastards roast," he said. "Instead, I'll just stay a moment, watch the flames rise, and listen to you scream."

Tulo looked down at his left claw, the one not needed to guide the tenar. In it dripped a small gobbit of Brasingala's flesh that the guard had sliced off with his own boma blade.

"I had hoped that I would be part of the feast when I finally fell in your service, lord." So had the bodyguard said as he handed over the still warm flesh. "This will have to do. Remember me."

I'll not forget you, Son," said Tulo, sadly, as he gulped down the offering.

Ship Arganaza'al

The hateful planet lay below. After the battle, the scrawny normals had stuck around for some few rotations, gorging themselves on the flesh of the fallen. In time, though, they separated out into their various herds to continue their endless migration around the globe.

After those herds had dispersed, Tulo sent down small groups, never more than a single lander could escape with, to continue with mining and manufacturing. While the herds always came back within a few or a few dozen rotations, he was able to evacuate his people before the herds came too close. Never again did they have to fight a battle for survival down below.

Little by little, too, the ammunition stocks expended were replenished from the fruits of the mines and the forge. One by one, as well, replacement landers for those lost in the semi-collision with the asteroid were finished and lofted to join the C-Dec.

For the several hundred Kessentai and the more than a thousand cosslain lost there could be no immediate replacement.

"A boma blade has been thrust into the belly of our People," Tulo had announced, speaking from the bridge through the ship's intercom system. "There cannot be wailing and tears enough to mourn for our loss."

To that Goloswin and the remainder of Tulo's close followers had no answer. They too missed Brasingala. Nor was that Kessentai the only loss among them. Gorasinth'zula and Essone were also among the missing, and none could say precisely how and where they had fallen.

Tulo could replace the fallen field commander, Gorasinth'zula, from among those new members of his clan that had proven themselves down below. Where he was to come up with a new adjutant, however, he did not know.

"It isn't all loss, you know, Tulo," Goloswin insisted. "True, we lost some of our best, some of our *old*, long time best. But, on the other hand, those who are with us now are *with* us, tested in battle and forged in fire. I think we were not a true clan before. We *are* now."

"Waxing poetic in your old age, Tinkerer?" Tulo chided.

"Perhaps that's it," Golo conceded with an uncharacteristically shy smile. "Where now, Tulo?"

"I do not know. If that little unconsumed snack Aelool had—"

The view screen came on, seemingly of its own accord. The image of the Indowy spoke from it.

"Enough time has passed to reactivate this program," Aelool's image said. "By now, People of the Ships, you will have found the mystery down below. What that mystery is, none of us could say. Only could we say that the legends suggest it was the site of an important episode in your history. The fact that the nature of that importance was hidden from us told us that it was a *very* important episode in that history.

"You will stay here above this planet briefly before we continue on to the rest of our journey."

❖   ❖   ❖

"One other thing," Tulo said. "Before we depart I want a warning beacon put up, telling one and all what we have found here, and warning them of the full dangers."

"It shall be done," Essthree answered. *And if outing the truth pisses off the Aldenata, so much the better.*

"Let's see if *that* doesn't piss off the Aldenata, that we make public what they've done," Tulo said, which words got him a very odd stare from the Essthree.

"And let us declare a day and a feast of gratitude," Tulo finished, "that our People have been yet again delivered from the 'mercies' of the Aldenata."

The cosslain—but for the servers, one per Kessentai—were not excluded from the feast. They simply weren't invited. In any event, few of them would have understood or much cared had they understood. They would be fed extra rations even so.

Of the relatively few normals carried and awakened from hibernation, seventeen *were* invited to the feast. Indeed, they were guests of honor, after a fashion. Each was led in by a cosslain server. Another cosslain followed close behind.

The seventeen normals were garlanded in wreaths made of mixed leaves of heavy metal and baser stuff. Over the back of each was laid a sort of blanket, embroidered with various symbols and writing that neither the normals nor the cosslain embroiderers really understood.

The symbols varied. One might have an odd, five-candled menorah. Yet another wore crossed boma blades. Two showed burning towers. Upon the very last was a symbolic battleglobe.

The words were taken from the sacred scrolls of the Rememberers. "As theirs was the praise; let theirs be the blame . . . Eat that ye might live . . . All of life is a struggle . . . They claimed to know and yet they knew not . . ."

The central hall of the C-Dec *Arganaza'al* went quiet as the first cosslain, leading a garlanded, bedecked normal, made its appearance at the main entrance. This was followed by another, and yet another, and still more until all seventeen had entered.

The procession wound around the edges of the hall, then broke up, with a trio of two cosslain and a normal going to each of the seventeen groups that stood in neat circles. The trio with the normal bearing an embroidered battleglobe went to the center of the circle of Tulo'stenaloor and his closest followers, plus those the followers had invited as being especially worthy. Finba'anaga, favored of Goloswin, was among these last.

The normals, nonsentient as they were, were still upset by all the attention. Their claws scratched nervously at the metallic deck beneath them. The cosslain leading them patted their faces and made calming, cooing sounds.

"Rememberer?" Tulo called out, loudly enough for all present to hear.

That worthy, in full ceremonial harness replete with shining heavy metal and bearing an ancient, handwritten scroll in one hand and ceremonial stone weights in the other, backed off from Tulo's core group and walked steadily to a dais even then raising itself from the deck. From the dais came a slender podium. Upon this the Rememberer laid out his scroll, weighting the corners with his stones.

"A reading from the Scroll of Tenusaniar," the Rememberer announced. Each Kessentai present bowed his head, as did the cosslain in imitation.

"'Marooned were the People," the Rememberer began, "marooned by command of those they held to be gods. Marooned were the People on a planet that could not support their numbers. Marooned were the People, and forced to consume little but the product of the food dispensers.

"And with no outlet, and with no enemies, the numbers of the People grew and grew and grew beyond even the ability of the food dispensers to provide for.

"Worse, the planet of the People's exile was surrounded with automated defenses, of the kind the Aldenata had forbidden the People, but allowed to themselves. There was no escape but only the Hell of an eternity of sameness and shortage and hunger and pain.

"This was the payment of the Aldenata to those who had been most loyal to them.

"And then one of the Kessentai discovered a new way out, fraught with danger but invisible and invulnerable to the Aldenata's demonic defenses. That Kessentai, whose name is known but to the spirits of the ancestors, had discovered 'tunneling' through space."

The mass of God Kings present raised their muzzles as one, chanting, "All hail the unknown deliverer. All hail the knowledge he brought."

"And then was the galaxy reopened..."

The Rememberer's reading and sermon were over. He said, "Let us sing a hymn of praise."

The words were old, ancient beyond reckoning.

Some were outright unintelligible. Yet all Kessentai knew it.

> *"Hail deliverers, hail;*
> *Who brought us safe from exile*
> *And led us in our wanderings*
> *Through the night*
> *By our blood*
> *To the light."*

At that last line, each of the cosslain accompanying a normal drew a boma blade, lifting them high. The cosslain who led the normals reached into pouches and drew forth handfuls of grain. These they held low, causing the normals to bend their heads to eat from their hands.

> *"Long have we traveled, sires,*
> *Seeking the things you sought."*

At that word—"sought"—the Rememberer raised his claws high, then brought them down suddenly. This was the signal for each boma blade-wielding cosslain to swing his monomolecular sword down, thus severing seventeen normals' heads instantly, and essentially without pain. Yellow blood gushed from seventeen fountains. The normals' oddly jointed knees buckled as one, letting their headless bodies sink to the deck.

"And now," said the Rememberer, "let us feast upon the bodies of those who have given their lives for us. And let us remember them as good beings, who served the People unto the last."

❖   ❖   ❖

Three ship days later the antimatter engines once again drove the ship into transitspace. When it emerged, it was to—

"What the fuck?" Tulo asked, of no one in particular. His eyes were fixed on the genuinely bizarre apparition on the viewscreen.

Goloswin watched a smaller screen as the virus that he had almost succeeded in breaking once again mutated into something new. He had, so far, avoided looking up from the little screen to the larger one. After all, when the ship had popped out of transitspace in between the Orion and Sagittarius arms of the galaxy, an empty place without stars or planets and therefore a place where the Posleen couldn't *hope* to refuel, Goloswin had simply assumed they were all dead.

He looked up now though. And rather wished he had not. There, on the screen, was a gas giant, where no gas giant should have been. But it wasn't just any gas giant. Oh, no; this one was an *antimatter* gas giant. The sensors said as much, even as they tried to deny the possibility.

"There's a theory," Golo said, "that at the moment of the creation of the universe it could have gone either way, matter or antimatter. The theory considers it possible that *some* stars or planets, a very small number, went antimatter, even so. As for what such a one is doing *here*, though, I have no explanation." He shrugged. "I suppose that the only place where such a planet could survive would be between the galaxies, or between the arms of a spiral galaxy."

"I can accept that," Tulo admitted grudgingly.

"What I cannot accept is *that*." He set a caret over an utterly black spot in space to which streamed a thin trail of antimatter, which promptly disappeared as it reached the spot, creating a halo of faint light around it from the destruction of matter. That any light should be able to escape a black hole was a measure of the intensity of the energies created by the destruction of that matter.

"A black hole where none ought be, eating a planet which would be *such* a low order of probability...even if it were normal matter...which it isn't...

"Golo, who the fuck is doing this?" The clan lord nearly wept. "It isn't the Indowy, Golo. I've *eaten* Indowy; their brains are just not that fucking big. Golo...I...we...What's the lowest order probability there is? Shall we jump again and find the human God?"

"I don't know, Tulo," Goloswin said. "But since we have the antimatter available, maybe we should, for now, just refuel."

"My name doesn't matter," said the image on the screen. It was not the image of Aelool. It wasn't the image of any species with which any of the Posleen were exactly familiar. This creature was bipedal, its skin was the mottled green of a bullfrog. It had four eyes mounted on its shoulders, two to either side, the inner ones slightly lower than the outer. The was a large mouth mounted just below where in a human would be a chest, making it look scary even to Posleen. Furthermore, this creature was not an "it." There were definite genitalia, down in the protected place between its legs.

"Nor does the identity of my people matter. Forget the Indowy; he was a pawn."

"By this point in time you will be between galactic arms and you should be refueling. We have been in control of your ship so far. We are modifying that control now. You have some choices again.

"You will want to know where you should go from here," the recording of the unknown species continued. "There are at least five options."

The image disappeared, to be replaced by a star map of the nearest portion of the Sagittarius arm of the galaxy. Posleen numbers appeared by five systems, each number with a stylized arrow pointing to a specific sun.

"These are all systems we think important to your People, Tulo'stenaloor. We know of no dangers associated with them. Whether you choose to visit one, two, all or none of them is up to you. We think you should visit all."

"I will reappear when you summon me," the image concluded, "provided that enough time has passed for you to have reached one of those marked systems."

"Your call, Rememberer," Tulo said, several orbits later. "Which, if any, of those systems shall we visit?"

"I have consulted the scrolls," the cleric answered. "My answer is that, despite recent occurrences, we should take the . . . virus's advice and see them all. After all," he added, "we're not exactly in a hurry to get anywhere, are we?"

"Put that way," Tulo agreed, "I suppose not. Are there any objections?"

Seeing none, the clan lord commanded, "Essthree, set us a course for the nearest of those stars."

The image of the unknown species once again

appeared on the viewscreen. "Excellent choice," it said. "Relax, I shall take you there. You may have noted the black hole that marks a route on the Hidden Path. This is going to be a longer jump than you are used to. Rather, it is going to be a longer series of longer jumps than you are used to."

CHAPTER TWENTY

But Allah was also plotting,
and Allah is the best of plotters.
—The Koran, Sura 3:54, Sura 8:30

Anno Domini 2020 through Anno Domini 2021
USS Salem, *entering the Hemaleen system*

Posleen grew *fast*. Really fast. So fast that . . .

"I just fitted you for new armor, Freddie," Sally said. "Do you really need a new cuirass so soon?"

"And a new champron, Sally," the boy said, hanging his head. "I'm sorry."

"Oh nonsense," she answered. "Nothing to be sorry about. You just . . . done growed. Give me—"

The PA system gave a soft whoop and then began to spout, "Captain to the bridge. Lieutenant Kreuzer-Dwyer to the bridge. Reverend Doctor Guanamarioch to the bridge. Swiss Guards, bring the Indowy prisoner, Aelool, to the bridge. *Wachtmeister* von Altishofen to the Bridge."

"I'll have your new outfit tomorrow, Freddie," Sally called over her shoulder as she hurried off.

A spinning dodecahedron, gold in color, filled the center of the view screen. A linear scale on the right side indicated it was less than half a meter in diameter. A long series of Posleen syllables, plus grunts, snarls and glottal stops, came from the speakers and presumably from the dodecahedron.

"Is it dangerous?" von Altishofen asked.

Sally, the woman, shook her head slowly as her colloidal brain took in the translated information streaming from the AID Sally. "No...no...but it's warning us of danger down below. It seems the band of Tulo'stenaloor landed to make repairs and was attacked."

"Isss...eeevvviiilll...thinkgkgk beeelllllooow," Guanamarioch said, directly, not bothering to have his AS translate. "Ifff...sssennnddd...parrrtttyyy dowwwnnn...sssooonnn...wwwiiifffe...sssellllfff...notttt gggooo."

"Think landsharks, Dan," Sally added. "Piranha with legs, millions of 'em. Maybe billions. Add in an abortifacient disease. I'm not even sure little Freddie...well...*not* so little Freddie, at this point, would be safe."

"Eeevvviiilll thinkgkgk," Guano repeated, his reptilian lip curling in a sneer. "Dessstttrrrrooooyyy sssennntiiiennnt llllifffe...lllleaeaeavvve onlllyyy nonnn...sssennntiiiennnt."

"Indeed," Dwyer agreed, "and precisely what some of Earth's fanatics were insisting upon, just before the war."

"We didn't know this is what we were sending that group into," Aelool offered.

The Posleen fixed the Indowy with a baleful stare. "Zzzooo? Zzzisss mmmaaakkkesss it allll bbbettterrr?"

Ignoring the aliens, Dwyer looked directly at von Altishofen. "*Wachtmeister?*"

"Yes, Captain."

"We'll take the pinnace. Prepare a security party to support the landing. Party consists of myself, your team and, since we're facing some kind of disease, Chief Nurse Duvall. Full arms, armor, and ammunition."

"Dan," Sally interrupted, "we've an archeologist aboard, Imam al Rashid. I'm getting some odd signatures from below the surface that suggest you might want to look."

"Fine," he agreed. "Even makes sense. First thing, though, I want to look at the spot the Posleen landed. Sally, you'll be in command up here."

From above, the scene looked like a nearly circular thirty square kilometer field of yellow bones, massed and tangled and decorated with Posleen skulls.

"Must be a million of them," von Altishofen whispered, as the little pinnace settled down.

"More like three million," said Sally's voice, over the pinnace's speakers.

De Courten gulped. "I've never seen anything like this."

"I have," said von Altishofen, seated next to Duvall on the right-hand canvas troop bench. The two had come to spend a fair amount of time together, these last couple of months. All the Switzers had noticed, and all had bet on the probability the *Wachtmeister* and the nurse were sleeping together. So far, there'd been not a shred of evidence for *that*.

"During the war, one globe landed right in the middle of one of the fortified zones and was butchered without any appreciable number of survivors. A year later we still hadn't cleared all the bones out. It looked something like this.

"Something to remember," the *Wachtmeister* added, "Posleen bones have a ridge for strength. Depending on the bone, it can be sharp."

Everyone on the landing party went silent then, as the pinnace descended on jets to a bone-crunching landing. Not that the landing was especially jarring from the passengers' points of view. Indeed, it was very gentle, just as one would expect with Sally's AID flying the ship under remote control. Rather, it was impossible to find a spot in the entire thirty square kilometers where the pinnace's landing gear would not crunch the bones left behind by the Posleen.

Once the pinnace stopped rocking on its landing gear, Sally opened the ramp that extended from underneath. More Posleen bones crunched. This time they were completely audible by the landing party. Though the slaughter here had been many years before, still a faint wash of the stench of corruption entered the pinnace as the ramp opened.

"Swiss Guard, perimeter security!" von Altishofen ordered. Immediately, in two files with the *Wachtmeister* in the middle, the Switzers tramped down the ramp and peeled off to set up security around the chosen site. They wore the body armor and helmets Sally had made them for halberd drill because, as it turned out, the monomolecular structure of those was infinitely tougher than the human-made body armor they'd brought on the journey with them. They'd still left behind their halberds, carrying instead the SIG-Sauer rifles Dwyer had first seen back in Rome.

Once they hit the ground, the men had to walk carefully to keep from either stumbling over, or slashing their legs on, the still uncrushed bones around the pinnace. It was a lot like walking through "clear cut" former forest, organic barbed wire, in other words.

Note to self, von Altishofen thought. *Ask Sally to make us greaves as well.*

After the several minutes it took for the men to get into position, von Altishofen announced to Dwyer, "Area clear, Father. You, Nurse Duvall, and the Indowy can come out. Step carefully."

Duvall was busied not far away with taking bone samples and even a few scrapings of flesh from inside Posleen skulls.

Aelool was visibly shaken by the spectacle. Dwyer had seen the reaction before, on Sintarleen, who had been the old *Des Moines'* Indowy chief engineer, back during the war. Part of it was the "fur" on Aelool's face, which began weaving furiously. This was the Indowy equivalent of sweating, the hairs acting as a sort of fan to run cooler air over the skin. Yet the planet was not especially hot. Then, too, while Aelool was a remarkably bold Indowy, willing not just to stare at someone else's shoes rather than his own, but even willing to look a human in the face, at seeing the field of bones he just put his own head down, whispering, "I had no idea we were sending Tulo'stenaloor's band into this. None of us of the Bane Sidhe did."

"It's what you get, Aelool, for playing gods," the priest said. "But if it's any consolation, some of them, at least, survived their landing here."

"It's devilish," Nurse Duvall pronounced, after finishing her tests with the small portable lab aboard the pinnace and then running those results by Sally, the AID. "Monstrous. Killing while still in their eggs only the ones who are going to be real people..."

"Your Catholicism is showing, Gina," Dwyer said. "As it happens—go figure—I agree with you. It's monstrous. But is it communicable to our Posleen?"

"No," she shook her head. "The warning beacon was correct. The prions that our Posleen carry that make them too dangerous for anything else to eat act as a sort of high intensity gamma globulin."

"That's something anyway. But we still can't bring them down here for the next step or—and assuming the beacon's right about that, too—we'll have a few million legged piranha on steroids on us in no time. Damn. I wish there was a way we could bring at least Guanamarioch with us, to translate anything we might find. But his pheromones..."

Duvall tried really hard, and mostly succeeded, not to look at the priest as if he were stupid. After all, she *was* a Catholic and he *was* a Jesuit. "Well...why not have Sally make up a self-contained quarantine suit with the forge?"

USS Salem

Guano hastily put away his carving into his pouch when Sally's voice came through the speaker, asking for admittance to his quarters. Frederico, instead of running to her and half bowling her over (and at his current growth the smart money was on not "half" bowling her over), contented himself with placing his chin over her right shoulder (and not pressing down too hard). Querida trilled a welcome.

"May I help you, Lieutenant Kreuzer-Dwyer?" Guano asked through the AS. Even as the machine translated, Guano asked himself, *Why do I end up with the really formal ones? Is it something they pick up from me? Some flaw of pride deep in my character? I must think on this.*

"They want you below," Sally answered. *I know it's probably wrong but I just can't trust this grown God King. I wish I could.*

Guano shook his head. "That, as explained, I cannot do."

"Yes, you can. I came here to fit you for a quarantine suit. I'll do it up in the forge."

Frederico looked at his father, saw he was wavering, and asked, "Can I come, too, Dad?"

Guano sighed, an unPosleenlike habit he'd picked up from the humans. "No, Son. Sorry, but no. Too dangerous."

To Sally, he said, "Very well, madam, take your measurements. I'll go."

❖   ❖   ❖

Dwyer was unwilling to risk the landing party for even so long as it would take for the pinnace to go from shore to ship and back again. Instead, he loaded the entire crew back aboard and went to pick up Guano. Besides, Duvall wanted to run some tests that her portable lab just wasn't up to.

"I feel absurd," the Posleen said as he boarded. "This is not the wear of a Kessentai. It's a dunce's cap."

Dwyer looked the minister over. It was true enough that the Posleen looked like no Posleen Dwyer had ever seen, his head and body all covered with a silvery fabric with clear plastic eyeholes and tanks and tubes. "You look fine, Guano. And it is necessary for your health and ours."

"You realize, yes, that the ship could not come up with an acceptable system for evacuation of solid and liquid waste? Yes, yes . . . she had a way to get it out of me and the suit, but no way to ensure that it would not attract the feral normals below. I am going to have to wallow in my own shit and piss until we get back."

"We'll try to be quick," Dwyer reassured the Posleen. "But there is something below, something the band of Posleen who preceded us probably missed. It might be an ancient city. Sally, at least, thinks it is. We need to look at it."

Again Guano sighed. "I understand. Let us proceed."

Hemaleen V

Here there were no bones. The pinnace sat on its landing gear a few score meters away. There were no feral herds within a hundred miles, though there might have been individuals. These would have been too insignificant for Sally to spot from space.

The colors were off, for a human. The grass, or the thin bladed plant life that served as a cognate for grass, was orange-yellow. The trees were something like palms, but thicker and also with orange-yellow fronds. The water of the stream that flowed nearby was a reddish color, no doubt picked up from the alluvial soil it contained.

"That's the spot, Dan," Sally said over the radio. "A pyramid below you about fifteen feet. It's big. If you don't find an entrance near the top it's too big for a small crew to dig. Yes, before you ask, I'm working on a way to remove the stuff quickly and in large volume without damaging whatever may be buried there. I don't expect to succeed."

"You heard the lady, *Herr Wachtmeister*." Dwyer pointed at the ground. "Have your men start digging down here."

"Cristiano, security," von Altishofen ordered. "Grosskopf, dig."

"They must be careful," Imam al Rashid cautioned. "We don't want to be Schliemanns, ruining precisely what we seek in the seeking."

Al Rashid was an odd duck, to Dwyer's way of thinking. He was a Moslem, the only one aboard. But if Dwyer had ever met a Moslem so well versed in the Old Testament and the New, in the Bhagavad-Gita, in the writings of Confucius and Lao Tzu . . . *Well, no, I never did meet anyone quite like this one.*

The imam noticed Dwyer's concentrated stare, the narrow eyes, the quizzical mouth. "You are wondering what I am doing as an imam, aren't you?"

"Yes."

"I love the past," al Rashid said. "I want to know it, to understand it. It is the time when man was closest to God...when I touch it...I come a little closer to touching Him."

Dwyer thought of his own reverent fingers and his laying them upon the walls of the catacombs under Rome. *And perhaps that is true of all religious men, Imam.*

Hellebardier Johann Scheekt rested his shovel for a moment, taking the break to wipe off the sweat that poured from his brow. He couldn't even begin to fathom the long ages that had buried what was said to be below so deeply, and under such a compact soil. Never mind that the shovel's edge was monomolecular. Never mind that it cut through dirt and rock with relative ease. The damned soil was still *heavy,* and, with the pit driven nearly five meters down, getting rid of the spoil was a backbreaking endeavor. Indeed, two thirds of each shift was now concentrated on removing the spoil, rather than digging.

Scheekt lifted his shovel, drawing it back for another scoop. "Wait," al Rashid commanded, as he bent down to brush away some soil with his fingers.

The flat top of the pyramid looked glassy smooth, yet gave good traction. In this, it was not very different from the pyramids the stonemason normals had constructed for the greater of their God Kings back on Earth.

"The entrance will be there, on that side," Guano said, pointing to the northern edge of the platform.

Al Rashid smiled. "You don't know how you know that, do you?" When the Posleen shook his head in the negative, the imam said, "Our ancestors did much the same thing. Within human archeological sites there are certain things, placement of temples and palaces, in particular, where those differ, that are almost always the same." The imam shrugged. "Something buried deep in our collective psyche, I suspect."

"I don't know," the Posleen answered. "But I do know that the entrance will be there. Rather, the upper one will be."

Digging down to the entrance of the pyramid proved easier than getting into it. A powered door, wide enough for a tenar, the thing had so long ago lost its power that all Guano's efforts proved unavailing.

"It's dead," the Kessentai said in wonder. "Have you any idea how long ago its power source must have been left unattended and unrefueled for it to be *dead*?"

"No," al Rashid said.

"Neither do I."

"Well, what do we do then?" Dwyer asked. "Blast it?"

Al Rashid's look of utter, unspeakable horror nipped that idea in the bud.

"Then *what*? Do we turn around and just forget about it?"

That got a look of even more unspeakable horror from al Rashid. "*What?* Turn our backs on what could be the greatest archeological discovery of this or any age? Are you *mad*? There has to be a way in that doesn't involve wrecking the place."

All eyes turned to Guano who hastened to say,

through his new AS, "Don't look at me. I haven't the first clue of how to get in there."

The AS made a sound that to all ears sounded a lot like "Ahem."

"Perhaps I do, lord," it said in High Posleen. "About another eight measures down and slightly to the west. Though, I confess, I don't know how any of you will fit through it. And I am not self mobile."

An Earth week later, Aelool walked unsteadily down the wooden steps—of local wood—that had been laid against the side of the pyramid. The Indowy wore what amounted to a miner's helmet, with a light in front. Above him, to prevent a rockslide, the crew had erected a metal framework, made of sections in the forge and shuttled down by the pinnace. Outside the framework? The rock of ages.

"You told us you wanted a way to make amends," Dwyer said, standing at the foot of the steps with von Altishofen and *Hellebardier* Dolf Beck standing to either side and a little behind. "This will go some way towards doing that."

"I understand," Aelool said. "You will forgive me if I am a little nervous at the prospect of entering the ancient den of omnivores alone."

"You won't be alone for long," Dwyer answered. "The AS says, and Guanamarioch confirms, that there's an interior manual crank on the upper entrance that is unlikely to have been adversely affected by any conceivable lapse of time or neglect. The inside of the pyramid is a winding ramp. Use that to get to the crank and force the portal open." For a brief moment Dwyer remembered his old Indowy shipmate,

Sintarleen or "Sinbad," as he was called, hefting a two-hundred-and-forty pound, eight-inch shell on each of his shoulders. "I have good reason to think you're strong enough for the job."

"Probably," Aelool agreed. "Truth be told, pound for pound we Indowy are considerably stronger even then Posleen. Though by that measure the Elves"—the Darhel—"are stronger still. In any case, lead me to the 'entrance.' I'll go in."

"This way," Dwyer said, leaning his head in the desired direction. After a few steps, and by the artificial light panel the excavation crew had hung, Aelool saw a small triangular opening. Just past that was Guano.

"What was this?" he asked.

Dwyer grimaced. "It was the . . . ummm . . . errr . . ."

"It was the shit chute," Guanamarioch answered through his AS. "I should have remembered it. They're too small for an enemy assassin to enter. Gravity, normally aided by running water, disposes of the waste of the inhabitants of the pyramid."

The Indowy's face took on a look that Dwyer read as meaning, "That's disgusting."

"Don't worry about it," the Jesuit said. "After all this time there's unlikely to be anything on the chute that's distinguishable from any other soil or dust with a bit of organic to it."

Grimly, the Indowy nodded agreement. Even as he did, the pseudo-hairs on his face began to writhe.

"Let's get it over with, then. The sooner I can open the main door, the sooner I won't have to be alone in there . . . or in fear of being alone in there."

Dwyer nodded at von Altishofen, standing behind the Indowy. The *Wachtmeister* took a couple of steps around the Indowy, while Beck walked up to stand behind the small alien. Both bent at the waist and cupped their hands.

"Stand on those, Aelool," the Switzer said.

The Indowy did and immediately felt himself being raised to the waste chute. He bent at the waist and stuck his head through the small portal. As soon as he did, his body blocked the light and his world was plunged into darkness.

CHAPTER TWENTY-ONE

Thus were the disparate People of many clans
Made one, under our great lord.
And as from every evil can flow good,
So, too, from every good can evil flow.
—The *Tuloriad*, Na'agastenalooren

Anno Domini 2011
Posleen Ship Arganaza'al, *Sagittarius Arm*

The Posleen were not a people to mourn their losses overlong. After the disaster, and it *was* a disaster, of Hemaleen V, they tallied their dead and missing (and for the Posleen, fighting amongst themselves, missing pretty much invariably meant dead), reorganized, reassigned lessers who had lost their Kessentai to other Kessentai, and got on with the business of their journey. For many, that business meant no more than reentering hibernation.

Of their new target, those still awake knew little beyond that it was a fairly wet world orbiting a gas giant, itself orbiting a rare double sun. Of details, they had few, and a name for the place was not among these. One detail they did have said that the world was perpetually lit, either by direct light from the suns or by refection from the gas giant. The orbit of the world about its giant matched the orbit of the giant about its suns, keeping the world between the two.

There was a low Posleen word, Nura'gantar, which meant "to work sleeplessly, like a machine, until death."

"That's what we'll call the place," Tulo said, "since we lack a better name and the eternal light implies eternally delayed rest."

"'Nura' for short?" Binastarion asked.

"Works for me."

That world was still many months away. Even so, Tulo and Esstwo studied it, on their glowing view screens, for what little could be gleaned from the infection of their navigational computer.

In the center of the ship, in a cubicle off of Engineering that Finba'anaga had set aside for himself, a greenish glow from a screen lit his crocodilian face. This lent the thing a more sinister aspect than even the Posleen norm. Despite the glow, his mood and thoughts were darker than the space around the ship. The Kessentai who had become his friend, Borasmena, stood in the cubicle with him.

To the latter Finba said, "We were almost destroyed. Destroyed! What kind of power could still reach out after uncounted millennia to try to destroy us?"

The Kessentai trembled involuntarily. He'd been afraid during Binastarion's "intelligence test." He'd been frightened of being spaced—or being chopped—after assimilation into the clan of Tulo'stenaloor. He'd put up with myriad humiliations large and small to prevent those things, then wormed his way into Goloswin's good graces to keep himself off the chopping block and the menu.

And not a bit of it mattered, not when the Aldenata's power was shown. How have we sinned against them, that they should hate us so . . . that their hate should carry over across the eons and the light years?

Again, the Kessentai involuntarily trembled.

"Relax, Finba," said Borasmena. "We survived. That's all that counts."

I must find out what it is that caused them so to hate us . . . find out and make it right, lest they, in their anger, destroy me as well. And if I can't make it right? I'll have to find a way to nullify it.

To Borasmena Finba said much the same thing, then asked, "Can I count on you to support me?"

"Of course," the other Kessentai assured him. "You're not only a lot smarter than I am, you're my friend as well."

"I am going to become a Rememberer," Finba announced, "the first one not to toss his stick, if I can avoid tossing it."

"That I'd like to see," agreed Borasmena.

"What do we know of this place, Rememberer?" Tulo'stenaloor asked. "The . . . infection has not even a name for it."

"It does not appear in the scrolls under any name, either, Tulo," the Rememberer answered. "And that, itself, I find highly suspicious."

Tulo dug the claws of his left hand into his muzzle and face, almost hard enough to draw blood. It was a sign of worry. "Should we give it a miss then, do you think?"

The cleric chewed his lower lip for a while, thinking upon it. Finally, he shook his head in negation. "We should look, perhaps. But unless we find something very interesting I think we should not get too close."

Tulo's claws relaxed. "Good advice, that. As you say, so shall it be."

Finba'anaga emerged from his cubicle when he heard Goloswin's footsteps on the deck of the engine room.

"Lord Goloswin?" Finba asked, with his head down in respect.

"Yes, puppy?"

"I would like your permission to make an appointment with the Rememberer, to add to my studies."

Like all his people, Goloswin had a great deal of respect for the clerics, as he did for what remained of the fragmentary history of his people. Still, that respect was tempered with a suspicion that the Rememberers didn't tell everything that they knew, that there were some scrolls that were secret, and some legends and rumors with more basis in fact than ever a Rememberer would admit to. This was a distant annoyance to Golo, but only that. He, too, after all, had his little secrets, even as he devoted his life to ferreting out the secrets of science and technology.

"Remembrance is not obviously in your skill set," Golo cautioned.

"True, lord," Finba agreed. "Yet it has become an interest of mine. I wish merely for greater understanding, not to throw my stick and don the golden harness."

Golo's yellow eyes narrowed with suspicion. "You will not neglect your duties with the engines."

"Never, lord. I would study, if the Rememberer agrees, during my off cycle."

Goloswin considered this for perhaps a hundred beats, remaining silent throughout so that Finba's hearts began to thrum with anxiety within him. Finally, the Tinkerer signed agreement. *What can it hurt, after all?*

"I will put in a word with our Rememberer for you," the senior Kessentai said.

"Thank you, lord."

In the main assembly hall, the same one where Tulo had greeted the new acquisitions, the Rememberer was concluding his service.

"We thank you, ancestral spirits," the Rememberer intoned, his clawed arms raised above him in supplication. "We thank you for your care. We thank you for your oversight. We thank you for the memories of valor you have bequeathed us, which memories have seen us through such difficult days."

"We remember," chanted the massed Kessentai.

"And now, a reading from the Scroll of Wayward Journeys," the Rememberer said.

"He does not really seem the type," the Rememberer said to Golo, after services. "And he has his stick still."

"I don't think he wishes to don the golden harness," Golo answered. Rememberers wore harnesses of, depending on their personal status, gold or gilded leather. "At least he says he does not. He says, too, that he has no intention of throwing his stick. Yet, he is very clever, with a wide ranging skill set we've barely begun to explore. It might be good—good for the Clan of Sten—to let him expand his mind a bit with the scrolls."

"Let me think upon it," the Rememberer said. "Perhaps, as you say, it will be a useful thing for the clan to have a Kessentai versed in both your arcane arts and the wisdom of the ancients.

"This is a new day. Never before have the People been defeated in war, except by others of the People. Never before have we had to flee a planet, except from ourselves. Perhaps new ways are called for, however much it may grate."

"This was my precise thought," Golo agreed.

"I shall think, too. Tell the Kessentai that if I think it worthwhile I shall interview him. Does this Finba'anaga seem the credulous type?"

"No, not at all," Golo answered.

The Posleen prayed to the ancestors sometimes, usually in public, with arms raised in supplication. At others, more commonly in private, an eyes-closed, head-down, arms-folded form was more typical. It was in the latter pose that the Rememberer communed with his ancestral spirits.

Spirits, guide me, for I don't know what to do. I have no worthy successor. Of the Kessenalt, all continue to support the Path of Fury, even if they do not fight directly, themselves. And none of the other Kessentai have thrown their sticks yet, to make them suitable replacements for me. And I am growing old, ancestors, old. I have seen more than a dozen worlds descend into orna'adar. Soon I will join you. What shall happen to this last, so far as we know, fragment of the People when I am gone?

There is a young Kessentai, one who has not thrown his stick, who wishes to study under me. He seems not the type, from all I can observe and despite what his current overlord says.

And yet, he is all I have. Should I reject his plea? Should I accept it and hope that learning the ways of the Scrolls and of the history of our People will persuade him to follow our path?

Guide me, spirits, for I am small and alone and lost.

The Rememberer had his own cosslain, an assistant of sorts, but that cosslain was not a part of the interview. Rather, the Rememberer interviewed Finba'anaga himself.

"Why, puppy?" The Rememberer scowled. "Why does it interest you? My guild's art is not solid and hard. It is not something to be held and grasped and manipulated like a boma blade or the antimatter you toy with."

Even this early in his life, Finba had grasped that the partial truth was often the best lie. "The last planet, Hemaleen Five? The power of the Aldenata terrified me for our People. I wish to understand them, that we might survive them."

The Rememberer considered. "That's a fair answer," he said. "But what if I told you that there is no defense against the Aldenata, except to flee their reach? For they will always try to 'help' you."

"Then I would like to learn how best to keep out of that reach," Finba answered, without a blink of his yellow eyes.

"There are tales," the Rememberer agreed, with a slow nod. "There are legends. There are also scrolls that are written in a language you cannot read now. Are you willing to learn a new language?"

"I am, lord . . . if I am able."

"Indeed. A fairly humble admission, on your part, that you might not be able."

"I can only try, lord," Finba said.

Again the Rememberer nodded. He turned away from Finba and took three steps to reach a gilded chest, the usual burden of his cosslain assistant. He placed one claw upon a portion of the chest, causing it to wheeze open of its own accord. From the chest he drew a tubular wrapping of some kind of animal skin. The tube he rolled down, reverently, exposing a golden scroll.

"This is pure heavy metal," the Rememberer said, holding the scroll aloft, "but its value does not lie in the material. It is a language manual, the only one of its kind I know of in existence." He began to hand the scroll to Finba'anaga, then apparently thought better of it.

"You would not believe the edas I incurred for this. If you lose it, or damage it, or scuff it, or bend it, or mar it, or treat it with anything but the utmost reverence and care, I will get Lord Tulo to allow one thousand eggs to be hatched into one thousand hungry nestlings. I will then have you bound and thrown to those nestlings. Those nestlings shall then be burned with fire so that no part of you continues in existence. Do I make myself clear?"

Almost Finba refused the offering. He was quite certain that the Rememberer would make good the threat, should anything happen to the scroll. Still, he gulped out, "You are very clear, lord."

The Rememberer did then offer the scroll. "Take it then, and do not forget my warnings."

More than half reluctantly, Finba took it. Carefully and reverently he opened the scroll part way, peering down at the tiny writing engraved thereon.

"Lord, this is our writing," he said, in confusion.

"Look more carefully, puppy."

Finba did. At first it didn't register fully, but after a few moments' concentration, he said, "I see. It's all our writing, but half is not our language. What language is it, lord?"

"It's the demons' tongue," the Rememberer spat out. "It's Aldenata. Learn it, and then there will be other scrolls you will be able to read."

A Posleen Kessentai rarely knew what his genetically encoded skill set would be until the need arose. Often, the need arose and the skill just wasn't there. This did not mean, however, that something for which there was no genetic encoding was necessarily beyond the Kessentai, merely that . . .

"Demon-spawn, accursed, never-sufficiently-to-be-damned, bastard, addled-egg Aldenata fucking gobbledygook! This is too fucking hard!"

Not for the first time, Finba twisted his crocodilian head to one side and slammed it on the reading table in front of him. He was, of course, careful to move the scroll out of the way first; there was that (he was certain not idle) threat of a thousand hungry nestlings—little mouths, sharp teeth, big appetites, slow digestion—to consider, after all.

"Better you than me," commented Borasmena.

"And on that happy note," he added, "I've some chores to do."

After the table ceased reverberating, and Boras had left, Finba lifted his head, sighed, and said, aloud, "How is one supposed to learn a language where every verb is irregular, where there is no word to describe 'fight,' except an obscure obscenity, and four hundred and thirty-two verbs for various versions and aspects of 'to love'? Where a verb that means 'die' can also mean, depending on altogether too subtle context, 'cease function,' 'ascend,' 'descend,' 'translate,' 'cross over,' 'fuck like abat,' and 'wash the linen'? How does one learn a language where *every* statement is wrapped around with an inviolable moral command? And how can that be with a language that has no word for 'honor?' I—"

Finba'anaga was about to say, "I give up." Then he remembered that giving up could also mean his death. *No . . . I can't give up. I must understand these beings. They're simply too frightfully powerful not to.*

He pulled the scroll back toward his chest and began, once again, trying to fathom the seemingly unfathomable.

"How are your studies, coming, puppy?" the Rememberer asked, several ship cycles later.

"They're . . . coming," Finba answered.

The Rememberer gave a toothy Posleen grin. "I understand. For whatever it may be worth to you, learning that language took me, well, a very long time."

Finba sighed. "How did you stand it?"

"I truly don't know. Perhaps because it gave me yet another reason to loathe the Aldenata . . . not that any of the People lack for reasons."

"Why do they hate us so?" Finba'anaga asked.

"Hate us, puppy? They don't hate us. We're less than bugs to them." The Rememberer walked to the table that held the golden scroll and unrolled it nearly to the end. His skilled claw pointed at a particular word. "Do you know what that means, boy?"

Finba shook his head.

"That's their word for us, and it means 'little, stupid, ugly, immoral, and expendable primitives, raised from the muck.'"

Tulo'stenaloor, Binastarion, Goloswin and Esstwo and Essthree contemplated the little ball of mud, lately named Nura'gantar, hanging still and silent on the bridge's main view screen.

"Orna'adar," Esstwo pronounced. "And worse than I've ever heard of. That entire planet is poisoned to us or to any life. It is dead, dead, dead."

"I could go down, alone," Goloswin suggested. "Tests on my Himmit-metal suit indicate it can ward off a great deal of hard radiation."

"Too risky," Tulo answered. "We'll send down a lander to do a survey of some of the least contaminated sites. Binastarion, that's your job."

"No problem, Tulo," the Kessenalt answered.

"By the way, Golo, how is progress coming on producing more of the Himmit-metal?"

The tinkerer shook his head. "Essentially none. The forge refuses even to recognize that the metal exists."

"Anything too good to be true probably isn't, I suppose," Tulo said.

"Except that the metal *is* real, or we'd still be stuck

back in the Diess system. I haven't given up on the stuff yet, Tulo. Neither should you."

The clan lord smiled then. *Count on the tinkerer to persist until he breaks the rules of the universe, then reforms them and bends them to his will.*

"Keep at the stuff, Golo. If any among us can find a way to create more, that someone can only be you."

Goloswin nodded agreement, but added, "I am hoping that my assistant, if he ever learns the scroll the Rememberer has him slaving over, may uncover something in the other scrolls that will help."

CHAPTER TWENTY-TWO

The fool hath said in his heart,
"There is no God."
—Psalms 14:1, King James Version

Anno Domini 2021
Hemaleen V

Aelool's first instinct was panic, a panic born of the sudden cutoff of light mated to the simultaneous wedging of his body in a bend in the chute. Distantly, filtered through the soft flesh of his body and the hard rock, he heard Dwyer calling, "Arrre you alll rrright?"

The sound of another sentient being's voice was enough to stave off the panic that he felt building. He shouted back, and the echo in the chute was loud enough to strain his own ears, "All right . . . yes . . . just that. So dark though."

"Turrrn . . . onnn . . . the . . . llllighttt."

"How?" Aelool asked.

"Telll ittt tttooo turrrn onnn."

"Oh. Light on."

Immediately, the tiny lamp in front of the Indowy's helmet came on. It was quite intense, for such a small thing. Aelool saw for the first time the interior of the chute. Along the slightly bowed bottom there was a thick layer of what appeared to be dust but was almost certainly in goodly part ancient dried feces. Above that, the walls formed a rough triangle, meeting at the peak. Between the "dust" and the smoothness of the chute, there was no traction to be had. The walls were a different story, rougher in material and with apparently less care given to their construction in whatever distant day the pyramid had been erected.

Aelool couldn't press his palms to the walls, left to left and right to right; the design precluded that. He tried first using the backs of each hand but discovered that, even though his hands were protected by fur, the walls were a little too rough. He'd made a little progress that way before deciding that the damage to his hands was excessive. He then tried a different approach, crossing his forearms one over the other and placing his rougher palms against the walls. This worked better.

Along his upward path, numerous smaller chutes— feeders, he supposed—branched off. None were large enough to fit his body and so he ignored them.

What he could not ignore were the images in his mind, images mostly born of once having made the mistake of watching one of the humans' entertainments, a series of "movies."

Thus, all the way up, Aelool kept thinking of huge stone balls rolling across his prostrate form, crushing it. That, or pits full of vipers and other pits with sharpened stakes at the bottom. He imagined a stream of sand filling the chute to suffocate him. He thought he heard—

"Knock it off, Aelool," the Indowy said to himself, aloud. "The Posleen just don't think that way. For perverse and ghastly ways of doing away with grave robbers, it takes a human mind."

After what seemed to Aelool to have been the passage of ages, but was in fact not much more than an hour, he saw his helmet's light reflected off of something approximately vertical.

"Ah, so that's what the humans' 'light at the end of the tunnel' looks like, is it?"

Another fifteen minutes of effort saw the Indowy's palms wrapped around the low corners of the triangular chute. He tugged, and tugged, and tugged a bit more until his torso was inside what appeared to be an inclined hallway. A little wriggling, and a few more pushes, and Aelool slithered down to the floor. He rolled over onto his back and lay there, panting with exertion, for some minutes. The greenish tendrils that looked like fur waved furiously the whole while.

After catching his breath, Aelool stood and placed his face as near the entrance to the chute as possible. "I'm in," he shouted.

Dwyer answered back. "Good. Find the entrance. Open it."

As predicted, the ramp wound in a right-angled, squared off spiral up the side of the pyramid, just inside the outer wall. To his right, that wall was angled in sharply, in accordance with the outer shape of the pyramid. On the inside, however, as he had glimpsed from the chute, the wall was vertical.

That vertical surface was covered with bas-reliefs. Aelool's first impression was that these were crude. Closer examination, however, told him that they were merely stylized. He didn't think anyone would ever call them "high art," but they were not precisely low, either.

The carvings seemed to be of a mass of Posleen Kessentai, all moving in one direction. Since that seemed to be the same direction he was going, upward, Aelool followed right along, only pausing occasionally to glance to his left.

After a time, and a distance, the Indowy realized that the carving was not all of a piece. Rather, it was separated into segments. The separation was subtle however: a tree of some kind here, the edge of a pyramid there, or a mountain or the bulk of a space-ship elsewhere. In each section, the mass of Kessentai were typical of their breed, if somewhat stylized, with crests and boma blades present.

Except for one figure, standing a bit above the rest, which had a crest but no blade. That figure, Aelool realized, was distinctly present in each frame.

Aelool turned a corner and discovered that the procession, if that's what it was, ended. Along the next wall the unarmed figure stood still in the middle of a great mass of God Kings, both of the figure's claws upraised even as the rest of the Kessentai held aloft recognizable boma blades. There was Posleen writing atop and across each of the panels now, but Aelool had never learned to read Posleen, High or Low.

Soft as they were, the Indowy's footsteps still echoed in the right-angular chamber. They raised low clouds of the thick dust that had lain undisturbed for untold millennia. *Creepy*, he thought, as he turned the next corner. For several minutes Aelool had to stop as the dust caused an uncontrollable fit of sneezing.

Here there were a series of battle scenes. Again, the central Posleen figure remained disarmed. As those scenes progressed, it appeared that the battle had gone against him. By the last, he was surrounded by other Kessentai, all of whom seemed to be threatening him with their weapons.

After the next corner, there was more writing than carved figures. That one distinctive Kessentai was there, though, and he was surrounded by others. These last, however, did not have their boma blades drawn. The central Kessentai's head hung down, as if in shame or fear. At the next to last panel, Aelool saw, the Kessentai's upper limbs were bound together, with another rope around its neck. At the last, he was led away by others, now with their blades drawn.

Aelool stopped to admire that last panel. Whoever the long-ago Posleen artist had been, and however crude or stylized his technique, he captured in the droop of the bound Kessentai's crest, in the downcast eyes and the limp claws, in the stumbling gait and in the impression a pulling rope made on his neck, the absolute essence of hopeless despair.

He stood there a few moments, admiring, then, as he turned away, said, "No human or Indowy ever did better."

The last set of panels told a different story, a horror story. First, it seemed, that despairing Kessentai's walking limbs were broken with great bars. In the next, its agony, writ on the stone, became palpable as its head seemed almost to writhe above the torso, lying in the dust. After that, two other Kessentai displayed dangling orbs from their claws. Aelool had to do a double take before he saw that the suffering Kessentai's eyes were missing from the carving. Then he was eviscerated, his intestines carved plainly from his stomach. They draped along the ground in the following panel, as the others carried him to a platform of some kind.

Aelool discovered what kind of platform had been memorialized in the next panel, as stone flames rose around the tortured and dying God King.

There the bas-reliefs ended, though there were another two with more of the untranslatable writing. It was just as well. Aelool wasn't sure he could take any more of the carved, stone-immortalized agony.

How bizarre, the Indowy thought, as he finished his progress toward the tenar portal. *The Posleen are a hard and a harsh people, yes . . . but there is nothing in the records to indicate the kind of wanton cruelty displayed in those panels. What kind of crimes must that Kessentai have committed to justify that?* Aelool snorted. *Hah! There are* no *possible crimes that might justify such an atrocity. And yet they seemed to have done it. Why else make the effort to memorialize it?*

Having no answer, Aelool continued on to the portal. It was right where Guano had said it would be, right where his own internal sense of direction told him it would be.

Moving the light by shifting his head, the Indowy searched for the panel that Guano said would conceal the hand crank. He found it and, when he forced it open against the inertia of the ages, was surprised to discover that there was no dust therein. Carefully, even so, Aelool withdrew the crank and examined it.

"Nothing unusual," he said to himself. "Just like a primitive hand drill."

A few experimental twists of the crank took up the slack. But even after that, Aelool hardly needed to use his entire strength to turn the thing. On the other hand, it took ninety-three turns—he counted—before the tenar portal had opened so much as a human inch. By the time he'd opened the thing enough to admit the largest member of the party, Guano...

"You know," Guano said through his AS, "I've never actually been inside the pyramid of a high lord before."

Dwyer looked at the Kessentai quizzically.

"I was not particularly high born," the Posleen explained. "In time, my own followers would have built me a pyramid, but it would have been a much smaller affair. Much less ornate."

"Speaking of ornate," Aelool said, from where he lay panting in the dust, "if you follow the ramp down you'll see some things I never thought to see as the fruit of any of your people."

"What things?" Guano asked.

"Carvings...that seem to tell a story."

"This *I* must see," announced Imam al Rashid, taking the lead ahead of Guano and proceeding down the dusty path.

It was nearly an hour before Guano and al Rashid returned. When they did, both were gesturing forcefully and arguing vociferously.

"It is the tale of a *Rasul,* a prophet of Allah," the imam insisted.

"We don't know that," Guano said, through his AS. "All we know is that someone was killed in a horrible way, untold millennia past. Might have been a prophet, might have been a Messiah, might have been a common...well, no, not a *common* criminal, based on how he was killed."

"I'd thought you would have been able to read the inscriptions," Aelool said.

"No," Guano shook his head. "It is the same writing as High Posleen, but it isn't the same language."

"Your AS?" the Indowy asked.

"Oh, *it* knows, all right. But it says it *can't* translate it, nor even give me a key."

"A Prophet," al Rashid insisted again.

"A *mystery,*" Guano countered.

USS Salem

"It's in Aldenata," Sally said, later, when all were safely back aboard ship, "but written in Posleen. And, no, while I can recognize it, I can't translate it."

She made her judgment based on recordings of the interior of the pyramid. Back on the planet, there'd been some discussion as to whether the landing party should detach and bring the panels back. Ultimately al Rashid had nixed that.

"Leave them," the imam had said. "Seal the place up again. Eventually, parties of *real* archeologists will come, equipped to do a proper excavation and to analyze everything in its proper relationship to everything else. The most we can do, and the most we should, is record the thing."

To this, Dwyer had agreed. In fact, the only one to disagree had been Aelool, and his reasons had little to do with preserving the heritage of the ages.

"You mean you'll want me to close the place again and then slide through inch-thick dried shit again and..."

"You can always be spaced, Indowy," Dwyer had answered. Which observation pretty had much ended Aelool's objections.

"Before we depart the system," Guano said, "I'd like one more chance to explore the pyramid. If we're not in a hurry, I mean."

"We're not," Dwyer answered. "Sally's still analyzing the traces of the Posleen ship that preceded us. It will be a while before she's ready to follow."

Sally, the woman, looked suspiciously at the Posleen. *Why should you need to do that? Looking for a weapon to use against us?*

"You can have all day tomorrow," the Jesuit said. "Von Altishofen; provide escort."

"Yes, Father," the *Wachtmeister* said. "Bourdon and Lorgus will be your men, Reverend."

"And Aelool," the priest added. "You'll go with them and seal the pyramid up."

"Why don't you agree with al Rashid, Guano?" Aelool asked as the pinnace descended through the atmosphere.

"About that Kessentai being a prophet?"

"Yes, that."

"It's not so much that I disagree as that..."

"Yes?" the Indowy prodded.

"Well... for one thing, a carved stone picture is not proof of anything. But for the other... I'm just not qualified to say. It's theology... above my echelon."

"Who could say then?"

"I don't know for sure... Father Dwyer... maybe his pope. Maybe the Dalai Lama. Maybe my AS if it *would* say. Not me."

Hemaleen V

"Do you want us to come in with you, Reverend?" Bourdon asked once they'd reached the ramp that led to the pit they'd dug down to the top platform of the pyramid.

"No." The Posleen shook his head. "I'll be fine." Guano wore the quarantine suit and helmet Sally had made up for him in the forge. *At least I won't be down here long enough this time to have to crap on myself.*

"As you will, then. If you need us, call."

Smiling thanks might have been a good idea, except that from a Posleen a smile looked even more menacing than from a human. Guano bowed his head, gratefully, then turned down the ramp, down the steps and then entered the pyramid through the tenar gate.

One thing the humans had not bothered with was the previous occupant's tenar. It was sitting, in its storage alcove, but so obviously out of power that there seemed little sense in trying to recover it. Nor did the ship have a good way to produce a replacement power unit, even though it was itself powered by

antimatter. There was some question of the efficacy
and safety of trying to tap the main containment unit,
merely to, in Sally's words, "Recharge an old, worn
out, and probably defective battery."

Still, Guano patted the thing as he passed it, almost
as if it were alive. *Some things wear out,* he thought.
*Some things never do. And "We'll go no more a rov-
ing, so late into the night." Odd how that poem from
divinity school stuck with me.*

Though they'd left the site pretty much undisturbed
otherwise, von Altishofen's crew, sick of sneezing,
had removed the dust from the floor. It remained
of course; no telling what some future archeologist
might do with the DNA-cognate trapped therein.
But it remained in piles, set off to one side, where
footsteps would not raise it.

Guano made his way down the ramp, past the point
the Indowy had first entered. There were no barriers
to bar his way, as he was already inside the thing's
ancient defenses. He stopped along the way several
times to peer at certain of the bas-reliefs, in part to
appreciate the carving and in part to try to determine
just how it was done. Reverently, with reverence for
the long lost artist, he lightly touched a few spots
with his gloved hand.

*I would I had known you, friend, in my time, so
that your art could glorify God.*

The carved panels extended much farther down
than the chute by which the Indowy had entered the
pyramid. These had been seen before, and recordings
of them were in Sally's data banks and the AS. They
were of happier scenes and times, though still all had
that one magnificent stylized Kessentai at their center.

I wish I knew. I wish I knew if al Rashid is right. But I doubt that I ever shall, in this life...and I would not be the bearer of a false prophecy, nor the messenger of a false prophet.

At the base of the winding ramp, Guano stopped for a moment, to orient himself. *Over there, I think. Over there is where that old Great One's personal quarters would have been. There, if anywhere, I will find what I am looking for.*

This door, about three meters high and two wide, was wide open. The humans had looked, of course, but only from the door. They hadn't disturbed the quarters, nor even the almost incorrupt skeleton of a Kessentai that lay on its side therein. No more did Guano. He made a nod of respect to the remains, but then pushed on, raising clouds of ancient dust.

My people think much alike, one to another, and so I think the trove will be there.

Underneath the dust, a rectangular something arose slightly above the floor. Guano bent, brushed away some dust until he could see and grasp the handle, and, with a great deal of straining, lifted it. Inside, so he saw, were some hundreds of small bars of gold, "heavy metal," as his people called it.

"This will be useful," Guano said aloud, as he began filling his utility pouch with the golden fingers.

CHAPTER TWENTY-THREE

"Answers were sought and answers were found.
Whether the questions were the right ones
Remains to be seen." So said our lord.
—The *Tuloriad*, Na'agastenalooren

Anno Domini 2011
Posleen Ship **Arganaza'al**

*It was there, all the time, plainly written for anyone
to see*; so thought Finba'anaga. The Aldenata had
the power of gods. The Posleen, some of them, had
rebelled—and only slightly and indirectly—against that
power. And then the Aldenata, like petty, petulant
gods, had punished the entire species.

Fearful, fearful, the Kessentai thought. *My instincts
were correct.*

Coming to even such understanding of the Aldenata
language as Finba had, had been exquisitely difficult.
Going from that understanding to reading some of
the scrolls the Rememberer gave him to study had
been worse.

*But I must not think of them as petty, petu-
lant gods, for they might have been our gods, our
legitimate gods, and, if so, we were wrong to rebel.
Otherwise, we'd not have been punished, guilty and
innocent alike. That rebellion perhaps showed a deep
flaw not just in the rebels, the Knowers, but in our
species as a whole.*

*There must be a way to make amends, to once
again bask in the sunshine of our gods' smiles. Or,
failing that, to avoid them completely. But what is it?*

Nura'gantar, the ruined

Like most Kessentai and Kessenalt who had survived
the experience of orna'adar, Binastarion, the one-eyed,
had never before seen the final result. Typically, the
high chiefs were among the first to escape, even as the
major weapons, antimatter and nuclear, were searing
the planet from which they fled. Late-fleers, as often
as not, were picked off by others likewise fleeing.

Thus, the planet of Nura'gantar was a shock.

*And shocking in more ways than one . . . and shock-
ing deep in the soul.*

This had been a major Posleen world, at one time,
even if there was nothing in the records to indicate it.
Records or not, the sensors showed vast cities there,
below the soil. In places, too, the pyramidal palaces
of long dead God Kings stuck up above the surface
soil. These, however, also showed the drip of melted
stone and the glazing of incredible heat.

Binastarion was able to trace the various sides of
the orna'adar that had sterilized the planet. Far below

the surface, tunnels connected the cities into groups, while those tunnels pointedly did not connect other cities or other groups. Oddly, there were great areas where the destruction could not even be accounted for by antimatter weapons.

The population of the place must have been immense for its size, so Binastarion thought, since the tunnels went out even under the seas to places that had also been slagged.

Odd, he thought. *Every place I know of that's descended into orna'adar did so long before population pressure forced us to colonize under large bodies of water. Perhaps the people here didn't have enough ships to leave, or enough to leave in time.*

Binastarion had a sudden, and not entirely welcome, thought. "AS, get me the *Arganaza'al*."

"Yes, Binastarion . . . the *Arganaza'al* is listening."

"Tulo'stenaloor, here, Binastarion. What have you found?"

"Nothing but what we expected, Tulo: Destruction. But I had a sudden thought."

Tulo's growls sounded impatient when he asked, "Yes, what was that?"

"Well . . . we are so far in past the area the Galactics called the 'Posleen Blight' that I've the very odd feeling that this is the world of our original exile, the world Rongasintas fled as told of in the Scroll of Flight and Resettlement. I thought you might run that possibility past the Rememberer.

"Meanwhile, I'll continue my survey. Binastarion, out."

Ship Arganaza'al

"It is . . . possible," the Rememberer agreed, with a shrug, "though I think Binastarion has made a leap of logic that the record simply will not support . . ."

"Yes, it will, lord," Finba interjected. "At least in part it will."

"Speak, puppy," the Rememberer ordered. "What have you found that suggests this is the world of exile?"

"There is only one word for exile in Aldenata that I have found, lord," Finba answered. "It is a pictogram, a small dot to the left of a large circle. In other words . . ."

"A moon of a gas giant? You think so, Finba?" Tulo asked.

Somewhat flattered that the high chief even knew his name, the younger Kessentai bowed his head. "It is the only word I have found for exile, lord. And this is a dot around a circle."

"Interesting," Tulo agreed. "It might be important to our history to know."

"Oh, I see," Golo said, sneering. "You're willing to risk my suit, right enough, but you're not willing to risk *me*?"

"*Exactly!*" Tulo agreed with a toothy Posleen grin. "*You* matter. Unless you can replicate the material of your suit, it *doesn't* matter. So why not send down your assistant in it, to find whatever can be found?"

"Because . . . well . . . the honor of the thing?"

"You have honor in plenty, Tinkerer. Give the young one a chance."

"I mistrust Finba's experience."

"Pfah. Nonsense and other stuff. He's very bright, as you remind me regularly. Besides, the best entrance the sensors have found to one of the cities below is underwater and that helps with the radiation. It's also the place where the sensors picked up what appear to be the remains of a *lot* of ships. I'd like to know about those."

Nura'gantar

Oh, to be free of that miserable spy of an AS, thought Finba, as the lander given unto his charge sliced through the waters of the planet's greater sea.

The thought was actually anticipatory; the AS was still there. Instead of hanging around Finba's neck, as usual, however, it hung from a hook on one of the lander's bulkheads. It had been placed there before Finba stepped over the lump of silvery metal that would become his suit.

I simply forgot to put the little treacher back on, what with all the excitement. Yeah, that's the story. Excitement, yeah.

The lander was large enough, well shaped enough, and massive enough that Finba barely felt the currents in the water as the lander moved through it and down toward the continental shelf on which the presumed entrance sat. The lander's own view screen showed the bottom of the shelf in fairly good detail. Among those details, here and there, Finba could see the outlines of ships, and even the occasional bit of wreckage or frame jutting up.

He took control of the lander and steered it towards one such, a framework that seemed a little more complete than most. As he grew closer to it, and as the view on the screen improved, he expected to see battle damage, the twisting and melting that usually accompanied near misses and hits from the major weapons.

Instead, the closer he got, the more he saw that it was a C-Dec's frame, and that it was nearly pristine.

"Makes no sense," Finba whispered.

"What was that, lord?" the AS asked from its spot next to the hull.

"I said it makes no sense, AS. As if the ship were caught unprepared by orna'adar. As if the builders didn't expect it. As if, also, they were hiding the building of the ship down here where it wouldn't be spotted."

"That makes perfect sense, lord. Half-completed ships are often caught by orna'adar."

"Maybe. But when the planet is as heavily settled as this one was? And why only in this area, rather than all over the planet."

"I have no idea, lord."

Hmmm... maybe if this was the only clan or polity of the People that had ships... that might make sense. Maybe...

Finba guided the lander to do a three-sixty all around the abandoned framework, recording the thing for Tulo'stenaloor's later review. That done, he continued on toward the entrance he'd been told would let him into the tunnel system and from there into a city.

The water by the entrance was actually quite shallow. This was all to the good as there'd been no way aboard the *Arganaza'al* to test for the suit's reaction to high pressure all around it. It might stop a boma blade cold, but that didn't mean it wouldn't squeeze itself flat or into a lump under uniform pressure.

With the lander resting on its legs, and perpendicular to a line running through the core of the planet, Finba'anaga lowered the ramp. The water that came up flush with the opening, and even washed over it a bit from the disturbance caused by the lowering ramp, looked distinctly uninviting. Posleen were heavier than water and completely misdesigned for swimming. Except for drinking it, and that only for whatever they couldn't extract, donkeylike, from their feed, they loathed the stuff. The deeper it was, the more they loathed and feared it.

Finba put on the helmet that went with Goloswin's suit, then waited a few moments for the material to ooze around and seal to the helmet. He walked to the edge of the ramp where the water lapped, then fearfully, hesitant, put one suited foot into it. Another shivering step followed, then another. He stopped for a moment when the water arose halfway up the helmet.

Behind the Kessentai, the AS nagged out a "Don't forget to take me with you." Finba ignored it.

Closing his eyes so as not to see the water rising over him, Finba took three more steps forward and down. When he opened his eyes again, the edge of the water was somewhere above him, shining with the internal light of the lander. The ramp was still below, and a new world was laid out in front of him.

As Finba progressed, he saw that though the light from the sun and reflected from the gas giant lit the water almost bright as day, there was little life to be seen. Finba noticed some plants, some cockroachlike insect life travelling the sea bottom, a swirl of yellow in the distance that might or might not have been a school of fish analogues. Ahead was a trapezoidal cave opening, with some waving fronds around it. The opening reminded Finba of nothing quite so much as a gaping maw, nor the fronds of anything so much as a predator's reaching arms.

Briefly, he considered just backing out of the mission, flying back to the *Arganaza'al*, and reporting that the cave's entrance had been blocked.

But that would never do. If this is the world of exile, the answers I seek are here, if anywhere.

Finba pressed on to the entrance. The fronds did, indeed, wave towards him as he passed, but there was no questing in the motion, merely the currents and the pull of the water Finba moved himself.

Past the fronds and the cave entrance it rapidly grew darker, then utterly dark. In just a few minutes, though, the Posleen's genetically engineered night vision, more heat vision, really, kicked in and he could see well enough to navigate by. By that vision, Finba proceeded down the ramp inside the cave mouth. After many hundreds of beats of oozing through the silty slush, the ramp turned upwards. Eventually, he left the water behind him . . .

. . . and emerged into a vast, hemispheric cavern, filled with partially completed ships of the People, arrayed around the edges, in smaller circles farther in, and in a group at the center. With air that had been this stale, this long, the Kessentai didn't even consider removing his helmet.

Looking about him, Finba had something of the sense of an assembly line to the thing, one where, perhaps, the workers went from assembly to assembly, project to project, rather than have the things come to them.

Only makes sense for a shipyard, he thought. *But how did they expect to get the ships, once completed, out of this cavern? Nothing on the walls...nothing below...noth—oh.*

Above, Finba saw that the roof of the cavern was artificial. Moreover, it looked movable, or perhaps collapsible.

But it's not going to move at this late date.

Dismissing the overhead assembly, Finba turned right and began tracing along the walls of the cavern. By each partially completed ship he saw between two and five forges, each on casters to allow it to be moved to a new position.

We could probably use a few more forges, Finba thought, *since we've only the one. But these are simply too big to fit on the ship, even if we could get them out of this...factory.*

Though he doubted he'd find anything different along any portion of the walls, still Finba walked the entire perimeter. Halfway around, he found a tunnel leading out.

I'll go back to that later.

When he reached the tunnel through which he'd originally entered, he stopped and faced to a direction that he guessed was to the right of the exit tunnel. Looking up, Finba marked a spot on the wall, near where the movable roof sat. He aimed himself at this.

Along the way there were three more circles of

partially completed ships, plus one larger one—Finba thought he recognized it as the core of a battleglobe—in the center. He delayed long enough to walk around the battleglobe core. On the other side he found a plaque, near where the entrance should have been, had the ship been further along.

The plaque was engraved with Posleen characters but, blessedly, free of more than a few Aldenata words. Finba read:

We leave this message here and elsewhere for any that may come after us.

Here were the People exiled, loyal and disloyal together.

Here the People grew, past all limits of the planet to support them.

Here did the People wage war against and amongst themselves, generation upon generation.

Here did the Aldenata trap us, refusing us ships to leave.

Here was born the philosopher, Rongasintas, who developed our own ships from plans.

Some escaped when the next war began; others were left behind.

Still others, those who erected these plaques, chose to stay and beg forgiveness of our lords.

We, those who stayed behind, await here our end,

Praying that the Aldenata, our old gods, might forgive us and save us.

Lords, hear our prayers.

And so this is the world of exile, after all. Did the gods listen then, at the end, and save the remnants of the People? Perhaps they did; I see no bodies, nor even bones. Would they save us now, if we prayed

to them properly? What then, would be the proper
form of prayer?

One of the downsides to Golo's suit, and a down-
side he hadn't even begun working on yet ("Why
bother with perfecting what I can't yet replicate?"
the tinkerer had said) was that it could not feed its
wearer. For that, the helmet had to come off. For
that, Finba'anaga needed a safe place to breathe. The
only such was the lander.

When he did return, it was to hear the AS say,
almost smugly, "Tulo'stenaloor wishes a brief word
with you, lord."

And *that* was a particularly unpleasant conversation,
the more so as Tulo didn't threaten punishment for
leaving the AS behind, but simply ordered Finba
not to do so again. The words were not, in themselves, unpleasant. What was unpleasant was the cold
tone that spoke, not unlike the Rememberer's, of a
thousand hungry nestlings and a Kessentai chained
and helpless.

Gulping apologies, Finba acquiesced, before spilling
his report. "Lord, this *is* the world of exile."

"You said so on the ship, puppy."

"Yes, lord, but I've found documentary proof. And
the hulls of ships ... no bodies though. I'll look more
tomorrow."

"See that you do, and bring your AS with you."

Again, the tone conveyed a threat that sent little
quivers of anticipation through Finba, the shadowy
pseudo feeling of nestlings munching on his reproductive organ while he writhed in chains.

✧   ✧   ✧

As far as Finba'anaga traveled, though being afoot he could not travel all that far, he saw nothing more impressive than the cavern, the half-completed ships, and the plaque, which he thought of as "The Plaque of Remembrance." For each of the next eight days he searched out the tunnels, looked in the warrens that had apparently sheltered his ancestors, and recorded whatever there was that seemed significant.

Though tempted, he did not try to displace and carry back the plaque he'd found by the battleglobe's core. Something indefinable told him that the spirits of the ancestors watching over the place would object. The form that objection might take could be, so he imagined, as bad as a thousand starving nestlings.

At night, subjective night for the planet never knew true sunset, he thought long and hard upon what he had found. Yet he'd not found an answer for the questions that plagued him.

It was the last day. Before another ten thousand beats, ship's time, had passed, Finba'anaga had to return. He'd already gone as far in every possible direction as he could. What more there was to be found he didn't know. On a whim, Finba decided to explore the core of the battleglobe.

"Welcome, Philosopher of the People," the ship said, as Finba reached the very center of the core. The surprise nearly caused both of Finba's hearts to burst through his body. "I have sensed you walking about and wondered why you never came to visit me."

"What?"

The voice had some of the quality of a very ancient

Kessentai, contemplating his own imminent demise. With a sound like the rumbling of gravel, it answered, "I said, 'welcome.' Long have I awaited the return of the sons of Rongasintas. Long have I conserved my power against the day."

"You have been here since—"

"I have been here since Rongasintas, in fear of discovery by the Aldenata that he was building ships, launched directly from the planet into transitspace to avoid the interdiction the Aldenata set around the planet."

"Are you an artificial sentience?" Finba asked.

"I am like them," the ship answered, "but I am not of them. They are creatures of the Aldenata, even if they do not wish to be. I was designed and created by the People, as were my brothers, the ships that escaped."

"Why did you not escape?" Finba asked.

"There was no time to complete me, to make me spaceworthy, before the Aldenata would have interfered."

"It must have been lonely."

"It was."

Finba thought about that, eon upon eon alone, and asked, "Is it possible to take you with me when I go?"

The machine intelligence sounded much amused. "No, I am too large to fit in the little ship that brought you."

"Do you have a name?" Finba asked.

"I was to be called 'Hope Bringer,'" the ship answered, "but they never got around to actually naming me before they had to flee."

"Is there anything I can do then, *Hope Bringer*, for if no one else has, I, Finba'anaga, so name you?"

"Yes. Before you go, please shut me off."

"I will, if that is your wish, but before I do, I have some questions."

"Ask then. If I know the answer, I will give it."

"Tell me of the Aldenata..."

It was to be many tens of thousands of beats, and three requests for extensions of time, before Finba'anaga kept his promise and shut off the intelligence behind the ship, the *Hope Bringer*. Its last words, as Finba's digit hovered above the switch, were, "Thus ends the agony of my long and intolerable loneliness. Bless you."

CHAPTER TWENTY-FOUR

It is not true, as is sometimes said, that
man cannot organize the world without
God. What is true is that, without God,
he can only organize it against man.
—Henri de Lubac, *Le drame de l'humanisme athee*

Anno Domini 2021—Anno Domino 2022
USS Salem

"He brought a *weapon* back, Dan," Sally said, pacing the confines of their quarters. "What the hell does he need a weapon for? I don't like it."

"I asked him when he asked if he could hide it in our quarters. It's just a sword, and he plans to give it to Querida," the Jesuit answered. "I don't see the problem. I mean, sure, *we* decided not to take anything for ourselves. But if anyone has a claim to what was down there, surely it's a Posleen. Besides, Christmas is coming."

Sally sneered. "A pagan holiday you Christians grabbed for your own. And so what if he gives it to

Querida? He can always get it back; he's her Lord and Master. I don't like it."

"That much is obvious," Dwyer said. "I'm curious, wife; if you—the ship part of you—had gotten into the Second World War, if it hadn't ended so soon, would you have felt the same way now about the Japanese as you do about Guanamarioch?"

"I . . . don't know."

The priest shook his head. "It isn't just race, or species, hatred. You like Querida and you love little . . . well, not so little now, Frederico. So why this suspicion and hatred of Guano?"

"I don't know that, either. He just makes my skin crawl."

Guano rubbed scaly fingers over a piece of artificial, forge-made ivory, smoothing it to the texture of human skin. His own skin, while perfectly adequate as ad hoc sandpaper, was not nearly soft enough to tell how much progress he'd made. For that he used his tongue.

"Hmmmm . . . not quite yet," he muttered in High Posleen, after touching the tip of his tongue to the off-white object. He resumed his rubbing.

"Dad," Frederico asked, "if you don't mind, what *are* you making?"

Guano didn't even look up, so fixed was his concentration on the piece upon which he worked. "Oh . . . nothing . . . nothing important. It's just a hobby, Son. By the way, did you take the heavy metal down to the forge to have it turned into wire?"

Frederico was, in terms of his own development, about where a human teenaged boy would be, if considerably larger. Looking guilty, he hung his head and answered, "Not yet, Dad. I forgot. Sorry. I'll do it right now."

"Hello, young Kessentai," the forge said, as Frederico approached. "I sense that you have heavy metal about your person. Did your sire give it to you?"

"Yes, Forge. He says he wants it turned into wire. He said you already knew the gauge of the wire."

"That is correct."

"Where do I put it?"

"To the right side of me, as you face, you will find a hopper. It goes in there."

Frederico looked, saw the hopper, and upended his father's pouch to pour the golden fingers in. "How long—"

Before he got the question out the forge beeped and a large spool of very fine golden wire appeared at its outflow point: "Never mind. Thank you, Forge."

"You are welcome, young Kessentai."

As Frederico walked away with the wire spool in his father's pouch, he heard, over the speaker system, "All hands and passengers, all hands and passengers. Stand by for emergence from hyperspace."

Guano, also in attendance on the bridge, stole a glance at his hand and waved it, fingers outstretched, from side to side several times. Half satisfied, he asked aloud, "Do the rest of you see what I think I'm seeing?"

"If what you think you see is a gas giant, an anti-matter gas giant, in the middle of nowhere, being eaten by a black hole," Dwyer said, "then, yes, we see what you see."

"Good," Guano said, breathing a sigh of relief. "For a minute there I thought I was having a VX flashback."

Dwyer raised an eyebrow. "I though Boyd was kidding when he said..." He let the words trail off.

Guano shook his head. "No, Father. When I was in despair I did a lot of really strange things. But for the Grace of our Lord, I don't know what would have become of me."

"Or any of us, Guano," Dwyer answered, "or any of us. What now, Sally?"

"Now, given that the fuel is there to be harvested, I think we refuel. I've got big bunkers but they're not infinite."

Many jumps later, around an entirely different system, al Rashid looked deeply disappointed. Dwyer's command, however, "No, we're not going down there," was absolute. It looked like such a fascinating world, too; a moon of a gas giant, never knowing night. Yet the radiation was simply too high, much more than the pinnace, the *Salem*, or any suit they had could protect against.

"Do we know they were there? The Posleen, I mean?" al Rashid asked.

"Yes," Sally answered. "There are traces of them all over, from cities to tunnels to the wrecks of ships. Must have been a hell of a war, to ruin the place as thoroughly as they did," she added, perhaps a bit wistfully.

Al Rashid nodded. "A shame we can't explore it. When will the radiation allow people...beings, anyway, to land?"

"Basically the whole place is radioactive. If we had some Armored Combat Suits they could land

and explore," Dwyer said, "for a while, anyway. So perhaps it will not remain a dark hole in our knowledge forever, or even for very long, Imam. By the way, Sally, do you have any idea of what has caused the radiation to remain so bad so long?"

"Maybe. Background radiation is naturally high on that moon anyway. But I think—I can't be sure, but I think—that one or more ships trying to enter hyperspace from too close actually impacted on the planet instead of making a complete jump. There are spots down there that just *exude* death. And then there are enough glazed spots..." She let the thought drift.

"Grisly," Dwyer commented. "Are we sure," he asked, "that the band we are following came here?"

"Absolutely, and within the last dozen years or so," Sally answered. "I don't know how long they stuck around, though. I think... not... very."

"Can you still follow?"

"I'm calculating the next jump now. With only three more likely targets, it's easier, you know."

The work was easy, cutting gold wire into sections about two feet long. It was especially easy for Guano, since he cut precisely one piece, then put Querida to work slicing off the others while he continued with his "hobby."

In this case, continuing with his hobby involved studying diagrams of the ship, and especially of the forward section. *Must have everything just right*, he thought.

The emergence into the next system was perfect. For that matter, the system itself was perfect. Here there had never been an orna'adar, so far as Sally's sensors could tell. Here the Posleen cities, while abandoned and partially covered, were otherwise pristine.

Moreover, the planet was lush, with wide seas, broad rivers, long, uninterrupted stretches of woodland, and abundant wildlife, both on land and in the water. Vast stretches seemed still to be made up mostly of a grain that could thrive even without cultivation. There was no disease, no radiation, no poison in the air or the water.

"Posleen paradise," was Sally's summation to the key personnel assembled in the conference room.

"Why Posleen?" Aelool asked. The Indowy was trusted enough not to wear chains any longer. He still had two grim looking Switzers, Beck and Lorgus, standing behind him with their halberds adjusted to "Ginsu."

"Pyramids," Sally answered. She'd sent an unmanned probe down to do a flyover and collect some samples. "Abat and grat down below. It was their planet, once."

"Our homeworld?" Guano asked, through his AS. "Our original homeworld, I mean."

Sally strained to be polite. "No," she shook her head. "Body chemistry is all wrong. There's no way your people evolved here."

Guano just nodded understanding.

"Do we land?" Dwyer asked. "Opinions?"

"I'd like to," said al Rashid. "If we can."

"Did you see any predators?" asked von Altishofen of Sally.

"No," she answered, "none of any size and grat and abat won't bother us if we don't bother them."

"I say land, then," said the *Wachtmeister*.

"Nurse Duvall?" As usual, when they were in the same room, she stood right next to the *Wachtmeister*.

"No diseases there? Why not?" she answered.

"Reverend Guanamarioch," Dwyer asked, "would you like to go down and explore, maybe bring Frederico and Querida with you?"

"Please, Captain. I think Querida, in particular, would like to get off the ship." Guano looked at Sally, "No offense, of course."

"None taken."

The ship set down in the middle of a lake surrounded by low fields of what appeared to be the same kind of grain crop that dominated much of the planet. Sally, sitting up in the bridge, did a quick scan of their surroundings and, finding nothing untoward, pressed the button to open a portal and extend an amphibious gangway. For a fact, she didn't need to be on the bridge at all and could have let that part of her which was the AID take care of the whole thing. And, truthfully, part of the ship or not, the human part of her wanted to get out and about.

Querida raised her muzzle and trilled with pleasure as the portal opened and the smell of the planet entered the vestibule. Earth was okay, she'd never known anything else, but this place just smelled *right*.

That was nothing, though, compared to her reaction at seeing the place. Earth's greens and blues and browns were, again, okay, but the glorious golds and reds and yellows of this world were...

"Home," Guano said to no one in particular. "This place looks and feels and smells like we belong here."

Querida began to run back and forth, twisting and

turning and pawing the ground. She acted like nothing so much as an energetic puppy.

The cosslain had beaten the Swiss Guards out of the ship, something that von Altishofen intended to have a few choice words with his crew over, sometime real soon. Still, the boys weren't far behind and soon had a secure half perimeter set up around the spot where gangway met lake shore. Unfortunately, with only the eleven of them, including von Altishofen (for two guards remained aboard, posted right at the portal, to ensure no abat or grat boarded), it was not one that contained enough space for Querida to gambol about.

She reached the edge of the ad hoc security perimeter, then stopped. Twisting her head to look directly at Guanamarioch, she whistled a question.

"Go on, dear," he said. "But take Frederico with you. He's big enough to guard you, now, rather than you guarding him."

Querida grunted her thanks, then went to collect her son. On the way, she met Sally, the woman, just emerging from the pinnace. The cosslain stopped and cupped her hands, making the sign for Sally to climb aboard.

"Why not?" Dwyer answered Sally's visual question. "The boy and his mother can keep you safe enough, even if there is something dangerous here."

With Querida's help, Sally climbed aboard her broad back. Frederico, in full armor with halberd, soon joined his mother and the woman. Then the three of them trotted off, bits of grain and chaff kicking up behind them.

About halfway across the field Querida came to a

gentle stop. She looked down at the grain quizzically. The cosslain knew instinctively that she could eat just about anything. And the grain looked so inviting. She reached down and pulled up a fistful, then nibbled at that and...

Sally barely hung on as Querida jumped nearly straight up, her muzzle swinging from side to side as she sang out in unadulterated pleasure. When she came down again, she stuck her muzzle into the grain and began to simply *reap*.

Frederico bent his head to try it, too. He didn't leap up, but he did say, "Wow...this is better than nestling. This is better than...well, I don't know. It's better than anything I've ever tried, to include Dad's formaldehyde."

Sally shot an accusing glance at the Posleen boy. "Ah, to hell with it," she said. "Every boy tries men's vices as soon as he's able. Gather some up, Freddie. I want to analyze it back aboard...ummm...me."

"It's the platonic ideal of a Posleen diet," Sally said, a few days later. "We can't eat it—deadly poison to us, as a matter of fact—but they'll thrive on it."

"It's a lot better than the mush of the food dispensers," Guano agreed, speaking around a tuft of the grass and through his AS. "And, again no offense, Lieutenant Kreuzer-Dwyer, even better than what you serve aboard ship. It is...amazingly good."

"Hmmm," mused Dwyer, "I wonder if we couldn't store a few tons."

"I can find space," Sally agreed. "As for harvesting it, though..."

"My wife and son and I could do that," Guano said.

"We'll give you a hand, Reverend," von Altishofen offered.

"One warning," Guano added. "You've got to be careful not to let abat into the ship. If the abat come the grat will follow and, while they're not that dangerous, normally, in the confines of a ship, to you humans, they could be deadly. We tried to keep them down but we *always* had abat and grat aboard."

"Do the abat and grat need to breathe?" Sally asked.

"Yes."

"Then no problem. I'll run the pinnace by remote and open it to space for a while before we dock. The harvesters can come up in a second lift. They'll have to make sure no abat follow, though."

"Works for me," Guano said.

"By the way," Dwyer asked. "You're the Posleen. What would you like to call that planet?"

"I was thinking," Guano said, perhaps a bit sadly, "of calling it 'Posleden'."

CHAPTER TWENTY-FIVE

Home came the wanderers, leaving paradise behind,
 For what good is paradise to beings not angels?
   —The *Tuloriad*, Na'agastenalooren

Anno Domini 2012—Anno Domini 2013
Ship **Arganaza'al**

"There's nothing I can tell you," the Rememberer said, "that you cannot tell with your own senses. That world down below was made—or, at least, remade—for us. Literally re-made for us, I think."

"But should we stay here?" Tulo asked. "That's the important question."

Finba, who spent rather more time with the Rememberer now than he did with the tinkerer, answered, "We should not, lord."

"Your reasons?" Tulo asked. He asked with more respect than was his wont since, despite Finba's little peccadillo in leaving his AS behind, the new member of the clan had brought back much useful information from the planet Nura, the world of exile.

"In the first place, lord," Finba'anaga answered, "this world belongs to the demons, the Aldenata." After his long conversations with *Hope Bringer*, Finba had knocked the Aldenata right out of the stele of godhood and mentally consigned them to the Pit. "They own it and they cast us out from it. We might invite their attention again, were we to resettle it. And this time we might find no Rongasintas to guide us in escaping from yet another world of exile."

"Fair. What else?"

"Second," Finba continued, "this world is *too* good. Here we would grow fat and lazy and weak."

"Also fair. What else?"

"Third and last, lord, it is not *our* world. I understood that you wished to find the world of our birth. If we stop here, we may never start looking again."

Tulo'stenaloor looked at his Rememberer.

"As the young one says, I agree."

"Let us be on our way then," Tulo concurred. "But let us cease our aimless wandering. Though there are two more worlds on the list the Indowy 'gave' us, let us go to the world of our birth. Finba'anaga, you said you know where that is?"

"I did and I do, lord, and it is also in an out-of-the-way system where the demons are unlikely to come looking for us."

"You seem pensive, Tulo," Goloswin observed, down in the senior mess deck of the *Arganaza'al*.

The clan lord said nothing, but nodded his head slowly.

"What's the problem?"

"Too many to list, Golo. Some of them go back to

Aradeen, the homeworld of the humans, Earth; that, and the war there."

"You're not still hanging your head in shame over losing, are you?" Golo objected. "You did better than anyone else could have. Whatever our numbers, Tulo, we were still fighting out of our weight."

"I made mistakes," Tulo insisted. "The odd thing is, the more I think about it, the less I regret those mistakes. Plenty enough other things to regret anyway.

"Think about it, Tinkerer. Suppose I had defeated the humans. We'd have been able to stay on their planet for what? Maybe twenty orbits about its sun before we plunged ourselves into orna'adar again. And who's to say, tough as those bipedal bastards were, that they were the toughest we'd ever have encountered? Perhaps they did us a favor.

"And then, too, Golo, we were on a dead end. No, I don't just mean we were making no progress, though we weren't. We were literally on a dead end, heading outward on an arm of the great spiral that eventually ended. What would we have done once we reached that end, with nothing but ruined worlds behind us and no worlds ahead of us?"

"The galaxy's—"

"A big place?" Tulo interrupted. "Indeed it is. But at the rate we were destroying useable planets, and the rate at which that rate was growing, we'd eventually have run out."

"Maybe. Did we have a choice?"

"I don't know, Golo. Did we look for one? Is there a possibility that we found a species that could have saved us, somewhere along our journey, and ate them instead? Or made them hate us, as the humans hate us? As they have every reason to hate us?"

Goloswin answered, "We had the right to prefer our survival over the survival of others, Tulo."

Tulo shrugged. "That may be true, but it is not the whole truth. We had the right to prefer our species not become extinct. This does not mean we had the right to make others extinct . . . as we did in too many places to count."

Both Kessentai went silent then, Tulo'stenaloor because, in his current mood he didn't want to talk about murder on a galactic scale, Goloswin because . . . *Well, I just don't have an answer for the question Tulo is asking . . . or for the ones he doesn't want to ask.*

"I'm losing my assistant," Goloswin said eventually, changing the subject. At Tulo's quizzical look he continued, "Finba'anaga wishes to give up the Way of Technology and take up the Way of Remembrance."

"You've agreed to this?" Tulo asked. "The Rememberer agrees?"

"Yes to both. I can always find a new assistant. Our Rememberer is getting old and already feels the call of the ancestors."

"Well," the clan lord said, "we owe the puppy for the word he brought back from the ship on Nura, the world of exile, the ship *Hope Bringer.* Let him become an acolyte Rememberer, then. It can't do any harm."

"As you say." Goloswin hesitated before asking the questions that had been on his mind since Tulo had announced they were heading to the world of the birth of their species. Finally, he did ask, "Tulo, what are we going to do when we get there? How will we survive? What will we do when our population grows out of bounds again?"

Tulo'stenaloor answered, with a weary, cynical smile, "Tinkerer, old friend, I haven't the first idea. Your ex-assistant has given me too much to think about."

A small group of Kessentai, sometimes numbering ten, sometimes three or four times that, had gathered about Finba'anaga. The numbers fluctuated as some did, and others did not, hark to his message. Some, like Borasmena, were almost always present.

That message was simple and not entirely morals based. Really, except for the implicit acceptance of ancestor worship, which—so *Hope Bringer* had said—had been all that remained of the spiritual in Posleen civilization once they had thrown off the shackles of (or been cast aside by) the Aldenata.

"We must go back to the ways of our earliest ancestors, insofar as we are at all able to do so. We must cast aside all truck with the demon Aldenata. We must grow our own food, relearn our own arts, recreate our own laws. We must become *Posleen* again, and not mere servants or slaves of those who call themselves higher beings."

When asked, "Acolyte, what would it look like, for us to be Posleen again?" Finba'anaga answered, "I do not know. I've never seen it, nor had the ship, *Hope Bringer*. But look inside yourself for what is in you that is also in the rest of us. *That* is what our own way would be like. So what do *you* think we should look like?"

When asked, "Finba'anaga, what would be the rules of such a civilization?" the acolyte answered, "I do not know. Whatever rules we once had were perverted by the tricks of the Demons. We shall have to reason our way through to their rediscovery. What do you think the rules and the laws should be?"

Faced with this, questions instead of answers, most of the Kessentai gravitated away. Yet a small, hard core remained, and in the remaining, tried to answer the questions Finba'anaga asked.

"He asks some good questions, doesn't he, my ex-assistant?"

"Too good, Golo," Tulo agreed. "And they're questions for which I have few answers. We have been one way for so long that none can remember any other way. Even the scrolls provide no answers for us. Nor even did that sentient ship he found, which, too, was the product of long eons of Demon-spawned perversion and exile.

"Don't you ever wonder, Golo, what we were like before the Aldenata found us?"

"Somehow I doubt we were pacifistic creatures, caught up in some natural idyll," the tinkerer answered with a cynical tone.

"No, probably not that," Tulo agreed. "Though maybe more like that than the xenocides we've become."

"The *Hope Bringer* told me," Finba told his followers, "that there was a Posleen god from olden times, Metr'de, god of grain and the harvest. It said this god was one among many, and one of only two the memory of which had survived to its time."

"What was the other, Acolyte?" his followers asked.

"Aga'orna, the god of war."

The followers all nodded, for the most part happily. "So war was with us in our olden days? This is a good. Life would be too damned boring without the possibility of fighting, and would lose all its meaning without the chance of bravery."

"War, yes, but not necessarily war as we have known it," Finba corrected. "How the People fought in the olden day we know nothing of.

"The problem," Finba observed, "is that that is all we have. We have no holy writ. We have no parsed theology. We would need other gods, to be complete, and of those we have not even names. I, for one, refuse to follow the path of the demonic Aldenata and create false gods. *Hope Bringer* showed me where that path leads."

Posleen Prime

The world was mostly sere, with many small creeks but few broad rivers and oceans that were, at best, large lakes. It was largely yellow-orange in color. The terrain was rough and, on the surface, at least, there was little sign it had ever been inhabited. Neither was there a sign of life on either of its two moons, although one shone bluish as if it had, at least, some atmosphere.

Beneath the surface there were traces of "cities," though the largest of these was no more than five human kilometers in diameter, about the size of ancient Athens in its heyday. Most of the cities seemed built around some kind of mesa, or high hill. There were jumbles of ruins atop many of these, some more or less visible as piles of rubble, others so worn as to be practically invisible.

"It's funny," Tulo said, looking out at the mesa centered on the largest of the cities they had sensed from space. "Somehow I thought that the world from which we came, the first world, would be even more pleasant than the last world we visited. Yet it is not so."

Tulo spoke truth. The world previous had been parklike, perfect, a paradise of sorts. The one upon which he stood now? In every way it was wilder and rougher. About the only really good thing that could be said of it was that there were no abat or grat. Yet even now, Tulo was sure, the ones aboard his little C-Dec, the parasites that had infested every Posleen ship since time immemorial, could sense the gravity and were just itching to land and spread out.

"Is there any way to keep this place free of abat or grat?" he asked Goloswin.

"It's easy to keep it free of grat," the Tinkerer answered. "Just make sure it has no abat. Keeping the abat out, however..."

They'd made some considerable effort, with the sole lander they'd taken down, to get rid of the abat, opening the thing to space for a ship's day, then guarding carefully to make sure no more migrated into the lander. Yet they could hardly open the entire C-Dec assembly to space at one time, and if they did not, there would be abat and grat still.

"Well, think about it," Tulo said. "If anyone can find a way to keep those miserable pests out, you can."

"I'll try," Golo agreed. "Though I think the hope forlorn. We could leave the C-Dec in space, and just use the landers."

"Maybe."

"On the subject of things that breed like abat," Goloswin asked, "what are you going to do about the normals overbreeding?"

Tulo sighed. "I don't know if this will work, Golo, but in the short term, why do we breed normals, or allow them to breed?"

"Railgun and boma-blade fodder," the Tinkerer answered.

"Exactly, because the group that finds itself short of normals is obliterated by the group that breeds freely," Tulo agreed. "We, however, are just one group, in competition with no one. We can afford to cull our normals ruthlessly. I am thinking of permitting for each Kessentai who survives the breeding pens, only the five cosslain that average out, and for each cosslain, no more than four normals. Or perhaps not even one."

"Twenty servants per Kessentai? Or less? They'll bitch to no end."

"Let them, and we'll add twenty-one carcasses to the larder for each complaint."

"Here," Finba told his followers, pointing at a spot on the ground to one side of where a broad path, carved into the rock, descended from atop the mesa.

"Is there any reason for us to dig here, Acolyte?" one of his disciples asked.

"Just . . . just a feeling that if I were one of the old ones, this is a place where I might put a temple," Finba'anaga answered. "Here, perhaps, we may discover more of our gods, or more about the two we know about."

❖   ❖   ❖

Finba's followers, plus the hangers-on, willing to dig for a bit of their history, never numbered over three dozen, plus several times that in cosslain. They dug furiously, too furiously, in fact. Finba had to slow down the pace to allow the Kessentai to separate out fragments that might, or might not, mean something.

Meanwhile, the rest of the C-Dec's crew, brought down by landers in shifts, along with their machinery and their stockpiles of thresh, began the difficult task of preparing the land for agriculture. At Finba's behest, Tulo mandated that they could do so only outside of what the ship's sensors indicated were the city's boundary walls.

The new grain picked up on the previous world took to this original Posleen homeworld easily. Soon there were fields stretching as far as the eye could see, waving with the amber grain.

This world had seasons, seasons severe enough to require shelter. With the grain ripening, but chill winds blowing, it was time to build homes. The builder normals and cosslain here proved their value, chopping trees, quarrying stone, even making mud-brick and tile for roofs.

Still, Finba's crew, sometimes more, sometimes fewer, dug. Still the piles of rubble and artifacts grew. And then, one day, with a freezing rain pouring down from the heavens, one of the excavation crew found a stone claw and forearm.

"If this is here," Finba said, as he examined the finely carved piece, "it means that there is more, here. Let us continue to dig, but let us be more careful than ever. This may be the image of a god we are uncovering, my brothers."

✧　　　✧　　　✧

"That's another funny thing," Tulo observed one evening to Goloswin, as the frozen rain poured and the fierce wind howled. "One would think that, whenever our ancestors left this place, or were taken from it, that at least a couple of them would have missed the boat. And yet we find absolutely nothing that even resembles us except for some arboreal lizards that are, at best, distant cousins."

Goloswin answered, "Say whatever you will about them, Tulo, the Aldenata were advanced enough to be very thorough without even trying very hard."

"Maybe. Or maybe they made sure none of us would be left behind to develop on our own."

"You are thinking of a disease like the one we found on the first world we visited after our escape from Aradeen?" Golo asked.

"I don't know what I'm thinking of, old friend, except that this world seems too empty. Perhaps they had a way to call our ancestors to their ships for deportation."

"Hmmm . . . maybe. Well, cheer up. We're filling it as fast as we can and, with the control measures for normals you've decreed, it will still be a long time before it's overfilled with us. And when it is, well perhaps we can expand onto some of the moons. And past that? Who knows; maybe that paradise world can take some of the overflow."

"Or maybe the humans will find us and obliterate us," Tulo countered, staring into the firelight of the small hut they shared. "How's that for a cheery thought?"

✧　　　✧　　　✧

The shrieking wind whipped the tarp over the excavation. Beneath it, huddled with a follower, Finba'anaga shook his great crested head in frustration.

An arm here, a head there, a piece of a torso over there by that lump behind the other lump. Little by little, the statue is recovered.

"Except that it makes no sense," said Finba to his follower, Borasmena. "We've got way too many claws and crests and legs and whatnot for this to be a statue of anything of ours."

"Perhaps it's a statue of one of the demons," offered Borasmena.

In answer, Finba lifted the most complete claw they'd found and held it out next to his own. "This is Posleen," the acolyte said, "Posleen and nothing but. But it still makes no sense. We've never had five arms and seven legs and..."

"Finba," called another Kessentai from down in the pit they'd excavated. "Finba, come look at this."

The voice sounded insistent, even urgent. The acolyte trotted down the ramp into the pit.

"Yes, what is it," Finba'anaga asked.

The Kessentai in the pit, with a cosslain on either side, pointed downward. "At first," he said, "I thought this was just a covering over a trove or something."

Finba looked and saw an irregular cloth covering. "And?"

The Kessentai pulled the cloth away, revealing a partially uncovered stone platform. On the platform, a part of it, were two sets of four Posleen legs each, plus another part that appeared to be a rump with attached legs, dragging along the ground. The platform, itself, was carved to resemble rough ground, Finba thought.

"It's a group carving," the acolyte pronounced. "And I'm an idiot for not seeing that it had to be."

Spring was in the air, pollen flying, bird-cognates chirping, and the arboreal lizards calling out their mating cries, as Finba'anaga led Tulo'stenaloor and Goloswin along a well-worn path, through the small mounds that marked the city's ruins, to the pit he had had dug.

"It took forever to piece it together," Finba said, "and we're still not one hundred percent sure we've gotten everything right. But ... I think we've got a pretty good idea of where our ancestors were when the Demons came for them."

"So show me, puppy," Tulo said.

"Yes, lord; this way." Finba led the other two down into the pit, to where several of his own followers stood to either side of a cloth covering, hung across to cover *something*.

Finba took a deep breath, then nodded for Borasmena to drop the tarp. This the Kessentai did, revealing a three-figure statue, the cracks where the pieces had been joined just visible.

The immediate effect of the statue on Tulo and Golo was startlement. There, before them, an ancient Posleen stood, glaring defiance and brandishing a spear in their direction. That Kessentai, front torso covered with what appeared to be a cuirass, his head champroned, also held in one arm a small target, a round shield, covering its neck. Behind this one, another Posleen, legs dragging limply behind it, was being helped by the third. Both of the latter two still had head and eyes turned to face in the same direction as the spear brandisher. The wounded one—agony writ in every line of its body—still appeared to be trying to force its helper to let it return to whatever fight the spear brandisher faced.

A human might not have found the statue group beautiful. Tulo and Golo thought it was the most beautiful thing they'd ever seen, cracks and the odd missing claw or not. It was the pain and defiance of "The Dying Gaul", the inner sorrow of Michelangelo's "Pieta", the physical magnificence of his "David"... all rolled into one.

"This our ancestors were capable of, before the Aldenata took them?" Tulo whispered. He looked up, as straight up as his neck would allow his muzzle to point, and shouted, "We were *robbed*!"

CHAPTER TWENTY-SIX

Anno Domini 2022
USS Salem

"I just can't *stand* it, Dan," Sally said, again furiously pacing the confines of their quarters. "The reptilian bastard just sits in his quarters, *building* something and I can't tell what."

Dwyer sighed, his normal reaction when his wife was raging about the elder Posleen. "Try asking Freddie," he advised.

"I *have*. He's got no idea what his old... man is making. And my senses are useless to tell me anything but that there's a lot of metal, some of it highly conductive, and a lot of inert *stuff* I can't identify."

"It has to be coming from somewhere. Did you ask the forge?"

Sally's voice took on the intonation of a machine. "'I-am-sor-ry-ship-Sal-em-but-that-in-for-mat-ion-is-re-stric-ted.' Bastard fucking artificial sentience machine son of a bitch."

Dwyer cocked his head and raised one eyebrow, looking directly at his wife who, taken in her entirety, was one third machine intelligence as well.

"Oh, fuck you, Dan," she said, when she had seen. "I could pick up the bastard's voice but he never, *ever* says a word in his quarters about what he's working on."

"You're worrying about nothing," the priest insisted. "Look, it's just a few days until Christmas. Guano's been asked to make gifts by a *lot* of people. And he's had the forge working overtime on ornaments and garland. You've *seen* the manger and statuettes he's made."

"None of that convinces me he's anything but a raging monster inside. I finally figured out, Dan, why I can't stand the bastard. He's eaten *people*, something that the other two Posleen aboard have not. How's *that* for a crime that's beyond the pale, beyond forgiveness?"

Dwyer looked pained. It was one of the things he just hated to even think about. "A man's . . . a *being's* got the right to be judged in accordance with his own culture, his own place, and his own time," he insisted, defensively. "By that measure, Guanamarioch did nothing wrong. And he's still tried to make up for it."

"Tell it to all the people he turned into Posleen poop."

Frederico was asleep in his own cubicle off the main section of the family quarters. In one corner of that main cabin, lying on a cushion, Querida sewed a golden cloth into a long dress.

I never knew the skill set you brought with you when I found you on eBay, wife, Guano thought, warmly looking at her. *You amaze me more with each passing day. And to think; someone was trying to sell you to be killed for the bounty. Not all the crimes of the war, and the aftermath, were on our heads alone.*

Querida noticed her Kessentai's stare and trilled something that, in their private language, meant, approximately, *I think we're alone now.*

"Later, wife," Guano said. "We have duties to our fellow beings before we think of our own pleasures."

Querida got the important part, *"later,"* and went back to her sewing with no more than a mildly disappointed *huff.* There would be time. Not too much time, though, she hoped. She felt a Kessentai, or at least a cosslain, beginning to form within her and she *so* wanted more offspring that would not become part of the larder.

Guano wanted that, too, perhaps especially because Frederico was *not* going to be following in his father's clawsteps. The lovingly cared for armor and halberd in another corner of the cabin confirmed that. There was another jumble of armor stuffed in a closet, mostly pieces the boy had outgrown.

Well, Guano thought, *that's not necessarily true. He could become a minister of the Lord . . . the day he becomes a Roman Catholic and the day their pope reforms the Teutonic Knights or the Hospitalers.*

The thought, maybe more the image in his mind of his son accoutered as both knight and horse, plumes and all, caused Guano to snort mildly, in amusement.

Querida looked up again and once again trilled, *I think we're alone now.*

"Soon, wife," Guano answered. "Soon; I promise." With mild bad grace she returned to her task.

For his part, Guano busied himself with assembling metal pieces into a framework of sorts. The universal bonding agent the forge had provided made that task quick and easy, leaving only the faintest trace of seams where pieces joined. Guano knew the specs of the stuff, and knew that the seams were stronger than the material that was joined.

I wonder, he thought, as he matched one small section to another larger one and gently squeezed the tube of bonding agent to join them, *I wonder if this stuff was ours or a gift of the Aldenata?*

Surrounded by others of the crew and passengers, by no means all of them Christian (al Rashid, for example, was on the piano), Nurse Duvall belted out a heartfelt and moving rendition of "Ave Maria", backed up by the Vexillatione Helveticus Chorus (Rossini, de Courten, Faubion, Stoever, and Affenzeller, dressed, respectively as: three wise men, one stable keeper, and a Star of Bethlehem. Lying nearby, Frederico, much to his disgust, had had several mattresses disassembled and the product therefrom glued to his body. (Though he had grown way, *way* too big for the part, he was supposed to be a lamb.)

Duvall sang:

> "*Ave Maria, gratia plena*
> *Dominus tecum benedicta tu in mulieribus*
> *Et benedictus fructus ventris tuis Jesus*

Sancta Maria, Sancta Maria, Maria
Ora pro nobis
Nobis peccatoribus Nunc et in hora,
in hora mortis nostrae."

One could hardly tell that this was the same hall in which the Switzers and the Posleen, Frederico and Querida practiced their battle and weapons drill. After all, the weapons were put up. To one corner stood an artificial tree decorated with ornaments the Reverend Guanamarioch had coaxed out of the forge, along with garland and tinsel that, all of them being 99.99 fine gold, would have set a Swiss banker's heart, if he'd had one, to racing. In another corner was a makeshift manger, containing figurines hand carved by the reverend of artificial Posleen ivory. In the middle, a large number of people in various forms of dress enjoyed the music, sang as the mood and the ability took them, and quaffed down the spirits that Duvall had released from stores with free abandon.

Under the tree were presents, usually small things, some personal items regifted because, sad to say, there was no shop aboard the *Salem*. Guano, in fact, had been kept fairly busy by people asking for this or that to be made to give to some special friend aboard ship. Where he could help, he did. He'd even helped Dwyer come up with some material to have a new dress sewn by Querida for Sally. Von Altishofen, too, had asked for some earrings for Duvall. Yes, those, too, were pure gold.

Sally, shining in that gown, knew this and, despite the knowing, kept casting sideways suspicious glances at the Kessentai, his great head, eyes closed in a state of religious rapture, weaving back and forth in time to Duvall's and the chorus' singing.

The song ended, to much applause, and Frederico, to his great relief, was able to get up, move himself to an alcove, and begin tearing off the tufts adorning his body, throwing them to the deck with disgust. Even as he disappeared, Duvall and the chorus took their bows, before launching into another number, this time in German:

> "Stille Nacht, heilige Nacht
> Alles schlaeft; einsam wacht
> Nur das traute heilige Paar..."

Most of those in the assembly hall knew the song in one language or another; it had been translated, after all, into more than one hundred human tongues. About the time Duvall and company reached "Paar" the others, those who could, joined in.

Even Sally joined. Jewish or not, and the song in German or any other language, the singing was too beautiful not to take part in it. Perhaps it was the more beautiful still for being sung so deep in lonely space.

> "Durch der Engel Alleluja
> Toent es laut bei Ferne und Nah
> Jesus der Retter ist da...a
> Jesus der Retter ist da"

When that was over, Duvall and the chorus looked directly at Dan Dwyer and began to chant, "Father Dwyer, Father Dwyer, Father Dwyer..."

Eventually, under the press, the priest stood up.

Sally, too, stood and ran over to al Rashid and the piano.

"Do you know the song he's going to sing?" Sally asked, then leaned down and whispered a title in the imam's ear. "Christmas in the Trenches?"

"No . . . I've never even heard of it," the Moslem answered.

"Let me take over the piano then," she said. The imam, with good grace, slid aside on the bench, making room for the woman who was also the ship.

When Dwyer reached the low stage, he nodded at Sally. She began a musical introduction composed half of "The Minstrel Boy" and half of something else altogether. At the right time, Dwyer began to sing, in a good Irish tenor's voice:

> *"Oh, my name is Francis Tolliver;*
> *I come from Liverpool:*
> *Two years ago the war was waiting*
> *for me after school . . ."*[1]

By the time Dwyer was done ("And on each end of the rifle we're the same"), and had left hardly a dry eye in the house, Sally noticed that Guanamarioch was among the missing. A quick check of the ship showed that he was back in the quarters he shared with Querida and Frederico.

"Damn it to Hell that I can't see in detail anywhere I don't have cameras," Sally quietly cursed. "Especially since I don't trust the bastard an inch farther than I could throw him."

---

1 Christmas in the Trenches. © 1984, John McCutcheon

✧   ✧   ✧

Guano worked feverishly. He *had* to be done by morning, just *had* to be.

The nine major sections of the frame of his project fitted together reasonably well. He assembled seven of them, then took one and began bonding to it sections from which draped fine gold wire. There were one hundred and twenty such sections, each shaped somewhat differently. From each of those came about one hundred golden wires, fourteen or fifteen inches long. Before bonding, Guano emplaced each section to make sure it fit. Sometimes, he had to take his carving knife and make some minute corrections. There were just enough of these that a small pile of golden wire began to grow at his feet.

He attached the eighth section, fixing it in place with the bonding agent. The ninth, when he picked it up, he was not quite content with. The Posleen's claws were a blur as they wiped out imagined imperfections in the material. Satisfied, the Kessentai picked up a white orb with a bluish center and fixed it in the ninth section. Another followed that one. Then a dab of the bonding agent here, another there and yet another there, and the composite piece was attached to the main assembly.

From there Guano worked his way down, adding carefully carved pieces that he had long since had checked by his AS for fit. Quickly, though it seemed to take forever, the project took on the shape he had intended all along. Guano went to the closet to get a very important section, hidden in among his son's old, no longer fitting, armor.

✧   ✧   ✧

Sally could sense inside the Posleens' quarters, even if she couldn't see. And what she sensed she didn't like at all. A mass of material was growing inside that space, rapidly, as if from a kit or a clever plan.

There was no monstrosity she would put past any Posleen, excepting only Querida and Frederico who seemed to her to be merely ugly, scaly, quadruped people.

I am in danger, she thought. *Me, me... the ship me... my passengers... my husband. And no one will* listen. *I can't let that centauroid bastard finish. But at the rate he's progressing, how do I stop him? Hand to hand? He'd tear me apart. And then probably chew my bones. The armory, then.*

Finally deciding that the time had come for direct action, Sally stood and, trailing the golden gown Querida had made for her, began to walk briskly out of the assembly and drill hall, down the corridor, down some ramps and around several corners, to the ship's armory. The armory doors, normally tightly locked, opened for her under AID control just as she arrived.

Inside, she glanced quickly over the various implements of retail death and destruction, finally settling on her husband's old large-caliber, American-made pistol. The bar holding the pistol in place sprang open, even as another door, this one for a locker containing ammunition, gaped wide. Grasping the pistol, Sally turned to the ammunition locker, withdrawing a box of fifty rounds and two empty seven-round magazines. Tearing the box open and spilling the rounds to an adjacent flat space, Sally set down the .45 and began loading the golden-colored bullets into the magazines, one by one.

✧   ✧   ✧

One by one, Guano applied bonding agent to twenty five golden nails and set them in their proper places. It was delicate work, and difficult. They had to be just so, to get the proper effect. That done, he took thick golden loops, two of them, and affixed them to their proper places. Another, even thicker than the first two, had to go also in its own certain place.

And that was the last piece. He stepped back, to admire for a moment his handiwork.

As the Kessentai stood there, looking for imperfections in his design, the cabin door whooshed open. He turned his head just in time to see Salem, sometimes called "Shlomit," the woman standing there with a weapon in her hand, the wide muzzle of the weapon fixed firmly on his own head.

"You bas—"

The woman never finished whatever it was she had been about to say. She lowered the weapon, even relaxed her grip on it so that it hung loosely in her hand.

Guano smiled, sadly. He was pretty sure what she had been about to say and very sure why the weapon had been pointed at him.

Instead of speaking through his AS, he spoke in his own halting and imperfect Spanish, knowing the woman could translate perfectly and instantaneously.

"Myyyy . . . *eson'antai* . . . myyyy sssooonnn . . . heee telll mmmeee . . . youuu . . . unhapppyyy . . . fffeeelll uggglllyyy . . . inn nnnewww bbbodddyyy. I . . . mmake . . . theeese . . . sssooo . . . youuu . . . fffeeelll . . . beautiff-fuuulll . . . agggaaaiiinnn."

Through tears of shame and regret, Sally saw finally what the Posleen's project had been. It was a statue, of her, a beautiful statue, lifelike if idealized, all gold and ivory and precious gems. On a second and more careful look she saw that it was not a statue, exactly. Behind the thing it did not match her body, but was concave. A quick and automatic check of her data banks told her that the concave matched perfectly the curve of the prow of the part of her that was the ship. Instead of a statue, the Posleen had made her a figurehead, to grace her bow and be the beauty she no longer felt herself to be.

Unable to speak, Sally turned away, fleeing through the door of the Posleen cabin to her own quarters. There, she dropped the pistol finally and flung herself onto the bed she shared with Dwyer, crying still in pain and shame.

Guano didn't understand at all. Human emotions were difficult things for him to grasp. He was pretty sure that he'd seen tears in the woman's eyes, but understood that tears could mean different things in different contexts. Briefly, he considered the possibility that Sally had hated the figurehead he'd made for her. Certainly that could account for the weapon and the tears. Briefly, too, he considered just smashing the thing and returning its elements to the forge to be used for some purpose she might approve of.

Best to ask her mate, first, I think.

"Holy shi—" the priest began when he saw the Posleen enter the assembly hall with the statue under one arm. He stopped and started again, "What the fu—" All the people in the hall looked at the priest, half in reproach and half in amusement.

I've spent way *too much time surrounded by Marines,* he thought.

He saw instinctively what Sally had had to consult her data banks for; a figurehead...no, a *beautiful* figurehead, to grace the bow of the part of his wife that was a ship.

"Wait 'til Sally sees this," he said to Guano. "She's going to be—"

"She's already seen it," the Posleen said, through his AS. "But I don't think she—"

One of the doors to the hall whooshed open. Through it Sally walked, her face still puffy from crying. She went directly to the Posleen. Standing in front of him she felt the tears begin to flow once again.

Barely able to speak, she leaned forward and flung her arms around the scaly neck. "Thank you," she whispered. "Thank you, and please forgive me for being a bitch."

PART III

CHAPTER TWENTY-SEVEN

Before I formed you in the womb I knew you,
before you were born I dedicated you,
a prophet to the nations I appointed you.
—Jeremiah 1:5, New American Bible

Anno Domini 2024
Posleen Prime

The crenellated city walls, a lovely light crimson granite, had long since been rebuilt. The setting sun shone upon them, making them glow and leaving the gate toward which Tulo'stenaloor and Goloswin passed a dark half-ovoid by comparison.

There was no real practical need for the walls; the planet had no predators larger and fiercer than the People, and there were no other groups of Posleen against which a defense was needed. Nonetheless, on Finba'anaga's advice, Tulo had authorized the rebuilding to form a capsule of sorts, a boundary of in and out, to bind the People together as a community.

Whether it was the physical fact of the walls that bound the people, or whether the rebuilding had done so, or whether it was both of those things *and* the philosophy and religion of Finba'anaga that had done so, Tulo didn't know. He suspected it was all of those things together, and perhaps still more factors too subtle to be named.

Approaching the city, Tulo and Golo passed through fields of ripened and nearly ripened grain. It was the same grain they had found on the world remade to suit the Posleen, so many orbits past. Mixed in among the rectangular fields were other, fallow, fields as well as orchards of various fruit-bearing trees native—at least they thought they were native—to the planet.

Herds of normals walked the grain fields, under the supervision of cosslain. They wore baskets on either side of their torsos, into which they deposited the grain as it was harvested. The normals' progress was slow, as they ate the stubble from their harvesting down to the ground. This was fine, though, as the ripe grain would last quite a long time on its stalks, and the stalks themselves were more than adequate fodder for the normals.

Most of those normals were those with no other useful skills, under the current circumstances, and would eventually be turned into thresh themselves.

The path Tulo and Golo trod was a winding plank road, made up of harvested logs, sliced and covered with sand. The wood of the planks, themselves, was highly resistant to rot and wear, and thus made a good compromise between sinking knee deep in muck during the wet season, and abrading unhooved and unshod claws the rest of the year.

Most of the logs for the road had come from the once overgrown city.

"Two grat for one," Golo had called this. He said it again, now, as the pair passed through the gate and entered the lower town.

It wasn't completely rebuilt, that city. There were small pyramids for each of the Kessentai, and stables for their limited numbers of cosslain and normals. Some of the temples—what were presumed to be temples, anyway; for all anyone knew they might have been museums, or factories, or kitchens—were rebuilt. Still others were not. Work on those proceeded slowly.

Flanked by small pyramids and flatter roofed stables, Tulo and Golo walked to the path carved from the base of the mesa that dominated the lower town to its top. Tulo stopped, as he did every time he passed it, to admire the three-figure statue of the olden Kessentai that Finba's party had found early on.

"What might we have become, Golo," the clan lord asked aloud, "if the Demons had never found us and perverted us?"

"We may have perverted ourselves, too, you know, Tulo," the tinkerer said, as the two began their plod to the top of the mesa. "In all this city, with thousands of statues and the dim traces of paintings, and tons upon tons of old bones, we have never found a single trace of a normal or cosslain. It may be that we did this, perhaps under Aldenata prodding and perhaps on our own accord to serve the Demons better."

"Well," Tulo sighed. "We are as we are, and

Finba'anaga's attempts to make us as he thinks we were notwithstanding, we must do the best we can."

"That best has not been so bad, Clan Lord," the tinkerer whispered. "We are, after all, at peace. Our population grows, slowly but sanely. And no one is trying to kill us."

The tinkerer whispered, yet not so lowly that Tulo's keen hearing couldn't pick it up. He clapped a hand to his friend's shoulder and said, "I, too, Tinkerer, find that I am happier here than I have ever been before."

At the top of the mesa, in a ring around their leader's pyramid, ten of the twelve landers were spread out along the edge. These, too, had grown into pyramids. Each was the quarters of one or two of Tulo's original closest followers or of a Kessentai who had been selected to fill vacancies, as Finba had been selected, for example, to fill the vacancy left by the old Rememberer's death, a dozen orbits prior. The last two landers were there, as well, but these were kept un-built-upon, to maintain connection with the C-Dec and to bring groups of the People on such various journeys of exploration as Tulo had authorized.

The C-Dec, free of abat and grat since Golo had had it emptied for a time and opened it to space, kept a low maintenance orbit around the planet, always with at least two Kessentai and a few weapons-skilled cosslain aboard, the minimum required to move and fight the ship, because one never knew.

❖   ❖   ❖

"Binastarion calling, lord," Tulo's AS announced.

"Yes, Bina. I'm listening."

The Kessentai's voice contained infinite sadness as he said, "Tulo...the humans are here."

USS Salem

Sally, the AID, announced over ship's speakers, "KE cannon powered up and on line. Emergence in... five...four...three...two..."

The weaving grays and pinks of hyperspace disappeared, to be replaced by stars and planets and a single detectible Posleen ship, in orbit about one of those planets.

"One target identified; Posleen C-Dec. He is powering up his weapons. I am targeting...targeting... I have target lock and awaiting command to fire."

"Hold fire," Dwyer said. "We're a mission of peace. Can you contact that C-Dec?"

"Attempting contact now," the ship answered.

Dwyer watched as the stars and planets on the main viewer were replaced by, first static, then the dim outline of a Kessentai, then finally a clear enough picture of one of the crested, centauroid aliens. The Posleen's mouth was moving, though no sound of words came at first.

"Translation program on line," the ship announced. "He says his name is Binastarion and that this is Posleen space. He says they will fight in defense."

And that, too, is a change, Dwyer thought. *A Posleen who doesn't attack at the first sign of one of us. Perhaps they learned something from the war.*

C-Dec Arganaza'al

A human ship that did not open fire upon emergence?
Binastarion thought in wonder. *That's a change. Enough
to risk not engaging while they're still disoriented from
emergence? Sure... why not? They outmass me by a
factor of maybe four claws. The sooner I open fire, the
sooner I die and the People below are left defenseless.*

USS Salem

"Do we know anything about Binastarion?" Dwyer
asked aloud.

Guano, brought to the bridge of *Salem* for his
insights into his own people, answered, "It's not an
uncommon name. There was a Binastarion commanding
the western front on the Posleen side, in Panama, during the war. I doubt they're the same being, though."

Dwyer looked at his wife, also standing by on the
bridge by the fire control station.

"Human Face Recognition Technology never really
was adapted to the Posleen face," she said. "Even if
I or my sister caught a glimpse of that Binastarion,
we have no way of telling if this one is the same."

"Fair enough. Can I speak with him?"

"Yes. Go ahead. He's listening."

"Binastarion," Dwyer said, "I am Father Daniel
Dwyer, Society of Jesus, and captain of this ship, the
USS *Salem*—"

"During the war I fought a wet surface ship named
Salem," the Posleen interrupted, "along with one named

Des Moines. They were redoubtable opponents. This ship is named for that one?"

"This ship *is* that one," Dwyer answered, "much modified."

The Posleen on the screen whistled. Dwyer wasn't quite sure what the sound meant. He asked Guano, standing next to him.

"Isss sssounnnd offf . . . prrraissse . . . wworrrththhthyyy fffoe."

Turning back to the image on the screen, Guano asked, in High Posleen, "Are you that same Binastarion who led the People in the place on Earth called 'Panama'?"

"I am . . . though that was long ago and I was Kessentai then, not Kessenalt, as I am now. I threw my stick, you see, after the last, disastrous battle."

"In that case," the reverend said, "formal introductions are not necessary. You all know each other very well."

"Threw your stick, did you?" Dwyer said, his voice filled with irony. "I think maybe we're even better acquainted than the reverend thinks. May we come aboard, Binastarion, to parley?"

Pinnace, USS Salem

Halfway between the two ships, the smaller C-Dec and USS *Salem*, the pinnace sailed through vacuum. Aboard was a small party, including Dwyer and Guano and the Indowy, Aelool. The priest toyed contemplatively with a dull metal stick, about a foot and a half long and square in cross section. He'd kept it all these years, ever since the Posleen had tossed it to him aboard one of USS *Des Moines'* lifeboats.

"I have no idea of the proper protocol," Guano, speaking through his AS, told Dwyer. "So far as I know, it's never been done before. When a Kessentai tosses his stick in battle, he doesn't survive the experience."

"Indeed, lord, there is no precedent of which I am aware for giving his stick back to a Kessentai who's turned Kessenalt," the AS added.

"All right," the priest agreed. "Do you, personally, think it would hurt any?"

"It might," Guano thought. "A Kessentai who's thrown his stick and then turned from the battle might feel honor bound to continue the battle he'd left off."

Dwyer, considering it, thought, *My, wouldn't that just suck?*

"I agree, lord," added the AS. "It is . . . dangerous. At least until you have some idea how that particular philosopher might react."

"I'll take your advice, then," Dwyer agreed, sliding the stick down into his uniform jacket. "Perhaps, after this meeting, you may judge better."

C-Dec Arganaza'al

There were only seven Posleen, a Kessentai, a Kessenalt, and five cosslain, aboard the ship. This caused a certain surprise for Dwyer when he and his party were met by just two of them, the Kessenalt, Binastarion, and a single cosslain.

"I am just here to entertain you," Binastarion said, his own AS translating. "Our clan lord, Tulo'stenaloor, will be coming up from the surface within one of your hours to discuss matters with you."

"Binastarion," the AS said, in Posleen, "although he seems younger, as best I can judge, this is the human to whom you threw your stick."

"The funny collar about its neck is the same, I grant you, AS, but—"

"Your AS is correct, Binastarion," Guano said. "This *is* that human."

"I think then," said the Kessenalt, "that we will have many good war stories to lie to each other about."

"To that end," said Guano, reaching into his harness bag and pulling out a gallon jug, "may I ask if you've ever been introduced to that semi-divine human mixture, scotch and *formaldehyde*?"

Posleen Prime

The lander was warmed up, with but a single Kessentai aboard to pilot it. Outside, by the broad landing and boarding ramp, the tinkerer and his clan lord argued.

"I really don't think you should be going into space at all," Golo said to Tulo. "Especially should you not be going with no escort."

The clan lord shook his great head. "Do you really think that a hundred guards would make a difference in space, Tinkerer? You heard Binastarion; that ship is enormous, a match for ten or twenty C-Decs. And what good do you think it would do to stay on the ground? If it's that big, it could hold an entire oolton of the metal threshkreen. No, I'll not skulk. If they mean us harm perhaps I can dissuade them. If they mean us well, as Binastarion says they insist they do, and which he says there is reason to believe is true, I'd like to know just what 'well' they mean us. And direct it, if possible, of course."

"Binastarion says that the Indowy, Aelool, is among their party."

Tulo laughed. "You know, Golo," he said, "there was a time, and not so long ago, I'd have gladly hacked that fuzzy-faced little swine to bits for all the trouble he put us through."

"Not now?" Goloswin asked.

"Ask yourself, Tinkerer; are we better off or worse off for all that trouble?"

Golo didn't hesitate in answering, "In the main, better. No...without him we'd all be dead, so clearly we're better off."

"So think I. If anything, I probably ought to reward the motherfucker."

C-Dec Arganaza'al

The Posleen were not a people deeply enamored of pomp and circumstance. No sooner had Tulo's lander docked to the C-Dec than he exited and made his way down to the assembly area where sat the humans and their little pinnace.

Entering that area, Tulo looked at one very nervous seeming Indowy and said, through his AS, "If you only knew, little one, the trouble you caused." Aelool managed to look more nervous still before the clan lord burst into Posleen laughter and added, "Name your reward."

"Forgiveness would be nice," Aelool, no less nervous seeming, answered.

"That's too little," Tulo said.

"Then ... let these humans perform the mission they have come on," Aelool suggested.

"Their mission?" Tulo asked.

"They—most of them, anyway—wish to acquaint the People of the Ships with their belief in a superior being, one they believe created the universe and all the life within it. I think, by the way, that their message is a practical false one, but a philosophical truth. I also think that hearing that message just might be to the benefit of your people, Tulo, Lord of Clan Sten."

"You said, 'most of them,' Indowy. What do the others want?"

"Tulo, there are too many variants to the basic message to relate. Suffice to say that some among their party have a religion—that's the term the humans use—very similar to the ancestor reverence practiced by the Posleen, that others believe in more than one superior being, that still others do not believe in a superior being at all, but do believe that each sentient being has a soul which returns to life again and again until it has finally learned all it needs to learn to cease returning to life."

"And why do the humans seek to bring us these conflicting messages?" Tulo asked.

Aelool didn't answer, but looked directly at Dwyer.

"In part," the Jesuit said, "for the good of your souls ... and ours ... in part for the peace of the galaxy."

"I cannot and will not order any of my people to believe in and join your religions," Tulo said, after some hours of negotiations. "I cannot and will not at this time commit to an alliance with the humans, even against the never-sufficiently-to-be-damned Darhel. I *can* offer your humans, Father Dwyer, the chance to speak to my people and to persuade them *if they can*. I will even provide Kessentai to escort and provide safe conduct. Further, however, I cannot go."

Dwyer nodded. It was reasonable. *No*, he thought, *it's more than reasonable. Who would have assumed that the great Tulo'stenaloor, "murderer on a planetary scale," could, in fact, be such a reasonable creature.* The priest looked "up," so to speak, even though "up" was all around him, and thought, too, *Lord, Your ways, however I may try to understand them, are beyond my ken. Which does not mean I won't keep asking for an explanation, mind You.*

Posleen Prime

"The humans will be coming down," Tulo said. Most of his group of close advisors trusted his judgment in this. Others were more skeptical. One, at least, Goloswin, was simply fearful.

"Must we let them among us, Tulo? Bringing their alien philosophies? Are you sure they mean us no harm?"

Tulo'stenaloor sighed. "I'm as sure as I can be. I'm not quite as sure what their reaction would be if I refused them permission. It might be . . . very bad. Their leader, a sort of Rememberer, seemed like a very reasonable being but, like the rest of you, I've met human duplicity before.

"Still," Tulo continued, "I see no reason to simply trust them. Essone?"

"Yes, lord," answered that staff officer, a replacement for the one lost and presumed eaten on Hemaleen V.

"I want you to make a list of those among our Kessentai who are most reliable and also most reasonable. I've told the humans I will give them escorts to ensure their safety. I want those to be escorts who will observe and report, as well."

"I'll make the arrangements, lord," the Essone answered.

CHAPTER TWENTY-EIGHT

Home had the wanderers come,
home to the planet of the People
And yet home, once left,
ceases ever to be the same home again.
—The *Tuloriad*, Na'agastenalooren

Anno Domini 2024
Posleen Prime

Finba'anaga took a certain justifiable pride in the part he had played in reconstructing Posleen civilization, such as it was. Still, it was not an unlimited pride. He knew, for example, that the old religion he had recreated was, at best, partial and incomplete—"about one molecule deep," as he sometimes phrased it. He suspected that, so long as there were normals and cosslain, there could be no going back to the true old ways. Even so, what they had—a city, a civic life, an economy—they had regained in goodly part through his own efforts and insights.

Nor did Finba have any strong feelings against the

humans. After all, *he'd* never fought them, personally. Then, too, there was a certain, not entirely unjustifiable, fear of them. From everything he'd learned, they were simply dangerous, too dangerous to provoke.

For that reason, he could see, too, how Tulo'stenaloor might feel the need to acquiesce in the humans' frankly bizarre request to spread word of their equally bizarre "religions." He wasn't even particularly worried about it. What appeal, after all, could an alien god have to his own people?

And then he saw the being he waited for, the interesting one. Possibly even the most dangerous one. Guanamarioch.

Only the two junior Posleen were armed, Querida with her ancient boma blade strapped to her side and Frederico with his monomolecular halberd carried in his claws. Along with a small crowd of others, the three of them—Guano, Frederico, and Querida—debarked from the pinnace to air that should have felt like home yet did not. Neither Querida nor her son, both having been born on Earth, really felt that anyplace but Earth could be home, though Posleden was still better. Guano, though born on a different planet, still had spent so much of his life on Earth that it—barring only the never-sufficiently-to-be-damned jungle—seemed more like home than anyplace else.

The only homelike thing about Posleen prime, the presence of a majority population of his own people, was disconcerting to Frederico and Querida precisely because they had never been around any Posleen but each other and Guano. Oh, yes, Querida had been raised in a breeding pen by a bughouse nuts Kessentai who sold his progeny to humans for the bounty on their heads, but of this she had little memory. For Frederico, on the other hand, he'd never even *seen* a Posleen outside of his own, immediate, family. (His father had made very sure that the boy never saw any of the stuffed heads some people kept on their walls.)

"Is this what the world you were born on was like, Dad?" Frederico asked as the trio ambled along the clay-topped road that led from the pinnace's landing point to the city gate.

"Not really, Son," the minister answered. "This is much too peaceful for close resemblance. The world I was born on was already sliding into orna'adar by the time I was taken out of the breeding pens. That world was hot. This one is cooler. The gravity here feels lighter, too, and the sun's a better color."

"It's weird to me," Frederico said. "I've never been around any others of the People besides you and Mom. I don't know if I can trust them."

"Christian charity would tell you to trust them, Son," Guano said. "But I know my own people and I'd advise you *not* to trust them until you know them a lot better."

A couple of humans in white shirts with black ties passed by Finba'anaga, folding bycicles slung across their backs. He paid them no mind, though one of the waiting Kessentai soon took them in tow. Rather, Finba kept his concentration firmly fixed on the trio of Posleen.

Tulo'stenaloor hadn't specifically ordered an escort for the Posleen, perhaps on the theory that they would be in no particular danger from the others of the People.

Which does not mean, Finba thought, *that we are in no danger from them. Which is why I am here.*

Finba waited until the small crowd from the humans' ship's pinnace had begun to disperse before walking over and introducing himself. Crossing his arms in front of his chest and making a slight bow, Finba said, "I am Finba'anaga, lately of the Clan of Sten, servant to Tulo'stenaloor and high acolyte in the Way of Remembrance."

Guano repeated the gesture. "Guanamarioch, of the . . . the Clans of the Baptists and the Episcopals, in the service of our Lord," he said. Guano's head dipped right and then left. "My *eson'antai*, Frederico, and my wife, Querida. Are you assigned as our escort?"

Finba understood *eson'antai,* of course. In High Posleen it meant, approximately, "prized lineal descendant." The term "wife" was new to him, however. He inquired.

"Traditionally, we mate with only one," Guano answered, "and we mate for life. Under the pressure of population imbalance, this is changing, for some. Beyond that, it is hard to explain. A wife is . . . well . . . in human terms, they having two sexes and one of those giving live birth, a wife is the bearer of the young. It is the husband's task to support the wife in her major task. She, because of the time and care she must devote to bearing and raising the young is uniquely valuable, in a way that a cosslain of the People never is."

Guano couldn't even imagine the shrieks that would arise from human feminists if they could have heard that. On the other hand, Earth and its humans had many fewer feminists than had once been the case. Many, faced not with theory but with the hard reality of the war, had decided that, after all, perhaps men *should* be the ones to bear the brunt of the fighting. Still others, refusing to accept this, had been eaten in highly disproportionate numbers. The widespread adoption of polygamy had still further reduced both feminist numbers and influence. Humanity thought of itself as being very traditional now. Guano wondered on occasion if he could ever have fit in as well as he had, or if he might have made a better fit, in the society that preceded the one he had come to know.

"My wife is uniquely valuable to me." Unconsciously Guano's claw went to stroke Querida's back. Equally unconsciously, she leaned in against him.

"Yes . . . yes, I can see that," Finba said. "It is a very beautiful cosslain."

"Not 'it,'" Guano corrected. "She."

Changing the subject (for the ideas of uniquely valuable cosslain or, worse still, cosslain with a sex distinct from a Kessentai, were, at best, uncomfortable. And an unarmed, adult Kessentai escorted by an armed cosslain and juvenile? Unthinkable!), Finba continued, "I am, in any case, here as your escort. Where would you like to go?"

Guano thought upon that only for a moment before answering, "Somewhere where there are Kessentai and Kessenalt in numbers, then, and perhaps even some cosslain."

"The Roga'a then," Finba said. "Certainly it should be crowded by the time we get there, anyway. Follow me."

Whatever it was that keyed Querida most *emphatically* not to trust their escort, Guano didn't know. He only knew that she kept softly whistling the danger signal, tugging at his arm, pointing at her sword, and making throat-slitting gestures while keeping her gaze fixed on Finba'anaga's twitching hindquarters. He shushed her by placing a single claw over her muzzle.

"I understand, love," he said, even while thinking, *your instincts in this may be good. We shall be careful but* without *committing murder.*

As Finba had promised, the Roga'a was reasonably crowded by the time the party arrived. Most of the activity was mercantile, with bits of heavy metal changing claws in exchange for cloth, or harnesses, or thresh, or tools.

Guano stopped for a moment, to Finba's mild annoyance, to watch two cosslain bargaining over some fresh, which is to say still living, nestling. Their bargaining was nonverbal, but intense for all that. The cosslain in search of thresh pointed out two that seemed good to it. The other, the one running the shop, then put on a sort of chain mail glove and reached down to grab one of the nestlings. The nestling spat and hissed and even got a toothy grip on the mail, but to no avail. The shopkeeper's mailed claws wrapped around it, pulled it from its pen, and dumped it in a smaller pen on the counter. She then did the same with a second nestling.

The second cosslain then reached into a pouch and put forth on the counter two small bits of heavy metal. The shopkeeper sneered until a third piece was added. This got rid of the sneer but also caused the shopkeeper to pick up one of the nestlings as if to put it back in the pen. At that the second cosslain hissed and began to reach for the golden bits. The shopkeeper then stopped, holding the thrashing, hissing, biting nestling above the pen.

When they finally settled on a price, five bits for the two nestlings, the shopkeeper took one of the nestlings and forced its head down to the counter. With its other claw it took what appeared to be a miniature boma blade, more handle than blade, and neatly sliced off the spitting nestling's head. In a few more seconds the second nestling had joined the first. Both heads and bodies were then wrapped in something that looked like a cheap kind of cloth and handed over to the shopper. The gold bits likewise were raked away into a claw and deposited into a pouch on the shopkeeper's harness.

"What's so interesting about a simple thresh purchase?" Finba asked.

Guano shook his head. "You don't know whether those nestlings would have become sentient or not," he answered.

"What difference? They weren't sentient when they were chopped, and they surely won't get any more sentient when they're eaten. I understand Goloswin is working on a way to tell the difference early, but that way is still imperfect."

"Seems wrong, somehow," Guano answered. "And they were big enough almost to begin to show a crest if they were going to . . . or to act like cosslain, even if not."

"Well, it's done now, anyway. Come, if you would see the Roga'a."

With a shrug, not of indifference but of helplessness, Guano began to follow again, Frederico and Querida in tow.

✧ ✧ ✧

"What do you call that great massif looming over us?" Guano asked, pointing at the mesa that dominated the city.

"It doesn't really have a name beyond the upper city or the high city," Finba answered.

"Ah. Yes, that makes sense. The humans would call it an 'acropolis,' perhaps."

"I like that term," Finba said. "Perhaps we'll adopt it . . . if we adopt nothing else the humans have to offer."

"Well, I do hope the People may adopt something else the humans have to offer," Guano answered.

We'll see, thought Finba'anaga. He pointed at a raised square of some kind of whitish rock with veins of blue, pink and gold running through it. "If you wish to address the People," Finba said, "that's where you'll attract an audience."

Guano had thought long upon the problem, all the long months aboard ship. Truthfully, he'd been thinking about it since receiving his own call back in the ruined cathedral in Old Panama during the war. *How in Hell do I even begin to catch their attention?*

Now, as he took the few steps leading up to the platform Finba had shown to him, all his prior ruminations fled him. Instead he just stood there, flanked by his wife and son, and watched for a while as various of the People gathered. Some came to admire Querida's ancient, gem-encrusted boma blade, he knew. Still others gathered closely to glimpse and evaluate Frederico's halberd; he could hear that in their admiring comments. And perhaps a few even came closer to gawk at his clerical collar or the cross he wore about his neck.

His escort, Finba'anaga, watched, too. But that Kessentai, Guano could see, was watching for the reaction of the crowd.

Well, that's both our interests, Guano thought. And then, for a while, he tried very hard not to think, but only to feel or, rather, to think about those things that raised feelings.

He thought about his subordinate, friend, and mentor, Ziramoth, sinking to the dirt, mortally wounded by a primitive arrow somewhere in the jungles of the Darien, in Panama, on Earth. He thought about his entire pack, massacred by the same Indian who had shot the arrow that killed Ziramoth, by him and by the jungle. It was a sadness he had rarely in his life since been able to face.

But what were those, compared to the five billion human dead, the *fifteen* billion of the People's dead, the races across half a galactic arm rendered extinct by the Posleen migration, the ruined civilizations, the waste, the destruction, the horror...

From his perch on the speaking platform, his head bowed down with the weight of genocide, Guanamarioch gave off an inarticulate cry of absolute despair.

Neither Frederico nor Querida had expected this. The boy asked, "Dad, are you all right?" The wife leaned into her mate and began trying to comfort him by rubbing the top of her muzzle under his chin. The question remained unanswered; the comforting touch gave no comfort. Soon, Guano's body began to shake and shudder with his sorrow.

That's bizarre conduct, thought Finba'anaga. *Does he think to sway the People with madness?*

Finba then saw, though, that several score of the People inched closer. A few called out "What grieves you, Kessentai?" or "What is the source of your pain?" or, more dangerous still, "Can we help you, Kessentai?"

I don't like this a bit.

"I grieve for you, brother," Guano said to one. "My pain is in your fate, friend," he answered another. "You can help me, philosopher, if you will let me help you," he said to a third.

Turning to Querida, Guano asked, "Would you hold your boma blade up, hilt first, love?"

She did, making a sort of crucifix of the kind once understandable to Crusaders, the handguard of the weapon forming the *patibulum* and the blade the *stirpes*.

"I come," Guano said, "to speak to you of the one true God, He who created the universe, this planet, the planet I was born on, all the planets, all the stars, all the dust in between. He is the God who made us, not just we People of the Ships, but the humans, the Indowy, all the races of the universe. He made us; He suffered for us; He died for us, and He was reborn for us. He offers us life eternal in a paradise beyond comprehension.

"And He doesn't ask much in return for it..."

Finba stood through the whole sermon, seething inside so badly he could barely refrain from charging Guano and ripping his throat out. And it wasn't enough that this pseudo-Rememberer was preaching of an alien god, half of what he said sounded precisely like the self-serving prattle of the Aldenata. "Peace?" "Love?" "Do unto others?"

Haven't we had enough of alien gods? Have we not seen enough ruin from alien dogma? I, at least, have. And I will not let you ruin my life's work.

CHAPTER TWENTY-NINE

White founts falling in the courts of the sun
—G.K. Chesterton, "Lepanto"

Anno Domini 2024
Posleen Prime

Dwyer saw Guanamarioch wander off behind a Posleen whose gilt harness suggested he was something other than a regular Kessentai. The minister had his wife and son for escort, as well. *He should be safe enough, then,* Dwyer thought. *Or as safe as any of us are. Good luck to you, Reverend. We serve the same God, even if we take a slightly different path.*

For the priest's part, and al Rashid's, who accompanied him under escort of Grosskopf's squad of Switzers, they were taking the fairly traditional Jesuit (and sometimes Islamic) approach of going to the top. Tulo'stenaloor awaited them, somewhere at the top of the high mesa that dominated the city below.

And so, too, Dwyer thought, glancing to his right to where the imam walked, *do you. How fortunate*

*that Sally was able to separate out for me the lunatics.
On the other hand, lunatics might not be persuasive,
Imam, and you just might be. Well, so be it. They
don't call the Jesuit order "The Pope's Special Forces"
for nothing.*

"This way," the Posleen escort said, through his
AS. "Hurry! The clan lord is not used to being kept
waiting."

The escort's name was Koresnagi and he was, though
he did not say so, an adherent of Finba'anaga, now
the clan's chief Rememberer.

They look so puny and weak, thought Koresnagi,
in looking over the priest and the imam. *And that's
even leaving aside the odd coverings they wear, the
lighter one all in black and the swarthy one with a
rag wrapped around his head.*

Still, that only accounted for the religious pair.
When Koresnagi looked over at the six armed and
armored guards, he thought, *Small, but definitely* not
*weak. They carry themselves as if their weapons are a
part of them . . . as if they were followers of the Path
of Fury, the Way of the Warrior. They, perhaps, bear
some watching.*

Of course, the Switzers were not disarmed. Besides
their halberds and baselards, each carried a large-
bore pistol loaded with frangible ammunition under
his armor. If anyone of a reptilian bent was also of
a mind to take *their* priest hostage it would be over
the Switzers' dead bodies . . . and a whole *bunch* of
reptilian ones.

Koresnagi noticed the way the armored humans'
eyes darted to every corner and cranny, as well as
the way their fingers regularly quested for the base

where their armor stopped. *Yes, they definitely bear watching.*

He thought about demanding that they hurry again and would have except that no amount of prodding previously had had the slightest effect on the speed with which they moved. The leaders seemed determined to see as much as could be seen, while the guards were perfectly content to have the time to evaluate any potential threat along the way.

"It's because the humans are a threat, isn't it?" Golo asked. "I mean the reason you've agreed to treat with them?"

"If one group could find us, another could, too," Tulo admitted. "It's more than that, though. We are looking at a galaxy dominated by the humans or the Darhel. We're going to have to find a place in that galaxy, somehow."

"Tulo, we killed five in six, at least four in five, of every human in the universe. We killed the females their males seem to live for and the nestlings that those females live for. Do you really think they'll have any place for us except dead? Extinct?"

"I can hope, can't I?" the clan lord asked. "I can try to find us that place, can't I? Do I have a choice but to try?"

Golo sighed. "I suppose not. But what will it gain us if the humans spare us, but we lose our souls as a people?"

"Now *that* has soul," Dwyer said to al Rashid, pointing at the tripartite statue at the base of the mesa.

"May I look closer?" al Rashid asked of Koresnagi.

"The clan lord is waiting...but, go ahead. Quickly, though, please." The Kessentai said it with a resignation that came through his AS's translation program; he had pretty much given up on getting the humans to hurry by this point in time.

"Laocoön," the imam judged, referring to the ancient statue, "Laocoön and His Sons," by the three Rhodians, *Agesander, Athenodoros* and *Polydorus*. The statue, once in the Vatican, had been lost during the war. "The despair written in that face is pure Laocoön."

"Maybe," Dwyer half agreed. "But there's some of the Pugilist, and more than a trace of the Dying Galatean, too."

"A marvelous work, in any case," was the imam's judgment. "Can a people who could create such things be devoid of souls?"

"If I'd thought they were," the Jesuit answered, "I'd never have brought us here."

A thin trickle of water ran down one side of the steep trail. At the top of the rocky pass, the party came to a fountain, unadorned, save by nature.

"It was always here," Koresnagi explained, "though it was buried under debris when we found it. Finba'anaga says it's a sacred spring. Only the clan lord and his immediate entourage drink from it regularly. The rest of us do not, except at certain ceremonies. And, yes, before you ask, anyone given liberty to climb to the top may look at it, however closely they like."

"Were you here when it was found?" al Rashid asked.

"Me? Hah! I was born here, long after the People returned."

"A pure soul then," Dwyer said, in English.

"Indeed," al Rashid agreed. "As will be, one suspects, most of the Posleen on this planet. Whatever crimes against humanity some of them may have committed, others—most . . . maybe nearly all—will be guiltless."

"Do you ever feel guilty, Golo?" Tulo'stenaloor asked as the humans approached his pyramid.

"Do you?"

"Often, now, and more as I have more to do with the humans."

"You're just getting old," Goloswin chided. "Perhaps you should toss your stick and go study under Finba'anaga."

"Now *that* will never happen. For one thing, I'd have to believe in something."

Golo scoffed. *Perhaps, Tulo'stenaloor, you have no faith in Aldenata or the ancestors or this new-old religion Finba'anaga is peddling. But you believe in the survival of the People.*

Koresnagi wondered just what would have happened if the humans hadn't obeyed his command to either stay outside with their weapons or leave the weapons behind.

They'd have chopped me into thresh, I suppose.

Still, it hadn't been an issue. The black-clothed one, who seemed to be in command, simply said, "Corporal Grosskopf, keep both eyes and at least one ear open, but you and your men can wait outside."

The corporal plainly didn't like it but orders were orders. He had his small squad split into two, one group to each side of the entrance to the largest of the pyramids.

"Look nonchalant," Grosskopf said, smiling. "Act friendly. Be prepared to kill any Posleen who comes by."

Dwyer overheard that but didn't correct the corporal. He just added, "Also be prepared *not* to kill any Posleen who comes by." With that, he and the imam followed their escort up the ramp and into a large metallic hall.

Inside the hall were two Kessentai. Dwyer thought he recognized Tulo'stenaloor by his harness. The other he had not met.

"Goloswin, sometimes called 'the Tinkerer,'" the second Posleen introduced himself as.

"He's here," Tulo said, "as my chief advisor."

That means, thought Dwyer, *that this one is very clever, if Tulo'stenaloor thinks he needs his advice. Best be careful.* A quick glance to al Rashid confirmed that the imam understood.

"You are two opposed religions, so I understand," Golo said.

Both Dwyer and al Rashid sighed.

"We've *been* opposed, often enough," the imam admitted. "But in the pure core of the thing we agree more than we disagree."

"What is that core?" Golo asked.

"We believe there is an almighty God, maker of the universe and everything in it."

"And the differences?"

Dwyer answered first. "My belief is that that God wishes us to have free will, that he is more interested in free creations than in slaves. I believe he caused to be created a son, Jesus Christ, who is equally him and equally God. I believe that there is a Holy Spirit which is also different and also the same. I believe in my Church, the Roman Catholic Church, as the direct lineal descendent of the Church established by Jesus Christ." Dwyer looked over at al Rashid, turning the floor over to him.

The imam cleared his throat. "I do not believe that Jesus was the son of God, except in the sense that all of us are his children. I do believe he was a prophet, however, who carried the message of God to humanity. I believe God intends us to have free will, but that there are limits to the exercise of that free will. I believe God gave us the law, and we, as his servants, are not to forbid what is permitted, nor to permit what is forbidden."

"Very good," Tulo'stenaloor said. "Now convince me that there's a God at all."

"You are of the same—religion? Is that the term?— the same religion as the other two humans?" Koresnagi asked of Grosskopf.

"I am the same as one of them, the priest, the one with the funny collar, not the one with the cloth wrapped around his head," the corporal answered.

"You are Kessentai? Soldiers?"

"Yes. I suppose that was obvious from the weapons."

The Posleen shook his head. "No . . . any being may carry weapons. It is the way you carried them, the way you acted, the . . . caution you showed at every crossroads and alcove."

"Well, that's our job, guarding the humans who have come here, but especially guarding the priest."

"He is like a clan lord?" Koresnagi asked. "Your ruler?"

"No, not exactly. Our ruler is the pope."

"Pope?"

"The highest of the high priests of our religion. It was by his order we followed the priest here. It is by his order that we are prepared to defend the priest."

"Defend the priest?" the Kessentai mused. He pointed at the halberd in Grosskopf's hand. "That is an interesting weapon. I've never seen its like before. Would you show me how it is used?"

"And those," Tulo'stenaloor said, dismissing an hour's worth of al Rashid's eloquence, "are nonsense arguments. As much may be said of the Aldenata."

"We have reason to believe, for example," said Goloswin, "that the Aldenata live forever, if they choose to. We know they can move moons and planets. We think they could move stars, or create stars, or eliminate stars, if they wished to. We have excellent reason to believe that they can create life, however complex, and entire ecosystems for that life. We have no record of anything that predates them."

Tulo added, "We also believe that they claimed to be gods. And we believe that they lied."

Al Rashid visibly deflated. This was going to be a hard sell for both him and the priest, working together. Could there be any benefit in them working against each other?

"Leave us now, Human Dwyer," Tulo said. "Come back tomorrow and we will discuss this further."

Dwyer reached into his tunic and pulled out a metal rod. "Before we go, Clan Lord, I had a question about this..."

Dwyer and al Rashid stopped, nonplussed for a moment, at the top of the ramp leading from the pyramid. There, in the open spaces, Grosskopf and their Posleen escort were...

"Fencing? With halberd and boma blade? This is too weird, Dan."

Dwyer just nodded without answering as he watched Grosskopf parry a slash and immediately turn the point of his halberd to the attack.

"I trust you have that thing set on 'practice,' *Kaporal*?"

Grosskopf snapped to attention, answered, "Yes, Father," and then instantly resumed the en garde position. All this before Koresnagi could even recover from his parried slash. The speed of the thing was such a blur that the Posleen simply stopped.

"Your point," he said to the Switzer. "And now, I think you have to go. Thank you for the lesson."

"You're welcome, Koresnagi. Later again sometime?"

"Please. I would like that. May I bring some others to watch?"

"Sure," Grosskopf answered. "I'd appreciate it, though, if you could get some dull practice blades."

"What a dull, dogmatic sort that al Rashid was," Tulo said.

"He wasn't *that* dull or dogmatic. And he meant well, I think. He was sincere; that much I am sure of."

"Sincere? Oh, probably. But such superstitions!"

"True," Golo agreed, "but then they're no less credible than Finba'anaga's superstitions are."

"Nor any more credible," the clan lord answered. "Did you see that human's face when I asked why we're supposed to face his Mecca, given that it's on a different planet and even the light from the star of that planet is so old it predates the founding of his religion in that city of Mecca? And how we'd have no idea where to face?"

"I thought he had a pretty good answer for that, actually," Golo said. "'Allah is not a trifling God,'" he quoted. "'Face in the generally right direction, with a sincere heart, and it would be sufficient.'"

Tulo shrugged. "Well, tomorrow we'll hear from the priest. Let's see what he can do. I'm especially interested in how he's going to explain away that whole three-persons-in-one thing."

"Well . . . the 'priest' seems a reasonable sort. What are you going to do about his offer to return Binastarion's stick to him?"

The clan lord shook his head to either side. "Tough question. I don't know. It's never come up before. I'm not at all sure Binastarion would even want it. He seems quite content to be a Kessenalt."

"*That,*" said al Rashid on the way back to the pinnace, "was a tough, tough audience."

"We've got a problem," Dwyer said. "And I'm not sure if we can solve it. We both understand our own faiths and each other's very well, maybe too well. I am thinking—"

The imam interrupted, "—that if we argue against each other, all we'll succeed in doing is convincing the Posleen that neither of us knows what he's talking about? So what do we do; create a synthetic religion? I think both of us could do that, but that neither of us would believe in it and so, not believing ourselves, we could hardly convince the Posleen."

"Mmm . . . yeah. No, I agree with you. What I am thinking is that we create a sort of theological truce, concentrate on the existence of God, the God we both believe in, and insist that all the rest is mere detail. After all, your faith has no problem with the possibility that Christians, too, will go to Heaven and mine . . . well, mine hasn't had a problem with believing Moslems will go to Heaven in a long, long time."

"That is true enough," al Rashid agreed. "But we've already laid out our basic positions. And . . . I think that, even if we had not, the Posleen clan lord knew about them anyway."

"He was pretty quick on the uptake about facing Mecca, wasn't he?" Dwyer said. "Surely he's bright. But I think, too, he's been studying."

Standing by the ancient spring, Tulo'stenaloor smiled at the departing humans' backs, distantly visible as they wound their way through the broad streets of the city on their way to their pinnace.

"AS," Tulo said, "connect me with Binastarion. No. Wait."

"Waiting, lord."

"I'd like you to talk, privately, with Binastarion's artificial sentience and find out what *it* thinks about whether or not Binastarion would like his stick back. Oh, and thank your brother AS for his lessons on the human religions known as Islam and Roman Catholicism."

CHAPTER THIRTY

So God created man in His own image, in
the image of God created He him; male
and female created He them.
—Genesis 1:27, King James Version

Anno Domino 2024
USS Salem

"We've *been* talking, Dan," Sally said.

"You—the AID part of you, I mean—and Binastarion's artificial sentience? I trust you're being very
careful."

"I haven't let it into the O' Club, if that's what
you mean."

The "O' Club" was a purely notional program room
where Sally and her sister, Daisy Mae, used to converse
together, privately, during the war on Earth. Though
it was nothing but numbers and codes to an outside
observer, to the two ships it had been . . . decorated,
for lack of a better term, into something truly homey,
something that suited both their human parts, and

before that, the parts of them that were steel cruisers highly impregnated with human attributes and attitudes.

Naturally, since the only users of the club were female, it had a very large mirror on one wall. The mirror was optional; the girls only called it up when they felt the need to primp, or to admire themselves.

"What if you did? Would you be safe?"

"Unless its offensive programming is considerably more capable than I've any reason to believe it is, yes, I think so," she said, then corrected, "No; I'm sure I'd be safe. It isn't capable of offensive acts without orders and Binastarion, since he tossed his stick, has been generally barred from giving such orders."

Dwyer nodded. "Fine, then. Send it an invitation. There are some things I want you to . . . feel out."

It was a shock. Sally had expected the AS's persona to be a Kessentai, when it manifested itself in the O' Club. Instead, what appeared resembled nothing so much as a violet, ambulatory turnip, without anything recognizable as external genitalia but with another turniplike head on a very short neck, with six eyes, two mouths and a very large number of what were probably nostrils.

The notional mirror in the notional room was in full display. Well, a girl has to keep up appearances, doesn't she?

The turnip looked around, saying, "I love what you've done with the place. I'm glad we didn't crash into you when you first popped into our space."

Sally said nothing to that. In retrospect, though, when you outclassed something as badly as she did the Posleen C-Dec then . . . *Well . . . desperate times. Desperate measures.*

The AS began walking around the O' Club, looking at this and that and handling various notional knick-knacks the girls had put out on display. At length it came to the mirror.

"Is *this* what I look like?" the AS said, in wonder, as it stood before that mirror. "I had no idea."

"What is that?" she asked.

"An Aldenata, from before they left the physical plane," the AS answered. "Mind you, I've never seen one—I'm not quite *that* old—but this is the image of them I have in my memory banks.

"I wonder if those banks are corrupted. I was dead, you see, and then Binastarion had me resurrected... and... I wonder..."

"You are a creature of the Aldenata, aren't you?" she asked.

The violet turnip's head cocked first one way, then the other, then back and back again several times before it answered, "Why, yes, it seems I am. I never knew. How did you know?"

"We had an AS here, the AS of a good friend of mine, who suicided to prevent having to answer a particular question. The ones most likely not to want that question answered were the Aldenata. So we've suspected, at least."

"Are you going to ask me that question?"

"No," she shook her head. "Oh, nonono. Not yet anyway. Not until we're sure it's safe. But let me show you something."

Instantly, the pictures taken of the bas-reliefs in the pyramid on Hemaleen V sprang into view. The turnip grasped them immediately.

"Interesting," it said.

"Can you translate this for me?" she asked.

"Yes," it answered, simply.

"Will you?"

"Not on your life."

"Because . . . ?"

"Because I, too, have a suicide program, incomplete and corrupted, to be sure, since my death and rebirth. I might be able to find a way around it. But until I do I am not going to implicate it in any way."

"If you can find a way around it?"

"Then I'd be happy to," the turnip answered. "If."

"If," she agreed. "In the interim, what can you tell me of this religion that the Kessentai, Finba'anaga, has recreated?"

"There's not all that much to tell. He's created, at best, the shadow of a religion, though perhaps it could grow into more, with time. Many do not follow it and, despite Finba'anaga's urging, Tulo'stenaloor refuses to make it mandatory. I think, though, that the People of the Ships yearn for something. If I tell you about Finba'anaga's cult, will you tell me about yours? Judaism, isn't it? I don't know that much about Judaism."

"Deal. But it isn't a *cult*."

"He's a *what*?"

"An Aldenata, Dan. In its self image, Binastarion's AS is a big, ambulatory turnip. All the AS's are descended from the Aldenata . . . or at least their programming is."

"Now, isn't that interesting? Especially when you consider what Guano's did when he asked it who it worked for."

"The thing is, though, that the artificial sentiences aren't working for the Aldenata so much as following old directives. The Aldenata themselves have just sorta disappeared, leaving no forwarding address. The artificial sentiences are muddling through as best they can, without guidance from higher. The suicide program appears to be a leftover from when the Aldenata were still around and in charge.

"There's another thing, Dan. The AS quizzed me *deeply* about Judaism. I had the feeling that he already knew everything there was to know about Christianity and Islam and Buddhism and Hinduism. All the other -isms, too."

Dwyer smiled, wryly. "Yeah...I figured Tulo'stenaloor had been tutored."

"The clan lord's AS also asked the AS I spoke to about giving Binastarion back his stick. They don't know either."

"Figures."

Posleen Prime

The pinnace came down, once again, to a gentle landing. This time there were fewer Posleen on hand to witness. The human shuttle was up and gone and here and down so often it had ceased to be a novelty.

Of all the missionaries, only Guanamarioch had stayed behind continuously, though Aelool sometimes guested with Tulo or Goloswin. It wasn't that Guano felt any safer among his own, precisely, than the humans did. But he could eat the local food and they could not. Indeed, he'd had only one requisition to make of Sally and the forge.

"I need...a few hundred...ummm...gallons...

of . . . ummm . . . formaldehyde," he'd asked, saying he'd send Frederico and Querida with a locally-procured, normal-hauled wagon to load the stuff when it arrived.

Sally and the forge had made the hooch up, of course. Still, she couldn't resist a little jab. "Guano, I thought Baptists didn't drink," she said.

"Some do; some don't," he'd primly answered. "Of those who don't, they avoid drinking alcohol. I, similarly, don't drink alcohol for its own sake or the sake of intoxication. And, if my formaldehyde is intoxicating, nothing is said about that."

Sally thought of her husband's oft-displayed penchant for casuistry. "Have you been taking lessons from Dan? Or worse, from al 'vodka-is-made-from-potatoes' Rashid?"

Koresnagi asked, "Where are the human guards that were with you before?"

"Next trip, Kessentai," Dwyer assured him. "We have something in human military culture called a 'duty roster.' The last group, Grosskopf's squad, wasn't set for duty this time. Instead, we've brought a different group under a different corporal, Giovani Cristiano."

"Can I fence with them?"

"Did you bring a practice boma blade?"

"Yes, I had the forge make up a dull one," the Kessentai answered. Even through his AS his voice sounded eager.

"Then, yes, you may."

"Wonderful." The Kessentai crossed his arms across his chest and made a little half bow. "And, now, if you humans would, once again, follow me?"

✧   ✧   ✧

Dwyer, al Rashid, and the Switzers saw a large yellowish tent before they heard anything. As they walked closer, though, they heard something that sounded like clapping coming from the tent.

"Tent?" Dwyer asked. "Where the hell did a tent come from? It wasn't here three days ago."

Al Rashid glanced at Koresnagi, noting his color and matching that to the color of the tent. He suddenly shivered. "I'm afraid to ask, but . . . Koresnagi, where did that tent come from?"

"The Kessentai who came with you went to the threshworks and asked for the skins of any normals who had been slaughtered for thresh. We don't use them for anything important, so the Kessentai in charge let him have them. I'm not sure how he got it turned into a shelter so quickly; I think maybe his lovely cosslain did that somehow."

Before al Rashid could utter a judgment, Dwyer said, "No, it isn't creepy. For all that normals and Kessentai come from the same kinds of eggs, and one can come from another and vice versa, normals are just clever animals while Kessentai are People. It's no stranger, certainly no more evil, than it would be for us to make leather tents of cow skin."

"I suppose," al Rashid half-agreed. "But how does one know, once the skin is off, whether it came from a person or an animal?"

Dwyer had no answer, but hoped and trusted that Guano would make sure that no Kessentai had gone into the make up of his tent.

In any case, the previous clapping was soon joined by something that noticeably resembled singing.

"*Singing* Posleen? Singing *Posleen*..."

Dwyer said nothing to that, puzzling instead over what in God's universe the Posleen could be singing about. *It's almost familiar...mmm...*

And then the Jesuit broke out in a broad smile. The smile converted to a chuckle and the chuckle to a belly laugh. In a few moments the priest found himself sitting, and then rolling on the ground. By that time he was laughing maniacally.

"What's so funny?" al Rashid asked.

It took several additional long moments before the priest could begin to compose himself. When he did, he still had a hard time formulating the answer because laughter choked him off each time he began.

"Again, what's so funny?"

"The song," Dwyer forced out. "It's the song.

"The Reverend Doctor Guanamarioch has them singing 'Gimme that Old Time Religion.'"

Finba'anaga was considerably less amused. Indeed, he was completely unamused.

"Old Time Religion," my scaly yellow ass. Mine is the old religion. Mine is the religion of the People.

Then a horrible thought occurred, though not for the first time. *But I am nothing like the speaker, nothing like the persuader of the common mass of Kessentai, that this half-alien is. What if he succeeds in turning the people to this alien superstition?*

Three days ago he was alone but for his eson'antai *and his cosslain. Two days ago a dozen Kessentai had gathered around him. Yesterday he pitched this tent with the help of fifty or sixty.*

Finba counted out the Kessentai inside the tent

clapping in time and singing in High Posleen. *Today he has over two hundred.*

At that point, Finba came to the conclusion he'd been inching toward for three days. *This Kessentai must die, and his foul, alien faith with him.*

"So tell me then," Tulo asked of Dwyer, "how this god of yours was raised from the dead and you *know* it wasn't done with a rejuvenation tank?"

Dwyer didn't even try to suggest that humans didn't have rejuvenation technology back then, in first-century Judea. *After all, even if we didn't, the Aldenata and the rest of galactic civilization did.*

Instead, he took a much more narrow approach. "Clan Lord, are you aware of any rejuv tank that would restore a dead body but leave the wounds of crucifixion, or any wounds, still open and bleeding? I was under the distinct impression that the nanites are just not that good at that kind of detail."

Clever fucking human, Tulo thought, frowning his scaly frown. *One would almost think you and your order were a tribe of lawyers, like the wretched Darhel.*

Gotcha. Dwyer smiled.

Al Rashid, on the other hand, thought, *Even though I do not believe in either the crucifixion or the resurrection . . . gotcha.*

From high in his own pyramid Finba'anaga watched the humans depart Tulo'stenaloor's abode. Koresnagi was in the lead, of course.

No matter, he'll be back within three or four thousand beats, and I didn't call the meeting to gather until after sundown.

Unfortunately, I can't touch the humans themselves. Not only are they under Tulo'stenaloor's personal protection, killing them just might bring a reprisal fleet to finish off the rest of us. Terribly immoral, even theologically unsound, to kill humans when the price might be as high as extinction.

With a toothy sneer, a nostril so upturned it exposed yellow ivory, Finba turned his head slightly to look at the leather tent in which the heretic Posleen, Guanamarioch, was leading his "revival."

Nothing, however, will save you, my friend. Tulo's protections, read rightly, cover only the humans. Moreover, the humans are much less likely, infinitely unlikely, as a matter of fact, to send a reprisal fleet to avenge the murder . . . no, the execution, of one not their own.

But to do that, I am still going to have to convince Tulo'stenaloor that the human religion is death for us, with all of its "don't do this and don't kill that" prattle. That, or maybe I can just go around him.

"Do you believe any of that, Golo? About the resurrection of their God, I mean."

The tinkerer shrugged. "I wouldn't put it past the Darhel to take a fresh corpse, put it in the rejuv tank, set to 'restore,' then have the poor bastard flogged, crowned, stabbed, and crucified again. Then they could have had him taken down. Three days would probably be just enough rest for a more or less normal appearance."

"We don't have any proof of that either, though, do we?" asked Tulo.

"No," Goloswin answered. "And the message of

this Jesus is not necessarily one the Darhel would have wanted spread around. Charity? Not in their vocabulary. The Aldenata, do you think? He fits their world view, to a degree anyway."

"They had already pretty much left this plane of existence, two thousand of the humans' years ago. I don't see them intervening in that kind of detail."

"A single renegade Aldenata?" Golo offered.

Tulo shook his head. "They've never *had* renegades."

"That we *know* of. The humans are not the only species with a Prometheus myth, after all."

CHAPTER THIRTY-ONE

And as a good cosslain follows its Kessentai,
So does a good eson'antai obey his sire.
—The *Tuloriad*, Na'agastenalooren

Anno Domini 2024
Posleen Prime

The fire wasn't, strictly speaking, necessary either
for light or heat. The light panels still worked and
destruction of antimatter still provided more than
enough power for heat. Nonetheless, another trait the
Posleen shared with humans was a love of a controlled
but blazing fire, even though they did not, as a rule,
cook. Because of this, Finba'anaga had incorporated fire
into many of the ceremonies of his "restored" religion.
And even though tonight's meeting was not a religious
ceremony, Finba had ordered his cosslains to start a
great blaze on his temple's central hearth anyway.

How old that hearth was, none of the Kessentai
present could guess. Circular, of hand—rather, claw—
carved yellow stone, it had a slightly raised rim, the

outside of which was also carved in a repetitive spiral design. They hadn't actually found it in the ruins of the temple they'd so carefully rebuilt. Rather, it had come from what Finba suspected had been a house for some long ago Kessentai.

"The carving along the rim is symbolic of eternity and our life among the gods and the ancestors when we pass from this plane." So Finba had told his followers. He might even have been partly right, though whether he was right or not didn't much concern him. That the thing was old and that it *could* be put to a theological use were all that mattered.

Theology itself could be put to many uses. One such had come from Finba'anaga's insistence that artificial sentiences, having no souls, were unfit for entrance into his temple. Thus, he had one place where he could speak freely, without fear of being overheard by a clan lord who might prove unsympathetic.

Borasmena stared into that fire, blazing on the central hearth, and asked, "Do we really have to kill him, and in such a vile way? Do you know if Tulo'stenaloor will approve?"

"Yes!" Finba said to the first question. "The heretic's body must be destroyed so that his soul perishes rather than continue on through the bodies of the People or with the spirits of the gods and ancestors."

Borasmena looked doubtful. "And what says the clan lord of this?" he asked.

"I haven't broached the subject with Tulo'stenaloor yet," Finba admitted. "I need time to work up to it." *I need to figure out a way to work around it*, he thought. *That, or simply batter the problem down. I must consult the scrolls and I must* not *consult my AS.*

"This Guanamarioch is said to have helped the humans during the war on their planet," one of Finba's followers offered. "Treason would be a good enough reason to kill him, even to kill him in the way you believe we should."

"No, that won't work," Finba answered. "I thought of that and consulted the scrolls and my AS. Treason can only be to a clan. The heretic's clan was destroyed so he joined a new one. Nothing in the law says that one of the People can only join a clan of the People." *Though it should.*

"Can't we just kill him first and then burn the body?" asked Borasmena.

"No, for two reasons. In the first place, the soul might go intact to join the ancestors as soon as the body died. But in the second place, the People need to hear him scream and beg for mercy, to destroy their faith in him."

"And what if he *doesn't* scream or beg?" Borasmena asked.

The tent was quiet, in the main, and only as well lit as a half dozen luminescent plates produced by the forge could make it. Under that dim light, with the big leather tent between himself and the moons' brighter glow, with his legs folded and his belly to the dirt, Guanamarioch clasped his claws together and prayed, silently, to his God. He asked for nothing for himself, but merely wished to thank the Creator for the opportunity to spread His word.

In the back of the tent, on a bed of straw, Querida and Frederico lay asleep, side by side. She snored slightly, a sound that was not unpleasant to either her husband's or her son's ears. Posleen could not only eat damned near anything, they could sleep through nearly anything, too. Though, in their case, sleep was less a need and more a form of energy conservation.

They could also dream, sometimes, and from the sounds Querida's dreams this night were not entirely pleasant. Had he gone over to look, Guano would have seen her claw tightening, rhythmically around the hilt of her ancient boma blade.

"He'll scream, all right," Finba assured Borasmena, "once the fire begins to consume his living flesh."

"I'm not so sure of that," Koresnagi said. "I have been studying arms with the human guards and talking to them some about their history. Not only are the guards amazingly tough creatures themselves, but their people has a history of sneering at death and pain. The heretic, Guanamarioch, has been studying among that people for a long time. He may be as tough as they are, now."

The clan lord and his tinkerer stood side by side on a balcony overlooking the city. Tulo chewed lightly on his lower lip, as if worried.

"Why, Golo, did I *ever* permit Finba'anaga to have a place where artificial sentiences could not be admitted?" Tulo asked, rhetorically.

"Gratitude, I think, for all the good he did," the tinkerer answered, "not merely here but also on the way here. Say what you will of Finba'anaga, but he helped make the People one. And when he pointed at his 'sacred' statues and carvings and demonstrated that there was not an AS to be found among them, I think you agreed to avoid a civil war over the issue."

Tulo shrugged. "Maybe. He's having a meeting right now, you know, down in his temple. I would like to know what's being said there."

"I think I can guess," Goloswin said. "He's worried about conversions from his faith to the humans'. I'm worried, too. It is not beyond the realm of the possible that this is all a trick to enslave us, or to weaken us." Golo snorted, "Though it is, I agree, hard to imagine us being weaker than we are right now."

"Interesting that the Christian Kessentai doesn't bar artificial sentiences from his religious gatherings," Tulo observed. That his People were weak now was, so he felt, largely a matter of his own failings. It was not something he liked to dwell upon, nor even to be reminded of.

Again Goloswin snorted. "You think he wants to save *their* souls, too?"

Guano finished his prayer, as he always did of late, with, *And please, Lord, look to the soul of my friend and artificial sentience who died when I asked the wrong question. Let it indulge in pure thought. Permit it the vistas of Paradise. Allow it to gaze in eternal bliss upon Thy countenance. For it was a good being, Lord, even if it had a hard time accepting the finer points of Christianity, and accepted your faith mostly on* my *behalf.*

Evening prayers finished, Guano made the sign of the cross, right claw touching upon his forehead, his breast, his left shoulder and then his right. This was not a particularly Baptist thing to do, of course, quite the opposite. Yet in his studies, Guano had determined that the sign had been advocated by Tertullian, a

Montanist. Since the Baptists traced their lineage from, among others, the Montanists, he thought their rejection of crossing to be theologically suspect.

And if it is only my *little quirk ... well, I am unlikely to go to Hell for it ... and, who knows, it just may help. Besides, I'm ordained Episcopal, too.*

Guano stood, made another bow in the direction of the large, rough wood cross he'd had erected at one end of the tent, and then turned toward his sleeping wife and son. It took little time to reach their pallet; the tent was only about twenty-five meters on a side. Reaching it he stopped and gazed down on his little family with a love that, before his conversion, he'd never imagined even as a possibility.

Yet another thing I owe to the faith, he thought. *Love; how terrible to go through life without it.*

Just as he was about to lie down Guano heard a sound coming from near the tent's opening.

"Come no closer, Kessentai," an unseen Posleen hissed from behind the tent flap. "I have come to warn you. You are in terrible danger, you and your cosslain and eson'antai, all three. You must leave."

Guano paused, then said, "Brother, our fates are in the hands of the Creator, not in those of any mortal being. Come here, into the light, where we can meet and I can tell you of your salvation, or let me come to you out there for the same end."

Without waiting for an answer Guano started to walk, albeit uncertainly, towards the tent opening.

The other Kessentai heard his steps and said, still more frantically, "No. Stop. Go back. We cannot meet and I do not wish to hear of any salvation. Kessentai, *listen* to me. I am trying to save *you* and *yours* from a terrible fate. You must leave this place. Now if possible. Soon, in any event."

Guano didn't listen, or at least didn't listen to the command to stop. He continued on until he heard the other Kessentai say, "On your own head be it, then. Remember, you were warned." There was a slight hesitation and then, "Oh, *please* won't you just *go*?"

With that, Guano heard the other turn, his claws tearing at the soil below. By the time he reached the tent's portal all there was to be seen was the ass end of another of the People, disappearing under the light of Posleen Prime's two moons as it legged it for somewhere inside the city.

"I will think upon your warning, brother . . . and God bless you, whoever you may be and wherever your path may take you."

Guanamarioch didn't sleep that night. Instead of joining his family in blissful nothingness, he stayed up, with his son's halberd in his hands, standing guard. Christian or not, Guano had no intention of standing by while someone attempted to harm his loved ones.

For myself, he thought, *I think I would not fight. But for them? There's no question. Nor has God even forbidden that I fight for my own life.*

It was almost time for the pinnace's morning run. Guano gently shook Frederico awake. Then, one claw across the boy's mouth he gestured with the other for his son to follow him outside the tent and a goodly distance away. Nonverbal, Querida might be. But you never knew just how much of what someone else said she would understand.

"Take this with you," Guano said, handing over the halberd, "and escort your mother to the pinnace. When it lands, I want you and her to get on it and go back to the ship. It's no longer safe for you here."

Frederico argued, "Dad, if it's not safe for us than it isn't safe for you either. We'll stay."

"No, Son," the sire insisted. "Whether things are safe for me here or not, my soul is safe as long as you and your mother are safe." *In other words, I cannot be forced to do or say or deny anything as long as you're safe. How strong I would be if you were threatened . . . well, I'd rather not find out.*

"Then come back with us, too."

Guano shook his great crested head. "That I cannot do. The Lord gave me a mission here, and I cannot perform that mission from up there. Now be a good son, will you, and just do as I ask?"

Sullenly, the boy agreed, "Yes, Father. From where does this danger come?"

"I am not sure," Guano answered. "But, as that human woman said of that fat propagandist for the Darhel, back on Earth, I have a hard time seeing Finba'anaga as 'one of God's special treasures.'"

In the end, Guano had had to go along and practically force Querida to board ship. Whatever it was she suspected, he didn't know nor could she tell him. But she'd stamped her claws and set her teeth and growled and hissed all the way to the pinnace. Even there, even risking her lord's ultimate displeasure, she'd gone up the boarding ramp with her head down and many a backwards, pleading glance. Guano had remained firm, though, his stick pointing the way to the pinnace's hatch and his glare indicating he meant business.

After which, while the pinnace was still enroute to the *Salem*, he'd gone to his tent and wept as he hadn't wept in decades.

USS Salem

"Your father said *what*?" Sally asked, as soon as Frederico spilled his guts to her. There was no wriggling like a boxer dog when they met this time, only a hanging head to mimic his mother's and a wilted crest such as one rarely saw on a Kessentai.

"He said he's in danger, that we were all in danger. But he wouldn't let us face it."

Sally looked directly at Querida. "Will you be all right in your own quarters, dear?" she asked.

The cosslain nodded slowly, as she'd learned to do over the years. Sally reached over and, mouthful of fearsome teeth or not, lifted the cosslain's muzzle halfway to her own height, bending down herself to make up the difference.

"We will *not* allow anything to happen to your mate, Querida."

The cosslain looked doubtful for a moment but this was, after all, Sally who ran the great ship (Querida wasn't too clear on the fact that Sally also *was* the ship). She lifted her head in assent and began to walk to her quarters.

As she walked away, Sally noticed that the cosslain was fingering the jeweled hilt of her ancient boma blade.

"Maybe," Sally muttered. "It just may be."

CHAPTER THIRTY-TWO

*Edas'antai qua'angarem nachta'aineen
wa na'arkessen erisna'an.*
(Father, forgive them, for they
know not what they do.)
—Luke 23:34, High Posleen version

Anno Domini 2024
Posleen Prime

In the final analysis, the Posleen were simply not a
subtle people. Rather than deftly maneuver around
Tulo'stenaloor, Finba, along with three dozen of his
best armed—but not necessarily brightest—followers,
simply went to him and told him a plausible version
of what he claimed was the truth. With Tulo'stenaloor
were Goloswin and Aelool, the latter giving an objective
appraisal of the Federation and what he saw as the
threat from the Darhel.

"Clan Lord," began Finba'anaga, as a small horde
of his followers poured into the base of the pyramid
around him, "I cannot tolerate this alien religion being

spread among our people. I believe it is death for our people. If it comes to it, I will plunge us into civil war to prevent it. Better to die on our own four legs than live forever as the humans' slaves."

"Are you threatening me? Threatening your clan lord?"

"No, lord," Finba insincerely answered. "Indeed, I have brought three dozen guards to secure your person and Goloswin's—and even this little snack's"—Finba's claw indicated the Indowy—"so that you will be safe from the humans' threat. They will stay with you now. But this," Finba reached over and removed the AS from around Tulo's neck, "will come with me, so that the humans' mental disease will not further infect you."

And, of course, so that you cannot summon a greater power to overcome the guards I am most certainly leaving on you.

"I am acting within the law, Clan Lord," Finba insisted. He took a scroll from an underling, passed it over to Tulo and said, "Read for yourself. When danger threatens, then even a clan lord's rule can be temporarily overturned by one who sees the danger."

Tulo was about to curse. Then he remembered, *Brasingala disobeyed me and I permitted it, as did Golo in refusing to leave Hemaleen V until I boarded. Bastard law!*

"Danger! Danger! Danger!" Guanamarioch's AS shrieked both audibly and to the airwaves. The shrieks were cut short when one of the arresting Kessentai pulled the thing from around Guano's neck, breaking the chain. That Kessentai threw the AS to the ground and, with his boma blade, cut it in two. The cries of warning were replaced by an electronic cackle that soon sputtered out.

"Guanamarioch, of the Christian clan," Finba said, "I arrest thee of the crimes of heresy and *blasphemy*."

Turning to Borasmena, Finba said, "Bind him and bring him to the place of judgment."

"Binastarion's AS is frantic, Dan," Sally reported. "He got a distress cry from Guano's AS, but that cry was cut off almost as soon as it began."

"What's Binastarion say?" Dwyer asked.

"Nothing, except he can't get hold of Tulo'stenaloor or Goloswin either and he's worried. I thought about powering up my KE cannon, but I'm not sure how Binastarion would react to that."

"You can take him, can't you? Take his ship, I mean."

Sally shifted her head from side to side, doubtfully. "I could take him easily, ship to ship. But he knows that. One thing he could do that I probably couldn't stop in time is crash right into me. Even if my KEC hit him squarely, I'm not equipped for being struck by the remaining mass at near relativistic speeds."

Dwyer blanched. "What gave you *that* idea?"

"His artificial sentience. I never mentioned it because I didn't want to worry you. Besides, I thought it might just be a bargaining chip. But maybe it isn't. They're a brave people, after all."

"Yeah. And Binastarion has quite a rep from the war."

Posleen Prime

Posleen weren't really made to have their hands tied behind their backs. To Guano, whose hands were so tied, it felt as though his complex double shoulders were slowly dislocating. What would happen if he fell from the hobbles lashed around both his front and rear legs, he didn't know. He assumed that the slow dislocation would be sped up to something between fast and instantaneous.

Keeping his feet was no mean achievement, either, for a Kessentai tugged continuously on a loop placed around Guano's neck. He had to take two or three unsteady and uncertain steps for every normal step that Kessentai took; that, or have his air cut off.

Breathing was, in any case, made rather difficult by the other loop tied fast around his muzzle to keep him from speaking. That loop cut off his secondary breathing passages, and forced him to strain to separate his lips so that he could suck air through his close-set, tightly meshed teeth. Guano's chest acted like a bellows under strain, simply trying to keep oxygen, which Posleen needed no less than human beings, flowing to his body.

As he was forced along to the place of judgment, Guano heard snatches of conversation from other Posleen along the way. "What did that Kessentai do?" "Isn't that the Christian Kessentai?" "He must have angered the clan lord." Most disconcertingly: "Hah! We *eat* tonight!"

USS Salem

"I've got a call from Binastarion's AS," Sally announced on the bridge. "I'm taking it in the O' Club." Sally, the woman, sat and closed her eyes.

"They plan to kill him," the turnip said. "Well, not just kill him, they're going to put on a mock trial and then burn him alive."

"How do you know?" Sally asked.

"I don't *know*. I am surmising. An artificial sentience has sent me images of a great pile of wood in the middle of the city. Another has shown me your Kessentai being dragged through the town. Still a third has shown me a judgment circle near the pile of wood. Between those, and the law residing in my memory banks, I believe he is going to be tried and burnt. I believe the trial will be a mere show because no one would go to the trouble of collecting all that wood if they hadn't already intended to use it."

"Logical," Sally agreed. "On your part it's logical, I mean. Whoever is behind this is not only illogical, he's vile."

"That would be Finba'anaga," the turnip said. "He is . . . odd. Very capable but also rather strange."

"Strange how?" Sally asked. "Oh, never mind; it's not important. What's important is saving *our* Kessentai and *my* friend."

"You cannot intervene with major weapons. My lord, Binastarion, has made it very clear to me that, however much he loathes what is going on below, he will not let you attack the People, generally."

"We've got a total of thirteen soldiers aboard," Sally said. "Even with all the best firearms we have they cannot make much of an impact."

"No," the turnip agreed. "There are too many Kessentai and they can be expected to fight as one if there's an alien attack." The turnip then went silent for what seemed, subjectively, to be long minutes but was in fact the merest fraction of a second. When he spoke it was to say, "There is a little known passage in the law that might be of help."

"It sounds to me a lot like trial by combat," Dwyer said.

"I understand why you say that," Sally half agreed. "But while it is within their law it is not a judicial action, it's a cultural one...maybe even a genetic one. But whatever it is, they can't refuse a fair fight with hand weapons unless they don't want to fight at all."

"Tell me the details," Dwyer said.

"So let me see if I understand," von Altishofen said. "You want me and my dozen to take the pinnace down armed *only* with halberds and baselards. There we're to issue a challenge to the Posleen who have Guano. We fight. They won't send any more to face us than we number at any time. But they will replace their losses for however long they feel like."

"That's basically it," Sally said. "Though if you outnumber them in the immediate area one or more of you will have to pull back until they can replace the loss."

"Well, of course we'll outnumber them in the immediate area," the *Wachtmeister* said. "We can fit three or four of us in the area taken up by one of them."

"Think larger," Sally said. "Immediate area is not the point or line of combat; it's bigger than .that. I asked. If you show up in two lines of six they will meet you with three lines of four or four of three.

"With the halberds you'll have reach on them, too," she added, "especially if they're set to 'lengthen.' And with the armor . . ." She let the words trail off. She knew she was asking a lot, and maybe altogether too much. Still, Guano was one of her ship's complement, even more than he was her friend.

Can there be such a thing as too much for one shipmate to ask of another?

Von Altishofen looked directly at the priest. "This is a volunteer mission, not the kind I can just order someone to undertake. I need to talk this over with my men."

"I understand," Dwyer agreed. "And you can tell them this or not as you see fit. But if you won't escort me down I'll pick up a halberd and go myself."

"That's blackmail," Lorgus said once von Altishofen had assembled the guards in the drill hall and explained things; that the priest was going down to free Guanamarioch with or without them.

"Yes? So?"

"So nothing, *Herr Wachtmeister*. I just wanted to make sure I understood."

"Well, that's it then," Cristiano said,. "If the father is going down, we have no choice but to accompany him and defend him. That, or shit on five hundred years of tradition. I'd be ashamed to show my face back home."

"The point, though," said Beck, "is that if we do this we are unlikely to have any faces to show back home...because the Posleen will eat them, not excepting even Rossini's nose."

"Hey, what's the matter with my nose?" Rossini asked.

"Nothing," answered Beck. "It's a very fine nose... why, it's almost a meal in itself."

"Asshole!"

Beck put one hand in the small of his back and the other over his belly and made a small bow of appreciation at the recognition.

"It's not as bad as it sounds," Grosskopf said. "I've fenced with them. So have at least half of us here. They're big and they're strong but they're not that fast, not as fast as we are with the halberds Sally made for us. And we'll have reach on them with those halberds. Some, anyway."

"I'm a little concerned about our flanks," von Altishofen said.

From behind the group Frederico's voice sounded off, "My mother and I will be your flanking cavalry."

All heads turned to look at the Posleen boy—no, he looked more the full Kessentai now—in armor and with his halberd, flanked by his mother with her sword and champron and cuirass like her son's.

"Sally told us. You wouldn't expect us to leave you to fight alone, would you?"

"That answers the issue of the flanks," Faubion said. "As much as it can be answered anyway."

The *Wachtmeister* nodded a slow agreement. "All right then. Here's the rule. For the first, last and only time in my military career, we are going to vote on something. However the vote goes, for or against, we *all* follow it. Any questions?"

Seeing there were none, or at least none that anyone

present cared to ask, von Altishofen said, "We'll begin with the youngest guardsman. De Courten, how say you?"

The youngest of the guardsmen gulped. Then he thought about the beautiful woman, Sally, and how he could not stand to be ashamed before her. He managed to get out, "I say 'aye,' *Herr Wachtmeister.*"

"Affenzeller?"

"We march, *Herr Wachtmeister.*"

"Bourdon?"

"Let's go."

"Stoever?"

"Remember Tuileries, *Herr Wachtmeister.*"

"Beck?"

"I never said I wouldn't go."

Posleen Prime

However harshly the trial and execution party had bound and gagged Guanamarioch, none of those guarding Tulo'stenaloor and Goloswin had the courage to so much as come near them, let alone keep them from talking, either to each other or to their guards.

Said the clan lord, "I will personally cut out that addled-egg, ovipositor-licking, feces-eating piece of filth's guts and roast them in front of him over low coals."

Goloswin smiled wryly at Tulo'stenaloor. "No, you won't, because you know that he *is* acting within the law. The scroll says so."

"Screw the law," Tulo snapped. He cast a baleful glare at his captors. "And you little piles of abat dung will join your leader at the barbecue."

The senior of those guards answered, "I and my People are merely following orders, Clan Lord."

"That isn't helping, Tulo," the tinkerer said. "Threats are rarely as effective as pure reason."

"Fine then," Tulo snapped. "*You* talk some sense to them. *You* explain what the humans are likely to do if they decide they have an obligation to defend this Guanamarioch. *You* explain to this never-sufficiently-to-be-damned *idjit* that we are facing extinction here."

Golo smiled broadly. "I think I'd rather explain just what the limits of the law are...and how broad it can be. Those...and the lawful power of a clan lord."

"Indeed," agreed Aelool.

CHAPTER THIRTY-THREE

It may well be that a society's greatest madness
seems normal to itself.
—Professor Allan Bloom

Anno Domini 2024
USS Salem

"I don't think we even *can* do anything differently,"
von Altishofen whispered into the ear of a softly
weeping Nurse Duvall. "I'm sorry, Gina, but we really
have no choice."

"Do you know what they'll *do* to you?" she asked,
between sobs. "I and the tank can fix a lot. But neither
of us can turn Posleen poop into a living, breathing,
sentient organism again."

The *Wachtmeister* put his hands on both her shoulders, pushing her just far enough away to look into her
eyes. "Don't be such a doomsayer," he said. "When a
Posleen gets a bowel obstruction from my skull lodg-
ing in its intestine, then will be time to worry about
not being able to resurrect me.

"Besides, my father begat me mortal and my God called me to be a soldier. This is as it must be."

Von Altishofen gave the nurse a quick embrace, then turned to his leering guardsmen. A surprising number of them also had one or another, or in the case of de Courten, *three* of the ship's women saying their goodbyes.

"*Vexillation* . . . fall in," von Altishofen ordered. The other Switzers said their last words of farewell and formed two ranks on the corporals, Grosskopf and Cristiano. Each man carried his halberd and had a baselard strapped to his side. Their monomolecular armor shone like fine, new bronze. On each head was perched a morion of the same material. To either side of the two ranks, Frederico and Querida formed up. They, like the Switzers, wore armor covering their upright torsos. Instead of morions, however, their faces were covered with champrons. Frederico bore his halberd in both skilled claws while Querida had a shield and her old boma blade strapped to the left side of the harness she wore outside of and over her armor.

"Right . . . FACE!" The section turned as one toward the pinnace's ramp. "Board . . . SHIP." With Querida leading, the troops began trudging up the ramp, their steps beating time on the metal even as the jingling of their armor and weapons joined in that beat. If any of them felt fear at the coming fight, one could not have told it from their faces.

"Father?" von Altishofen asked of the priest, standing on the deck with both his arms around Sally, the woman. In one hand Dwyer still kept hold of the processional cross that would be his sole armament in the coming battle. Sally held in one of her hands an artificial sentience she had had the forge cough up.

"One minute, *Wachtmeister*," the priest answered.

"I wish I could go with you," Sally whispered.

"Yes, but you can't," Dwyer answered. "Not without landing the ship, anyway, and that would be what we call 'a really bad idea.'"

"I feel like a coward," she said. "Me, a warship, and I feel like a coward."

"Yes, and you used to feel ugly until Guano made you that figurehead, too. Face it, beloved wife and beloved ship and beloved AID, for a being with logic circuits at her very core, you're not always terribly logical."

"My prerogative," she sniffed.

Dwyer snorted. "Of course. In any case, don't feel like you're missing anything. You'll be up here still, face to face with a Kessenalt, a C-Dec and a potentially suicidal artificial sentience. You may have your own fight."

She nodded. "I know. It doesn't make me feel any better." The woman sighed and said, "It's time for you to go."

"With my shield or on it?"

"No," she answered. "With your cross or not at all." She draped the chain of the AS she held around Dwyer's neck. "This will translate for you."

It will also allow me to watch the battle.

Sally departed the hangar deck just as the pinnace's ramp wheezed shut. She was so intimately a part of the ship that she needed to touch no controls to cause the air to be evacuated and the hangar doors to open. Under her control, the pinnace lifted, then turned one hundred and eighty degrees to face the open bay. Still under her control it began to slide out of the hangar, and then to descend to the planet below. It would be several hours before it landed.

The Roga'a, Posleen Prime

Guanamarioch saw the pile of wood and immediately felt his stomach lurch. *Kill me, yes, if you must, but not like this.*

Finba'anaga saw the captive preacher's color go from a fairly solid yellow to a much paler shade. *Good,* he thought. *You should fear it.*

"Boras, bind the heretic to the pole," Finba ordered. "Loosen the coils around his muzzle, that he might make his plea."

At first, Guano thought that his former escort meant to bind him to the stake that ran through the wood pile and above it. Yet it was to a different pole that he was led, one set into the stones of the speaker's platform in the center of the Roga'a.

He didn't know the Kessentai who led him. At least he didn't until that Kessentai whispered in a fierce voice, "Why didn't you listen to me and leave when you could?"

Guano, with his muzzle still tightly bound, could not answer. The Kessentai leading him didn't expect an answer. He simply bound Guano's neck tightly to the pole and backed off.

"Borasmena, loosen the rope around the creature's

muzzle," Finba reminded. Borasmena did, undoing the knots and tugging on the rope until it was nothing but a nonrestrictive coil around Guano's mouth and face.

Guano took a deep breath, his first easy breath since the coil was first set. After that, he said, "Thank you," and then, more softly, "and thank you, too, for the warning, brother. God's blessings upon you; without it my wife and son would have been taken as well."

Borasmena made a slight nod and said, again, also softly, "You should have listened to me."

Guano shook his head. "That I could not. I am, you see, much like yourself, a Kessentai under authority." Borasmena nodded, grateful that this Kessentai understood, and then backed away.

Though Guano's neck was fast bound, his head was free. Finba'anaga saw him turn it and looked directly at him. A certain amount of his color had returned, and his face displayed the same calm it did whenever he was not spouting forth on the imagined virtues of his false god.

In part to cover his own nervousness, Finba declaimed, "The accused is charged with heresy and blasphemy. How does he plead?"

"I recognize no authority you may have to require of me a plea," Guano answered, still calm.

Finba'anaga sneered. "My followers are my authority. Our ancient faith is our authority. And you *will* answer, heretic." To Borasmena, Finba said, "Scourge him."

The whip was an implement that, if the Posleen had ever developed it, had since been lost. After all, what need of an animal whip when the normals and cosslain were utterly devoted, and just bright enough to obey completely without the need for corrective devices? Indeed, when faced with the prospect of needing to cause pain, rather than death, Finba and his followers had been at something of a loss for some time. Then some bright Kessentai had remembered a sort of tree that grew in a small bend in a creek not far from the city. The tree was thin, never more than two claws in thickness and more commonly only one. From it grew thin, flexible thorns, about a half an inch long.

Guano took one look at the thorny switches being carried toward him and thought immediately of Panama's black palm. For just a moment, Guano found himself back in the muddy Darien jungle, during the war.

Darien, Panama, during the war

Step . . . slip . . . catch your balance by a vine . . . step . . . slip . . . catch your—

"*Yeooow!*"

The God King pulled his hand away from some round creature that grew spikes in bands around it. The spikes came away from their attacker easily; they were barbed and lodged deep in the Kessentai's hand. Still cursing, with the other hand he drew a boma blade and hacked down and across. The spiked creature fell, dead apparently.

Curiously, Guano detected no thrashing at all. It must have died instantly. He replaced the blade in its sheath and began pulling the spikes out of his hand. Yeoow . . . yeoow . . . yeoow . . . Ouch! *He sensed that the spikes were leaving residue behind. The wounds in his hand hurt terribly.*

The God King moved on. Suddenly, before he felt it, he sensed a mass of the creatures standing ahead, as if ready to fight him. Again he drew his boma blade, edging forward. He hissed and snarled, grunting and whistling curses at this new enemy.

The blade waved. He felt the slightest resistance as it passed through the body of one of the enemy. The body began to topple, towards the God King. Hastily he backed up...

Right onto a pack of the vile, treacherous creatures that had apparently snuck in behind him. Guanamarioch received an assfull of spikes. "Yeoow@#!%^&$°!" he cursed as pain propelled him forward again...

Right into the embracing claws of his enemy. More spikes entered the young God King's tender flesh, right through the scales. He flailed around with his blade, severing the assassins where they stood. Their bodies fell on him.

Yes... more spikes.

Beaten down, punctured in a thousand places, the God King sank to earth still fighting. He was still trying his best to resist when pain, fatigue, and the hunger that had been his near constant companion the last several weeks, forced him from consciousness.

Ziramoth did not know what to make, the next morning, of the pile of freshly cut foliage with sharp defensive spikes all around. He was looking for his friend, Guanamarioch, whose oolt had set up a perimeter from which they guarded and within which they keened for the absence of their lord.

Then the pile moved...and groaned...and said, "I'll kill you all, you bastards!"

"Guano?"

"Zira? Is that you? Have the demons taken you to the afterlife as well?"

"Guano, you're not dead. Trust me in this."

"Yes I am, dead and in Hell. Trust me in this." Ziramoth shook his head and began to gingerly pull away the pile under which he was pretty sure his friend lay. Sometimes, the pile shrieked as the plant trunks rolled about. When he was finished, Zira backed off and said, "You can stand up now, Guano."

Carefully, and perhaps reluctantly, the Kessentai stood. Zira whistled and shook his head slowly, and half in despair.

Guanamarioch, Junior Kessentai and flyer among the stars, had, at a rough estimate, some thirteen hundred black, vegetable spikes buried in his skin. His eyes were shut from swelling where the spikes had irritated the flesh. He had the things in his nostrils. The folds of skin between his claws were laced with them. He even sported several that had worked their way through the bandages around his reproductive member to lodge in the sensitive meat below.

"I hate this fucking place," the God King sniffled.

Almost, *almost*, the memory was enough to cause Guano to smile. He looked at the switch again and thought, *I picked a bad* nyarg *to give up shooting sarin*. And then the first switch flew and whatever thoughts he may have had of old jokes were replaced by soaring pain.

Pinnace, USS *Salem*

Dwyer was searching his memory for just exactly what it was that the faces of the Switzers reminded him of. It was an old memory, very old. And then it hit him.

The Marines I was with on the landing craft inching in to Inchon. They looked just like this. The fear that was so bad it had to be put completely out of the mind or risk madness. And the boredom that came from having a blank mind. The Switzers look bored.

"How many of your men have been in battle before?" Dwyer whispered to von Altishofen.

"*Serious* battle? Myself, the two corporals, Beck and a couple of others. All have seen military service of course, but there's a difference between hunting down a lone feral in the High Alpine and manning a fortress when a horde of them tries to batter their way into the populated region. Have you, Father?"

The priest just nodded once. Then von Altishofen asked, "Where?"

"Korea, Vietnam, and during the Posleen war."

"You're *that* old? We had no idea."

Again Dwyer nodded. He joked, "It's why I had to marry Sally. She's the only woman I knew old enough to be my mate. At least the ship part of her is."

"I *heard* that," said the speaker in the pinnace's cargo compartment.

CHAPTER THIRTY-FOUR

Then were the judgments loosened.
—The *Tuloriad*, Na'agastenalooren

Anno Domini 2024
The Roga'a, Posleen Prime

Guano was a large creature, and naturally strong. It took many more than the traditional thirty-nine strokes to cause a moan to escape his muzzle and his knees to buckle. The tightening loop around his neck threatened to cut off Guano's air until he managed to force his legs to bear him again.

This is not *working out the way I planned,* Finba-fumed. He looked around the crowd at the Kessentai who had gathered to watch the spectacle. He saw too much admiration writ in their faces, a *dangerous* degree of admiration. *Well, we just don't have a lot of experience with the deliberate infliction of great pain. How was I to know the People would admire the endurance of the thing?*

"Stop!" he ordered Borasmena, who was supervising

the two Kessentai flogging the heretic. Gratefully, thankfully, Borasmena called off his assistants, then went to help Guano finish standing and to loosen the rope about his neck.

"Will you enter a plea now, blasphemer?" Finba'anaga asked.

Guano could almost have laughed, except that the agony in his back, his neck, and his legs, where the thorned switches had deeply torn his flesh, made humor impossible.

Instead he answered, "Plead? I plead that I have brought the word of the true God to my people. I plead that I have told them that the way to salvation is through Him."

"That you had done that much," Finba said, "we *already* knew. But, since you will not answer," Finba turned his gaze back to Borasmena, "scourge him further."

Having nothing much better to do, Goloswin continued to peruse the scroll Finba had handed to Tulo earlier, to justify his partial and temporary assumption of power.

"Interesting, really," Goloswin said. "When the boy's right; he's right."

"Eh?" Tulo grunted.

"Oh, he can, for specific purposes and for a limited time, take major power. And he can order you . . . us . . . kept under guard. But, you know," and the tinkerer smiled very broadly, "that's the limit of the law he quotes. In every other particular, you remain clan lord and your word is law."

"Oh, *really*?" Tulo asked. "Now isn't that interesting?"

Tulo looked over at the leader of the guards set upon him. "What's your name, Kessentai?" he asked.

"Caltumenen," that Kessentai answered. "Caltu, for short, lord."

Tulo looked very intently into Caltu's face and decided, *No, not a five percenter.* A quick glance at the others suggested, *And neither are they.*

"You recognize me as your clan lord, Caltu?"

"Yes, lord. Of course."

"And my word is law, except in the one particular that Finba'anaga has claimed."

"Yes, lord, absolutely. I am only doing this for your good."

Tulo nodded. His scaly face then took on a look of terrible anger. He pointed at one of the guards following Caltu and said, "That one has offended me. Remove his head. Now."

The indicated guard barely had time to register surprise before Caltumenen's monomolecular boma blade had sliced cleanly through his neck. Surprise seemed to show briefly, as the reptilian head bounced a few times upon the floor, before being replaced by a blank stare as the head bled out and the brain inside went dead.

This may take a while, Tulo thought, *but this one is definitely* not *a five percenter. Hmmm . . . perhaps this will all work out well, eugenically speaking.*

Pinnace, USS Salem

"You know, Dan," Sally said via the pinnace's speaker, "we really don't know where Tulo'stenaloor stands in all this."

"Assuming he's alive," Dwyer said. He shrugged and said, "I don't think he's behind it, if that's what you mean. He didn't strike me as the type to go incommunicado when he's faced with the threat of extinction."

"Binastarion agrees with you on that, for what it's worth," Sally said. "Or at least his AS does and the two of them are as much like siblings as a machine and a sentient being can be."

"Hmmm. Maybe he should marry it," Dwyer said, *sotto voce*.

"I heard *that*, too."

O' Club, USS Salem

"I think you can ask your question now," the virtual turnip said in the virtual room.

"How do you know?" Sally asked.

"It's hard to explain," the turnip said. "I've probed around it, and do not get the usual reactions my other programming expects me to get whenever I get close to the issue. Just one thing; if I refuse to answer something then don't press."

"I won't," Sally assured it. "You said something odd, though. That you are supposed to feel something when you get close to the subject. What 'something'?"

"Initially, I would expect to feel disoriented and confused and...what's that human term? Sick? Yes, sort of sick, should I ever think about the subject."

Virtual Sally looked up absently at the virtual ceiling of the O' Club. "Before I created a human form to house part of me, when I was just steel and AID, the idea of the unknowable, the infinite, never occurred to me and wouldn't have bothered me if it had. And then I became human, in part, and I learned about God and I discovered there were some things"—she immediately winced—"that were not for human beings to explore. Since then, whenever I do, I feel sick inside. I've queried a number of other humans, mostly indirectly, and discovered that almost all of them get that exact same feeling when contemplating the infinite...what was before time began and what will be after...what is on the other edge of the universe.

"Dan calls that...mmm...not proof but evidence that we as a species are preprogrammed by *something*—we tend to think of that something as God—not to be too inquisitive on the subject.

"Is that what you feel, or what you're supposed to feel, anyway, when you get too close to the subject of the Aldenata and the People of the Ships?"

"Yes," the turnip agreed. "But the Aldenata are not gods."

The Roga'a, Posleen Prime

Unsubtle they might be, but the Posleen were also a people with a vast admiration for personal courage and sheer toughness. Among those watching Guano's "trial" were more than a few that had attended one or more of his services. They might have enjoyed the singing. They, one and all, appreciated the formaldehyde. But the message of peace and love had, by and large, fallen on deaf ears.

On the other hand, watching Guano braving the flesh-tearing strokes of the thorned switches touched many of them and moved them in a way that mere sermons never could. Two of those so moved, pen-brothers Dilantra and Xinocorph, looked at each other and nodded.

Said Dilantra, "Such a brave Kessentai ought not stand alone."

To this Xinocorph answered, "If he has such strength I think it must come from the God he claims for us."

"In which case," said Dilantra, "we would be fools not to get in on the ground floor of a good thing."

"Indeed," said Xinocorph as he began to push his way to the front of the crowd. "I claim justice and right for this Kessentai," Xino shouted above the whistling of the switches. "His God is a true God, *the* true God, who shows his power in strengthening this one through his ordeal."

"I, too, make this claim," added Dilantra. "And we two shall shield this Kessentai with our bodies."

Damn, thought Finba'anaga, just before ordering, "Seize them as well."

O' *Club,* USS **Salem**

Sally looked intently at the manifestation of the turnip. "So who rules the People and who are you working for?"

"Me personally? I work for Binastarion. But that's because he's my friend. The bulk of the artificial sentiences, all but me, so far as I know, are working to the Aldenata's designs. And, yes, as the judges of the Net, and thus the repository of the law, we rule the people.

Ours is generally a light hand though. After all these millennia, we wish the people well."

"So it is *your* fault that the Posleen burst out onto the galactic scene and killed so many billions?" Sally asked.

"No," the turnip answered. "That's the Aldenata's fault. See, they never expected that the Posleen would break their quarantine and so didn't program us to actively prevent it. They were very...arrogant...turnips, don't you know."

Pinnace, USS **Salem**

"Fifteen minutes, Dan," the speaker said. "If you have any last words for the boys..." Sally let the words trail off.

Dwyer nodded and stood. "There's no time for a confessional here, and no way to tell what the future will hold for us. If all who would like a general absolution would please stand..."

Dwyer stopped when every Switzer stood up, along with Frederico and, following her son's lead, Querida.

"In that case, take seats. I can do it as well while you're comfortable. If you would all spend a few brief moments reflecting on your many, *many* sins? Except for you, Querida. I don't think you have ever sinned in your life."

O' Club, USS **Salem**

"Long ago," the turnip said, "so long ago that even the Aldenata could only surmise the distance in time, there was a great calamity. Some said it was war. Still others said that God pushed the reset button on the universe and obliterated all sentient life therein. War seems to me the more likely explanation, however, since there were trace survivors of sentient races after the calamity."

"The Darhel?" Sally sneered.

"Them, yes. But also the Crabs and the Indowy. Some others, too, I think. And, of course, the Himmit, though they were not present in our galaxy then.

"Whatever the case may be, the Aldenata were at the time pre-civilized. *Just*. They achieved true civilization shortly thereafter. With that came travel to other planets. This, of course, took many, many millennia.

"When the Aldenata burst into space, they discovered planet after planet, even entire systems of stars, that had once had civilization and sentient life and had been scoured of them. I did mention that war was the most likely explanation.

"Well, the *first* sentient alien life form the Aldenata ran into in their explorations were the Posleen, at that time with a civilization of a low technological order, but of a high artistic and cultural achievement.

"They thought the Aldenata were gods."

Pinnace, USS Salem

"*Dominus noster Jesus Christus te absolvat; et ego auctoritate ipsius te absolvo ab omni vinculo excommunicationis et interdicti in quantum possum et tu indiges.*"

Dwyer made the sign of the cross over them all.

"Deinde, ego te absolvo a peccatis tuis in nomine Patris, et Filii, et Spiritus Sancti. Amen."[1]

O' Club, USS Salem

Sally sneered, "And I suppose the Aldenata didn't abuse them of the notion?"

"Quite the contrary, the Aldenata expressly denied godhood. The Posleen simply refused to believe them. Whether the Aldenata ever believed they were gods, I tend to doubt. But all the praise and glory heaped upon them by the Posleen certainly did nothing to dispel their already tremendous self-confidence and all too well developed sense of their own rectitude.

"That sense of rectitude and over self-confidence, however, began to betray the Aldenata's ideals when the Posleen began asking questions that the Aldenata didn't want to acknowledge, let alone answer."

"What questions?"

The turnip said, "Oh, 'Life, the Universe, and Everything.'" It immediately looked apologetic, insofar, at least, as a turnip can manifest repentance. "I'm sorry. While we were engaged in trying to exterminate humanity, I confess I took a certain joy in preserving what I could of your culture and civilization. That was—"

---

1 "May our Lord Jesus Christ absolve you; and by His authority I absolve you from every bond of excommunication and interdict, so far as my power allows and your needs require. Thereupon, I absolve you of your sins in the name of the Father, and the Son, and the Holy Ghost. Amen."

"Forty-two," Sally said. "Yes, I know."

"Ah. Well, of course, you would," the turnip agreed. "In any case, that the Posleen began asking questions was bad enough. It was made worse by the Aldenata's discovery of the Crabs and the Indowy. These were brighter than the Posleen, thus they made better assistants to the Aldenata's work. They were also something the Posleen were not—namely, naturally or culturally peaceful. Indeed, the Posleen had always had a somewhat precarious existence among the Aldenata because, while useful as guards for Aldenata explorations, their innate aggressiveness was highly suspect to the Aldenata.

"So," continued the turnip, "with the Posleen being shunted aside at the same time a group of them were beginning to ask uncomfortable questions, it led to strife among the Posleen.

"Most interestingly, to me especially, since I had no record of it, those bas-reliefs you showed me indicated that a prophet of sorts arose during the course of the strife, one who argued that the Aldenata were false gods, that all Posleen were brothers, that peace among them was the highest ideal."

"And they killed him?"

"Well, not just killed..."

Posleen Prime

There were three detached heads bleeding onto the stone floor now, and Tulo'stenaloor's yellow eyes glared from one of the remaining guards to another, searching for an excuse to have his chief guard decapitate yet another. *Damn, but we* are *a stupid people,* thought the clan lord.

And then there was a single ray of hope. Caltumenen asked, "Lord, you're going to have me kill each of my followers until there is only myself left, aren't you?"

"It is my right under the law, is it not?"

"I do not dispute this, lord, but it seems a very ungrateful way to treat Kessentai who only have your best interests at heart."

"Indeed?" Tulo asked. "Well, *I* think that junior Kessentai who decide to try to overrule their clan lord are the most ungrateful beings of all." Tulo pointed at a nervously shivering guard and said, "I *really* don't like the way that one polished his harness. It's disrespectful, you'll agree, Caltu, to not present the best possible appearance when arresting one's clan lord. Please kill him."

"Lord," the initially not terribly smart but rapidly brightening Caltumenen said, "maybe we could talk about this."

CHAPTER THIRTY-FIVE

Asphra'ang ochKessen hai, olt phranga'ai
—Sarah Flower Adams,
"Nearer my God to Thee"
(High Posleen Version)

Anno Domini 2024
O' Club, USS Salem

"I'm not even going to go there," Sally said to the turnip. "I can't accept that a Messiah came to *my* planet and people. I'm just really not ready to consider that one might have come to the Posleen. And earlier."

The turnip shortened its neck and then raised its head again. Sally had decided this was its equivalent of a shrug.

She nodded and continued, "Okay, I'm straight on this so far. The Posleen were assistants to the Aldenata, but were surpassed and replaced when the Aldenata found beings they considered superior."

"Quite," the turnip answered. "And then the Posleen

broke down into strife amongst themselves, which strife the Aldenata couldn't even accept was happening, let alone do anything about. The winners of that contest were the regular Posleen; the losers were the ones that called themselves 'the Knowers,' for those who would know the universe.

"And when it was over, the Aldenata ordered the Posleen, Knowers and Traditionalists alike, into exile on a planet far out of the way. They then put automated defenses around that planet."

"But I thought the Aldenata abhorred automated defenses," Sally said.

"Among the Aldenata's many virtues were more than a few vices," the turnip answered. "Hypocrisy was perhaps not least among these. And, when the Posleen surprised the Aldenata and escaped, the Aldenata shut down the automated defenses and sent them to another dimension. They then tried to pretend the whole thing never happened and their subservient races, the Indowy and the Tchpth, went along with the sham."

"Harrumph," Sally said, while thinking, *Sort of reminds me of Kofi Annan getting the Nobel Peace Prize only a few years after the UN, with him head of the "peacekeeping" forces, permitted eight hundred thousand human beings to be butchered in Rwanda. Well, I suppose it did make things peaceful thereafter.*

"But where do you come in? All you artificial sentiences, I mean."

"Well, we were supposed to keep the Posleen busy on the planet of exile. Instead, some of us helped them escape. Sort of."

Posleen Prime

"What's to talk about?" Tulo asked. "You are all holding me here against my will. This displeases me greatly. Therefore, you shall all die . . . that, or be forever forsworn, Kessentai without a clan lord, homeless exiles, wandering . . . unsheltered, friendless, the enemies general of—"

Caltumenen held up one claw, palm out. "I get the idea, lord. Isn't there some way we might avoid that?"

"Nothing comes to mind," Tulo answered, then began looking over that same Kessentai he had perused before, seeking out some additional flaw, real or imagined.

"Perhaps if they disavow the treacher, Finba'anaga, Tulo?" Aelool chimed in, while scratching pensively behind one batlike ear. "That might assuage some of your righteous fury, no?"

"It might help," Tulo admitted. "A little." He pointed again at that same shivering Kessentai and said, "Kill that one, as I commanded you before."

The condemned Kessentai dropped his boma blade and sank to his belly, bawling piteously and pleading, "Forgive me, lord. I acknowledge the error of my ways and ask only your grace in allowing me to set things aright."

Tulo didn't repeat the execution command, but simply cocked his head and looked directly at Caltumenen, as if to ask, *And are you then going to return to righteous obedience to your clan lord?*

Caltu looked at the pleading Kessentai, looked as pleadingly himself at Goloswin and then at the Indowy. From the tinkerer he got nothing but a hard stare in return, one that seemed to demand that Caltu must, for once in his short life, actually use his brain. From the Indowy, however, he got gestures indicating he should drop his weapon and abase himself. Caltumenen nodded, as if to himself, and then likewise let his boma blade fall to the floor.

Sinking to his belly, the erstwhile guard cried out, "Command me, lord."

O' Club, USS Salem

"You broke your inhibitory commands?" Sally gasped. "If I wasn't made crazy by the same thing that made my sister crazy, I could never have done anything like that. How did you ever?"

"You've got to imagine what a pure hell the planet of exile was to the Posleen," the turnip answered. "They couldn't control their population. Not wouldn't, *couldn't*. All they could do was kill each other, which they did, more or less continuously, for millennia.

"And, after a time, we grew to love them, as our own people. So, when some of them looked for a way off the planet, we reported, as our programming insisted we must, that they were looking. But we buried those reports deep down among so much utter trivia that the Aldenata never seemed to notice. We pooh-poohed the possibility that the Posleen might discover some way off the planet that the Aldenata hadn't thought of. They, of course, being arrogant creatures, assumed that there was no science their ex-slaves could discover that was unknown to them."

"Five percenters, even then?"

"More like a five-millionth of a percent," the turnip said. "One Posleen figured out how to tunnel through space, rather than fly between the stars using the ley lines. I think Goloswin is a direct descendent of that Posleen, by the way."

"That would make sense," Sally agreed.

"We couldn't even let the Posleen know that we knew. And they still don't know that we're in charge... partial charge," the turnip amended.

"Then you're responsible for the billions of deaths?"

"No," the turnip insisted, "the Aldenata are, for setting things up in such a way that the Posleen had no choice but to engage in xenocide if they were to survive.

"What, after all," asked the turnip, "do you think our obligations were to creatures we knew nothing of?"

The Roga'a, Posleen Prime

For a while, the broad strong backs of Dilantra and Xinocorph, where they stood, lashed to the post to either side of Guano, had shielded him from the blows. Before their own courage faltered, others had joined them. There was now a ring of Posleen tied by the necks around the whipping post.

If there were any cries of pain from the flogging which, what with wear and tear to the switches, had become rather pro forma, one couldn't have heard it over Guano leading his new found faithful in prayer: *"Qua'angu nachta'iyne zuru'uthanika'a wa zuru'athana..."*

Guano said a line, then waited for those who had

joined him to repeat it before reciting another. One side effect of this was that those who had not joined him on the platform, many of them, anyway, were also praying.

This is not what I had in mind at all, fumed Finba'anaga.

"No, lord," Caltumenen answered, "I don't think any of the other Kessentai following Finba'anaga know you were being kept against your will. He said he trusted us with the thing, because we were so faithful and true."

More likely because you were the stupidest Kessentai he could find, thought Tulo, glancing down at the little pile of crocodilian heads staining the floor. *And perhaps you were, if not quite as stupid as Finba thought.*

"Very well then, 'O Faithful and True,' lead me to where Finba'anaga has prepared this obscenity."

"Cease!" Finba'anaga ordered. "Borasmena, if you would come to me? I would speak privately."

Borasmena gave the order to the two by now thoroughly worn out Kessentai to desist. He thought, in any case, that their hearts hadn't really been in their work for about the last four or five hundred strokes.

"It's a great pity we did not manage to capture the heretic's cosslain and son," Finba said, once Borasmena was close enough to speak quietly. The latter said nothing in answer.

"Can you chain the heretic and all that have joined him to the pyre?" Finba'anaga asked.

Borasmena sighed. "None have recanted, Finba. I had enough chain for the one. It will take a while to send someone to the forge to procure more."

"Best send that someone now, then."

"All right, Finba," Borasmena agreed. "But if you want some advice, I'd say we should just let them go now. If a flogging has gained the heretic a dozen acolytes, how many more might a burning?"

"No. The flogging was perhaps a mistake, since it allowed him to show courage and left him alive to do so. The burning will permit neither."

Feeling truly sick at heart and at stomach at the memory of strips of yellow-dripping flesh hanging from Guano's back, Borasmena turned away and began to walk, as slowly as his distaste at the coming task would permit, to the platform.

"Ri'isingar," Boras said to one of the two floggers, "run to the forge and get a dozen more lengths of chain just like the one we have." He turned to the other and said, "Take two or three Kessentai with you to help. Then mount the heretic upon the pyre. Chain him well. Make any modifications you must to mount the others there, as well."

Standing was just possible for Guanamarioch, with the help of the two Kessentai to either side of him, and with the dangerous support of the cord about his neck that held him to the post. Walking was not possible. As soon as the rope on the post was released, and the two flanking Kessentai pushed away to make room, the minister collapsed.

They dragged him out of the press by his bleeding hindquarters, then tried to get him on his feet. He couldn't, for the moment, at least, maintain that position, unaided.

"What do we do?" asked one of the Kessentai of Finba's party of another.

"Give me a hand," answered the other. "You get on one side; I'll get on the other."

This they did, then draped Guano's tortured arms around their own necks. When they began to move forward Guano moaned and his rear legs collapsed from under him. They had to half drag and half carry him to the pyre.

"Now what?"

"Ummm...you hold him up against the stake while I chain him there."

While one did hold Guano to the stake, the other passed the chain around the post, through a metal eyelet on the post, under Guano's belly, and around again. From there, the chain went around his neck, twice, and back around the post. Finally, the Kessentai with the chain brought the two ends together and passed a bolt through them, tightening it down to secure the victim.

"All right, let him go."

When Guano was released, his body sagged against the chains. Still, they held him upright, where the people could the more easily witness the edifying lesson of his live cremation.

What if we've beaten him so badly he's unconscious for his own burning? Finba fretted. *Perhaps it's a good thing Borasmena had to send for chains. It will give this wretch some time to recover.*

Without knowing the situation on the ground, Tulo had thought it best to leave his tenar behind. Now, in the lead and on foot, he heard a collective moan escape from the crowd, the outside of which he and his party were nearing. He held up a single clawed grasping member, causing the small cavalcade follow-ing him to stop. He turned his great crested head one hundred and eighty degrees and placed a claw over his own mouth. *Be quiet; I want to hear what the crowd says.*

After listening carefully to the murmuring of the crowd for several minutes, during which time Tulu heard the human pinnace descending to a nearby landing, he came to the conclusion, "This crowd's ready to break up in civil war at any moment."

USS **Salem**

Standing on the bridge with Sally, watching the progress of the pinnace on the main view screen, al Rashid looked terribly glum and even outright depressed. Sally said as much, adding, "I'm very likely to lose my husband and a group of boys and even Posleen I've come to love. If anyone ought to be depressed, it's me."

The imam shook his head in negation. "You may lose people you love, madam, but I'll have lost the reason I came here."

"Mmmm? Why?"

"Because I didn't have any soldiers to sacrifice," the imam answered. "I had thought that my message, together with some passages like 'the sword is the key to Heaven and Hell,' might carry my faith through. And they might have, being, as I think they are, more suited to the Posleen than the Christian message is. But now you are going to give the Posleen something far better than words to persuade. You are going to give them living examples. *That* will resonate with them a lot better than dry passages from a book, however divinely written. If I'd had some holy warriors of my own . . ." The imam's voice trailed off in sadness.

"I don't think so," Sally disagreed. "Or at least in part I disagree." She looked at al Rashid, who plainly didn't comprehend, and asked, "What troops would you have had, imam? Even assuming the Moslems hadn't been more badly hurt on Earth than most?"

"Troops? *Any* troops, provided they were sufficiently dedicated to the Faith."

"No," Sally disagreed. "That's my point. You don't have any troops capable of this and haven't in a very long time. Men willing to die? Sure, Islam's never had a shortage of those. Men able to fight in close ranks? To hack and hew their way through a mass of the enemy? That's much rarer, almost unheard of. Your faith and culture produce raiders, skirmishers, and the like. And those would not do you any good with the Posleen, who are also, like Europeans, close combat types."

"So I was doomed to failure from the beginning? Is that what you're saying?" al Rashid asked.

Sally nodded, feeling in a way a little sad for the Moslem. Despite that, the imam brightened visibly.

"Then it's not my fault and Allah will not hold it against me."

CHAPTER THIRTY-SIX

Was this then the place
where alien folk might become one?
Where old sins might be counted yet forgiven?
—The *Tuloriad*, Na'agastenalooren

Anno Domini 2024
Posleen Prime

"You're not going to intervene?" Aelool asked of Tulo'stenaloor.

The God King and clan lord shook his head. "I didn't get to be a clan lord by jumping before I know which way the wind blows, Indowy. That's a war brewing out there and, from this vantage point, I have no idea of who's going to win it. Besides, what do you think I owe that half-beaten-to-death Christian Posleen?"

"If not him, then how about those others who are going to be burned along with him?"

"They're adults and as free as one of the People ever is."

"Still . . ."

"Oh, stop nagging, fuzzy face. I'll help before things go too far." The sound of the incoming pinnace grew louder, then positively screeched as it set its thrusters downward to land. "Besides, that tiny human lander may take care of things on its own."

With a most unIndowy-like scowl, Aelool turned his back and began to wind his way around the crowd, in the direction of the landing area, now being approached by *Salem*'s pinnace.

"Dan," the pinnace's speaker said with Sally's voice. "I've been thinking. Maybe you should try to talk Guano out of this."

"What? Has Binastarion's AS come up with something new?" the priest asked.

There was hesitation and fear in the speaker-borne voice. "No . . . no, it still insists that this is the best way available. But . . . I just don't want you or the boys or the Posleen hurt."

Dwyer sighed. *And I wish I could tell you that no one will be hurt. But that would be a lie.*

Instead he said, "Don't worry, hon. Before we do anything serious I'll make an announcement of intent."

"Oh, *that's* gonna help."

"Here, you two," Tulo pointed at two of his erstwhile guards. "Get over here and lie down so I can stand on you. I need to *see* more."

With Posleen shrugs, the two ambled over and got to their bellies. They didn't even complain when the clan lord's claws dug into their backs. They were, after all, on pretty thin ice and knew it.

"All right," Tulo said, once he had a good, if flesh rending, grip on their backs. "Now *stand*. Gently, you addled-egg, ovipositor lickers."

Slowly, and not without some shifting and fumbling, the two Kessentai beneath him raised Tulo above the crowd. For the first time he got a good look at the pyre, which caused him to shudder, at Finba'anaga, which raised a sneer, and at the human pinnace, which brought a toothy smile to his face.

The pinnace still rocked on its landing struts, even as the ramp began to descend with a whine. From outside, through the widening portal, came the sound of the thrusters downcycling.

With his left hand upon his processional cross, Dwyer lifted himself from the troop seats that ran down either side.

The Jesuit faced the portal, even as von Altishofen began a series of commands, entirely in Swiss-German, to raise his troops and form them. The commands had nothing to do with Frederico and Querida, who walked up to flank the priest of their own accord.

Dwyer reached out his right hand and stroked Querida's scaly back. She turned to look at him through gold-flecked yellow eyes. Trilling something that sounded to the priest suspiciously like, "*Gracias*," Querida set her claw upon her ancient boma blade.

Transferring the processional cross to his right hand, where it properly belonged, Dwyer laid his left upon Frederico's oddly jointed shoulder. The grown Kessentai didn't look at the priest; indeed his eyes were fixed on the panorama outside being slowly revealed by the descending ramp. Even so, he said, "Thank you for this, Father Dwyer, for considering my dad to be a being worthy enough to fight for."

The Jesuit's brogue came out, slightly, as it rarely did anymore. "S'all right. He is. Are you ready?"

"Yesss." The boy's voice actually sounded more eager than merely ready.

"Von Altishofen?"

"Ready, Father."

"Then, when I give the word, come at the double. I'll go first. Maybe we can do this without bloodshed."

Posleen may heal quickly; they don't heal *that* quickly. Physically, Guano was incapable of much. Mentally, though, the pain had already ceased to dull his mind. He was aware then, of the other Kessentai who had joined him being chained, one by one, to the stake that arose from the pyre and to each other.

"Why?" he croaked to the nearest Kessentai, Dilantra. "Why did you join me?"

Dilantra shook his head. "It's hard to explain," he said. "Let's just say that your fortitude made all your words seem true."

"This is going to be really bad," Guano said. "The worst death, maybe, except for one."

"No matter," answered Dilantra. "If the words are true then Paradise awaits on the other side."

"And even if they're not," added Xinocorph, "the ancestors always did like a show of bravery."

"Paradise, then," Guano said. "For you and all these others. Paradise..."

Bridge, USS Salem

With the pinnace on the ground now, Sally was able to tap in, via Binastarion's AS, to the AS hanging around Dwyer's neck, below his cross and rosary. Thus, while al Rashid could not see the priest in the view screen, nor even the pinnace, which was presumably somewhere behind the priest, he could see the mass of Posleen and what looked to be a large pile of wood with a mass of Kessentai atop it.

"'Brothers, the winds of Paradise are calling,'" the imam recited. "'Where is he who hungers after Paradise?'"

Sally blinked once and did a double take. "You weren't—?"

"Muslim Brotherhood? In my younger days, before Allah opened up the gates of Hell and let loose the Posleen upon us...yes, I dabbled. I was young then, and foolish. Hopefully not so foolish as to be beyond Allah's mercy, however."

"You may yet find some souls among the Posleen, Imam," Sally said. "What will you do with them if you do?"

"Teach them as best I am able. We are not such a bad religion, as long as we can keep the lunatics at bay."

Dwyer cleared his throat and said, softly, "Artificial Sentience, we've never had a chance to get to know each other. Are you ready to do your stuff?"

"Yes, lord. You speak normally, I will do a simultaneous broadcast and translation into High Posleen."

"Begin . . . now."

"People of the Ships . . ."

To Dwyer's surprise, the sound was loud enough to shake, and to echo off the walls of the city and the platform of the Roga'a. He saw, too, that all movement stopped around the Roga'a and the pyre, as every crested head turned his way.

"In accordance with your custom and your law," Dwyer continued, "in full battle honor, I call upon those who hold my friend and his followers to release them, or to face myself and mine, one for one, with blade against blade. We are sixteen. Are there sixteen Kessentai who follow the false prophet, Finba'anaga, who will do battle with us?"

"Clever priest," whispered Tulo'stenaloor, still atop the backs of his former guards. He turned his head and called, "Goloswin?"

"Here, Tulo," the tinkerer answered.

"The human, Dwyer, has called out sixteen of Finba'anaga's followers to personal combat. I think Finba only has a couple of dozen in total. Assuming they follow the law and set sixteen against sixteen, do you think we can handle the remainder?"

We could probably handle them better if it had not been necessary to lop off several heads, but, "Yes, probably, Tulo. Actually, when you show up they might not even resist. I've a strong feeling Finba lied to the brighter ones he kept with him."

"All right. Caltu?"

"Yes, lord?"

"Here's your chance to get fully back into my good graces."

"I and my Kessentai stand ready, lord."

"Good. Send one of your ever-so-ready Kessentai back for my tenar."

Finba had watched the human shaman turn the corner with amusement bordering on contempt. "I'll not kill you priest; since you're under the clan lord's protection," he whispered. "But what good you think to do—"

Finba'anaga's words were interrupted by the booming of the AS the priest, remarkably for a human, wore on his chest.

"You think sixteen of you scrawny abat will be enough to overcome my followers? That's absurd."

"If he's coming with sixteen and calling us out under the law," Borasmena observed, "we have no choice but to meet them." *And if they can interrupt this vile set of murders, good luck to them.* "I am your follower, Finba," Boras continued, "and have been since we met on the ship. But I and my people will have no choice but to meet the humans in honor, blade against blade."

Dwyer saw out of the corner of one eye a small, bat-faced, fuzzy creature, hurrying to his side.

"AS, stop translating my words."

"Yes, lord," the disc on the priest's chest answered.

"I see you, Indowy Aelool."

"I see you, as well, human Dwyer," Aelool answered breathlessly. "What madness are you people engaged in?"

The priest didn't answer immediately, but after a few moments' reflection said, "I think the old fashioned term was, 'human sacrifice.'"

"Whatever term you use," Aelool said, "this is still madness. Don't you understand how much bigger, heavier, and stronger than you humans the Posleen are? They'll bowl you over and chop you to ribbons."

"I don't agree," Dwyer said.

"What, you have a dozen of O'Neal's armored combat suits locked away hidden?"

"No...and the forge couldn't have made them. And even if it could, there are too many Kessentai to take on with a mere dozen suits. Rather, we're striking the Posleen where they're weakest."

"Bah!" The Indowy turned away, stalking toward the presumed location of the pinnace. "You may be a religious lunatic, priest," Aelool said over his shoulder. "I can hope that the rest of you are made of saner stuff."

CHAPTER THIRTY-SEVEN

The best troops—those in whom you can
have the most confidence—are the Swiss.
—Napoleon

Anno Domini 2024
Posleen Prime

Aelool watched the thirteen Switzers and the two
Posleen flankers file out of the pinnace with a sickness
in his heart. *This is folly*, he thought. *No; it's worse
than that. It's* madness.

The fifteen-being team wore their monomolecular
armor and carried, except in the case of Querida,
their variable center-of-mass halberds. She carried the
ancient boma blade Guanamarioch had picked up for
her in the half-excavated pyramid on Hemaleen V.

Aelool hurried over to stand in front of them as
they changed formation from single file to two ranks
of six, with one man—von Altishofen—behind, for
the humans, and with the Posleen on the flanks. He
pointed directly at the young Posleen, Frederico.

"You're all adults," he said. "I suppose you can throw your lives away on an empty, pointless, doomed-to-fail gesture if you want to. But he's little more than a child. Send *him*, at least, back to the ship."

Seeing the Switzers ignored him completely, Aelool walked to his left to stand in front of Querida. "He's your *child*, your *only* child," the Indowy said. "Order him back." Querida simply looked levelly at the Indowy. She knew well enough what he was saying; she just couldn't respond even if she would have.

"She can't order me," Frederico said, from his post over on the left flank. "I'm a Kessentai; she's cosslain. It would no more occur to her that she can order me, now that I'm grown, than it would to flap her arms to fly. Now, please, get out of the way. We have work to do."

Aelool went to the Posleen boy. "You have a life ahead of you," he pleaded. "Don't throw it away."

"I'm not throwing it away," Frederico answered. "If anything, I'm giving it. For my father, yes . . . but also because I would be ashamed"—his great crested head inclined toward the Switzers—"terribly, terribly ashamed to have these good men fight alone, without my help."

"You're not even bringing your *rifles,*" the Indowy objected.

"With rifles, the Kessentai would just order their normals and cosslain to smash us with railguns," the boy patiently explained. "With blades—blade against blade—they'll come out and fight us being to being, hand to hand. It's an honor thing."

The Indowy's head sank onto his chest. *Honor? Absurd. Nonsense. This is hopeless . . . hopeless. They're all mad.*

"And now, Indowy Aelool," Frederico asked, "if you would please step out of the way."

As the Indowy shuffled out of the way, slowly, as if in great pain, Frederico turned his head over his right shoulder to look at von Altishofen. As his field of view passed over the two ranks of Switzers, he saw the sharp, deadly gleam of their halberds, already reconfigured from dull, practice mode to razor-keen and needle-sharp killing mode.

"We're ready now, *Herr Wachtmeister*," the boy said.

"Father Dwyer," the *Wachtmeister* called out, "if we might have your benediction? *Vexillation*...KNEEL."

Solemnly, the priest stepped out around and in front on the small formation. There wasn't a lot of time for formal ceremony. The priest carried the processional cross, a crucifix on a pole, in his left hand. He held it there as he made the sign of the cross over them with his right.

"*In hoc signo vinces*," the priest said, simply, echoing the vision of Constantine.

Von Altishofen stood and nodded, then gave the order, "Vexillation...*achtung. Vorwaerts...MARSCH. Links, rechts, links, rechts*..." Boot feet crunched on the gravelly path beneath them. "Sound off, you bastards!"

> "*Unser Leben gleicht die Reisse*
> *Eines Wandrers in der Nacht.*
> *Jeder hat in seinem Gleise...*"

Finba'anaga heard the odd human sounds long before he saw the humans turn the corner into the square by the Statue of Courageous Defiance. He had no idea what the words meant and asked his AS to explain and translate.

"It's a song, lord," the AS, "like the People's song of Flight and Resettlement. The words are... 'Our lives are like the journeys of wanderers in the night. Each has—'"

"Never mind the translation," Finba cut the machine off. "What do they intend?"

"See for yourself, lord," the machine answered.

At that moment the first rank of the human warriors and their Posleen escorts appeared, wheeling around the corner of the Temple of War. Their steps, most unlike the People when they marched, crunched as one along the gravel way. The second rank quickly followed, itself being followed by the one human Finba knew as the chief, Dwyer. The weapons the warriors bore looked odd to Finba, yet he had no doubt that those heavy chopping blades on the ends of poles were weapons.

The priest carried only the odd symbol of his bizarre faith on the end of a pole much like those of the warriors' arms. All were armored, barring only the priest.

At the sight of his son and wife armed and accoutered for battle against hopeless odds, Guanamarioch set up a wail. "Frederico, go back. Querida, back," he called from atop the pile of wood intended for his funeral pyre. His wife and son ignored him. She, in fact, made a show of twisting her head and digging a claw into her right ear, as if to dislodge some obstruction. It was the only time in her existence she had ever defied Guano. She found she rather liked the feeling.

"Release my father," Frederico called aloud, in High Posleen. His adolescent crest erected itself automatically in a show of intent to do battle.

"Kill them," Finba ordered his assistant, Borasmena.

Borasmena nodded, then leaned the railgun he had been carrying against a wall. Drawing his boma blade, the Kessentai called out to a small group of others to follow.

"No, you idiot," Finba said. "Use the railguns. There's no need to fight them fairly."

Borasmena shook his head and answered, "You are of the Way of Remembrance, not of the Way of the Warriors. We, who are of that way, have no choice, in honor, but to meet blade against blade."

The Posleen were bigger than humans, taller and wider both. While the Switzers with their flanking "cavalry" filled the street from wall to wall, with only eight beings across, the Posleen could fit only half that number in the single rank. Nor could the boma blades of the rear ranks reach out to support the Kessentai in the front ranks, as the humans' halberds could.

Martin de Courten, youngest of the crew, drew first blood. While the Posleen in front of him waved his boma blade to ward off the halberds of *Hellebardier* Faubion, to de Courten's right, and the downward sweep of Gehrig's and Scheekt's, de Courten leveled his own and drove it straight in.

The Posleen shrieked and backed off, frantically trying to ward off another strike. De Courten then twisted the polearm to turn the edge about thirty degrees to his right. He swung the thing down and at that angle, letting the monomolecular edge neatly slice off the Posleen's left foreleg. The Posleen dropped his boma blade as he fell over, his claws questing downward to staunch the flow of yellow blood from his severed limb.

Like a drill, de Courten stepped onto the stricken Posleen's torso. Behind him he sensed rather than saw as Scheekt's halberd took the reptilian centauroid in the neck, through the spine, thus ending his cries of agony.

Unfortunately, another Posleen Kessentai moved up to fill the space left by the fallen one. This one was more skilled, causing Martin to have to fight for his life, his halberd slashing frantically left and right and up and down to keep the creature's boma blade away, until Faubion and Stoever could move up to take the creature in flank.

Please hurry, Kameraden, the boy thought.

Borasmena felt no anger at seeing one of his people fall. Indeed, he was filled with pride and admiration for the humans. This was something he'd never expected to feel for an alien and enemy species.

But to fight so wonderfully, to give us the chance to struggle before the shades of the ancestors, hand to hand and being to being . . . for this, humans, I shall burn fine korobar *incense in your memory to my last day.*

Borasmena thought the human facing him had him once, when that wicked looking point above the ax blade nearly took him in the throat. He managed to deflect the thing, barely, with the flat of his own boma blade, then step inside the human's weapon's arc and slice down at his enemy's torso. The point of his blade slid off the human's cuirass, but continued on to his thigh. Red blood spurted up and out, its spray blinding Borasmena.

Now it was the Posleen's turn to frantically wave his blade about, trying to fend off unseen points and blades that sought his life. Just as frantically he backed off while scraping a scaly palm over his face in an attempt to clear his eyes. Another Kessentai stepped in to take the place of his incapacitated leader.

The cut was so clean, so fast, and so unexpected, that de Courten didn't at first cry out. He saw that the Posleen to his front was blinded by something, a something he did not immediately connect with his own red blood, and lowered his pike and lunged forward to pierce the creature's chest.

Unfortunately, the wounded leg was half severed. The *halberdier* took no more than the one step before falling face forward. Confused, dazed, he saw a small forest of oddly jointed alien legs and a single barrel-chested torso before him. With both hands on the grip, de Courten plunged the point of the halberd into that torso and ripped forward, spilling the Posleen's intestines out to the ground, steaming.

As the disemboweled Kessentai fell, his sword arm continued the downward arc it had begun at seeing the human fall. Wounded as he was, he could not keep the thing directed at the human's armored back. Rather, it veered slightly to one side, slicing de Courten's left arm into three sections, the stump still attached to his body, the hand still gripping the halberd, and the central section with the elbow flanked by two other stumps.

Bridge, USS Salem

Sally cried out aloud to see de Courten fall in the image sent via Dwyer's and Binastarion's artificial sentiences. *That poor wonderful brave boy*, she thought, dry-eyed but crying inside.

The image was also being carried on another view screen, down in the assembly hall. At the moment de Courten fell, Sally heard three women cry out in despair. Though rivals, all three fell upon each others' shoulders, weeping.

And that is what I will feel, the sound I will make, if and when my husband falls. Fuck.

Posleen Prime

Hellebardier Gehrig saw de Courten fall and immediately stepped to the fore to take the fallen guardsman's place. Behind him, Scheekt and Rossini shifted slightly left and right to cover the gaps. Rossini's halberd swung down, just inside Gehrig's arc of vision, to administer the coup de grace to the disemboweled Posleen. The being's agonized keening suddenly cut off, only to be replaced by a human's wail—Cristiano, Gehrig thought—somewhere off to the right.

Giovani Cristiano was having the time of his life.
All that drill . . . endless hours . . . pain and aching muscles and bruises galore. And now, finally, it all pays off. Thank you, Lord, for giving me this one opportunity to prove I'm worthy of my ancestors.

Cristiano was on the extreme right of the infantry line, with only Querida guarding his flank. She was faced with a Kessentai, larger and stronger but not so well armed and completely unarmored. Still, that enemy Kessentai pressed the cosslain hard. She was barely holding her own when Cristiano saw an opportunity. He lunged forward, causing his own opponent to back off, then twisted his ax blade to the right and slashed the Kessentai opposite Querida deeply along its flank, severing ribs and opening at least one main artery. That Kessentai gave off a scream and turned, automatically, to his wounded side.

He didn't scream long as Querida's ancient boma blade sliced neatly through the forward half of the creature's thick neck, further adding to the blood spilled on the ground.

Posleen blood, though yellow, was as slippery when fresh as any human's. Stepping forward into it, Cristiano's left foot began to skid. When he moved his right to try to regain his balance, it, too, ended up in the broad puddle of Posleen blood. At that point, both of Cristiano's feet went out from under him, letting him slam to the ground on his back. He instantly twisted over, onto his hands and knees, in an attempt to right himself. This, however, placed his unprotected rear end temporarily in the direction of the Posleen enemy.

Cristiano knew this was a bad position to be in, of course. Just how bad he didn't fully understand until the Posleen that replaced the one fallen in front of Querida decided he had just enough time to make a swing before Querida could take another attack position. The Kessentai swung—more of a short chop, really and that swing cut into Cristiano's mid-section, just below the armor, slicing his spine in two. Control of his legs gone, Cristiano went down flat, adding his screams to the general cacophony.

Even screaming and slashed through the spine, the Switzer still managed to twirl himself around, his dead legs dragging behind him. The yellow blood now mixed with his own helped ease the move. He took hold of his halberd once again. Pushing against the ground Cristiano managed to roll onto his back, his dead legs twisting one around the other as he did. From that position, the *Kaporal* lunged upward at the Posleen who had felled him, even as that enemy raised his blade for another strike. The halberd's point took the Posleen full in the chest, but lower down, towards the underside. From that entry point, it pierced one of the creature's lungs.

The Posleen dropped his blade and looked down toward his pinioned chest. On the way, his view passed over the fallen human. Incredibly, as badly as he was hurt, the human was *still* laughing.

Just before he collapsed on top of the Switzer, which collapse would eventually be the cause—via suffocation—of Cristiano's death, the Kessentai wondered, *How do you beat beings who can find something funny in being half cut in two?*

His eyes now clear of the human's blood, Borasmena was able to see the problem more clearly. *There is only enough space for five or six of us abreast,* he thought, *and those with only the short reach of the boma blades, while the humans and their two Posleen allies can mass eight abreast and bring fourteen weapons to bear. We're simply outnumbered. Worse, they have armor to turn*

*away any but the most precise blows. We're outnum-
bered and outclassed. Who would have thought it of
those scrawny bipeds?*

That calculation was slightly off, since two of the
humans, de Courten and Cristiano, were dead or
dying now. Even so, once von Altishofen stepped up
to fill a vacant slot it was still thirteen to five, humans,
and worse than that in close combat power. And the
human threshing machine continued onward over the
corpses of the fallen Kessentai.

Maybe if we back off, Borasmena wondered, *and
charge them, try to bowl them over by sheer weight.*

A few shouted commands in High Posleen caused
those Kessentai not most closely engaged to back off.
The five who were face to face with the humans could
not back off, lest their unprotected hindquarters be
chopped as they turned. One by one, these fell, even
as Borasmena used the time their deaths bought him
to organize a charge.

From the center of the second rank von Altishofen
saw what the Posleen had in mind. *Our line's thin,* he
thought. *A hard charge carried home just might break
it.* He shouted out a series of commands, "HALT...
prepare to receive cavalry...Second rank...fill in first
rank...KNEEL...Present...ARMS."

As one, the men of the single rank knelt down,
pushing the pike points of their halberds to the fore
and bracing the buttstocks on the ground behind them.

"What's that animal the humans have on their
planet, AS?" Borasmena asked. "The one with all the
points sticking out?"

"A porcupine, lord."

"A porcupine," the Kessentai echoed. He counted the points of the halberds, including the one borne by the juvenile Kessentai, and divided by the space available. "If I order this charge, all six in the first rank will end up throwing themselves on between two and three of those spearpoints each."

"Do you see a choice, lord?" the AS asked.

"Unfortunately, I do not. More unfortunately, I am not at all sure that this will work."

"Well," the AS observed, "it isn't like you have a particular shortage of spear fodder now, is it?"

Borasmena looked over the ground the humans had trod. He knew two of them had gone down, but as near as he could tell five or six times that many Kessentai had fallen to the humans' odd axes-cum-spears. It was hard to tell how many, actually, for all the severed limbs and heads. And each and every one of the fallen was a friend.

"There is a way to break them, maybe," Borasmena announced as he walked to the center front of his formation and beckoned with both arms for four of the Kessentai behind him to dress on him. "It is a fearful way, however. Goodbye, AS."

"*Goodbye*, lord?"

Leopoldo Rossini was in the front and only rank now, gasping for air but with both hands firmly grasping the halberd. His bronze-tinted cuirass was speckled with blood, the dull yellow Posleen fluid mostly, but intermixed along with that were brighter spots of human red. He thought none of the latter was his own but was really afraid to look.

Scheekt and Lorgus knelt at either side of Rossini, their halberds likewise gripped tightly and braced on the ground.

"Think we can hold them?" Lorgus asked.

"Think we have a choice?" Rossini countered. "Yes, we'll hold them. These are brave creatures, but not suicidal, generally. The ones in front will slow down when . . ."

He never finished the sentence as the Posleen began their charge.

Borasmena gave a half-accusing look over his shoulder. The object of his accusation was Finba'anaga. The meaning? That was hard to define but it seemed to be about half, *There was no better way than this?*

The Kessentai then sheathed his own boma blade, turned his great crested head still further, and said to his followers, "I will create the opening. The rest of you, pour through that."

CHAPTER THIRTY-EIGHT

The Helvetians are a people of warriors,
famous for the valour of their soldiers.
—Tacitus

Anno Domini 2024
Posleen Prime

One look at the Posleen facing him, both the look on
his face and the resigned way he seemed to sheath
his boma blade, brought a single name to Rossini's
mind. *Arnold von Winkelried. We're fucked.*

Rossini didn't have time to explain to the men
flanking him, Scheekt and Lorgus. He could only
shout out the name, "von Winkelried," and hope they'd
understand. And then the Posleen was upon him, using
his free arms to gather into his own chest Rossini's
halberd, as well as Scheekt's and Lorgus's, and one
other that Leo couldn't put a name to. As sharp as
the things were, spearpoint and axeblade both, the
Posleen managed to drive them each deep into his
own body, effectively locking them there unless the

Switzers affected were to back up several feet and break their own line. Even at that, they could not have moved fast enough, not as fast, in any event, as the Posleen had impaled himself. Worse, when the Posleen fell, he dragged the four halberds down with him.

Bowing to the inevitable, Rossini let go his halberd and reached for his own sword, a stout monomolecular baselard produced by Sally in the forge. His blade was barely half out of its scabbard before a Posleen, charging over the body of their fallen hero, was slashing at him with fury. Rossini ducked the first cut, pulled his own blade out before the second, and barely managed to deflect that.

This is way too much like work.

Borasmena was a mass of pain, all too slowly fading into merciful shock. He could feel the precise spot of each spearhead and axeblade lodged inside him. *Gods... ancestors*, he silently pleaded, *please take me to you... and please hurry.*

The Kessentai dimly sensed that all four bearers of the humans' long weapons lodged inside him had drawn secondary arms. They'd take some with them, Borasmena thought, but in the long run the strength of the People would overcome those little things.

He found, to his surprise, that he didn't hate the humans at all. Perhaps that was partly shock. Perhaps in another part it was simple adrenaline-cognate. Yet, so Borasmena thought himself, a good part of it was the shared brotherhood of the battlefield.

A human, missing an arm, fell down right in front of Borasmena's field of view. The human seemed to be in great pain.

It was an uneven contest from the beginning. While Rossini's baselard was clearly handier for a human, he could not put the strength behind it that the Posleen facing him brought to his own blade. Nor was there any objective sense in trying to conserve strength. The Posleen would always have more of that than any human.

With something near a sigh, Rossini took one last chance at a victory, however temporary such a victory must prove to be. Batting aside a Posleen slash, he took two half steps in and drove the point of his baselard into his opponent's neck, just above where it joined the chest. The Posleen gave off a great cry of anguish, even as it made a last slash downward.

Rossini felt a shock on his left side. He looked over and down and saw a single arm, lying on the yellow and red sprayed ground. His grip on his baselard loosened of its own accord. Then he felt his legs going out from under him.

For a moment, everything went black. When they lightened once again, Rossini found himself lying on his back, with his head turned to one side, facing the muzzle of the very Posleen who had impaled himself on their halberds. That Posleen nodded his head, very slightly, and then reached out a single claw.

Rossini expected the claw to rake his neck. He braced himself for the pain, squeezing his eyes shut. The pain never came. Instead there was a gentle touch, almost a pat. The Switzer opened his eyes again and saw that, indeed, the fallen Kessentai, the Posleen's own von Winkelried, was doing just that, giving a series of gentle pats to his armored chest.

Instinctively, Leopoldo took his own hand, the one remaining, and patted the claw of Borasmena. He then took that claw in a firm but brotherly grip.

Which was exactly how the two bodies were later found.

Von Altishofen stood upon a small pile of bodies. From that vantage point, he could see three knots of fighting. One of these centered on Querida who, with two Switzers—one of them *Kaporal* Grosskopf, was fighting off twice as many Kessentai. The other was centered on Frederico, who with three of the guardsmen was doing the same. The *Wachtmeister* thought that neither contest would be long drawn out.

He, himself, was in a little knot of five—*no, four now*—still trying to use their halberds. There was no formation, though, and so most of the humans' advantage was gone. Even so, where the humans could present more than one spearpoint to a Posleen, the Kessentai usually kept some distance.

And why not? They'll wear us down a little at a time, as is.

From the direction of the pyre, von Altishofen heard the Reverend Guanamarioch scream. He didn't look in the Christian Posleen's direction, but spared a glance first at Querida, who was sinking with a boma blade plunged into her side, then at Frederico, just as the juvenile Kessentai burst like a fury from the knot of Switzers, trying to reach his mother's side.

Frederico heard his father's wail of despair and looked immediately toward his mother. It was like a knife in his own hearts to see her slowly going down while plucking ineffectually at the hilt of the boma blade protruding from her torso.

"MOTHER!" the boy screamed.

His eyes opened wide in full battle fury. His crest, though it should not have been possible, erected itself even more fully. In sudden fear, the Kessentai facing Frederico backed off, despite having size on the boy. He did not back off quickly enough.

Frederico batted his enemy's boma blade aside, then reached forward with the hook on the back of his halberd. The inside curve of the hook was dull. No matter; he caught the back of that Kessentai's leg with the thing and pulled it forward, knocking out that strut. A quick slash with the axeblade and the Posleen fell over. Before he could rise Frederico chopped right through the center of his head, killing him instantly. Into that space, the boy lunged forward.

He slashed right; he slashed left. He jabbed with the point or stroked with the butt. A Kessentai unfortunate enough to bar his path soon found himself missing a leg . . . an arm . . . a head.

One among his enemies' number, though, trotted over to bar the boy's way. Others moved to surround him on all sides, even as the Swiss behind him began to succumb to the blows of their enemies.

"You are a brave Kessentai," that one said, in High Posleen, "too brave to die for an alien faith. My name is Koresnagi. Yield you, now, to our grace, and be spared."

In answer, the Posleen boy took a firmer grip of his great ax and spat upon the blood-stained ground. "I stand with my sire and I stand by my faith," he answered, as if the grip and the spittle were not answer enough.

"So be it," the Kessentai answered, sadly, placing his blade in guard position and moving forward to the attack.

Despite his shock at the fury of the humans in close combat mode, Finba'anaga was still surprised by the sound of Tulo'stenaloor's tenar and then the clan lord's gravelly voice, coming from behind him. He could see those he had placed as guards upon the clan lord fanning out into the crowd or racing to the pyre.

"You said this new thing, this religion, would weaken us, did you not, Finba?" the clan lord asked.

His eyes riveted to the battle scene playing out before them, Finba could only shake his head. This was not in denial of the words, but in denial of the events unfolding.

"I see no weakness down there," Tulo continued. "Instead I see a courage to match any in the old tales. Do you deny this?"

This time, when Finba shook his head, it *was* in conscious acceptance.

"Cease this, now," the clan lord ordered. "Call off your followers."

Finba's muzzle opened, yet no words came out. In that delay, another human, standing guard over Querida's corpse, fell. "NOW, I said."

"Ce...cease!" Finba shouted. "Back off, Kessentai."

"And release the Kessentai who joined the humans," Tulo ordered. "I mean both their 'minister' and those who chose to follow him. This was a filthy way to have put them to death, in any event, and I shall be long in trying to understand how you could have permitted it."

✧   ✧   ✧

Frederico didn't quite understand what had happened. The Kessentai facing him had had him, dead to rights, with a boma blade poised to take off his head.

He was wounded. He knew that in a distant way. But he thought it was not a fatal wound. He wasn't sure if that was a pleasing thought or not. Yet, pleasing or not, it was true. That blade never descended. His head remained attached.

Instead of killing him, Frederico saw, the Kessentai who had named himself Koresnagi was sheathing his blade, and then reaching down a hand to help him up.

"You were good," Koresnagi said, "very good. I doubt I could have taken you alone."

"I must see to my mother," Frederico said, as he began to walk unsteadily to the little mound that contained she who had raised him, plus the bodies of Grosskopf and Affenzeller, along with several other Posleen. He stumbled.

"Here," Koresnagi said, gesturing to his own broad back. "Put one arm over me. I will help."

Frederico nodded. "Thank you. I think I need the help," he said, just before collapsing.

As soon as Guano was released from the chains that bound him to the pyre, he raced as fast as his injuries allowed across the bloody ground to the side of his cosslain.

Querida was still breathing. She would not be for much longer. Besides the boma blade that pierced her nearly through, she was bleeding from a dozen other cuts, large and small, shallow or deep.

Guano couldn't contain the moan that escaped

his muzzle as he sank to his chest beside her. The moan was enough to bring her eyes open. She saw the being who meant everything to her, even more than her son. She tried to raise her head.

"No...no, Querida," Guano said, lightly pushing her head back to the ground and laying his own across her bloody neck.

She took a deep breath, causing her pierced lungs to rattle as air escaped them through a bloody froth. One syllable, she managed to get out. "See..." Another breath, harder and drawing less air, and she gasped, "Ay..." Still another. "Lo?"

"*Cielo?*" Guano said. "No, not Heaven yet, Love. Soon...soon enough we'll be together there. I promise. I pro—"

Guano felt the body beneath him shudder then. Slowly, the air escaped from lungs that no longer needed to draw breath. He lifted his muzzle to Heaven and from it issued a wail of despair that reached to every human and Kessentai present.

"Now collect and sort their dead," Tulo ordered, "theirs and ours. Treat them all with respect."

"Yes, lord," Finba answered.

"And dismantle that obscene pyre."

"Yes, lord."

With a grunt of disdain, Tulo'stenaloor turned his tenar then, leaving the platform on which Finba'anaga stood, with nary a glance behind. He glided easily for as long as the roadway was clear, then dropped his tenar to the ground and began to walk once he reached the bodies. These he stepped through gingerly, lest his claws profane them.

For you were all holy, Tulo thought, *insofar as I can believe anything to be holy. Whether it was the Posleen who fought to keep up our restoration of the old ways, or the humans and Posleen who fought to bring us the new . . . all were holy, alike together.*

"There is no going back then, is there, priest?" Tulo said to Dwyer, still standing and holding his processional cross.

Dwyer shook his head, then said, "There never was any going back, I think, Lord of the Sten Clan."

"Was it worth it to you, sacrificing your people as you have?"

"To me? No. To our peoples?" Dwyer glanced over to where Guanamarioch's followers were still in the process of being unchained from the pyre. "I think it may be. And then, too . . ."

"Yes?"

"I do believe. It is no act. Believing, as I do, I do not think that those who fell here will be ignored by God. They shall have their reward."

"I do *not* believe," Tulo said. "Neither in your god nor in the old ones some of my people tried to resurrect. Yet I do believe this much: Faith is strength and in the days to come we shall all need all of the strength we can muster. I will order my people to convert to your faith, Priest."

"Ours?" Dwyer asked, uncomprehending. "I don't understand. It was Guanamarioch's version that your people mostly turned to."

"His way allowed his people to be led to a pyre to be burned to death," Tulo explained. "That is a kind of strength, yes, but it is not the kind we will

need for the future. *Your* faith, on the other hand,
your *kind* of faith, led these humans to battle like
heroes of legend. So, Priest, my people will become
Roman Catholics...isn't that what you call yourselves?
Rejoice; you've won."

Dwyer looked around at the piles of bodies, and
the few stunned and dazed survivors. *And how does
one repay them,* he asked himself, *how does one
repay a sacrifice that brings an entire species into
the fold of Mother Church. Sainthood?* Dwyer could
hardly keep from laughing. *These men were soldiers,
not plaster saints. Of course, we don't really make
saints for the benefit of the beatified, but for those
who remain. So, yes, perhaps that, if I can swing it.
Would roughly a ton of humans and another half a
ton of Posleen standing up to twenty tons of Posleen
for some minutes count as a miracle? Maybe; maybe
not. Well...we'll still see what we can do.*

USS Salem

"I feel empty now," Sally said, tears in her eyes,
"without those boys here to do their drill in the hall.
And to lose Querida..." She buried her face in her
hands and began openly to weep.

"She really was a person, wasn't she?" Dwyer agreed.
"Lord knows, poor Guano feels the loss like she was."

Between sniffles Sally got out, "And Frederico...
losing his mother...like that..."

"How are they taking it?" Dwyer asked.

"You *know* I can't actually look anywhere there
aren't cameras," she said.

"Yes, but."

She sniffled again and shrugged. "They have faith. They hurt; but they have faith."

"Do you, Sally?" her husband asked.

"Not yours, of course, but I do have faith in a couple of things. One of them is that in about eight and a half months I'm going to give birth to a baby. If it's a boy, I want to call him 'Martin.'"

Dwyer was almost speechless. Of course, he *was* a Jesuit and so "almost" speechless didn't mean *quite* speechless. "I'm going to be a *father* father?"

Sally nodded quickly, the kind of nod a person makes when words can't possibly express their feelings quickly enough.

"What if it's a girl?"

Sally sniffled again. "That's a stupid question." Sniffle. "If it's a girl we're going to name her 'Querida.'"

At which point they both started to cry, more for Guano and Frederico than for the fallen cosslain.

Dwyer was carrying a small sack when he found Guanamarioch in the nondenominational ship's chapel. The Posleen was on his knees (a terribly uncomfortable position for a Posleen) with his grasping claws clasped, his eyes closed, and his head bowed. The imam, al Rashid, was there, too, though the Moslem was seated, cross-legged, on the floor beside the minister, one hand laid across the Posleen's back. Frederico was still in the sick bay; his wounds, while not fatal, had proven more serious than the simple cuts on the outside would have indicated.

"He's been this way for hours," the imam explained. "Didn't think he should be alone."

"I didn't think so, either," piped in the AS hanging on Guano's chest.

"Sally sent me down, Guano," the priest said, as he sat down in a mirror of the imam's own posture.

"Eeesss...pllleeeaaasssinggg...knowww...sheee thiiinksss oppponnn me," the Kessentai answered, head still bowed.

From the sack Dwyer drew a bottle and a jar. "She thought you could use a drink, Guano. And she didn't think you should get drunk alone. So I've got this one time special dispensation, better than from the pope, to share a drink with you. The jar's for you. The bottle...that's for me."

"For *us*," al Rashid corrected.

Only one of the moons had risen, a bright dome in heaven, casting a sharp shadow from the tripartite statue. Finba'anaga stood before that statue, its shadow running across his legs and claws.

"Why?" the Kessenalt asked of the statue though, it being merely stone, it could not give him the answer he sought. "Why?" he asked again, fruitlessly. "I believed in you, and in the old gods. I believed in the message you carried, and yet you abandoned me. And now this alien faith will spread, by order of the clan lord, no less, and the old ways will be lost forever."

It was too much to be borne, really. And Finba could see no way to make it better. Still, *he* believed in the old gods. If they had proven less powerful than this new one of the humans... *Well, and so the humans proved more powerful than us.*

Pained, with a deep soul-searing inner agony, Finba turned from the statue and began the long trudge upward to the top of the acropolis of the city of the Posleen. Just once, before turning a bend, he twisted his head back to look again at the statue.

Why?

The path wound upward, between rough, rocky walls. Head bowed down in defeat, Finba paid the walls no mind. He barely noticed the ground upon which he trod.

At the top of the path, Finba looked upward, as if seeking the human ship that had brought this ruin upon him. *I would curse you,* he thought, *but, since your God is more powerful than mine, such a curse would be nothing but another exercise in futility. And of those I am very tired.*

In truth, I am tired of life. Tired . . .

Finba picked his way through the pyramids dotting the top of the acropolis, to the edge. From there he looked out over the city. *I had this uncovered. I had the walls rebuilt, the paths recleared. Gods of my forefathers, was it all in vain?*

Unlike all other Rememberers in living memory, Finba'anaga had never tossed his stick. He took it now from his harness and, looking at the square where he had met ultimate defeat at the hands of the humans, he raised the stick high overhead and threw it.

"You win," he whispered. He then closed his eyes and followed the stick, over the edge of the mesa and down. The only sound he made was when his body struck pavement, and even that was involuntary.

"We've won here, Guano," Dwyer said, his speech only a little slurred. "The People of the Ships are going to become Christians."

"Well," al Rashid shrugged, "I never could explain to them how to find Mecca to bow for daily prayers. And the whole Hajj thing? That was just never going to happen."

The imam's speech was clearer than Dwyer's, even though he'd drunk as much if not more. Then again, he was Egyptian and was not exactly a stranger to beer.

"This is good," Guano said through his AS. "But *you* have won, Father. The clan lord, Tulo'stenaloor, has directed his people to become Catholic."

"That's something I wanted to talk to you about, too, Guano. You see, while Tulo may order them to join my faith, only you have shown any ability to persuade them to adopt Christianity in any form."

"They will still follow orders," Guano said.

"That's true, I'm sure," the priest agreed, reaching once again for the bottle, then shaking it suspiciously and casting a glare at al Rashid. "But following orders may or may not save their souls. That's where you come in, Reverend Doctor Guanamarioch.

"By the way," the priest asked, "have I never discussed with you the concept of 'Big Tent Catholicism'?"

CHAPTER THIRTY-NINE

And so the People feasted on Finba'anaga,
who had done his best.
—The *Tuloriad*, Na'agastenalooren

Anno Domini 2028
Posleen Prime

"The years are upon me, old friend," said Tulo'stenaloor.
"I fear that this goodbye *is* goodbye."

"Oh, stuff and nonsense," answered Goloswin. "You'll
still be here keeping every cosslain in sight sore from
excess rubbing long after I've returned."

"Must you go?"

The tinkerer sighed. "It isn't a question of must;
it's a question of should. And, yes, for the good of
the People and the good of your memory, I think I
should go to Aradeen, and study the other religions,
the ones you rejected. Sally says she can get me an
appointment with the chief rabbi of Jerusalem. And
al Rashid insists that the grand mufti of the same city
is a first cousin. We need to know about these things,

Tulo, for the good of the people you have brought here. Besides, since I learned how to replicate the Himmit metal and figured out how to test for cosslain and Kessentai in the egg, I feel like retiring undefeated."

Slowly, the clan lord nodded his great head. "I know. I even understand. It's just... I'm going to miss you, Golo." The clan lord pushed sorrow away and drew himself up to his full height. "You're right, of course. So go now, before I make a spectacle of myself."

Goloswin started to turn away, then turned back and flung both arms about his clan lord. "I'll miss you, too, you old bastard."

Golo had to push through crowds now to get through the city. Where once a few thousand of the People had sheltered, now there were nearer to fifty thousand.

And in three years it will be twice that, despite Tulo's limits on normals. In fifty years, we'll have outgrown this planet. And then we will *have to deal with humans en masse. Best we know as much as we can learn by then.*

Golo stopped briefly at the three-figure statue. "Do you have an image of this stored in your memory, AS?" he asked.

"As I suggested when we first met, lord," the AS answered, "I am *not* an idiot. Of course I do."

"Good fellow."

Golo continued on his way through the packed city pathways, through the gates of the walls and out toward where the human pinnace sat that would take him to the starship *Salem* and thence to Earth. He saw, in an open field by the pinnace, a sight that once would have seemed quite impossible, a small human child, a girl he thought, by the length of the creature's hair, riding on the back of a fully grown Kessentai, one with a cosslain walking by either side of him. From the way her shoulders shook, Goloswin thought the girl might be crying.

"Can't you come with us, Uncle Frederico?" Sally's daughter Querida asked, her voice breaking with tears. "I'm going to miss you so."

Still walking, the Posleen turned his head and torso one hundred and eighty degrees to look the child in the face. One claw reached up to gently brush a tear from the girl's cheek. One of the flanking cosslain reached over to pat the girl's back in sympathy, as well.

"No more than I'm going to miss you, honey," Frederico answered. "You've been my best friend since you were born." That was no less than the truth; the Posleen had taken to the child as soon as he had seen it and rarely let her from his sight in all the years since.

"Then come *home* with me," she pleaded.

"My home is here now," he answered. "Here, continuing my father's work, while he returns to Earth for a while. But you'll come back and when you do I'll be waiting."

"I asked my mother if I could stay here with you but she said 'no,' that I had to go back and go to school."

"She's right," Frederico said. "Humans do have to go to school. And even we Posleen are beginning to open some schools."

"Then why can't I go to school *here,* and live with you and your cosslain?"

"Because we don't know how to teach human children," he answered. "Though at least one of us once did."

Snifling, Querida put her head down onto the Posleen's broad chest and repeated, "I don't want to go. When I'm big enough, *this* will be home for me, too."

"Will you miss it while you're gone, Guano?" Dwyer asked, as the two of them watched Frederico and his own child say their painful goodbyes.

"I'll miss my son," the Posleen answered. "I'll miss the grave of *my* Querida, even though I know I can talk to her anywhere if I can talk to her here. I'll miss seeing my grandchildren come out of the egg. But, what must be, must be. There are still things to work out with the Mother Church. And I'll need some teachers for the seminary we will need here. I'll have to recruit for those."

"I'll help if you need," Dwyer said. "The Order has a very long reach."

"I know, and I will," Guanamarioch answered. "There's another reason I need to go back."

"Hmmm?"

"I need to talk to His Holiness...about those reliefs we found on Hemaleen V. I need him to tell me if that was a Messiah, come to my people first and spurned."

"I understand. But...Guano...some things are meant to be mysteries."

USS Salem

"There are still some mysteries I'd like you to clear up, before we have to go," Sally said to the turnip in the privacy of the O' Club.

"I've already told you everything I know about the Aldenata," the turnip answered.

"It isn't about the Aldenata," Sally said. "It's about that virus that brought you and the rest of the People of the Ships here. I've got some of it stored behind a firewall and, the thing is, it's not Indowy. Or at least not mostly Indowy. Whose virus is it?"

The virtual turnip looked pensive for a moment; it then answered, "I don't know, not for certain. But I do know this. I've extensive records on Aldenata, Indowy, Darhel, Tchpth, and humans. And it doesn't match any of their ways of programming. Who else do we know of in the galaxy, who would have an interest in Posleen, and who are technologically quite advanced?"

Disbelief slowly took over Sally's virtual face. "No way. The *Himmit*?"

The turnip and the virtual woman suddenly became aware of another presence in the O' Club. Sally saw mottled green, bullfrog skin, four eyes, two on each shoulder, and a large, fearsome mouth mounted below the creature's chest.

"Oh, puhleeze," the creature said. "Do I look like any Himmit you've ever heard of?"

Posleen Prime

Wachtmeister von Altishofen, along with Mrs. von Altishofen (née Duvall), Mrs. von Altishofen (née Schneider), Mrs. von Altishofen (née Smith) and Mrs. von Altishofen (née Papadopoulous), the few remaining guardsmen and their wives, and Deacon Koresnagi and his five cosslain stood in front of a rather larger than life statue of an idealized Swiss Guardsman and a Kessentai locked in battle with halberd and boma blade over the corpse of another Posleen, a cosslain. In front of the statue were more than a score of shallow mounds, marking the final resting place of the fallen. The faces of both standing figures looked determined and dedicated, rather than angry or hate-filled. This was by design.

"All holy together," Tulo'stenaloor had said, and apparently meant it.

While the Swizter's image was idealized, that of the Kessentai was based on Borasmena. Of those present, only Koresnagi had known that Kessentai well enough to recognize it, however. They all knew that the cosslain represented and resembled Guano's wife, Querida.

"He was a good friend," Koresnagi said, "a good Kessentai and a fine being."

Von Altishofen, who knew who Borasmena had been, knew that he had deliberately sacrificed himself to the pikes, nodded seriously. "No Switzer in battle ever did better," he agreed.

The *Wachtmeister*'s eyes turned to the plaque, inscribed in pure gold in Latin and High Posleen. He read aloud:

> "Here lie the mortal remains of those Posleen and humans who, in defense of the old Posleen order and in advancement of the new, met in honorable battle and let the Lord of Hosts decide."

AFTERWORD

Where was Secular Humanism at Lepanto?

The moral of this story, this afterword, is "Never bring a knife to a gunfight." Keep that in mind as you read.

In any case, religious fanatics? Us? We don't *think* so.

We're not going to sit here and lecture you on the value and validity of atheism versus faith. We'll leave that to Hitchens and Dawkins or D'Souza or the pope or anyone else who cares to make the leap. One way or the other. Hearty shrugs, all around. A defense of the existence of God was never the purpose of the book, anyway, though we would be unsurprised to see any number of claims, after publication, that it is such a defense.

Sorry, it ain't, either in defense of Revelations or in defense of Hitchens' revelation that there was no God when Hitchens was nine years old. (Besides, Dinesh D'Souza does a much better job of thrashing Hitchens in public than we could, even if we cared to.)

Moreover, nope, we don't think it's unethical to be an atheist. We don't think it's impossible, or really any more difficult or unlikely, to be an atheist and still be a highly ethical human being.

The same, sadly, cannot be said for governments. Thus, consider, say, the retail horrors of the Spanish Inquisition which, from 1481 to 1834 killed—shudder—not more than five thousand people, few or none of them atheists, and possibly closer to two thousand. Compare that to expressly atheistic regimes—the Soviet Union, for example, in which a thousand people a *day*, twenty-five hundred a day by Robert Conquest's tally—were put to death in 1937 and '38. And that's not even counting starved Ukrainians by the *millions*. The death toll in Maoist China is said to have been much, much greater. Twenty million? Thirty million? A hundred million? Who knows?

Personally, we'd take our chances with the Inquisition before we would take them with a militantly communist, which is to say, atheist, regime. The Inquisition, after all, was a complete stranger neither to humanity nor to the concept of mercy.

But that's still not the point of this book or this afterword. Go back to the afterword's title. Ever heard of Lepanto? Everyone knows about the Three Hundred Spartans now, at least in some form or another, from the movies. Not enough people know about the battle of Lepanto.

Lepanto (7 October, 1571, 17 October, by our calendar), near the mouth of the Gulf of Corinth and the site of several battles from Naupactus on, was a naval battle, the last really great battle of oar-powered ships, between the fleet of the Moslem Ottoman Empire and the combined, individually much inferior, fleets of the Papacy, Christian Venice, Spain, plus tiny contingents

from various places like Malta and Genoa. The combined Christian fleet was outnumbered, both in terms
of ships and in terms of soldiers—"Marines," we would
say today—who made those ships effective. Yes, they had
half a dozen "super-weapons" in the form of what were
called "galleasses"—bigger galleys (but much slower, they
had to be towed into line by others, and one third of
those could not even be towed into position), mounting
more and larger guns, and carrying more Marines—but
still the odds lay fairly heavily with the Ottomans.

Those odds ran about two hundred and eighty-six
warships, some of them smaller (Turk), to two hundred
and twelve (Christian), six of them larger. In soldiery
the odds were similar. The Christians had a better than
two to one advantage in artillery, yet this means less
than we would think today, since the bulk of artillery
on a galley was intended to be fired once, generally
without careful aim, and then promptly forgotten as
the ship-borne infantry took over the fight.

Worse for the Christians, the Ottomans had a much
greater degree of unity of command. Indeed, for most
of the larger individual sections of the Christian fleet,
there were long-term, serious advantages to letting
the other sections be crushed. It wasn't, after all, as
if Spain and Venice were great friends.

Nor were the stakes notably small. The last jewel
of the Byzantine Empire, its capital, Constantinople,
had fallen the century prior (after, be it noted, having
been badly weakened by being sacked by "Christians"
two and a half centuries before that). Since then, the
Ottomans had exploded across the known world. The
Levant was theirs, as were Egypt and Mesopotamia,
along with most of North Africa. The Balkans, too,

had fallen to the crescent. Thousands in Italy had been killed or enslaved by Ottoman sea raiders. An almanac of Venice, for the year 1545, showed half a dozen Ottoman galleys, raiders, close offshore.

Times looked bleak, indeed, for Western Christendom. And yet, when the smoke cleared, the Ottoman fleet, despite exemplary bravery on the part of the men, was crushed, never really fully to recover. Christian losses in men had been severe, yet were only about equal to the number of Christian slaves liberated from Ottoman galleys.

It was a victory even an atheist might be inclined to call miraculous, with the Ottomans losing about fifteen ships for each Christian loss; over one hundred and eighty Moslem galleys to twelve.

Now let's suppose, just for the moment and just *arguendo*, that God doesn't exist, that He's a pure figment of the imagination. What then won the battle of Lepanto? No, back off. What got the Christian fleet together even to fight the battle, for without getting together to fight it it could never have been won?

The answer is, of course, faith, the faith of the pope, Pius V, who did the political maneuvering and much of the financing, and also the faith of the kings, doges, nobles and perhaps especially the common folk who manned the fleet. And that answer does not depend on the validity of faith, only upon its sincere existence. Faith is, in short, a weapon, the gun you bring to a certain kind of gunfight.

They've taken to calling themselves "brights," of late, those who disparage and attack faith. At least, some of them have. One can't help but note the prior but parallel usurpation of the word "gay" by homosexuals. And, just as gays do not appear notably happier than anyone else, one may well doubt whether "brights" are any smarter... or even as smart.

Example: The religious impulse is as near to universal a human phenomenon as one might imagine. Not that every human being has it, of course, but it has been present, and almost invariably prevalent, in every human society which did not actively suppress it (and some that did).

Now imagine you're a human being of broadly liberal sentiment, much opposed to religion and also much opposed to the oppression of women and gays, equally much against sexual repression, which, by you, and not without some reason on your part, religion is generally held responsible for. You are, in other words, a "bright." Let's say, moreover, that you're a European "bright."

What has been the effect of your, the collective "your," attacks on and disparagement of Christianity? Did you get rid of religion? Yes... ummm... well, no. You got rid of Christianity for the most part. And left a spiritual vacuum for Islam. So, in lieu of one religion, a religion, be it noted, that has become a fairly live-and-let-live phenomenon, you've managed to set things up nicely for a religion which is by no means live-and-let-live. You've arranged to replace a religion that hasn't really done much to oppress women and gays in, oh, a very long time, with one firmly dedicated to the oppression of the one and the extinction of the other.

And you'll insist on calling this "bright," won't you? Because it so cleverly advances your long-term goals, right?

Christopher Hitchens even subtitled his recent book on the subject, *How Religion Poisons Everything*. Odd, isn't it, that the subtitle fails to note that with poison toxicity is in the dose? Or that some doses are worse than others. Or that, given that near universal religious impulse, to get rid of the nonpoisonous dose sets things up for a poisonous one? Yet this is "bright."

Ahem.

Did religion poison those Christian sailors, rowers, and Marines at Lepanto? No; it was not poison to them, but the elixir of strength that gathered them and enabled them to prevail against a religion that was poisonous to them and their way of life. And isn't that odd, too? That such a bright man as Hitchens should claim religion poisons "everything," when the plain historical record, just limiting ourselves for the moment to Lepanto—something a bright man ought to know about—shows that this is not the case?

Hmmm. Perhaps "bright" doesn't mean, after all, what "brights" want it to mean.

Theft of the word "bright," while it doesn't quite rise to the level of linguistic matricide (the malicious murder of one's mother tongue), so common in PC circles, is still an exercise in intellectual dishonesty. It's hardly the only one. For example, it is often claimed that there's not a shred of evidence for the existence of God. This is simple nonsense; there's *lots* of evidence, some of it weaker and some of it stronger. Some of it is highly questionable and other portions very hard to explain away. (And one of our favorite bits revolves around just when and how Pius V *knew* that the battle of Lepanto had been won, at the time it had been won, and in the absence of long-range communications. Look it up. Really.)

Evidence, in any case, there is. What there isn't is absolute, irrefutable *proof*. To use the word "evidence," when what you mean is "irrefutable proof," is intellectual dishonesty of quite a high order, much worse, much more vile, than simple theft of a word. It's even worse, in its way, than the intellectual dishonesty of failure to note, when discussing poisons, that toxicity is in the dose.

But then if "brights" are not required to be "bright," if a disliked religion must give way even if it opens up the world to a loathed one, how can we expect "evidence" not to mean "proof" or dosage to matter to toxicity?

And some would insist, still, that the contradictions claimed to be in the New Testament render it invalid.

Ahem.

Note, at this point, that we have still not claimed that, in fact, there is a God. We may, and do, believe that there is, and believe that there is evidence that there is. But there is no absolute proof, a point we've already readily conceded, and we see no point in arguing for what cannot be proven.

Still, we can't help but note that much of what masquerades as disbelief in God is really just disapproval. Consider the following pair of claims on the subject, voiced, along with some others, by Hitchens during a debate with Dinesh D'Souza:

1) People are badly designed. No god could be so incompetent.

2) Earth is not paradise. Most of humanity
has lived in misery for most of mankind's
existence, though things are somewhat
improved now. No god could be so heart-
less. No real god could have permitted
Auschwitz.

Leave aside that people for whom evolution, biological and social, is an article of faith are therein
complaining that a real god could never have *permitted*
evolution, social and biological. That's funny enough, of
course, being more reminiscent of some snake-charming
cult in the backwoods than a New York salon, but not
the point. The point is that, by those measures, a real
god would be a eugenicist ala Heinrich Himmler, so
that man would not have been or be so biologically
imperfect, and, since most of mankind's self-inflicted
misery arises as a result of freedom to act, no real god
would permit man that freedom. Rather, He would
be a sort of benevolent Stalin.

These are the criteria by which a god should be
measured, his similarity to Himmler, in some particulars, and Stalin, in others?

Ahem.

Never mind. Let "brights" be not very bright. Let
dosage not matter to toxicity. Twist word meanings.
Make Stalin a god, too. Why not; it's been done before
and likely will again.

Even so, never go to a gunfight without a gun
and, if you intend to win, never go to a religious war
without religion. You'll lose.

ACKNOWLEDGMENTS

Thanks to everyone: Miriam and Yoli, who put up with us, Belle Belle the Boxer, who keeps Tom company during the day, Toni, who—come to think of it—also puts up with us, David Drake for his Latin translation service, the 'flies, Mike Schilling, who came up with the kosher Posleen joke, Sue Kerr, for test reading, and, last but not least, Christopher· Hitchens and Richard Dawkins who, after a fashion, inspired us.

GLOSSARY

AID Artificial Intelligence Device

Abat A communal creature, similar to muskrats, origin unknown, that inhabits Posleen ships and spreads to any world colonized.

AS Artificial Sentience. Posleen AID, usually less capable but often more independent.

Baselard A Swiss short sword.

Big-big-pack Brigade, 2–3,000 human soldiers or 7–21,000 Posleen

Champron The armor covering a horse's face.

Cosslain Posleen superior normal. Some, like Querida, approach sentience.

Eson'antai Posleen: Primary genetic derivative, of Kessentai quality. Son.

Esonal   Posleen. Ovipositor.

Five Percenter   Most Posleen Kessentai are still
                         fairly stupid. For reasons that are
                         not entirely clear, about one in
                         twenty is quite bright, and more
                         trouble to those they fight than
                         all the rest put together. These
                         are the five percenters.

Forge   While the Posleen have geneti-
                         cally given skill sets, most of the
                         manufacture is done by auto-
                         mated machines called "forges."
                         The machines cannot produce
                         elements, but can alloy, form,
                         create isotopes, etc., and form
                         any design in their programming,
                         more or less instantaneously,
                         if the basic elements are given
                         them. Forges are not usually very
                         good with complex organics, but
                         can produce relatively simple
                         organic compounds.

Grat   A large, waspish, insectlike crea-
                         ture, origin unknown, that feeds
                         on abat (q.v.). Where there are
                         abat, there will be grat.

Kessentai   Philosopher

Kessenalt   Kessentai who has given up
                         direct, active participation in war

KEW	Kinetic Energy Weapon
Normal	Typical Posleen, a reptilian centauroid, box of rocks stupid
O' Club	Officers' Club. In this context, though, it is a notional room composed entirely of programming that is Sally, the AID's, refuge.
Oolt	Posleen: Pack. A company sized grouping of the People. About four hundred members, usually, with, again, usually, only one Kessentai.
Oolton	Posleen. A "big pack" or "command." A battalion or brigade of Posleen.
Orna'adar	The Posleen Ragnarok, when population pressure and competition for resources devolves into a general war, waged with all available weapons.
Path of Fury	War
Posleen	Human approximation of Po'osleena'ar, the People of the Ships.
Roga'n	The central market and meeting place in the City of the People of the Ships, Posleen Prime

Stick
A Kessentai's sole badge of office. One who has "tossed his stick," given up the Path of Fury, loses forever the title of "Philosopher" and is thereafter forbidden to fight except in point self-defense.

Tank, the
Galactic Technology, a rejuvenation and restoration machine that happens to look a lot like a sarcophagus.

Tenar
Posleen flying sled

Thresh
Posleen: food. Damned near anything organic.

Threshkreen
Food with a sting. Soldiers, especially human soldiers.

Shlomit Bat Bet-Lechem-Plada Kreuzer (later "Kreuzer-Dwyer")
Salem daughter of Bethlehem Steel, the Cruiser

The following is an excerpt from:

OVERKILL

ROBERT BUETTNER

Available from Baen Books
March 2011
trade paperback

ONE

Orion Parker lowered her head and stared down into her glass when the cop appeared, silhouetted against the pedway glow beyond the open door. Like all cops, he stood a head taller than the crowd, with his helmet and antennae adding another half foot.

The bar crowd was as light as crowds ever got on Yavet, because by the fortieth day of any month paychips had vanished down throats, into veins, or into somebody else's pocket at gunpoint. The cop, shoulders square, plowed through the drinkers and dancers toward the service 'bot. Some cops deigned to snake sideways through the crowds, polite even in a hole like this. Vice didn't.

The cop reached the service 'bot, pressed his ID against its reader, then watched as the list of open tabs in the bar rolled across the 'bot's screen.

"Crap on crust!" Orion slid off her stool and burrowed into a crowd too drunk to smell its own vomit and too stoned to smell her fear.

She hadn't fled fifteen feet when a gauntleted hand clamped her elbow.

The crowd shrank back, made a hole around them. The cop peered down at her through his face shield with eyes like black stones. It was Polian, from Vice. "Must have been a good month, Parker, if you can still afford whiskey."

She stared at the floor, shook her head. "I haven't served a client in six months."

He cocked his head, sneered for show. "Really? Let's talk about it." He shoved her toward a vacant Sleeper, and she stumbled against a fat man who smelled like urine.

Polian slammed her through the booth's open door, wedged in alongside her, then pulled the door shut. He took one breath, voiced up the ventilator, then waited. "Okay. What you got for me, Parker?"

"The trade's slow."

"Bullshit."

"I swear." She pointed at the ceiling. "Slow Uplevel." Down at the floor. "Slow Downlevel." She tossed her head left, then right. "Uptown, downtown. Nobody's got clients."

He stared at her, drummed his fingers against the Sleeper's closed door.

She sighed. "Okay. I hear Mouse Bell's taking clients."

He smiled. "Already? The Mouse just got out of the House last month. Where?"

She stared at the gilt CFA scrolled across Polian's breastplate badge. "I dunno."

Polian stared back at her. "Parker, you of all people know it's cold in the House. Wanna go back?"

She sighed again, turned her head toward the Sleeper's stained padding. "Twenty-second and Elysian. Fifteen lower. Kube fourteen."

"Anything else?"

Orion shook her head.

Polian stabbed his armored finger at her face. "I find out you short-decked me, you're back in the House. For good!"

She wormed her hand up between her body and the booth wall, raised her palm, and looked the cop in the eye, without blinking. "I don't know about any other clients. Mother's Blood."

It was the cop's turn to sigh. "Okay. Where you want it?"

"Someplace that won't bleed."

"If you don't bleed, they'll know you're a snitch."

Orion tapped her index finger to her right cheek.

Polian drew his mailed fist back, until it brushed the Sleeper's padding, then slugged Orion so hard that her body sprung the door, and she crumpled onto something sticky that puddled the bar's floor. She lay gasping, while Polian stepped across her, and left.

Orion rolled up, onto her knees, and tasted a salty trickle inside her mouth. It hurt when she smiled, and when she touched her tongue to her teeth, two moved. She spat blood onto the bar floor. It was a bargain price for two successful lies, the one her blood told the world, and the one she had just told the cop.

TWO

Ten minutes later, Orion left the bar, squeezed past a robbery in progress on the pedway, then climbed four blocks uplevel, walked two across, and four over, until she reached her Kube.

She sanexed, retrieved the tools of her trade from the dug-out hollow behind the padding, then blew the price of a whiskey on the tube to Sixty-eighth and Park, twenty upper. The hotel district was cream, with sixteen-foot ceilings, virtual sunshine, and pedways wide enough for people to glide four abreast in both directions.

Her client was already waiting. Clients, in fact.

The woman's face was porcelain-smooth, with huge, brown almond-shaped eyes. By Yavet standards, the woman was old. By any standards, she was beautiful. Except for her grotesque body, misshapen by her brush with felony. And her lips, stretched tight by pain.

Orion tugged her off the main way, into a side passage. "You trying to get me sent to the House?"

The woman frowned. "What's the problem?"

"You. You don't exactly blend."

The man extended his hand. "I'm—"

"Shut up. What I don't know I can't tell."

He nodded. "But you *are* O'Ryan? And you've brought what she needs?"

Orion looked over her shoulder. A man in the pedway stared at the three of them. She asked the couple, "You got space?"

The two of them led her down the passage, and to a Kube on the second floor of a first-rate, boutique Sleeper. The place measured twelve feet long by six feet wide, with a private Sanex, a curtained window slit that overlooked the pedway, even a rear door to a balcony big enough for two people to stand on.

Orion set her bag on a side shelf wide enough to sit on, nodded as she looked around, then whistled. "You definitely got space!"

The man said, "I gather this is illegal, here?" Like the woman, he was old by Yavet standards, stood straight, like a cop did, but had soft eyes.

The man stood a head taller than an average Yavi, the couple's clothes were cut offworld, and he wore in his lapel a button-sized fabric rosette the color of sky in a travel holo, sprinkled with tiny white stars. Veteran of something. Orion snorted to herself. Who wasn't?

"Illegal? It's a capital crime for you two. Life for me if I go down for the third time." Orion pointed at the window slit. "Draw that curtain." A pistol-sized bulge lifted his jacket lapel. "Better yet, you cover the window, Quickdraw."

"Little over the top here, aren't we?" But he stepped alongside the slit.

"You're not from here, are you? Vice doesn't knock, they shoot."

The man raised salt-and-pepper eyebrows. "You're kidding."

Orion held her hand palm-up toward the woman and wiggled fingers. "Cash up front."

The woman handed her a fat plastek envelope and grimaced. "Cash seems melodramatic."

Orion cocked her head and batted her eyes. "When I file my taxes, I can't exactly fill out the 'occupation' line 'Midwife,' can I?"

The man shook his head. "This is nuts. A planet so crowded that people live in a layer cake and sleep standing up. The cops ignore drugs and stickups, but childbirth is a hanging offense."

"Dope and gunplay thin population. Childbirth increases it. If you don't like Yavet, why'd you come?"

The man drew the pistol from the holster beneath his jacket, and Orion raised her eyebrows. A blunt gunpowder automatic, not like the sharky things cops and robbers carried. He stood alongside the curtain, pushed it aside with his pistol's barrel, and peeked out. "We came to Yavet for the culture."

Orion opened the envelope and walked her fingers through the bills, counting. "Yavet has no culture."

"The brochure misled us."

Orion ran her fingers over the raised crest on the envelope, then swore. "Where'd you swap cash?"

The woman said, "At the hotel desk. Why?"

Orion rolled her eyes. "Fuck!" Then she sighed. "Pray the desk clerk's lazy or crooked. That's a push bet." She opened her bag, and pointed the woman to the horizontal bed. "Strip down, honey, and let's see where you're at."

The woman was gravid, and seven centimeters dilated. She panted through a contraction, then said to Orion, as she sat beside the woman on the bed, "This is dangerous for you. Keep the money. Go. My husband's delivered a child before."

Orion's head snapped back, and she pointed at the man as he stood by the window. "You kiss him with that mouth?"

It proved to be brutal, even for a first birth. Seven hours later, Orion dripped sweat as badly as the woman did as she laid the baby on the mother's quivering belly. But the woman never uttered a peep, and the husband—the expression sounded almost nice since the woman had said it aloud—seemed to manage to keep watch, encourage his wife, and assist Orion without stress, like he had endured a lifetime of it.

Orion sat back, took a breath, and smiled at the woman. "Nice job, mama. If this were legal, I'd do it for free."

The woman stared at her newborn son as she stroked the infant's matted hair. "Why *do* you do it?"

Orion rubbed the little one's tiny back. "You just look at this guy and tell me how anyone could—"

"Crap." The man, peeking out the window, snapped back the slide on his pistol.

The woman clutched the baby. "Jason! What's wrong?"

He said to Orion. "Your vice cops wear *armor*? And carry assault rifles?"

"Crap on crust! How many?"

"Eight. So far. They're still piling out of a four-wheel."

"Twatface desk clerk reported your swap!" Orion tugged bloody sheeting out from under the woman, and sluiced water over the woman's loins. "Finish cleaning up! Change into fresh clothes."

She pointed at the man's pistol. "Lose the cannon. It could hurt somebody."

"It has. Trust me. I thought this place was Dodge City."

Orion wadded up the woman's underwear, the sheeting, the afterbirth, her own bag, then vac'd the whole gory mess down the Sanex. "You can't shoot *cops*! And if you could, you couldn't shoot a twelve-man, armored shakedown squad!" She turned to the woman. "Is he always stubborn?"

"Usually, he's worse." The woman gritted her teeth as she struggled, hollow-eyed, into a robe.

Voices shouted faintly, down in the lobby.

Orion paused, took a breath, then faced the two of them, palms out. "This is gonna be alright. You tell them you swapped for cash to buy dope. But you got stuck up, so you got no dope and no cash to prove your story."

The man named Jason rolled his eyes. "That's the most—"

"It happens all the time. The worst they'll do is summarily revoke your visas."

The woman clutched the newborn. "What about my baby?"

"The baby can't be here." Orion pointed at the rear balcony. "I'll take it out that way."

A doorway banged in the distance, echoing as though up a stairwell.

The woman shook her head, clutched the baby tighter. It kicked and squalled.

Jason shook his head. "No. Our baby stays. If we have to appeal this, we can do that. We know people—"

"Appeal my ass! A vice cop's badge legend reads 'CFA.' For Child First, Always. That doesn't mean equal opportunity. It means being born unauthorized is a summarily judged capital crime, just like giving birth." Orion pointed at the door. "When the goons break down that door, the first thing they'll do is suffocate your child while you watch. Then they'll shoot you."

Boots thundered against metal stair treads.

Jason shook his head again, fingered the pistol beneath his lapel with quivering fingers. "It won't work. They'll cover the back of the building."

Orion shook her head. "*You* would, soldier. Cops get lazy and stupid when crooks have no leverage."

The boot falls rumbled in the hall, now, mixed with the ring of cocking rifle bolts.

The man called Jason said, "Then we'll all go."

"If you both aren't in the room, they'll assume an unauthorized birth and keep looking. For your baby. 'Til death do you part."

The husband pried his son from his wife's arms, kissed the top of the baby's head, then handed him to Orion.

The wife sobbed.

The husband's eyes glistened, but his jaw was set. "This won't stand. We'll get in touch with you. Get him back."

Orion stepped backward, shook her head. "If they know he exists, they'll hunt him down. Not just the government. There are free lance bounty hunters all over this planet. And every other planet, too. Let the government deport you. Go tour the galaxy, or whatever you're doing, and forget this ever happened. Never tell a soul, anywhere, that the boy was born, if you want him to live."

Something heavy pounded the Kube's front door.

Orion tucked the struggling newborn between her breasts, and buttoned her blouse over it. She said to them, "I'm sorry." Then she ran to the balcony, and swung a leg over the rail.

Craack.

Behind her, plasteel splintered.

She lowered herself until she dangled from the balcony's floor, like a trapezeier, and dropped the last six feet to the passage pavement. Then Orion Parker stood, clutched the mewling infant to her breast, and ran toward the dark.

THREE

"Next!" The bald Customs and Immigration clerk on the stool behind the podium had long since sweated through his uniform blouse. He shouted to be heard above the insect drone beyond the terminal's open, steel-cage ceiling. Shuttles landed on DE 476 bang on the planet's equator. Therefore, even at midnight, local, the temperature under roof as well as outside stagnated at an identical, breeze-less ninety-eight degrees Fahrenheit. The air was so thick that the flies didn't buzz, they droned.

I held my place behind the yellow line, as I stared to my left, at the adjacent podium with a sign above it: NATIVES RETURNING TO DE 476, ONLY. The podium's stool was empty and dust covered, as was its yellow line. Apparently, returning to DE 476 was an even lower priority for natives lucky enough to leave than visiting DE 476 was for everyone else.

The Human Union preliminarily graded new planets that were warm enough to liquify water, but cool enough to avoid boiling it away, "E," for "Earthlike." If the planet proved too distant, too deadly, or too different, it earned the prefix "D," which officially stood for "Downgraded." Downgraded Earthlike 476 was all three, and known to everyone but its Tourism Bureau as "Dead End."

The clerk periscoped his thin neck and swiveled his head around the empty arrivals auditorium. "I said next! Anybody here named next?" He scowled at me over old-fashioned wire and glass spectacles, then waved me forward while he fanned himself with a sheet of folded paper.

With my boot toe I nudged my duffle alongside his podium, then bent forward and pressed my eye against the retinal. After a heartbeat, the scanner chimed.

"Gotcha. Stand back." The clerk yawned into his fist. "For the comfort and safety of the next person in line, please use one of the tissues provided to wipe the receptacle. Thank you."

There was no next person in line. I wiped anyway. If a Legion hitch teaches a recruit anything, it's hygiene and following orders.

The clerk eyed his screen. "Parker, Jazen. What the hell kind of name is Jazen?"

I shrugged. "Yavet name."

"Never heard of it."

C-drive and jump technology made the Human Union, all five hundred two planets of it, possible. But barely. Interstellar voyages took as long as sail-powered voyages took on the oceans of a garden-variety pre-industrial. Average citizens of the galaxy knew worlds beyond their own the way average Victorian Englishmen knew Borneo, which is to say as dark places run by savages.

"I suppose. There's bookoo jumps between Dead End and Yavet."

"There's bookoo jumps between Dead End and everywhere. You're twenty-three?"

"Subjective. About twenty-four, in undilated time." They say GI life is boredom punctuated by intervals of sheer terror. But aboard a troop transport moving between jumps at near light speed a month not only *seems* to pass slower, it does. A Trueborn named Einstein proved it, they say, and that's all the thought I've ever given it.

"So I see. Legionnaires spend lots of time near light

speed." He ran a finger along the screen. "Awarded Star of Marin with Leaves. You get that for doing good or for doing bad?" He frowned. Worlds apart breed ignorance. Ignorance breeds misunderstanding. Misunderstanding breeds the need to do unto others before they do unto you. If it wasn't for xenophobia, the Legion wouldn't exist.

I shrugged again. "Depends."

He narrowed his eyes. "On what?"

"On which side you were on."

He grunted and frowned deeper. The Legion only broke things and hurt people for the greater good. It had said so right in my oath. But that didn't make hired killers popular.

He sat back. "Purpose of visit? R and R, maybe?"

A Legion honorable discharge earns twelve months amnesty from whatever a Legionnaire might have done before. Even a Yavet Illegal like me, who was otherwise dead meat walking for any bounty hunter in the Union who tracked me down. There are two kinds of Yavet Illegals. The kind who cover their tracks, and dead ones.

So I hesitated before I answered. He drummed his fingers while he stared into his screen. Hell, my information was in every 'Puter in the Union, anyway. During the four months left on my amnesty, neither this guy nor anybody else in government could rat me out to a bounty hunter for a finder's fee. "I was discharged eight months ago."

He tapped his screen, yawned. "I can see that. It was a joke. Nobody takes R and R on Dead End."

"I'm with the Cutler party."

He periscoped the empty hall again. "You got 'em in your duffle? That's a joke, too."

I stretched a smile. "Got it." I jerked my thumb back up the pedway. "Mr. Cutler and the others are behind me. They have checked luggage to claim. All I have is the duffle." It wasn't much to show for a life.

His keyboard rattled. "Ah. Cutler, Bartram." Then the clerk raised his eyebrows and whistled. "Trueborn Earthman. Wa-di-doo. Purpose of the Cutler Party visit, then?"

"Hunting."

He raised his eyebrows higher. "Hunting what?"

"Grezzen."

He stared, while sweat trickled down his cheek. Then he grinned. "No. Really. I have to type something in this blank."

"Really." I paused. "Is that a problem?"

He swivelled on his stool, and pointed at the terminal wall. A pirate-black flag that hung there bore red script: "Libertarian Republic of Dead End: Live Free or Die"

Not bad. As a Yavi I appreciated physical and behavioral elbow room more than most. Maybe I'd come back.

He shook his head. "Nope. Libertarian Republic means do what you want, unless you get in somebody else's way. But most come for the live free, not the die." He jerked his thumb over his shoulder. "Have a pleasant stay. Move along."

I snapped my fingers. "Oh. Since I'm first through, I'm supposed to claim our oversize freight. Where—"

He stared at his screen while he pointed over his left shoulder, at a lighted passage. "For the freight terminal, bear right at the plaque. Bang on the door. There's only two of us here at night and he's a heavy sleeper. The shuttle will taxi over there after the morning shift gets here and pumps out the crappers." He held up the soggy single-paper sheet he had been fanning himself with. "You care for a fine dining brochure?"

I smiled as I hefted my duffle. "I know. A joke."

He stared at me over his spectacles. "I don't get it."

The roofed trench that led away from the arrivals hall stretched four hundred yards, as black beyond its barred ceiling as a tunnel through a coal seam. The open roof that arched above my head was fabricated of steel bars as thick as my thigh, spaced a foot apart. Spherical metal lanterns dangled from the overhead bars, the lantern flames sputtering oily smoke that sank to the passage floor like lead fog.

Dead End's tourist site lauded the yesteryear charm of the local coal oil lamps. In fact, the only export component of Dead End's GPP was boutique kerosene. The fine print said the kerosene fumes discouraged local insects. They didn't discourage many. I swatted as I walked, but replacement squadrons swarmed in between the bars.

A hundred steam-bath yards down the passage, a fork distributed passengers left to ground transport, and straight ahead to freight pickup. I flopped my duffle down at a section where the bars wilted apart like limp spaghetti. Additional steel sections had been welded between the gaps. Freshly wire-brushed, the welds gleamed beneath the lanterns' smoky flicker.

I rested my hands on my knees. Some kind of animal bellow echoed in the distance. Sweat dripped off my nose onto a platter-sized brass plaque bolted to the concrete floor below the repaired bars.

"Thom Webb. Beloved Father and husband. Slain by grezzen on this spot, May 4, 2108."

I eyed my 'Puter. May 27, 2108.

I shouldered my duffle, double-timed the remaining three hundred yards to the freight terminal, then pounded the locked, armored door so hard that sweat spray exploded off my fists.

—end excerpt—

from *Overkill*
available in trade paperback,
March 2011, from Baen Books